About the Author

Colin Wiltshire grew up a chauvinist, when all the women in his extended family appeared happily domesticated. However, as a young man he matured with a generation of women who knew they were intelligent, capable, competent and confident, and although, blessed or damned, with the procreative anatomy, did not see why that should hold them back. They set about seizing the wider experience.

Inexorably his ingrained attitude moderated, and watching his daughters grow and take a choke hold of their lives and worlds, polished his conversion. He sees even the world's most subjugated women, one day joining the diaspora of the liberated, and rising to rule.

A pilot and adventurer, he has crossed continents and deserts, but as a father of six, he regards his contribution to their notable achievements, as his most gratifying accomplishment— Horden, Richard, Katherine, Kelly, James and Stephanie. colin_wiltshire@hotmail.com

Sisters and Surrogates

Colin Wiltshire

Sisters and Surrogates

Olympia Publishers
London

www.olympiapublishers.com
OLYMPIA PAPERBACK EDITION

A CIP catalogue record for this title is
available from the British Library.

ISBN: 978-1-80074-362-5

This is a work of fiction.
Names, characters, places and incidents originate from the writer's imagination.
Any resemblance to actual persons, living or dead, is purely coincidental.

First Published in 2022
Olympia Publishers
Tallis House
2 Tallis Street
London
EC4Y 0AB
Printed in Great Britain

Dedication

I dedicate this book to my wife, Estrella Sta. Ana — 'Til death do us part.

Chapter 1
Before Breakfast

Affinity awoke each morning easily. She was never tempted to snuggle back, with an eye bickering with the clock, until rising was imperative. This morning was no different, and wide eyed she glanced indifferently at the snoring, unshaven, and heavy breathing frame adjacent, and repelled by the sight, she cast aside the bedding with a sweeping arm, swung her legs over the edge of the bed and stood up. She stretched, took a breath of air and paused momentarily to notice the scene outside the window. It was early spring, the plants and trees were awakening, green shoots were abundant, the early blossoms already out but Affinity's appreciation was cursory, her concerns not for nature's beauty, but for her own. She turned away, shook her head until her fair hair, layered with horizontal blue bands, lay behind her square shoulders. She headed for the adjoining bathroom, its double doors sliding open as she approached, the room illuminated, and a synthesized voice spoke:

"Good morning, Affinity, nice to see you, how are you?"

"Shithouse, probably," she conceded.

"I'm sorry to hear that, Affinity."

"No, you aren't! You're just a bloody android."

The bathroom's early morning self-cleaning had finished, and its overall white veined black marble, with floor to ceiling mirrors on opposite walls, all gleamed. The trimmings were silver gilt but neither the outdoors glory nor the indoor splendour detracted Affinity from another morning's anxiety. It was her tiffanys, which each morning for weeks had enticed her to the mirrors for examination. Each morning had begun with hope but so far had ended forlornly.

Now again, naked, she stood erect amid the mirrors. She stiffened, hollowed her back, tightened her rate one alice, tensed her rate one stomach, pulled her shoulders back, and clenched both rows of flawless crowns. Readied, she presented her minus three-quarter tiffanys to the mirrors in profile, and then rotated enough to examine each meticulously, desperate for any hint of improvement. Surely the weeks of programmed tiffany exercising, and the massaged cell constricting therapy, should have helped by now, and she perused hopefully. How much sag lazed on her chest, had the dewdrops looked up, even a touch? She threw her head back, and bounced on her toes hoping to encourage some lift, but again sadly, she had to concede, there was no joy this morning either. The apparent was demoralizing, and despite her sisters' reassurances she worried needlessly; her bedtime resolve to be positive had remained in bed.

She turned for recourse to other features of her early-forties figure, which in defiance of her tiffanys had maintained her jaythree status, and for now she'd resorted to that comfort. With her hands on hips, she rose on her toes and smiled at her long legs, slim ankles, sweeping high calves, fine knees, cambered thighs, a backside to die for, all honed, subtle and smooth, while above her nulliparous waist, her contoured shoulders and firm fleshed face, was swathed in unblemished silk. But there were a couple more checks to go. With angry fingers Affinity clasped the cheeks alice, shook vigorously, and when they passed the wobble-less test, as she knew they would, she turned to her stomach, punching it severally, severely. Probably it lacked all the supple strength of twenty years ago, but it was still rather good. Thankfully, she'd never jeopardised her body with pregnancy.

The abstracting self-admiration was brief, as her tiffany distress recaptured her unblinking gaze. She lifted her arms sideways until they touched above her head. They were handsome arms, but she was watching her dewdrop dewdrops. Lowering her arms to her side, Affinity turned to the opposite mirror and repeated the manoeuvre, only to ascertain identical data. Gauging dewdrop travel revealed nothing new. Her head drooped, she was fed up, not only with her predicament, but also because she felt alone, no one else seemed interested or cared. "Bugger them," she yelled turning towards the bedroom.

"Summit!"

There was no reply. Her impatience boiled, so she screamed.

"Summit!"

It worked; there was movement nearby, and after a short while a muffled enquiry wafted from the bedroom.

"What?"

"My fucking tits have definitely sagged," she called, her voice inimical.

He did not respond. Incensed at being ignored the pronouncement was repeated, with acrimony and emphasising the "f" word and the "t" words. For a moment there was still no response, and then, "Turn the bitch off, Affinity, it doesn't help, and your obsession with your tits is becoming tedious," Summit announced, as he dragged his apathy to the bathroom.

Affinity stared unamused at her lethargic reba (registered breeding affiliate), slumped against the doorway. 'Disgusting,' she thought.

"Hell, Affinity, what are you screaming about, that I haven't heard before?" he mumbled, begrudgingly.

Affinity glared, straightened up and thrust her tiffanys forward.

"Look at these," she shook her shoulders and chest, "The bloody things have sagged so much I'm going to fail my next annument, the way they're going."

Although Summit knew the problem had been brewing, exasperatingly, this morning he suspected she could not be dismissed easily, and scheming a speedy extradition would be achieved by showing some interest in her distress, even be commiseratory. He straightened off the doorjamb and moved closer for an examination. It had been ages since he'd eyed her physically, but this morning he was reminded of the times her tiffanys had been one of her alluring features, and how often, the mere hint of her cleavage spurred his libidinous ambition. They still possessed a sense of the innocent gentility of that teenager girl, and were still inviting.

He eased back for the panoramic. She was still beautiful, and it was unfortunate he'd grown so accustomed to her body, but other incongruities were responsible for their antagonisms. "Well, they may have drooped slightly, Affy, but since you're forty plus, that's to be expected. It's natural, and we have to accept these changes. But damn, they're still gorgeous, and you'll pass easily."

An empathetic and encouraging Summit was refreshing, and she wanted more.

"Summit," she said solemnly, "A couple of things, I'm only forty-two, and who said it had to happen, how do you know they'll pass? You were only interested in them when you wanted a bit of rough, and it's long since they felt your soft caress or a warm kiss."

"That's unfair, Affy," he protested, "You've been protecting them for years, ever since your downgrading to a jok (just okay), I've not been allowed to touched them. But you'll be all right when the time comes," he emphasised again.

Affinity took a deep measured breath, and as she slowly exhaled felt some stress drain but it was a short respite.

"Summit, I need to hold my threejay for years yet or I'll be R rated and in a dunville before I'm fifty. I want my jay status even as a jayfour, for at least another ten years."

Her early morning persistence was testing Summit's commitment to her distress, "Stop moaning Affy, no female fails over her tits these days. Technology can put twenty-year-old tits on a ninety-year-old, you know that!"

"Yes, provided my skin is suitable and I don't scar."

"There's cell restoration. I think you're being melodramatic, even masochistic, Affinity."

"And that can go wrong too, you know that. All I know I'm afraid this may be the final step to the slippery slope."

"Nothing's going to happen to you Affinity, not for years," he snapped.

"That's easy for you when you males don't have to measure up like females. The specifications for males aren't tight enough, I know that, you know that" Affinity's uncompromising tone persisted.

"Well, there's no point upsetting yourself until you know if they'll pass or fail. Have a pre-annument appraisal then we'll know if you need to worry."

Summit moved up to her with an exploratory hand, and his amorous gesture was tasked principally with diverting her preoccupation, but then, unexpectedly he toyed with another outcome. She shrunk away, sweeping aside his groping hand.

"Don't touch me, Summit. Piss off!" her hands pushing his chest, "the sight of you unshaven, the odour of your sweaty grubbiness, and the thought of your dishevelled bulk trying to hump me, is repulsive. Piss off, I said!" she held him at an arm's length.

He'd achieved his first goal but her insults had dissuaded his plan B, persuading him to withdraw to the shower. However, Affinity was unable to dismiss her obsession, returned to her mirrors, took her tiffanys loosely in her hands and bounced them lightly.

"They're definitely lighter, but flabbier," she nagged vehemently but the shower was running so Summit either did not hear or pretended not to.

Finally, Affinity compelled herself to move into the day, firstly with a shower where the warm flowing water doused her worries, somewhat, temporarily. She pulled on the shower mask, lay in the hammock and let the multiple spouts do their work. Her thoughts drifted to what to wear; what outfit to print out, and what style of body makeover would improve her mood? It was a long time before enough was enough, and she called for the water to stop but stayed lying in the hammock.

"Affinity, do you wish to be dried there or will you stand?" the voice asked.

Affinity was inclined to deliver a profanity but did so silently.

She clambered out of the hammock, and stood awaiting. Two flexible arms reached out and began systematically tracing her body, blowing her dry.

"Can you lift your arms please Affinity?"

She did. "You're too hot, cool it down a bit?" she snapped.

Immediately the air flow cooled and Affinity felt livelier for the change.

"Can you part the legs Affinity?"

She did.

A few moments on, "Will I apply rejuvenating moisturizer Affinity?"

"Of course!"

The air stopped, and fine mist applied the lotion.

Summit stepped from the shower and found himself in front of a mirror unintentionally inspecting his own physique, probably a rejoinder to Affinity's disparagement of his specification. At age forty-eight he tightened his stomach and while it was not what it once was, pleasingly a ripple persisted, albeit only a hint; his raised arms were as muscular as ever, and devoid of any sag or flab; his under chin sag would only be detected by a pessimist; the same pessimist might frown at his forehead wrinkles but they were faint; his legs were objects of power as they had always been; and in summary, with an inflated chest, taut stomach, flexed muscles and a clench jaw, it was easily a satisfactory picture.

As Affinity stepped out of the shower, he turned to her in peacock pose: "Look." he crowed, "looks awfully good to me, Affinity!" he declared grinning broadly.

She stared panly, her scrutiny fleetingly. Now showered and shaved he looked more amenable but she was in no mood for his exhibitionism, and instinctively she was not going to be complimentary.

"Go to work!" she instructed dismissively.

"Don't take out your frustration on me Affy, you've nothing to worry about," he retorted but with a slight grin, which was becoming lascivious, a look she knew well, and he was looming again.

"Piss off Summit," she turned away, and moved away.

Against the mirror she turned back, and waited while he imprisoned her with an outstretched arm each side of her shoulders. Her antagonism faltered, and unannounced a once familiar quiver inspired a new attitude. 'What the hell', she thought but with their accrued enmity she could not surrender, easily. However, looking into his eyes she saw fun and avarice, and with the touch of his chest on her tiffanys there was a journey underway, for the first time in a long time. Habit though ensured Affinity disguised her pleasure.

"I told you to piss off, Summit," but it was a directive they both knew, this time, was symbolic.

While Summit had embarked on this path without expectation, the hint of passion in her disguised smile, he sensed desire stirring within her, he was pleased to be pressing against her.

He looked into her eyes and smiled, for despite her pretend poker face, he knew devilment was dissolving her resistance. Finally, she surrendered, smiled and wrapped her arms around his waist, pulling him closer.

The touch of his presumptuous erection on her lower stomach surprised her with its warmth and strength, whipping her enthusiasm, and

14

provoking her chemistry for the encounter. Suddenly everything was forgotten, as she decided this assignation was going to be purely self-centred. She pushed in off briefly, looked down, smiled and still grinning looked back at him, pulled him close again, and with one foot on its toes, she lifted her other leg high and around. He grasped it, and slid his other hand around her waist, while caesar's rummaging for her destination was brief. Now it was he, who was surprised. Her abrupt transition, had come with his sudden transition from distraction to enthusiasm, and now, as caesar foraged not too politely into a silken, savoury and supplicating vivian, he was impatient.

Affinity reminisced that once they enjoyed a high demand, and plentiful supply of carnal comfort, and surprisingly this morning a sense of that indulgence was back. She relaxed, rested her arms on his shoulders, lay her head back on the mirror, and let him fulfil her. But he pummelled her against the mirror, held her leg uncomfortably high, and was obviously on a self-service mission. Disappointingly his affection had only been ephemeral, and in the end, his rush left her with an episode not for consignment to her memory bank. But there had been some pleasure in his pounding, and when she sensed his selfishness was imminent, she managed to coax a small nefertiti for herself. Finished, Summit flashed a smile, pecked her on the forehead, abandoned her to dart back into the shower.

"That was nice Summit," she called out sarcastically, "you should try to find some style, sometime." She was ignored.

Out of the shower and dried Summit took the spray nozzle from the bench, closed his eyes, sprayed a blemish concealing and skin toning treatment over his face and neck, then over each lower arm and hand.

"Why don't you use the cavern and do the job properly? And while there, it's about time to get rid of your body hair again, it's a turnoff Laser it, then it's gone for good. I don't understand why you didn't do it years ago, even before your alphaspection," she said watching him from the comfort of the shower hammock again.

Again, he ignored her, the observations, comments, aspersions and advice.

He checked his finger nails deciding yesterday's polish could carry him through today. Yesterday's shave would also do, his facial presentation; foundation (lemon), lipstick (light amber), just needed touching up.

Back in the bedroom he dressed in a fitted, floral patterned white and jade green open necked shirt. His suit was in narrow vertical stripes of blue and green without buttons and contour cut. Two yellow gold and diamond rings on his right hand, two yellow gold and emerald rings on the left.

He stepped back into the bathroom doorway, smiling, "How do I look?"

Now, Affinity ignored him, but from her eye's corner via a mirror she was looking, 'he still had it', she thought but that was classified.

"Right then," he quipped and was gone.

"I'll be here for a while, so tell Essence and Wraith to go when they're ready." she called out.

Affinity was relieved to be solitary, in silence, and since Summit persisted in being aggravatingly unhelpful, his departure was an escape from the friction and tension of their relationship. Affinity sat slouched at her dressing table, leaning on her elbows, once again staring at herself in the mirror, unintentionally this time, but captivated anyway. She straightened up, finger combed her hair off her face, and holding it out turned one side of her face to the mirror for a moment, then the other side. She leaned closer searching for crows' feet around her eyes, for fine lines from the corners of her mouth, and for neck wrinkles. Her finger and thumb darted about her face and neck pinching, pulling, seeking any deterioration in texture or consistency. She couldn't complain, it was pretty good, she thought. She dropped her hair to her shoulders and continued to gazed in the mirror. It was mostly more than satisfactory.

Suddenly Affinity had had enough, she was over it, for the moment anyway. She bounced to her feet, pirouetted on the marble floor, and strode off towards the cavern. Although she'd deny being fickle, her mood had turned and now the thought of an hour's self-indulgence in the cavern was invigorating. She called for the cavern and printer bay and a large mirror slid aside revealing an alcove of more black marble, a cushioned air bench, a control panel and several stainless wall fittings. As she entered the control panel illuminated and the voice was ready with more.

"Welcome to your cavern and printer bay Affinity, it's nice to see you. If you're planning to be outdoors today, I've the weather forecast if you wish it."

"Not really but go on anyway."

"Fifty-five percent overcast early this morning, dispersing until full sun by one o'clock, the temperature rising from the present 18 degrees to the maximum of 29 degrees at three-o-four. There is a seven knot breezes from zero-seven-three which will move around to zero-eight-eight and decrease slightly by this evening. The humidity is stable at 34 percent. This forecast has an accuracy rating of 92 percent."

For Affinity the information was mostly ignored, rather she concentrated on the display menu and choosing her days' exhibition. Her thinking finger tickled her bottom lip, her work finger cruised aimlessly about the keypad, while her imagination deliberated on what body work and outfit she wanted. Something spirited, something strong, something with a statement, something stimulating, even sexy? She tapped in Ho2, activating a half size hologram of her naked self at the back of the cavern. Her finger was waving hurriedly backwards and forwards. How adventurous was she feeling, and as a picture formed in her mind there were lots of colour and flounces?

She began testing ideas on the hologram, trying skin colours, tonings and patterns, face designs and hair styles. The underlying skin shading she selected would lighten her natural tone slightly, and allow her to selected fine blue lace pattern as the stand out. She would apply the pattern full body, feet to face. She would highlight her cheek bones with solid blue of the same shade, and her eye shape and brows would be decorated in dark blue, with glitter, and when she tried black contact lenses, she liked them. Her lips would be the same dark blue, without glitter but high glossed. Affinity stepped back to better assess her body makeup and was pleased; now to dress herself.

Her temperament was for something refreshing, and a departure from her usual proclivities. This eliminated anything suggestive but she still wished to expose a generous amount of her bodywork. Another tap at the panel and the accompanying screen displayed a menu. Affinity gazed thoughtfully and began programming choices: soft, colourful, blue compatible, fifty percent coverage, no; sixty percent, flares and frills —

yes, sensual rating: conservative — no; moderate — no; flirtatious — no; moderate — maybe; moderate Mark II — Yes!.

Images from the inventory began steadily parading across the screen, with Affinity sporadically pausing them for a second thought. Then an outfit induced a broad grin, and an assurance it was what she wanted. The light blue crop top had wide capped sleeves and a modest V-neck, with trimmed edges in navy blue, burst into unpretentious reds and yellows in flowers over each tiffany with stretched petals extending over the shoulders, she smiled. The hipster wrapped skirt in blue with floral hips, dipping below the rump, while shorts fell above the knee and down each outside leg was a row of miniature flowers. Overall, she thought it subtle and classy but she wanted to modify the blue to that of her chosen skin blue and wanted the same patterning.

With the adjustments programmed she stepped back, called for the hologram to go full size and parade.

The image rotated looked back over its shoulder at Affinity, smiled, placed its hand on its hips then its waist, in Affinity's gait it walked a few steps. 'Let's do it', she thought, and set the printer in motion, but the device had another opinion.

"Excuse my interrupting, Affinity, but I suggest your flower colours of yellow and red clash unreasonably with your blues. Taking into consideration your personality profile and behavioural pattern, It is suggest you either reduce the extent of these colours or you reduce their intensity."

She was in no mood to argue, and the program was probably right anyway. "Whatever, just change it."

When the hologram amended it, Affinity was pleased and called for the printer proceed, to be informed her outfit would be ready in twenty-seven minutes, while her cavern choice would take about the same, so all seemed satisfactory.

With the data entered Affinity lay on the grooming bench, closed her eyes and relaxed. She wiggled more comfortably into the bench.

"Affinity, the wellbeing scan shows you're stressed, the reading is at level three which has a remediation recommendation."

"Not required, just get on with the job."

"I reiterate, your wellbeing needs attention, if you wish to enjoy the day."

Affinity ignored the advice, closed her eyes, and as the soothing perfume woofed into the chamber she took a deep breath, then another. The faint hum of equipment setting about its task quickly faded as Affinity's thoughts drifted to her tiffanys again. Then undirected she found herself reminiscing and reflecting back through various stages of her life, arriving finally at the fifteen-year-old girl she'd been. It was the age her tiffany's conformation first became the subject of a family discussion. It was still a year until her opportunities in the adult world would be determine, when her beauty would be assessed, and so dictate her life's journey. Her beauty rating was to be the sole consideration in establishing her social status

Over the decades class divisions had evolved, until finally society was divided into two main categories, and it was an individual's physical attributes, or the lack of, which determined if they were beautiful or ugly. The two consortiums, were further divided, with four levels of beauty, and three levels of ugly. The beautiful reside in jots (jays only territory), while ugliness was confined dunvilles. All residents were reassessed annually, to discover those needing reclassification. Aging was the nemesis, as it ensured everyone slipped down the ladder, unless of course, for those who started on the bottom. Naturally most people wanted the jot life, and responsible parents spent considerably intervening if their child was found with defects or inadequacies. Most parents wanted physical enhancements irrespective of their child's base line.

Affinity wriggled on the air bed and smiled to herself as she recalled those times of excitement, of youthful expectation, and recollected her nervousness before her approaching alphaspection, when she was officially measured, and assessed, quietly confident of being delivered into a high status. Unsurprisingly the event had been a priority topic for months, even years, among relatives, peers, friends, school colleagues, but mostly within the family. Imminent hopefuls interrogated recent graduates about their best scoring features, and those not rated so well. They wanted to know what affect juvenile interventions, eating regimes, exercises with and without bindings, hormone injections, dental and physical surgery, hair removal, and skin blemish correction, had had on their final grading.

Shortly after Affinity's birth her parents sought to engage a reputed Judco (Juvenile Development Company) to orchestrate her childhood and adolescent growth. Cost was inconsequential as the kudos of a high-ranking daughter, was only outranked by the censure of a low ranking progeny. After weeks research her parents handed the responsibility for her physical production to the Just Jays Company. For the first few years she needed little more than diet control and examinations but when at ten her puberty was nigh, the program intensified. For Affinity there had been three years sleeping in a neck brace but she had been fortunate enough not to need surgical adjustments to her eyelids, ears, nose or lips. Nor had she undergone tiffany adjustment, although there had been minor concerns about their development but finally it was decided intervention was unnecessary.

At fifteen a preliminary assessment indicated her alphaspection would rate her jaytwo, a jil (Jealously Is Likely). Such a rating, for most families was satisfactory, but in her private moments Affinity dreamt of the prized jap (just about perfect) ranking. The dream was likely a common one; hers based on her statistics revealing she exceeded the mandatory height of 177cms for a jayone by one and a half centimetres, her torso/leg ratio was well within specification, her rump exceeded requirements, while her mouth/nose/eye ratio were satisfactory, her ankle/calf/thigh ratio was excellent, her hips were satisfactory. Although her tiffanys location and dewdrop ratio was well within parameters, her tiffanys density rating was below specs slightly. Alone this would not prevent her obtaining the jayone.

However, candidates who were initially assessed jayone still had to face a final hurdle, and it meant submitting to Obac (overall body appraisal committee) which would determine if all zonal dimensions merged harmonically to give a 'yes', or 'sorry'. Candidates who failed the jayone appraisal by less than five percent could appeal to the Obac tribunal.

Just Jays preliminary assessment disappointed Affinity. Regardless, her dejection was brief before she refocused on becoming a jap. Neither of her parents had graduated as japs, her mother Sagacity came through a twojay, as did her father Sanguine, but Sagacity was later assessed up

20

to jap but only held it for two annuments. Affinity's ambition married well with her recently emerged body consciousness, self-awareness, self-confident independence, which all ignited when she discovered carnal cavorting. The discovery that happy endings were more gratifying in company, than solo, was an enlightenment which elevated her to new aspirations, and she set an audacious sail to forage for all the exhilarations she suspected were suspended within the gambit. She believed being a jayone would help her to the zenith of her fantasy. She was just fifteen.

Affinity decided the only potential for last minute improvements lay with her tiffanys but what to do was the problem. Unfortunately, Just Jays, in discussions with her parents had decided, twelve months earlier against any further interventions to her tiffanys, apparently content with a jil rating, with an outside chance at jap. Her parents' seeming untroubled acceptance of this, after years of work and funds, saw Affinity disappointed so she decided to act independently. However, her two months of excessive chest exercising and tiffanys binding had little effect.

Suddenly Affinity's reminiscing was disturbed when the cavern's musical alarm and the voice, "Your back's done and dried Affinity, I'll roll you over to do your front," it announced. She waited for the manoeuvre to be completed, jiggled into comfort again, and closed her eyes again.

"That's fine Affinity; are you ready to continue?"

Affinity's ruminations resumed, her mind returning to the day of her alphaspection, three days after her sixteenth birthday, a delay of three days caused by heavy bookings at the Mac (Measurement, and Appraisal Centre). The assessment was expected to take an hour and Affinity was booked in for eleven am but arrived at ten. She wore regulation attire, in a colour of her choice which was pale orange with fawn pin stripes. The one-piece garment of fine, body clinging fabric, was neck to ankle, her body features exposed undistorted. Her hair was tied on top with a yellow band.

At the centre others also waited; like Affinity nervous and early, half a dozen in all, their apprehensions an impediment to conversation, total silence a fugitive thanks to the boy sitting opposite her. Affinity attributed his assurance to his belief in the certainty of a jap rating. His body was outstanding, and his language intoned success, justifiably she thought. Her assessment included fascination with his male anatomy, obvious within his outfit, and she was pleased he noticed her noticing. When her flagrant gaze settled on his jewels, propriety inspired him to cross his legs.

However, Affinity's libertine self-amusement was shattered when suddenly her name was called, like a scream, and every nerve in her body skipped. Instinctively she sprang to her feet, almost embarrassingly so, and once outside the waiting room, the door opened, above which an illumination read, "Welcome Affinity, please enter. My name is Endeava."

Affinity's gazed into the devouring opening, the rest of her world fading, and for a moment she froze. Mechanically she stepped towards her future. Inside, the room was off white, the fittings and equipment were of stainless, including the desk behind which sat her examiner. Affinity's looked at her and wondered, 'how was this female eligible to be working in a jot, since she was unattractive and surely would not have a jay rating. She was heavy set, stooped slightly, was almost waistless, had what were at least double four-quarter loveless tiffanys, and her short neck and face were wrinkled.

"How are you Affinity, not too nervous, I hope? One look at you and I can tell, you've nothing to worried about, so just relax."

Her voice was sociable and reassuring, and Affinity's disapproval dissolved, as her mind quickly returned to self-interest. Did she have nothing to worry about making a jay rating, or nothing to worry about becoming a jayone? Grudgingly she assumed the former.

"Well, I am nervous; a lot really," a little quaver audible.

"That's natural Affinity, I was a nervous wreck at mine, but that was long time ago. I only ever made a Jok (Just Okay) but now I've been a twoR, for a long time. I have a work time exemption from my dunville to be here," she smiled and with that explanation Affinity relaxed slightly.

The procedure commenced with weighing, and she came in a few grams below 60 kilos, as planned by Just Jays. Then into the scanning chamber where she held the bar above her head for the initial survey, and was scanned again with her arms by her side. Each time a green light beam circled her body charting the progress of the laser. Although it only took a few minutes, it seemed ages to Affinity, her mind having epicentered on the features she thought could be better. Small flaws were suddenly major concerns. There was slight underarm scaring which until this moment had been irrelevant, and her left foot was off setting a few degrees. It seemed to take forever. When the beeper finally sounded the finish, the chamber door swung open, and Affinity's emotional reservoir bust, her body drained, weakness invaded her and her legs were on the cusp of collapse.

Her distress was obvious, "Would you like to sit down for a minute?" Endeava asked.

"Yes please," she replied with a relieved smile, and quickly headed for her chair. Endeava began pursuing the data on her display and Affinity studied her expression hoping it would give a hint as to the favourability, or not, of the results she was examining. Her expression failed to enlighten her.

After a few minutes she looked up at her subject, "Now to the next stage Affinity."

'Hell! I thought it was over,' her mind mumbled.

"I need to test your skin's ductility and check for blemishes, examine your teeth for stability, take a body odour measurement and a head hair count, so just slip out of your outfit for me Affinity, please. I need you naked."

She did, and after a few minutes, she did.

"That's fine Affinity. Just get dressed again, then wait outside. Your results will come through shortly. You'll be called back."

Finally, thankfully, it was all over and walking back to the waiting area she felt a breeze of weightless emptiness overcome her. Her evolution through the alphaspection had been theoretical but now in reality, she found herself unprepared for the passage. The most important event of her young life was done, abruptly, a sixteen years long obsession, dispensed with in minutes, leaving the glare ahead a blank sheet of whiteness. There was no horizon, and while she began toto sense freedom's birth, she could not distinguish between relief and excitement. Maybe they were the same thing.

Like a chick from the shell, she now wanted to shake the legacy. After all the years, all the discussions, all the disciplines, the sacrifices, all the worry. It had come down to this hour, and for a moment her appearance was unimportant, as she began to resent being subjected to the necessities, and finally the examinations. After all the time, all the work, all the discomfort, all the cost, all the years, suddenly it was over, in minutes, had it been worth it? Not at the moment, it hadn't. Her consolation though was in the promised guarantees it would all pay dividends, in the mythical happinesses Which awaited her. However, there were still the results to come, and as she waited, some reasonless foreboding returned too.

How long would she have to wait? Then there it was, after only a few minutes, her name above consultation room number three. The butterflies erupted, her heart began to beating and as she rose from the chair, she held her chest. She was coffined again. The door slid open, this time to reveal a broadly smiling jayster behind the desk, whose pointing finger directed her to sit. She did, uneasily, stiffly and straight backed, her eyes flicking about the room. Oh no, she had to cross her legs urgently, the threat of embarrassing herself a symptom of her nervousness, but not now, she pleaded within.

"Do you need to go somewhere?" the incisive consultant asked.

"Yes, but tell me anyway, how did I do?"

"I'm Adele, Affinity, and congratulations not only have you been rated a jay but preliminarily you're jayone," she announced clearly, looking piercingly into her eyes.

Affinity went blank, she'd almost forgotten about the Obac, but for now a breaking wave swamped her. How could she respond, what should she say, she wanted to laugh, she wanted to cry, she wanted to collapse exhausted. She wanted her mother.

Adele expected an excited yelp, a disbelieving exclamation or platitudes of appreciation, and thanks but instead Affinity sprang to her feet, grasping vesuvius, "I need to pee, quick! Where?"

The office door opened and Affinity rushed to the end of the hallway and turned left. A couple of minutes later she was looking again at Adele across the desk. The interruption had afforded her the chance to collect some thoughts and come to terms with her news.

"What happens now I'm a preliminary jayone?" she asked firmly, a feeling of form and formality finding quarters in her consciousness.

"You'll be notified when to return for the appraisal but Obac only meets weekly so you'll need to wait upon them but it could be later this week or next week, as there've not been many qualifiers recently," she said and turned her attention to her screen.

"I thought it would happen today," Affinity said, disappointed.

"No Affinity, sorry. In the meantime, I've all your statistics which you can examine in detail in your own time, but briefly your torso came in at 8.5/17; your figure is plus 3, your neck head is also a plus 3; your tiffanys are satisfactory stage 2s with very good dewdrop placement of 50/50; your hands and fingers are 3.5/3/4; your hips and buttocks are type C and measured at 65%. Yours legs are a splendid 90 over 90 and your above neck made category 1. You lost seven points altogether which is not enough to affect the final result. However, I do have one concern about your future Affinity."

"Yes," Affinity beckoned, but her concentration was counterfeit, since absorbing the veracity of her achievement required all her mental faculties for the moment.

"Your density scan revealed some tiffany tissue fragility, and I would recommend immediate treatment while there's time, while they appear to be still developing. I think you'll likely end up with three-quarters. I am surprised your management company didn't take some corrective measures early after puberty," she said.

"It was talked about but unfortunately it was decided they were not serious enough to need action," Affinity explained, apologetically, her disappointment clear.

"Well, they were wrong," Adele announced bluntly, "But it's not too late I hope, so I suggest you talk to your parents again if you hope to maintain you jayone into your thirties.

"There's still a couple of other matters we must attend to before we're finished," she continued.

"You need to be scheduled into Capa (Control and Policing Agency) for a microchip data implant, and you also need to have an AP (anti pregnancy) implant. The AP is effective for six years during which time it is illegal to become pregnant. After that you can apply for a pregnancy permit or have the AP renewed. If and when you decide to have children a pregnancy permit is required, whether you plan a personal confinement or chose to exploit a surrogate. Think carefully before ever deciding on getting pregnant yourself, since it will likely have a detrimental effect on your body, particularly your tiffanys, and therefore on your annument. Do you have any questions, Affinity?"

"No. I won't be having babies," she replied impatiently, anxious to be finished.

A week later Affinity's hovering apprehension varnished, with confirmation her jayone rating had been confirmed.

Even now after all the years the memory produced a tingle of delight but the indulgence was brief, and now twenty-eight years on, her tender tit tissue had taken its toll and trumped her tendings, potentially bequeathing some detestable correction procedure or rating disaster.

Affinity mumbled to herself, "Fucking tits, sometimes endowments but always threatening. For men titillating toys; for women merely a narcissistic display of feminine confusion, that's all. Any pleasure they provide is paltry pay for potential problems."

Affinity reached across her chest to the inside of her left arm, just below the armpit and felt the lump under the skin which was the latest of half a dozen she'd had since her visit to Capa all those years ago. They had been replaced each time improved technology made it compulsory. The microchip held all the information required to authenticate identity, including her DNA profile; and were a tracking device which ensured people remained within their zones. As well, it held a history of their status, along with any exemptions to which they were entitled. Chips were updated at each annument, non-intrusively using micro waves. As a person moved through their daily life scanners regularly checked their identity verifying compliance. The whereabouts of scanners was generally known, such as throughout government buildings, most public venues and transport thoroughfares. Capa patrol warders randomly scanned iffy individuals, searching for counterfeit or expired chips.

Penalties for having bogus identity chips could result in forced re-locations or movement restrictions, but repeat offenders could be subjected to chemical personality adjustments. Jot scanners also identified r-raters with visiting exemption who strayed beyond their confinements, or who remained in the jot after hours. People with exemptions were those vital to jot life, and fell into two principal categories; the first being for employment, where a person's qualification or experience could not be found among jays. The second most common group of exemptees were surrogates, who could live with their employer/patron but must be identifiable in public and whose movements and hours were controlled, according to the stage of their pregnancy.

Affinity's post teenage AP implants were now necessities from the past, ever since technology had absolved females from the prime responsibility for preventing pregnancy. Males became responsible with the development of inert sperm implants.

The voice suddenly interrupted and wrenched Affinity from her memories, plonking her back into the world of a forty-two-year-old, clutching at absconding eminence.

"You're finished Affinity, is there anything else you want."

"Nope!"

She lingered on the bench for a minute, initially reluctant to return to the present but then she grew eager to be in the mirror again., not to study her tiffanys this time. The cavern's work delighted her and the patterning had worked particularly well, she thought. Her face would be fine once the lashes, lines, sapphires ear clusters were fitted. The printer had completed its couturier work, and it lay on the tray. She took it by the straps and held it up and smiled, it was as attractive as it displayed, and she pulled it on, jiggled it into place, then stepped into the bottom and jiggled again. She stared at herself from all angles including a paused look over her shoulders.

"That's a nice alice," she gave it a pat. Affinity decided not to bother with the hair booth. She'd have it done at the stylists' where the intercourse would be human, and where her ache for some platonic human understanding was more likely to be found. And on the way, she'd stop off for a double modco.

Chapter 2
Finding Balance

Sunday lunches for Affinity were always taken at the Green Gardens (C) Restaurant, with her sisters, Enamour and Prudence. Affinity was the elder, then Enamour, then Prudence and they were all born female because they were what their parents wanted, and for whom they had obtained permits. They had not been alone in choosing female offspring, as a preference for females had evolved in sync with growing female authority, superiority and societal control. It was an evolution which brought parents to realise female children had the best prospects for the future.

However, when the numbers reached sixty percent females, or one and a half females per male, and projections suggested a continuing increase, the GC was left with no alternative, and moved against the burgeoning imbalance, by introducing controls.

However, a sizeable legion of females opposed any reversal of the trend, arguing that ultimately the only need for males in society was to have enough of them to maintain a selected and healthy gene pool. All other traditional and not so traditional functions, roles and obligations typically sheeted to males, could now be undertaken by females, and in all instances could produce better outcomes. Already females had usurped many male responsibilities and directorships, and there was no reason to disturb the thoroughfare to female destiny. In the end though, the counter debate carried sway, with an equally vocal portion of females favouring more equality. The GC bent in favour of what it considered common sense. Males had remained rather mute on the matter, and while they saw losses either way, there were obvious gains either way as well.

Under the new protocols five out of six couples were refused a female child first time, and three out of six second births had to be male also; but parents deciding to apply for a third, were not restricted by quota, so a female could be chosen, and usually was. The one in five parents who were granted a female first up were ineligible to apply for a female the second time. Mathematically the new regime should have produced eight males for every five females, based on the premise that seventy percent of parents would have a second child, while only thirty percent of parents who already had two male children, would opt for a female. Since large scale surrogacy had become part of the social norm, decades ago, the size of families had grown from one point two children, to two point four.

However, these interventions were only enforceable where the embryos which were fertilised in vitro, and when a surrogate was to be the gestationist. Though there was an anomaly, since couples deciding to have a child naturally, and without the Harlequin Program intervention, would deliver whichever gender arrived. In these cases, when potential parents chose a veritable pregnancy but wanted gender selection, then they became subject to regulation. It was possible for these couples, although fraught, to venture into clandestine gender selection, and harlequin embryo supply, but females going down this path were usually not interested in connivance, and the number of jays interested in this family building avenue was small, and had little impact on the figures.

While couples grumbled, in the end most accepted a boy in preference to the veritable alternative or childlessness, consoled by their sacrifice to the beautiful society. However too few parents chose to have a third child and guaranteed female, so eventually the amendments reversed the ratio to fifty-fifty females and males, and this produced the desired result.

After twenty years of gender management, the ratio of over twenty-year-olds and under thirty, was 55 percent female to 45 percent males, while for the under the under twenties and over tens, the figure was near enough fifty/fifty, but a decimal in favour of males.

The pendulum had swung too far, especially as females belatedly realised their dominance in society was threatened by the re-emergence of males challenging for influential positions. The facts hit home with the release of the five-year Employment Situation Report, which was a statistical categorization, and listing of the employment demographic. The revelations were disturbing, especially high-ranking females. In Rank Three positions, there had been a stunning twenty-three percent increase in males winning these jobs, lifting their share in the category to twenty-six percent; while in Rank Two; there had been a twelve percent increase in males, increasing their percentage to thirty-one; and while Rank One was the least effected, the male increase had still been a disturbing 8 percent, bringing them to 19 percent.

The deduction was simple and obvious. There was a male whale wave washing into society and while it had not yet seriously impacted the top echelons, the inevitable was concerning. The doomsayers were convincing, alarming the female cohort with predictions that males were marching back into control of the beautiful society. And another disturbing aspect of the trend was the fact males were returning to influence, largely utilising the same devices females had exploited in their ascendency.

Unfortunately, re-adjusting the gender regulations to restore a female mass would not end the threat forthwith, as the correction flow through would take another twenty years. However, in the absence of any obvious quick solutions, the GC had set about rewriting the controls. A total abandonment of the program was considered but dismissed, foreseeing it as an open gate to another explosion in female births. But with the all-female GC fearing any return to male eminence would result in a paralleled revival of their predatory instincts, it resolved to firewalled the danger with a moderate surplus of females. It settled on a fifty-fifty split for first child permits, and eight out of ten second permits allocated for females. Third child permits would remain uncontrolled. If family sizes remained high any excess of females should moderate.

Affinity, Enmour and Prudence were conceived before gender allocations and as young adults the sisters slinked into the morass of massing females oblivious to any struggle for identity, or concerned by any innate rivalry for status or attention. Affinity lost her chance for a visa pre-alphaspection, by which time she was well familiar with the single tracked motivations of males, young and old. Pre-alphaspection she'd honed a flamboyant style of presenting herself provocatively, and with quarry waylaid, she'd take control of the rapport, be it brief or extended. Her irresponsible years were brazened, fun and unaccountable, until she was released from her second AP, when unexpectedly her dynamic forces ploughed virgin soil, fertile soil, and her fornicators became lovers, and procreation became a perception.

It was now nearly sixteen years since a surrogate delivered her daughter, her arrival causing consternation, investigation and demanded an explanation, for while her permit said male, the delivery was female. On advice Affinity shammed astonished ignorance, and was unable to offer an explanation, blaming a mix up in the laboratory documentation which would have made feasible if the DNA had not matched the parents. Her insistence on ignorance finally saw the inquiry fizzle. Two years later the same surrogate carried another of Affinity's babies, again with a permit for a male, which was duly delivered accordingly.

Affinity's preference for blue was on display again and this Sunday since she wore it totally, in varying shades. An aspect of the trio's behaviour when they were cocooned in their security triangle, was to be provocative, flaunting themselves and relaxing in their own mirth. And while for the moment nothing was said, Prudence and Enamour were glancing at Affinity, thinking the same thing. Although every detail of her presentation was immaculate, as usual, she'd breached their unwritten code and dressed a voluptuously, too much so. For the moment they wondered silently.

Enamour, like most second children, was of a different chowder and although her early swathe through her peerage lacked any vulgarity, she was disdained by some for her intellectual superiority, and aloof beauty. She was two years younger than Affinity, tall and firm, always cutting a graceful figure, moved elegantly, and her long-legged gait was rhythmic and assured. She'd graduated her alphaspection a comfortable onejay.

As a onejay, suitors, lecherous and virtuous, swarmed in her trail but for most, her conquest was an impossible dream, while her acolytes were content to loiter, pleased for being within her ambit. As maturity began to mould Enamour the elbows in her disposition were checked, leaving an intelligent and sophisticated female, with a subtle determination anchored in self-confidence. She'd had a son in her early thirties, and regardless of some uncomfortableness at trusting her embryo to a surrogate, she had complied with the convention.

Despite the expense Enamour preferred handmade garments of natural fibre rather than those computers fashioned and printers synthetized. Today was no different, her dress was of silk, flowing, in muted multi-coloured florals, the neck line fell to a high waist, her back was bare and below a broad waist band the dress flared slightly to just above the knees. Her unsupported tiffanys occasionally revealed dewdrop beneath the soft fabric, large hooped earrings in stainless dangled almost to her shoulders and around her neck a matching stainless hoop rested. The body makeover was in a touch of burgundy, with fine purple pin stripes running vertically toe to a fading neckline. Her face highlighted the brows, lips and eyelids but they were somewhat subdued under a pair of large bubble shades with faint amber lenses and white rims sitting on her high cheek bones. A fitted but rippled cap in aquamarine reached her ears and beneath it long black hair burst out.

Prudence was more of Affinity's ilk, and like many families youngest, grew up with ripened and relaxed parents, who subconsciously and consciously delegated sundry rearing tasks to her sisters. She escaped the tyranny and obligation to prove perfect parenting, and the innate personality of the female who emerged from this conduit, had been tampered with more by siblings, than parents. The sibling influence had been positive, and Prudence became the trio's glamour girl, vivacious with the broadest hips, narrowest waist, long necked, legs like Enamour's, and A-grade alice, minus three-quarter tiffanys, all of which meant whenever the three went cavorting, she was the ogling magnet. It was taken for granted, she would follow her sisters and become a onejay, and so she did.

She loved pretty things, colourful clothes and objects, and admired interesting shapes, and as a young person she was a standout for her creative displays. Social imperatives were an anathema, and she was reassured finding friends on the fringes.

The contradiction in her personality was her passion for female superiority, spawned more as a reaction to distressing experiences, than out of observation or conversation. She graduated from childhood, carefree, happy, relaxed, but unfortunately, she materialised from under her sisters' umbrella somewhat innocent, with a low-level preservation instinct, or an acute barometer for danger. As a middling teenager she was gullible, a vulnerability sniffed out by an opportunistic male, who subjected her to degrading and disillusioning selfishness. She'd buried the injury in effervescence, and retained a recovery rational, but internally she was convinced female superiority was the only defence against male predation.

Normally Prudence's presented lively and vivacious, and on this luncheon occasion nothing was different. She wore ankle to neck a vivid white with fine red spots, translucent, one-piece suit, with bright red blazes bursting from her crotch upwards and outwards, under and passed each tiffany. Similar bursts from the centre of each tiffany streaked over her shoulders. From her heels thin red straps latticed their way almost to her knees, while above the neck line her skin was whitened with exaggerated red eyebrows reaching mid-forehead. Her lips and eye surrounds were whitened but the eyeballs bore red lenses. While the outfit was stunning it was not one, one would warm to easily, unless you were a sister.

The Sunday lunches were the weekly event for which the sisters were impatient. They were always punctual, and reconnected with cheerful embraces, which morphed quickly into laughter and banter. The salutations continued until the kinships were reaffirmed, their relationship reassured, their affections verified, and all was in order, then with Affinity in the middle they joined arms and strolled into the restaurant. The meal usually extended into an afternoon of comradery and conversation, sometimes ending with a girls' night out, with visits to haunts selected according to the amount of mood enhancing substances ingested, principally by Affinity and Prudence. While these forays could inspire misbehaviour, Enamour always remained stoic and demure, though her sisters knew she was having fun too.

The Green Gardens (C) was aptly named as it was a large and luscious indoor garden with tables sprinkled throughout. The background sound of fountain water flowing and rippling over rocks safeguarded all but the most ruckus conversations from eavesdroppers, intentional or not.

"Good morning, ladies, it's a pleasure to welcome you all again and how are you this beautiful Sunday?" came the welcome, from the stereo-typical restaurant mine-host, in his neck to ankle outfit of black with silver lame, a pixie neck and ankle line.

"Fine Crispen, thank you."

Crispen led the way to their usual corner table, with its view of the rural landscape and then taking charge of the chairs, seated his guests one at a time.

"Would you like something before ordering?" he asked glancing at each of them.

Prudence was the first to respond, "The usual and iced water," she smiled at Crispen knowingly.

Affinity thought briefly, then ordered the same, while Enamour wanted nothing.

Enamour usually imbibed a little but her sudden abstinence had Affinity and Prudence glancing quizzically at each other, guessing. They stared at her, demanding an explanation. With eyes fixed on the menu Enamour's sensed their intrigue, and without raising her head, looked up from under her eyebrows and announced casually, "I've given up all that sort of stuff." she paused teasingly, her silence irritating.

"Well, you've never done much anyway," Affinity noted.

Prudence leaned into the table, her eyes wide, smiling open mouthed, her arm stretching out a begging hand, "Yes Enamor, and?" she stopped, enough said.

"And! Yes," Affinity too demanded.

"I going to get pregnant," Enamour announced coolly, then raised her head, her eyes scooting between them. A stunning silence seized the situation, Affinity straightened in her chair, her expression pained, while Prudence eased back contemplating.

"We'd better talk about this!" Affinity responded immediately academically, her voice vexed. It was a measured and calculated response, plucked from flabbergism, but she knew it was the only approach for this intercession.

"Yes, I'd like to talk about since I'm not getting any support from Maxim. He won't even discuss it."

"Of course, understood," Prudence said, wanting to contribute but struggling to be immediately constructive.

"It's very simple, I have this deep and consuming passion to be pregnant. Well, it used to be deep but now it's surfaced, and I going to have a child which grows inside me, and comes from me, not out of someone else. I know there's a difference," she said glaring at Affinity, dissuading her from interrupting. "Justice is ten now and while I love him very much, I've always felt our bond suffered because I never carried

34

him," her voice was deliberate but her explanation was a path of broken glass. She was hoping neither Affinity or Prudence would contend.

Just the same Affinity wanted urgently, to nip this bud. "Fuck Enamour, I don't understand, you'll need to explain yourself because I'm dumbfounded," she spluttered.

The conversation was disrupted by the arrival of two glasses of water, two tubes and three menus. It was a convenient pause as the oldest and the youngest needed time to comprehend middling's intentions, and to conjure a convincing common-sense contention, inferring her plans were absurd, without being offensive. Prudence took a glass of water and swallowed the cap, Affinity did likewise while Enamour studied the menu. With the ordering done, and despite being aware of Enamour's bid to curtail criticism, Affinity returned to the subject, anxious to find a self-destruct button in Enamour's reasoning.

"How long have you wanted this?" she enquired looking intently into her sister's eyes.

"When Justice was born, I knew straight away I'd been cheated. While he was biologically mine, I'd not borne him, so was he truly all mine; or did I only have a share of him; maybe the surrogate was just as much his mother, probably more emotionally? It left me nebulous and bonding with him was not straight forward, it took time and a conscious effort. Now I want a brother or sister for him, and I want it from me; I want the morning sickness, the discomfort, out of sight and swollen feet, the diet, the medication, the delivery pain, and all the other penalties of pregnancy. I know medication can placate the symptoms but I may find settlement in paying the piper.

"The problem is Maxim says I'm stupid, irrational, even mentally disturbed, and won't even discuss the idea. He's happy about another child but he's adamant we use a surrogate again, and he won't have his infertility implant switched off until there's a test tube for him to impregnate, and a surrogate in the wings."

Affinity's wished to lambast him but knew that would be counterproductive, since she agreed with him. "Enamour love, for goodness' sake, you're so beautiful, at forty-two you're still a jayone; you're exceptional, and you could still be a jil at fifty; don't you worry that pregnancy might ruin those prospects? Pregnancy now could consign you to jayfour or worse, very quickly Are you really ready to risk your body and status by getting pregnant?" her frustration no longer disguised.

Enamour was not interested in the debate. "I'm looking for support Affinity," she said adamantly, unruffled by her sister's argument or dismay.

Prudence's emotional sinews were plodding another path, and it was her sister's immediate impasse which livid. "Let's look at first things first ladies! For the moment, forget about using a surrogate or not," she said staring at Enamour then Affinity, "Maxim is the issue for now, and his refusal to even negotiate with his reba about such a fundamental yearning, needs challenging. Even more, he's been insulting as well," her tone vexing, "and don't think about defending him En," she concluded, staring.

Enamour was unsurprised by Prudence's outburst, and she smiled softly, tickled, pleased her sister seemed to be seeing her problem from one standpoint. "Unfortunately, Pru, it's one of the few things we females have no control over. No regulation can be brought to bear forcing his compliance, and I've tried charm, reasoning, patience, connivance, and bullying, all without any hint of success. Sadly, for him, the concept is foreign, inconceivable," she explained.

Prudence sighed, looked aside, and averse to persist, and for the moment surrendered to Enamour's apparent impossible predicament. Then, "But if Maxim won't cooperate what's the alternative?" Prudence enquired, probing for an off ramp.

"I not sure Pru, as long as it arrives via my birth canal I don't care, and Maxim is not the only male in the universe," she pronounced, again quietly but defiantly.

Prudence's face ignited. "You wouldn't!?" she paused, grinning, "Would you!?" her voice rang with enthusiasm for the alternative.

"I think she would!" Affinity concluded, studying her sister's expression.

The seafood entrée arrived, offering another opportunity to dwell. Prudence's shuffled in her chair. She felt uneasy, thinking she had dismissed Enamour's predicament too easily. She eyeballed her victim, her expression hardening.

"Who the damn does Maxim think he is sis, the days of the male dictatorship, even choice, are long gone, so if you want to be pregnant, he'd better deliver his half; end of story!" she paused. "These days most males have accepted their new role, and it's incumbent on females to ensure all renegades are re-aligned," Prudence's sentiment was as expected.

"He's not a renegade, and there is a bond between us; I believe that he just thinks I shouldn't jeopardise myself, when a surrogate could do the job. Some people would interrupt that as love," Enamour said, hoping to quell any emerging enmity.

"You might think it's love for you, but really, it's your body he loves, principally it's fucking your body he loves, but now from the depths of incredulity, you're imperilling the optical quality of his carnal pleasures. He's just fears your post pregnancy topography will not be as picturesque as before, and that's all he's worried about. Typical male," Prudence suggested. Then she continued, "if he loved you, he'd help you get pregnant. It's that simple!"

Affinity lay down her utensils, looked up at Prudence, "Pru, you're missing the point. Pregnancy is the issue, and it doesn't matter who initiates it, Maxim or someone else," she explained. "So, it's just a matter of convincing our sister to use a surrogate, but I sense you and I won't achieve that."

Prudence agreed, "Yes, well! It's En's body and her choice, besides she'll probably keep a high jay rating post pregers, anyway," Prudence said, her resignation consoling.

But for neither sister this was not the end of the matter, despite the platitudes, and Affinity now resorted to a subtle approach, hoping Maxim's opposition may be an embryo worth nurturing.

"Maxim's disregard for your instincts, and his refusal to share your dream, leaves you with no recourse but to employ the only alternative, doesn't it?" she asked sympathetically.

"There are occupational live shooters touting, and the idea of abusing one goads the mutineer in me, stimulating my sensual nymph. And a search for an alternative male lets me peruse for the perfect specimen," Enamour said exposing intimacies, something she rarely allowed.

Prudence and Affinity glanced at each other again, "That's a rather libertine and mercenary approach to such a profound and far-reaching undertaking, and you surprise me, since I've never seen this mutineer you're claiming," Prudence said, but her eyes were glinting at the prospect. "Anyway, there's another way, mundane and surely not as much fun, but it comes with all the safeguards. You may not qualify, but you should consider artificial insemination, which even if you're ineligible, can be secured for a price," she suggested.

"No Pru, I considered that briefly, but no. It's not my vision of conception; on a clinic table, my legs hooked up and spread eagled, while some functionary with syringe and laparoscope, peers into vivian, probing academically. I see a natural occasion, with a least a nefertiti or four, maybe more."

"You're a funny girl En, good on you, if you're determined to do this" Prudence conceded, "I'm seeing a side to you which surprises me. One thing about it, we'll have lots to talk about in the coming months. Already I'm anxious about your seeding, and you must promise to keep us up to date with all the intricacies."

"Maybe Max will come around, I'd prefer that but either way I'm determined, and you'll hear," Enamour conceded.

The arrival of the main course saw them fall silent again but not for long. Affinity glanced up from her meal examining Prudence for a few moments.

"You've something on your mind Prudence, what is it?" she asked looking backdown at her food.

Prudence looked up and paused, her sisters sensed something was afoot but said nothing, but stared pointedly, awaiting their baby's news.

"Well, I'm hesitant after to hearing about En's plans," she paused, smiling.

"Come on Prudence, spit it out," Affinity demanded.

"I can't believe the coincidence, I feel a little embarrassed, even a thunder thief," she stopped, unsure how to proceed.

"Not pregnant, are you!?" Affinity snapped, gawkingly eyed.

"No Affinity!" she paused again, "Stone and I applied for a pregnancy permit more than two years ago, and we've up onto the A list for a surrogate, so we're expecting some news in the near future," she announced apologetically

"That's all I need, two pregnant sisters to mother" Affinity announced sulkily.

"I'm not getting pregnant. Just getting a baby!" Prudence rebounded abruptly

"Well, Pru, it's not a big surprise. I knew you two were thinking about it, but it's out of the blue just the same," Enamour said, delighted. "Have you got a time line yet?"

"Once we receive a surrogacy agreement and the pregnancy permit it should only take days if all our files, DNA compatibility, physically soundness, and the physiological and social reports are acceptable. However, that won't happen until we're at the front of the surrogate queue, and that shouldn't be long now," she replied.

"How long?"

"Months, maybe less, maybe longer."

"What gender do you want?" Affinity wanted to know.

"Well, we'd like a girl, and now they've eased the quota a little we might be lucky. But whatever, we'll be happy. I think Stone would like a boy but he's not insisting."

"And what about a harlequin?" Affinity wanted all the details.

"That's a silent but brewing topic at home. Stone thinks like En, and wants to leave it largely to nature but we're not thinking much beyond the surrogate at present. However, since neither of us are perfect physical specimens, I want to all the adjustment allocation to upgrade him."

"You might not be perfect; nobody is, and even the harlequins never turn out exactly as planned, but since you're both very attractive people, and I can't see why nature wouldn't do an excellent job," Enamour reasoned.

While Affinity had found the conversation stimulating, even concerning, she had arrived for the lunch unusually anxious, something which her sisters noticed, and she had expected her problem would be the conversation's main topic, and she'd hoped for the normally reliable empathy and sympathy from her sisters. She'd dressed hintingly and had been disappointed her display had been ignored; well, not entirely as she'd noticed silent glances. However, in view of the surprise disclosures hitherto, it was possible her anguish may garner only casual acknowledgement, and could even be regarded trivial.

"Well sisters, changing the subject from babies to baby feeders; that is, tits, specifically my tiffanys," she proclaimed, leaning back presenting a better view, then waited for their reactions.

She didn't have to wait long as two pairs of eyes, which had been reluctant, flashed and locked onto her blue pattern fully exposed three-quarter tiffanys, the centre pieces of her immaculate turned out

Public tiffany display was not common but it was growing in popularity, and was already widespread among the young, especially at entertainment venues, at nocturnal cavortings, at arena events, and at other places of play. For Affinity though, today's excess was a first. She sat upright, straightened her back, lay her shoulders back, and looked down her face at her problems.

"Look at these," she demanded stabbing the sides of her tiffanys with her index fingers.

"What do you think?" she looked up wanting her sisters' to respond.

Unsure where the subject was headed Prudence retorted, "They look great Affy, always have. What's wrong?"

Affinity frowned, "No, Prudence, I want the truth," she said looking to Enamour hoping for a more considered response, but she had decided sitting on the fence was wise, for the present.

Her hesitancy caused an impatient Affinity to continue before either sister could reply. "I've always known my tiffanys were my Achilles' heel, so I've always protected them, and until recently they've held up. In fact, until I was thirty-four, they supported my jayone rating, and have stood well enough for my jaytwo, but I think the picnic's over."

"What's wrong with them?" Prudence demanded, mystified.

"They've lost substance texture and weight, the dewdrop which were once 45/55 have drooped to 52/48, the roots have narrowed a bit, and with raised arms I still have tiffany on trunk."

Enamour loved her sister but when she occasionally rolled out her drama queen, she was inclined to dismiss her. This could be different though, even if it was emotional rather than factual.

"There's nothing to worry about Affy, just have an intervention if they are letting you down. Most females end up requiring help, everyone expects it finally."

"Not at my age, and please don't sound like Summit too," her annoyance obvious but it was quickly displaced by self-pity, "I'm only forty-two En."

"You can't deflect aging Affinity, all you can do is be thankful medical science gives us the ability to stave off the inevitable, even delay ugliness until we're quite old," but Prudence's attempt at logic made little impression.

Prudence stood up. Leant over the table and reached for a handful of her sister's tiffanys. She squeezed gently and released, then again. She straightened up, and looking down at herself took her tiffanys in her hands and applied the same test to herself.

"You've amusing Pru, people are watching and wondering," Enamour said a little embarrassingly and glancing around the restaurant.

Prudence checked around but was unbothered, then sat down.

"Yours have let go a bit more than mine Affy but I'm five years younger, so that's normal I'd guess. En's right, just have them inflated a touch, or whatever. You shouldn't need us to tell you that."

It wasn't what Affinity wanted to hear; she'd heard it before, repeatedly at home.

"That's easy to say, but some females have had bad outcomes from that sort of intervention," she said leaning forward, her hand stretching across the table to stroke Prudence's arm.

She withdrew realising unhappily her comrades' interest was cursory, but still she could not let it rest. "I've always been envious yours Pru. They're still as gorgeous as ever."

"Simple, Affy, find a good technician," Enamour tried to disguise her rising irritation.

Affinity had hoped the lunch tattle would have comforted her obsession but in the light of the unexpected revelations, and the fact her tiffanys had generated only casual interest, her attention switched to the other pair which concerned her, "En, if you finally decide to have your baby yourself, you won't breastfeed it, will you? That would be the final disaster."

"My decision is done Affy! And yes, I'm taking the whole voyage."

The response served to compound Affinity's dejection, and although she had only enquired as a diversion from her own impasse, there appeared no redress at the end of this corridor either.

"Changing the subject again ladies, are we interested in a night at the arena, because I am. I'm disposed to a bit of brutality, some bouncing in the stalls, punching some air, screaming some abuse?" Prudence asked her eyes flashing between them

"Men or women," Enamour enquired.

"Both I think."

"Yeah, Pru, sounds great. What about you En?

"Yes, sounds like an idea?"

"Right, that's an appointment then. I hope it'll be an official red night, with cloud," Affinity explained wistfully.

"Even better."

Chapter 3
Watching Brilliance

As the Bustohe (Buck Stops Here) of the Pregnancy and Surrogacy Authority (PASA), Summit sat at the head of the table in the Nognog Nownow room, as he did whenever he called management team meetings. His chair was grandiose, more so than the others around the table and it reclined, whereas the others did not. Usually, he was in situ ahead of schedule awaiting the four section managers for their weekly confab, and today was no different.

It was tactical, and instead of making them await his pleasure, he preferred to cast an intimidating eye over his subordinates, as they entered. The four underlinings underlined their proficiency by arriving exactly on time, 10 am. As a survivor in the diminishing ranks of male bushies, in the beautiful society and now in his latter forties, Summit was acutely aware of the precarious nature of his situation. A popular rumour circulating the office was he'd be downgraded to jaythree at least, at his next annument, weakening him further, and making a putsch seem delicious; and he knew to whom.

His survival methodology was basic. Command from a bolt-hole; keep any and all perceived or possible rivals in the dark; attack at every opportunity employing his experience, competency, and cunning; and assert his authority aggressively where feasible. As he awaited this morning's meeting Summit pondered his style, while his eyes lazed around the familiar scene. The conference room's walls were red flock panels with timber dividers, the carpet brickish red, and the table and leather cushioned chairs were grey. The table held a digital screen at each placing which popped up as the companion chair was sat upon. The lighting was diffused.

At the far end of the room, staring at Summit from the life-sized hologram, were a near naked couple. They were the current Most Beautiful Male and Woman of the Year, a title granted, purportedly, to the two most beautiful specimens in the land, an accolade which secured them financially and socially forever, and even when aged and ugly, society would continue to tolerate their presence in appreciation of, and in memory of, their once supreme beautifulness, albeit with restrictions. While title holders, they were referred to as Nog-Nog (Number one guy) and Now-Now (Number one woman).

At meetings he often directed from beneath his eyebrows. He didn't like his management team much, in fact not at all, and while he accepted they were all deserved onejays, they were not superior operatives, and he found their sometimes patronising and pretentious manner grating. The conference door opened at exactly ten, and as the three females and a lonesome male spilled into the room and dispersed around the table, Summit watched them intently, especially the one he knew was scheming an ambush. His telekinetic rays could not destroy her ambitions but as he stared intently at her, there was some hedonistic satisfaction in the dream. They were a young, colourful quartet, one in tones of green, another in tones of red, then blue and yellow. Their morning's cavern presentations were all different, one in fine stripes, another with swirls, fades, and a fine and subtle checking. Their colours never clashed as they decided each week on theme colours and the accentuations for the following week.

The tradition had produced some startling, even pioneering turnouts and while Summit was difficult to surprise, today his steely grimace concealed a surprised expression. When the current Nog-Nog and Now-Now were first unveiled publicly, their near nude dress code influenced a trend towards more personal asset exposure, and it now had caught on with this group. Summit's eyes were on his nemesis, Brilliance, whose colour theme of red seemed appropriate. She was tall, attractive, and despite her lithe beauty, a physical strength coursed with her every movement, while beneath her flagrant superficiality lay self-confidence and an intellectualmetier. Her red was shaded to accentuate her features, while from her face a disconcerting pair of black eyes watched out. She sat, peeled off her tice (totally integrated communication encrypter) from her arm, placed it on the table, and turned to Nog-Nog and Now-Now, without acknowledging Summit.

The four were seated quickly, and as their settling subsided

Summit's eyes toured the faces, fixing again on Brilliance, who still chose to ignore him. The contest was apparent and silence descended, the other three glancing between themselves amused, but ultimately coming to watch Summit and wait for his solution. Brilliance toyed with her keypad, then rested back in her chair, folded her arms, then finally turned her eyes to Summit, but not her head. He smiled; she remained stum.

"Good morning everyone, thanks for coming. You all look great, as usual. By comparison my presentation looks a little drab."

"Your age and rating are your alibi," came the commiseration.

Summit hesitated, then ignored the comment, straightened up and pushed a key on his panel, readying for the morning's business.

"What about the assurance?" came a an abrupt demanded from a pair of black eyes, beaming at Summit.

"Do we really need that, Brilliance?" he questioned dryly.

"It's fucking compulsory before all meetings, you know that," she snapped.

Resigned to the banal interruption he leaned forward to speak to his screen, "present today's assurance," he demanded, and all eyes turned to the hologram. Nog-Nog and Now-Now came to life. Now-Now smiled, turned about, paused, then looking back over her shoulder spread an open hand over alice, "Good morning beautiful people, today I wish to remind you of this month's assignment. Your buttocks," she hesitated, patted hers, then turned back to the front.

"We encourage you to have a density reading, be measured for spread, shrinkage and slump, and recommit yourself to the maintenance of its ride, shape and texture. For females it's especially important since we are more vulnerable to its deterioration than are males, so keep up regular cellulite tests. If unfortunately, any deterioration is detected, seek remediation immediately. Remember staying beautiful takes time and effort but no one needs to end up in a dunville prematurely, so don't let this month escape until you're sure alice is okay."

It was Nog-Nog's turn, and with a precise voice and a fading smile announced:

"Yesterday's figures are satisfactory with 159 candidates undergoing alphaspections. The break up is 38 to be confirmed onejays, 45 made twojay, 34 made threejay, 19 made fourjay, and 23 unfortunate youngsters were rated Rs, three of them were graded the lowest at threeRs. The prognosis for the onejays is that all are expected to be confirmed by Obac, and 24 are predicted to maintain their rating for ten years or more, while ten should survive until age thirty-five. Overall, a satisfactory day for our young people.

"Once again, we thank you people at Pasa for your contributions to our beautiful society," he said and looked to Now-Now.

With the propaganda finished the hologram resumed statue status, three pairs of glistening eyes returned to Summit, while the fourth lingered on the hologram.

"Damn, she's beautiful," Brilliance sighed. "She makes me feel so fucking inadequate."

No sympathy was forthcoming, least not from Arrant who leaned towards Brilliance, his biceps, deltoids and pectorals featuring, beneath a square set jaw and joules, all shaded in blues, with brown eyes,

"Yep Brilliance, she sure does," he said grinning wide eyed, "I certainly wouldn't crawl over her to get to you."

She responded with a sneer, as she gazed unblinking at her antagonist, her mind scheming to respond from her self-assured position of personal and intellectual superiority.

"Here's some advice Arrant. Look for some other engagement, as your tenure here is soon to expire, because your position is about to be challenged," she said knowingly. "There's five people around this table, only three of them female, which is an unfortunate but temporary disorder, since within six months it'll be all female. Don't worry about that." She flicked a glance at Summit.

"The number of males returning to senior positions is increasing Brilliance, so the era of the female takeover, is over," Arrant prophesied.

This was not the first time Summit needed to defuse friction between these two, and in doing so stepped over Arrant's comments and addressed Brilliance's.

"Be that as it may Brilliance, today we need to confront a problem requiring immediate attention. The serious backlog of rebas waiting for surrogates is a subject we've skirted for too long, and it's reached the point where we must act decisively. It's an impasse of which we've been cognisant for too long, and have pretty much ignored; wishfully

46

rationalising, or hoping, that nature, or a self-correcting phenomenon would materialise to rescue us. Stealthily and relentlessly the problem has crept upon us for several years, until now, the GC's (Governing Council) hand has been forced and has now directed us, in no uncertain terms, to devise a remedy, post-haste."

Summit reached out and touched his screen, peered at the information for a moment, and without looking up read out the details: "This month's figures are: District A1, currently has applications from 112 licensed and approved rebas for surrogate but we'll only have approximately 78 surrogates available over the next three months; district A2 requires 79 surrogates but only 42 are available; District B1 needs 174 but at best we'll only supply 54; etc. For all districts 984 surrogates are required but at best 502 are all we have available. In districts such as A1 with its high proportion of onejay females, the situation is not as critical as it is in other districts such as B1, where threejays are prevalent, while surrogate availability is only around 30 percent."

"Fourjays can't currently exploit surrogates, and we should exclude threes too!" Brilliance cracked.

A gentler voice secure in competence was thinking, and Summit looked at Vertex, her eyes and dewdrops amber, while much of her upper somatic exposure was eclipsed by the flurry of orange and blonde striped hair falling over her soft shoulders, and over her upper femininity. Her body was pastely, patterned in undulating blood-orange, with fine light twirls, and her lips in white, black outlined.

"Can you post those figures to us?" she queried firmly, her finger tapping her screen.

Summit glanced around the faces, it was a moment for sand bagging against compatriot scrutiny, and risking any mistakes or miscalculation being discovered.

"No," he responded abruptly, and looked back at his screen, planning to nip the subject by moving on too quickly for potential interjectors.

"Here's the root of our dilemma! The number of jayfour females, jars, (join a recovery scheme) prepared to become surrogates has diminished considerably, as has the oneRs, raps, (recovery a possibility) group. The only category which has maintained a stable flow of surrogates is the twoRs, runs, (recovery unlikely now). There are still rofs, (rubbed out forever), females available, but more than a few are deemed unsuitable or unfit for exploitation, while embryo parents are quick to reject some, alleging obesity, indolence or have a poorer medical history. None of these demerits effect the development of an unrelated embryo, but prospective parents too often hang out for a surrogate of better conformation. It's delusionary wanting an attractive surrogate, a ridiculous perception and an oxymoron. But there we have it!"

"Do we have any information about why the rap group is shrinking. Have we done any surveys or analysis?" a clear deep male voice asked.

"Yes Arrant, for the past twelve months I've had all threejay, jok (judged okay) and below, at their annuments, answer a questionnaire about their prospects of becoming surrogates. In all, over two and a half thousand surveys were completed and the results were pretty clear. Joks, almost universally were insulted they were even in our surrogacy range finder, with only five percent acknowledging that nullipara may not, or need not, be forever. Most, joks still regard surrogates as mere mercenary amenities, and most have availed themselves of their uteruses. Even the thought of becoming surrogates is seen as a denial of the jay ethos, and therefore abhorrent.

"In the meantime, while the feelings among jars females is not as hostile, the group size has diminished and is continuing to shrink, and while the survey found the majority still desire a jot life, a significant number are accepting that the dunville is inevitable, and just a matter for time. It may even have benefits. This belief, apparently, is gaining traction in this diaspora, and it should be a concern for others, not us. The survey indicates that when these females arrive in dunvilles, some will be more inclined to surrogacy, especially if they are financially needy, and are physically suitable. It's estimated three-quarters would be suitable but unfortunately, they have failed to enlist in the numbers which would go anyway in dissolving our problem.

"Fuck Summit, I don't believe anyone wants to become an R. Your survey is bullshit. I just don't believe it," came a raucous, and dismissive response from a wondering expression.

Summit paused, staring at his sceptical twenty-three-year-old colleague.

"Brilliance," he said and pausing until she glanced sideways at him, "the survey has a two to three percent error factor, since before questioning all subjects enjoyed a modified modco, ensuring their honesty."

Brilliance looked away, withdrew her arms from the table, and eased back in her chair.

"Well, the sooner those have-beens end up in a dunville the better, because I don't want them holding back our beautiful society," she pouted.

"There is some evidence that a percentage of former jay females discover a maternal hankering once the pressures of the jot lifestyle passes. However, they are usually nulliparas responding to flushes of activated hormones, oestrogen and progesterone, and invariably, they have their own babies," he said.

"Selfishness, if they've already had children by surrogates, I'm with Brilliance on this," Vertex exclaimed. "They obviously expected a long jot life and enjoy themselves, while surrogates did their breeding but now; they're too selfish to help other young women extend their jot lives. It should be a condition of their initial contract, that those utilising a surrogate, must return the same number of surrogacies, when their jay lives have spluttered out." she said.

"Unenforceable, but if so, would be counterproductive," Summit pronounced, bluntly

But Vertex wasn't finished. "If jay females were required to return surrogacy, it would go a long way towards neutralising the present imbalance. Jayfems would have fewer children, and more would end up baring their own, particularly when they become resigned to their decline. I'd be interested to know how many jayfems are aged between forty and forty-five, and still acceptable for pregnancy."

Arrant stared across the table, at Vertex, "So Ver, when do you think it will be your time to be a surrogate?" he was watching her intently.

She did well to conceal the shudder which speared its way from her shoulders to her feet, and for a moment her mind went blank. Her pregnant! It was a prospect so foreign as to be preposterous, even in the distant future but when her thoughts reassembled, she sensed a belittling in the question, and contesting Arrant's stare; she leaned forward.

"By that time Arrant, probably males will be neutered five minutes after their first ejaculation is popped into liquid nitrogen. That is if you're any good," she paused watching him working on a comeback but Brilliance injected "Fuck no, they'll always be of some use, certainly 'special purpose' specimens need to be preserved, fully fuelled, and with all their instinctive impulses, and repugnances intact."

But Vertex wasn't finished. "They can still get it up and perform when they've been sterilised. When they only have the journey and no destination they should last longer," Vertex said, defending her suggestion.

"No Vertex, that wouldn't work. Their brothers are their dynamos, and if they're anxious to unload that last extra bit of oomph makes it worth tolerating them. As long as they stay in their place, then that's okay," Brilliance said, contented.

Vertex looked to Summit, "All that aside, some sort of contractual obligation is worth investigating, and it should include exploring feasible sanctions against recalcitrant. Impractical it maybe, but let's investigate."

Summit ignored the banter and the suggestion, "Of all the groups, the ones which offer some immediate potential are the twoRs, and the threes. These categories already supply the most surrogates but it appears there remains within that group unsourced resources. Most of these females have never been jays, having been born to veritable mothers in dunvilles, and grown up there, and it's a reservoir of fit, healthy and a younger group of females which can be further utilised. However, while there are some opportunities in these groups, they cannot dissolve the shortfall, or even come close. We need to work towards a plausible, long-term solution."

Brilliance inhaled the white contents of a capsule, held her breath for a moment and sank back into her chair.

So far, the morning's meeting's most startling and intimidating pair of eyes had flashed lustrous silvery about the room but Fraternity had remained silent, content to listen. Now her pastel pink on pink camouflage designed body wriggled forward in her chair.

"We need to divide this problem into three sections and find answers one at a time," she said glancing at the faces around.

"Firstly, we must examine supply, and it seems to me there is

50

probably some uptake to be had there. Secondly, let's not overlook demand. Are there options for reducing demand? And thirdly, who is really in control of the program? I believe at present, the parents right to choose or reject, an otherwise suitable surrogate, gives them too much say, when, if they want a surrogate, they should accept whatever is available," she said hoping she had injected sufficient provocation to agitate the group beyond the rhetoric.

"If we appoint surrogates arbitrarily, that would take up some of the spare capacity in the r-threes," Summit admitted.

"By how much?"

"I'd be guessing, but probably around 50 immediately, could be double that."

"Doesn't your private file tell you exactly," Brilliance sniped, pointing at his screen but she was ignored.

"Taking away parental choice could deter some potential parents from the program, and thereby reduce demand slightly, which helps Fraternity's proposition," Vertex suggested.

Two hands slid into the middle of the table, intending not to be ignored again, "We must avoid anything which encourages or obliges beautiful females to get pregnant," Brilliance nagged, forcibly. "I saw a pregnant onejay the other day," she exclaimed and paused, glancing around to ensure she was being heard.

"It was not a pretty sight," she sighed. "And she seemed unashamed, striding or struggling past people enjoying drinks and lunch in the sunlight, her bugling spectacle destroying the ambience completely. It didn't appear to bother her; she made no attempt to disguise her condition and in fact I think she may have been flaunting it. It ruined my day anyway." She paused, "I didn't think they were allowed in public in day light, at that stage, even if she was a jayone."

"Compassion is not your strong point, is it Brilliance?" Summit queried.

"It has nothing to do with compassion; I'm just reminding this meeting that our duty is to protect the beautiful society, and we should, at all times, maintain the standards which have taken decades to achieve. When I see a once beautiful female so destroyed, I'm upset, that's all," her tone petered.

"It's not our commission to uphold beauty standards, Brilliance, we've just supply them with surrogates," Arrant reminded her.

"There is no reason why, why after giving birth, a female, with some effort, cannot retrieve her former beauty, especially with today's technologies," Fraternity reasoned.

Brilliance glanced at her dismissively, "Five in ten women aren't that lucky, while only one in ten have no after effects at all," she retorted.

Summit was keen to get on with business.

"I have some propositions for considering. First; increase payment and privileges to surrogates.

"Second; raise the eligibility aged of females entitled to utilise surrogates from twenty-seven to thirty-five.

"Third; allow rebas to use surrogates only once every ten years.

"Four; as Fraternity suggested, withdraw parents' right to assess and approve or reject surrogates. Either accept the offer or go back to the end of the queue.

"Five; withdraw the rights of threejays and fours to use surrogates, especially the fours who we need as assets, not liabilities.

"Six; reduce the eligible age of surrogacy, from the present 18.

"To what?" Vertex interrupted.

"I don't know. You tell me,17," he glanced around enquiringly.

"Sixteen," Brilliance announced blasély.

"They're only kids at that age," Fraternity objected "Physically, ideal probably, but immature while mentally, emotionally and socially still children. For a couple years after sixteen they should just have fun, not moribund in pregnancy. And while at sixteen they don't have to get pregnant, just because they're Rs, they're vulnerable to conniving and unreasonable persuasion. For me, that's not a consideration."

"We can talk about that, in due course" Summit suggested dismissively, and moving on.

"Seven; reduce the eighteen-month layoff between pregnancies for surrogates, say to a year, or nine months, thereby getting more production from the existing pool."

Brilliance had loaded her ammunition in readiness, and it was items two and three on Summit's list, which were targets.

"What we are talking about here are female rights, jay class females, that is. We've no moral authority to dictate to a female she cannot have a surrogate until she's thirty or thirty-five, just because she's beautiful. Of course, very few couples want children before thirty-five but still, it's the principle, and it's already bad enough with the twenty-seven limit. Pushing it to thirty-five is out of the question as far as I'm concerned. And also, what fucking right do we have to say a female can only have one child every ten years just because she's beautiful?" Brilliance demanded.

"After the age of twenty-four they can have veritable babies as young and as often as they like," Arrant said attempting to balance the argument.

Brilliance scowled; her eyes shot daggers but she was too disgusted to respond. Instead, she reached again into her waist band for another capsule.

"Brilliance, you should cut back on that stuff, you're already scratching. How do you get so much anyway, you must be using more than your legal quota?" Arrant advised and questioned.

"Bugger off Arrant. It's none of your damn business how much I use or don't use, or where I get it." She reached into her waist band again took out another capsule holding it up, "anyone want one," she enquired looking at everyone except Arrant. There were no takers.

Fraternity had been mulling the options, "I agree; let's consider increasing financial rewards and privileges, let's withdraw parental right of surrogate selection, let's deny fourjays surrogacy access, let's set a new minimum age for surrogates, and shorten the time between their pregnancies. However, I agree with Brilliance that interfering with mothers' ages and the number of children they can have, could cause more trouble than we expect."

Vertex was thinking differently, "We're concentrating on two things; restricting demand and increasing production from our current inventory, when we should be directing our thoughts more on new supply sources. We know we can increase supply somewhat by fiddling with ages, layoffs and incentives, etc., but it's likely, despite your survey Summit" she said looking at him, "I believe there'd be significantly more females available for surrogacy, if the environmental and contextual factors of the profession, were held in higher public esteem.

"The reason these opportunities didn't appear in the survey, could simply be a matter of females shying from the perceived relegation to subservience, even serfdom, and a substantial status downgrade; rather than a matter of not wanting the rewards for surrogacy. I know, if I was contemplating surrogacy, I'd be off-put by the lack of regard with which the vocation is held by the community, both in jots and dunvilles. While we all understand the importance of their contribution, we fail to afford the surrogates the station they deserve. Surrogates and dunvilles are seen as synonymous, and since dunvillians are regarded inferior, there lies the dilemma," she concluded.

"You are probably right Vertex, but correcting that problem is a long-term propaganda program, and should be part of our planning but we need solutions which will have an impact sooner, or at least in the predictable future, or at least give that impression," Summit said.

"Of course, we could look at enticing recruits by offering surrogates a lifestyle commensurate with that of a jayones or twos."

Brilliance's simmering furry exploded again, and she sprang upright in her chair, "No fucking way!" she blurted.

"Having a jayone lifestyle doesn't mean they cohabit with jayones in a jot," Summit said attempting to neutralise the objection, but Brilliance showed no sign of acquiescence.

"So how do you think it could work?" Vertex enquired.

"I'm not sure, but we should examine possibilities."

"Surrogates are already permitted in jots if residing with the parents, so why not house the others in special facilities, where they can live in similar conditions, but with some restrictions," Vertex suggested.

"Restrictions or not, we're still talking about letting ugliness circulate in our community, and pregnant ugliness at that! The thought is horrific. Already there's far too many incompatibles with exemptions in jots," Brilliance remained dogmatic.

"There could be a way to make the compensation package more attractive to jayfour females, other than just by increasing remuneration," Arrant said, looking at Brilliance. "Your probably won't like it, but anyway; if a jayfour surrogate delivers full term, she could be guaranteed her ranking for, say, two or three more years, and if she has a reba, his annuments could be suspended for the same period. And I know this might be a stretch, but why not allow oneR surrogates back in the jot for a couple of years, after confinement."

"You're right Arrant, it's a shit idea. A lot of what I've heard here today means lowering the jot specifications and standards, and I'm fed up with it," Brilliance waved a dismissing hand.

The others pondered but it was Summit who pointed to the obvious, "We don't have the authority to do that, anyway. We'd need GC to amend the Specification Charter, and while I'm fairly sure they'd reject it, it's a strategy for unloading some responsibility onto the GG to help solve the problem. At least that would mollify the need to defend ourselves, so vehemently" he mused.

Fraternity felt visionary. "Let's extend our thinking, step outside the square, where the answer often awaits. Farming is the solution, baby farms, where controls are stringent, and production improvements are found through research and development," she headlined. "I see standalone institutions where surrogates reside, under constant medical, emotional and social care, in a place where baby production is relegated to a by-product of the lifestyle. It would necessarily be an active lifestyle, mentally stimulating, and self-enriching. It could be promoted as a career choice for young females, where they undertake higher education, graduate, and who at the end of their engagement, say after ten to fifteen years, could retire financially secure, self-assured and comfortably as young as thirty or thirty-five. Or, with the benefit of qualifications, could pursue fulfilling careers, even from the dunville. What we would be offering would be a pathway to personal fulfilment, via five or six or more pregnancies."

"And the measure of their reward could be in ratio to their production," Arrant suggested.

"So, we'd need surrogates to deliver up ten times in a career, to justify what is likely to be at a very expensive operation," Brilliance said after making a quick mental calculation or a wild stab. But it was the ten gestations which was the hook for her.

"At present surrogates produce, on average, two and a half babies before withdrawing from the program, and while doubling this figure would go a long way towards resolving the problem, long term it would not be sufficient. Maybe farming is the answer," Summit agreed.

"As devil's advocate let me ask, what happens if such a project becomes so successful, we ended up with a farm over supplied with underutilised and unpregnant would be surrogates, to whom we've made commitments?" Vertex asked.

"I think we should first deal with current shortage and worry about a surplus if that unlikely event ever arises," Brilliance rationalised.

The discussion honed in on the probability that surrogate husbandry could solve the supply dearth, while not immediately, but certainly in the medium term. First up though, the priority was more research, as they needed to discover the reason so many eligible females were uninterested in surrogacy. Even without research they recognised the perception of surrogates needed enhancing, and therefore it was agreed the term 'baby farm' be erased from their jargon forthwith, and with more professional terminology, be adopted

Setting production targets would be simple, estimating unit costs would have limited variables, and retail pricing, being easily adjustable, would be straight forward. However, resource recruitment was problematic, since surveys would likely carry high error factors. The difficulty lay in projecting how many surrogates could be enticed or cajoled to enlist, what was a reasonable production rate expectation, or could any production tally be reliably forecast?

"For farming we need to find a different type of female than those we normally deal with. It's an opportunity to promote institutionalized professional surrogacy, by creating a female collective whose only desire for male attendance comes solely courtesy of a contractor. With that human prerequisite sorted, surrogates would concentrate on personal achievement and fulfilment, leaving the foetal creation a secondary factor, even a biproduct"

"I've a suggestion," Brilliance interrupted, "How does Progenitive Lodge sound for a name," her suddenly smiling face searching for approval.

"Yes," a surprisingly convivial Arrant agreed.

"What about Progenitive Palace, the PP," came Vertex's suggested amendment.

"Yes, I like Palace," Fraternity voted.

Summit raised his hand approvingly, "sounds good but let's keep thinking. I like what's coming out of today's discussions but it's a long-term plan, and if we start the preliminary work forthwith, I imagine it would take at least two years, probably three, before the first product take's a breath. Not the least of the obstacles will be the funding, when we can't give guarantees, only formulate capital and operational costs, based on projection surveys with an error factor below five percent."

"The funding won't be a hurdle, whatever it amounts to, because the surrogate shortage has the potential to seriously damage society and the jot lifestyle. It will go ahead if we coalesce into strong team, and remain determined," Brilliance declared.

"And of course, if the funding is not available, then we'll be blessed with the perfect escape clause, and it'll be our turn to point fingers and attribute blame," Vertex noted.

"In the meantime, we're burdened with a waiting list of disgruntled want to be parents and a Governing Council demanding we do something about it," Arrant reminded the meeting.

For Fraternity attempting to solve the impossible was implausible, "We do three things. First, we more or less ignore the current impasse, maybe announce an improved compensation package, which will coax a few more, hopefully, but the offer would be nothing more than appeasement. Second, we agree that industrialised and institutionalised production is the way forward, and plunge into making it happen; and third, we announce our proposal for two reasons — to divert attention from the present bottleneck, and commence a propaganda program aimed at enticing a much broader cohort of eligible females to start thinking and talking, about surrogacy as a career."

"Even if initially it only increases offers from a dozen of so females, this along the Progenitive Palace proposal should divert GG coercion," Vertex suggested.

Summit stared at Fraternity as did another three set of eyes, all silent.

"What!" she exclaimed raising an upturned hand to Summit.

"Give us something formal to deal with."

Fraternity's gaze drifted as her mind worked to frame something substantive. After a moment, "I move, that the establishment of an institution for the industrial utilisation of surrogates in large scale baby production, becomes Pasa policy, and that work on the project commence immediately. she said looking around for approving expressions.

There was considered silence for a moment, then Summit's was the first hand to rise, then one at a time Vertex, Fraternity and Arrant followed, but Brilliance hesitated.

"Come on Brilliance," Arrant whined.

She glared at him, then slowly raised her hand.

"That's great people."

Chapter 4
Raising Maws etc.

The office was extensive. For visitors the journey from the entrance to the head honcho's desk, could feel awkward, even intimidating, and the unblinking stare of the slouched figure behind the distant desk could intensified the discomfort. Of course, it was designed to do so, and once having breached the 'Are You Sure You Wish to Continue' sign on the door and entered, not only was there the unnecessarily long walk, but the hard underfoot surface echoed every step. To the indigenise, the walk was known as the 'Omgo' (Only Masochists Go On), while for those hapless enough to cross the Rubicon in the afternoon, an additional assault on their composure came from their gawking stares of an avenue of dishonour, a line of hulks lounging on couches along the side walls. The sense of interference from a dozen stares, and the subsequent feeling of strained ears bugging any conversation, all guaranteed the visitor struggled to overcome a kowtowing manner.

Once arrived at the expansive desk, a plaque prominently revealed:

THE BUSTOHE — Fortitude Armstone
Academy of Combative Sports
Male Division

However, not all visitors succumb to this menacing, there being exemptions for affectionate associates, bearers of favours, and officials of superior rank. Once aware of the identity of the approaching arrivee Fortitude would adjust the welcome accordingly. For fellow industry professionals there'd be concessions, and she'd come from behind the desk to wait, resting against its front edge, while for certain others she'd advance with a hand extended. Close personal friends and members of the aloof echelons, might even be met at an open door by a welcoming Bustohe.

The four walls of the office were adorned with full-sized relief images of maws (male arena warrior) groin clad, chemically constructed muscle males, the imagery capturing vital fight moments, or a delighted winner. However, overlording all shrines, in double life size, on the wall behind Fortitude's desk, was an immortalised moment of her fighting life. In G-string, her stance braced, fists raised, stretched up from atlas shoulders and triceps, wide glazen eyes, muscles bristling, angry veins in profile, sinews string bagging her body, tiffanys lacking any mothering potential, shoulder length blonde streaked and stressed hair, slightly bloodied over an eyebrow, her entirety trickling with sweat, an exhausted joy obvious, and a large trophy at her feet. The image inscription read: Fortitude Armstone, World Champion, All Comers, Grade 1, and with the title had come a handsome pay day, improved social status, and her decision to retire from the arena as the champion female, with a litany of victories against males.

Several years had crept by since that day, and now in her late thirties Fortitude, was still a jayone, despite considerable opposition to her body type being considered beautiful, and thereby eligible for any rating. Although statistically her body dimensions fell within parameters, a significant opposition complained that a female body shaped lump of flesh, undulating with seams of coagulated muscle, disfigured by inflated veins and tendons, and having cannibalised most suggestions of femininity, did not comply with the ambitions or spirit of the beautiful society, their contention being that despite their statistical compliance, Obac should reject them. The opposition had formed themselves into a group known Asib (Always seeking improved beauty) and worried some dubious persuasion or devious patronage was at work. As stars of the arena, they were glorified for a capacity to inflict pain, draw blood and overwhelm opponents, but outside the arena they were no asset to society, and should be rated Oaos (out of arena, out of sight), and only allowed in a jot conditionally, and with a permit.

Fortitude seized the academy's Bustohe position by way of challenge but only after surviving an appeal to Obac instigated by Asib. In dismissing the appeal, the committee said sufficient people admired the body type for them to remain jays, and as arena sports were society's preeminent entertainment, this added weight to the acceptability of the type.

If the appeal had been upheld Fortitude's position as Bustohe would have been tenuous, and encouraged challenges from jays, albethey less qualified. However, she was not unfamiliar with the ways of a fight, and saw combat as inspiration. With the appeal dismissed she plunged into controlling the academy and its associated enterprises, including arena fight betting, chaperon auctions, substances supply, and taag supply.

As well as being maws, most of the giants loafing in the afternoon office, flaunting and chatting were taags (Tested and Approved Gigolos) as well, and for most spent more time at the more profitable engagement of taaging, than mawsing. Arena bouts were irregular, and tallied less than twenty appearances a year, while taaging usually meant severalling a week. Having finished their day's training and work outs, they then idled, some hoping for a booking, some hoping not, but if listed to be available anyway, and waited along the office walls, until scheduled.

Body patterning and facial makeup were considered distractions to their physiques, so they had none, and the dress code was a basic anatomically revealing midriff fitting trunks. Hair styles and jewellery, were their only avenues for self-expression, resulting in extravagantly worked and vividly coloured hair dos, atop their otherwise hairless, and glistening shapes. All were adorned in ear rings, bracelets and finger rings, with a prolific quantity of gold around their necks, wrists and ankles. Like all groupings, humanoid and beastly, a pecking ordered dictated rights and behaviours. Fraternity's constellation churned with rivalries, manoeuvrings, and connivings and frequently with skulduggery. When the natural order functioned, the two factors which designated hierarchy were; success in the arena, physical proportions, statistical ratios, and strength.

Although excluded from going to arena bouts, pre-alphaspection young people watched the action by hologram, and many fell victim to the hype, the hoopla, and the cult of personality it promulgated. Many pre-pubescent adolescents were in awe of arena heroes, while frequently post-pubescent females and males envied the fighter/fornicator's audacious careers, feeding their maturing imaginations with eroticism and fascination. The majority of budding males supposed it was all fantasy, but for the odd few with the potential and ambition necessary, needed to be at least two metres tall, with chest circumferences equal to at least their height; biceps 60 centimetres around; neck in excess of 80 centimetres around; quadriceps a minimum of a metre around and hands 14 centimetres across. They needed to weigh 140 kilos or more, and be assessed founded, of excellent soundness and be Obac approved. An extraneous characteristic sought and highly valued, was a potential for exuding murderous determination in the arena, and a flair for the arrogance which would inflame audiences.

While most dreamers were young males, a few pre-alphaspection females fancied arena stardom, but as spectators, females were the most belligerent. And females attended arena events in much larger numbers than males. Also, female fighters who became arena warriors, were more ruthless and ignited more passionate audience reactions than did maws. While fewer taaps (Tested and Approved Paramours) than taags were demanded, those with ingenuity and were relaxed about dispensing brutality, often attracted customers of the neurotic paraphiliac and deviant type, and not dissuaded by extortionist pricing.

The easiest path to the arena began at around the age of two or three when parents submitted their child for a Fopha (Formative Physical Appraisal), a non-compulsory review devised to identify traits, positive and negative, of the child's physical and behavioural future. Parents used this information to select an appropriate Judco to capitalise on their child's natural assets, while teaching them to manoeuvre around weaknesses. If the Fopha report showed a child would grow into a large, tall and heavy-duty person, with a synopsis suggesting potential combat capability, it was a powerful lure for mums and dads to embark that boat, notwithstanding a horizon littered with the wrecks of 'would be's. Mothers, usually, were the protagonist in dispatching children onto this narrow, bruising, fenced and secretive conveyor but tended to be more protective of sons. Fathers, on the other hand were more likely to be reluctant about consigning daughters to an oestrogen munching, testosterone swamping regime. But they were inclined to see status in a boy's fighting future.

Potential combatants who graduate successfully from their growth management years, could apply to the academy provided their bodies had finished, or almost finished its natural growth, and after their alphaspection. With only five males and five females inducted annually, competition for positions was fierce. For the successful it would be a career lasting no longer than ten years or not after their thirtieth birthday, but promised a decade of glamour, accolade and wealth.

Once admitted to the academy's "Formation College" they entered an extreme regime for which they had been forewarned, and their life's devotion was to becoming warriors of combat. They were embarking on a three-year program of medications, supplements, body sculpting, fight training and ancillary learning, including carnal technique, mental control and fighting creativity. With zone specific growth hormones now allowing trainers more control of shape and strength, ever more formidable specimens were graduating, somewhat to the chagrin of older combatants.

While females too were eligible to apply for entry after alphaspection, they rarely met the strength requirements, even if they'd been suitably managed, but if the college determined the prerequisite could be achieved in time, candidates would be monitored to the age of twenty. This was an encouraging proviso for late aged applicants, when older females could still expect a ten-year career.

It was made clear to budding male and female arena warriors, from the get go, that every comfort, facility, avenue for advancement and attention would be provided, provided they submitted to the regime and the work ethic. The selection process had historically proved effective, with less than one bud from each intake failing to finish.

Each bud was accommodated in their own deluxe unit, and attended to by a day housekeeper, and a night jackal (usually permitted dunville staff). About the only task trainees needed to undertake were the very personal ones. Even so, the minions had few work obligations other than to grovel, a requirement strategically designed to cultivate an aloof arrogance in the buds. In concert, self-admiration was inculcated, with recruits scarcely able to move about or indulge in any activity, public or private, without seeing themselves in reflection. In the beginning the mirrors could be confronting even overbearing, but within weeks self-admiration became a passion sport, and good time was spent in self-examination, self-assessment, and in exuberant pleasure at the slightest physical improvement, real or imagined. The minions constantly streamed praise, compliments and tended congratulations, the program proving exceedingly successful in ghosting exaggerated, often irrational egos. It didn't matter, so long as self-delusion controlled their ego.

At the day's high protein breakfast, the housekeepers were responsible for administering prescribed medications, physically enhancing formulations, and aggression fostering substances, as well as any personality adjusting interventions, where deemed necessary. At the end of the day's work, away from the designed cold and harsh environment, they'd migrate to the warm and convivial environs for the meal, where they'd mingle, genders separated, while under visual and sensory scanners, were checked for any social and behavioural shortcomings.

One of the first assignations for fresh recruits is the Chaperones' Auction, at which selected females bid to become cucems (Chaperons undertaking carnal and emotional mentoring), and accept responsibility to report progress, positive and negative of their novices, for a year. Only females are permitted to make purchases, be that for males or females, and before participating, were required to establish their credentials before a panel. Candidates vying to mentor a female needed amazonian features, be lesbian or bi and harbour a hatred of males. Included in their contracted was an obligation to foster that hatred, with the expectation the characteristic would become evident in the arena, and another spur for audience reaction.

Before their auctioning the recruits are made available for private viewing, allowing hopeful cucems to peruse the merchandise, consider their obligation, but more importantly, wonder about opportunities and probabilities. There was a cost benefit assessment needed, and with potential buyers mainly in their mid-thirties, and motivated by sensual excesses, the presence of a young, large and powerful body, usually stimulated their ribald imaginations. With air filled, artificially, with the hormones of the fornicating variety, the stimulation reminded them, that while their normal corporeal extravagances, should have been fulfilling, they still suspected, and hoped, there was more to a complete nefertity than they'd so far discovered. They were well familiar with the frantic and the multiple, but the strains of their libido continued to insist true euphoria lay even deeper. Was it real or rumour? Could this powerhouse pawn, under direction, be the discovery channel they imagined? For bufaws (budding female arena warriors), retired faws were often the keenest bidders at auction, with nepotism and corruption regularly responsible for purchases by fellows of the coterie.

Throughout their college years bufaws and bumaws, were isolated, with separate training and indoctrination syllabuses. Bumaws' journey a path based on the premise males were instinctively aggressive, responded intuitively to physical threats, and believed revenge normal; while with bufaws the underpinning strategy was to cultivate and inculcate a desperate desire to dispense distress. When successful their vengeance could be furious, blinding, and irrational, but successful. Fundamentally, the stick was waved at bufaws, but for bumaws the carrot was the methodology.

While cucems of bumaws are charged with illuminating their charges with an ability to identify female sensitivities, assess female emotions, and be expedient with response techniques, the imperative of self-control, and other factors, academic instruction in fornication is delivered whenever opportunity presents, but carnal consorting is permitted only as a reward.

However, on admission bumaws are deluged with an array of sexual activity and felicities, far beyond anything their boyish imaginations had envisioned. Unaware their galloping good fortune was chemically enhanced, and libidinous triggers were being hypnotically installed using external influences such as odours, light and sounds; the college's carrot quickly becomes irresistible. Chemicals, libido and cucems quickly become addictive. If a bumaw returns to his unit at day's end, with a 17-year old's loaded weapon, to find only his jackal home and no cucem, he learns quickly the college was unhappy with his effort that day.

Cucems submitt reports monthly, detailing the recruit's morale and emotional status, along with the details of any idiosyncrasies, tendencies or preferences noticed. If cucem identifies any of nature's shortfalls, these are usually corrected medically, by manipulation, or in surgery. If in the end a bumaw's carnal prowess or technique fails to attain performance requirements, his implant is programmed CO (Combat Only), and while failure to make taag affects incomes, such graduates typically focus more intently on their fighting potential, and often reach greater heights in the arena, than was predicted.

After a year, each recruit is auctioned again and found themselves with a new cucem, and another at the beginning of year three. Cucems were not permitted to buy the same trainee twice, and the demand for third year bumaws falls away, as they are far more likely to want control and dominate Also, by now, for bumaws and their self-centred and rampant egos, the arrival of a fresh body is manor for their inclination to dominate, and with it comes danger for the new cucem, if she is unaware or unprepared for his idiosyncrasies

For bufaws the experience could be different. While most accept the loss of an intimate associate as part of the big plan, and just another stone on the thoroughfare to success, some found the loss difficult. When this was identified, they are isolated and left friendless until they appreciated, someone, anyone was better than no one. Medication intensifying the desire for sexual companionship, and while self-help mediates for a while, awaiting the new cucem slowly become a preoccupation.

For the last year of college, with fight training almost completed, the emphasis, for bufaws and bumaws, moves to the techniques which fuels audiences into emotional irrationality; and to pain tolerance, an essential ingredient for good endurance. For the first half of the year trainees are subjected to rising pain levels, while trainers watching stress monitors, coach them in mental acceptance, while striving for mental and physical separation. Pain suppression is achieved through zonal isolation, and attention diversion, fostered by resilience. In the second half of the year the lessons from the first half were fused with sensory deprivation substances, and each trainee is assessed for optimum dosages and endurance. One of the side effects of the program leaves trainees with memory gaps, and vague notions, but provokes them to continue to brawl, when ordinarily they would have been rendered or would have capitulated. Stupefied combatants, help provoke audience hysteria.

By the end of three years, the graduates bare scant resemblance to the individual inducted. Their physical elaboration shocks mothers, while the personality rearrangements surprises fathers, but with family relationships having been deliberately discouraged and diminished, the ego riven graduates are little affected. Their cultivated obsessions are now entrenched; their universe blinkered and defined; all the vortices of

66

their lives lased in; and the mesmerising factors promising an ordained future, installed.

Fortitude straightened from her desk keyboard, pulled back her shoulders, stretched her chest, arched her back, glanced at the ceiling, then fell forward in her chair, her gaze framing the taags agitated in their lethargy, and growing impatient by the delay in receiving their evening's appointments. Fortitude learnt onto her elbows, and began surveying her inventory, slowly. None of them were as good as she once was, but they were making her a lot of money, so she tendered them carefully, and was scrupulous in scheduling their activities for her greatest benefit. While she revelled in lording over her gofers, and while it meant keeping them distance, occasionally she wished for a compatriot in whom to confide.

Fortitude was disturbed from her wistful lament by the sudden hum of her tice on her desk, and the image displayed was of a close female face. She pushed back from the desk, delighted and smiling,

"Hi sweetie, you're just what I need at the moment, how are you?" her usual deliberate and determine delivery, displaced in favour of genial familiarity.

"I'm good Fort, what's wrong?" the voice concerned.

"Nothing really Aurora, I'm just bit frustrated, that's all. Are you coming to see me?"

"If you're free, I'll be there in fifteen," came the snapped response.

"Great, want something when you get here?"

"Nope, thanks, some other day. I'll see you soon," and the apparition was gone. She reached for her tice, "Display Aurora in rigout, 50 percent," she instructed

The delay was momentary, then Aurora was there, dark, bristling, and with all the usual gleaming lines of muscle and cords of sinews and veins etc, smiling. Her rigout was customary and minimal. Calf high boots in sparkling red, G-string in sparkling red and a sparkling red head band, collecting most of her rampant curly red hair.

She and Aurora had met the day they entered the college, for Fortitude that was a year after her alphaspection and for Aurora it was two years after hers, making her the elder, technically, at least. Their apartments had been adjacent and they first meet when both stepped out their front doors, to absorb their new environment. They saw at each other, and turned with outstretched hands of introduction, smiling. A friendship was born, a dependable alliance which was always supportive, one which never judged or challenged, and which persisted even in absence.

As their physiques developed it became obvious Fortitude was going to be the stronger fighter, while Aurora's advantage turned out to be agility and tactical thinking. In their ten odd years of arena performances, they never fought each other, something they resisted strongly, and which the promoters happily avoided, aware they lacked mutual malice. Not unreasonably since they became lovers within days, a relationship their cucems encouraged and which frequently found fun and fulfilment for four. After graduation the absence of cucems allowed their affair to consolidate and blossom spontaneously, directed now by an inclination for love.

However, the end of their fighting careers left them with residual masculinity, thought patterns, excessive testosterone, and bawdy eyes for the delights in cucemsing, and both were drawn to the salubrious offerings at the chaperon auctions.

Both secured bufaws and became cucems but when Fortitude was bushtoe at the Male Academy her priorities mutated and their relationship dwindled. Aurora, however remained a cucem for a further two years, until she also successfully challenged for a position with the academy, the sign on her desk reading:

The Bustohe — AuroraTrim
Academy of Combative Sports
Female Division

While their estrangement persisted for a period their friendship rebounded with Aurora's appointment, since they needed to regularly collaborated over arena matters such as event scheduling, bout matching and associates matters. Their bond remained reliable, but was now relaxingly platonic, and the reduced zones for interaction helped it continued in comradery rather than carnally.

When Fortitude's tice announced Aurora 's arrival in the building, and was one minute away, she rose from her desk and strode to the door.

When it opened she stepped into the corridor, watching. At the sight of each other they hurried to close their gap, the two big females seized each other in embrace. With arms still holding the other, they parted enough to look into their eyes. They locked gazes momentarily, then instinctively they fell into a brief lovers' kiss. Aurora's tongue made an enquiry, and her lure was alluring, but Fortitude ignored the invitation, broke from their kiss, and took Aurora's head in her hands, "You're very tempting my love, but our time is over really, and I think we should leave it that way; don't you?"

Aurora's disappointment was evidenced by her firming grip. Fortitude broke away, but still holding her hand, led her into the office, to the audible amusement of the lounging lumps. She pulled her chair to the front of the desk and they sat facing each other.

"I've a monster female I want to introduce at the next event," Aurora announced. "She's going to be a headline act even though she's still a girl but she's a beast."

Fortitude looked at her with widening eyes, but before more details were forthcoming and unannounced, the office door swung open and Fable, the taags' Assignment Curator strode in, head down her finger tapping her tice. Her entrance sparked an immediate response from the dozen and half taags, some of whom had been waiting up to an hour, hoping to execute their carnal commitments early. As Fable strode down the echoing Omgo strip, the hulks limbered to their feet, and draughted behind her, in a rag-tag procession.

"I've twenty bookings for this afternoon and this evening, but only seventeen gonads available," she announced on arrival at Fortitude's side.

Fortitude looked up and thought for a moment, "Don't call them gonads, Fable, they're taags, who earn your wages," she said pointedly.

"Well gonads are what we're flogging, they're just merchandise, that's all the fuck they are," Fable retorted, but was ignored.

"Fable, you should know the routine and what to do, so get back to them and sell some threesomes," she said smiling.

"Well, I could have done that, but you insist on knowing these things," Fable said as she turned about, pushed her petite frame through the grumbling congregation, and strode out, titivated by teasing the eyes watching her bobbing alice.

Fortitude turned to Aurora "Getting back to this monster you've found," she said.

"She just fifteen, an absolute monster whose been in training for two years and who I've gone to a lot of trouble to keep hidden. She's ready to demolish the best you can put up," Aurora boasted, her excitement obvious in her smile.

It was enough to rouse Fortitude from indifference but for the moment she was going to remain oblique, "I'd need a good reason to commit my best man to this, and you'll need to convince me she's competitive, and if she is, it could be an expensive exercise ensuring her victory, if that's the way you want to play it." she said.

"You wouldn't need to organise anything Fort, this beast can defeat anyone, without help. Besides I'm sure you could recoup your costs by way of gaming."

Fortitude was thoughtful, Aurora's confidence needed verifying. "Give me a look at her, or is she still a secret."

"Not to you," Aurora peeled her tice from her arm, "Display Romance, naked at 25 percent," she instructed and placed the tice on the desk.

The hologram morphed a figure, a huge, heavy, neckless, muscular, young, an angry looking female.

"That's a big girl, and only fifteen," Fortitude conceded, glancing at her colleague, and for the first time showing real interest, "But big doesn't mean competent, capable or crowd pleasing."

"This female is almost two metres at the withers, weighs 210 kilos and is stronger than my next two faws together. She'll crush any male you can produce."

"All right," Fortitude acknowledged, "I'm not going to argue but I'd like to make a couple of suggestions."

"Sure, that's what I'm here for."

"Are you sure she's only fifteen?"

"Fifteen, that's right."

"Hell, Aurora," Fortitude's attention was now fully summoned, and she sat forward to examined the hologram more closely.

"Enlarge her." She waited, "Where did you find her," she enquired.

"It was before my time, but she came to us as an eleven-year-old, sent by the Social Court, after almost killing her parents," Aurora revealed, her eyes excited. "And she was only eleven. She was almost two metres tall and weighed 110 kilograms. At her assessment hearing Jadaps identified a list of her personality disturbances, which can basically be summarised as her being severely irrational, schizophrenic and an uncontrollable psychopath. After that her story is shadowy but apparently undue influences, and mysterious decisions directed her future. Normally it would have been expected Jadaps should have directed chemical adjustments, a treatment, which at her age could have been effective.

"However, she was handed her to the academy after purported expert evidence, explained her evils were not as serious as Jadaps determined, and a regimented routine would mitigate her anxieties, and significantly correct her dysfunctions. She would finally be able to return her to her parents, and allowed movement in the dunville community. Of course, everyone who was aware of her and her analysis, realised there were unseen forces directing events.

"But even before then her story is shrouded in mystery and rumour. The official explanation for her mutating into the abnormal, is she's the result of a harlequin stuff up, and by the age of two she was double normal size, and by seven was adult size and as strong as her father. However, the gossip suggests she is not the product of a harlequin mistake but a deliberate embryotic formulation designed to produce exactly what she is, an enormous fighting female, expected to be a financial goldmine. The corrupt ghosts in her shadow must be smiling. Her parents show no interest in her, and while they are bottom tier, they are now unaccountably substantial, and they have another child apparently quite normal.

"All that aside, after the years of academy cultivation and training her creators have what they designed. She's feels no pain, hardly sleeps, is devoid of empathy, and is the fighting monster whose only amusement seems to be injuring people.

"Right!," Fortitude was still not one hundred percent on board "How do you train her?"

"I've been paying well, three retired fighters to enter the circle with her but even then, injuries occur regularly, but not to her. We've found locking her up for several days and feeding her only food she dislikes, followed by methedrine infused meals for a day, is a recipe for releasing an enraged fighter, which I defy any opponent to overcome. She's ready for the world, as am I for a pay day. What do you think?"

Fortitude was growing fascinated with the potential but still, she was slow to respond as she mulled for ways to fully exploit the apparent potential.

Her thoughts came slowly: "I think Aurora you should dehair her, including her head," she paused, staring at the hologram. "She might only be fifteen and a close look confirms that, but have some work done on her face and get back to thirteen or fourteen again. We should then enlighten the rumour mongers she's a fourteen-year-old savage. If she's as good as you're claiming, the sight of her crunching a couple of maws, could be the biggest event we've ever staged."

"Shit, Fortitude, that might be going too far."

"Aurora, just do it, because you're on a winner here. Blood, Cloud and Romance could make an incredible event, and leave an audience physically exhausted and psychologically destitute. And, she could be a headline act for several years to come."

"Yes, I'm aware," Aurora had more, "I think as well as Cloud it should be a red night. I know most spectators normally go red anyway but still we should make a point of advertising it."

Fortitude didn't have to think, "Yes, of course."

It was half an hour since Fable went to fit twenty into seventeen, and now she was back striding down Omgo, exuding her usual competence.

"Problem solved, I lost no bookings, so three gonads are booked to six females, so it should work out. Of the six females going threesome, four have used us before, three regularly, so I have their sensual responses recorded, and have matched likes to likes. For two, this will be their first threesome, and were enthusiastic about the prospect, and thanked me for making the offer. However, they did need reassuring one taag was capable, and I've three, one-four; two-twos available for them, so that went down rather well too. And I charged a premium, upping the minimum hour and half, to two and half hours.

"So, this is the schedule," she said turning to face her operatives.

"G1, 47 and six get the double acts, and I'll post everyone's schedule on their tices shortly," her eyes went back to her tice.

"Shit Fable, this is the second time in two weeks you've done this to me. Give me a break for fuck's sake," came a protest but Fable just conceded a flashed glance at the complainant, then continued.

"And I've sold them a lot of cece. One client declined it and wants a live shooter."

"We don't do live, Fable, you know that," Fortitude complained. "But well done anyway, good work."

Fable continued on her tice, marking off the taags she'd allocated, then instructed the device to match the remaining taags with customers, according to fetishes, idiosyncrasies and requests. When booking, clients answer questions designed to ensure they experienced a satisfactory episode, and are asked about kissing, vaginal licking, fellatio, anal, bondage, and the use of stimulants, sensitivity intensifying devices such as the Fers (Frequent endorphin release stimulator) and/or the Nas (Nefertities achievable sensor). All wanted Fers and Asas; four ticked anonymity and would be masked; fourteen wanted debauched conversation; fifteen declined anal; only six wished to give fellatio; while two wanted facial ejaculation. Two clients ticked for the most expensive service, to dominate a restrained taag, but the academy only had two taags prepared for that, and neither were available today.

Another five customers want to be restrained, one extremely so, while three ordered a paddling. Three had asked for two taags but with the supply problem one switched to the threesome, with another female, while the others settled for one. As usual the most desired bonbon was licking and all but one client ordered it, fifteen wanted at least one nefertiti by it. Finally, customers had to decide what pricing bracket they wanted, or could afford. All clients were informed that while the academy made every effort to ensure satisfaction it could not guarantee outcomes, and no refunds were made. With the day's appointments delegated, the office emptied quickly, much to Fortitude's relief, thankful for the quietness, to be alone with Aurora.

"What was that business about 1–4, 2–2, Fortitude?" Aurora asked quizzically.

Fortitude broke into a self-satisfied, ear to ear grin, a mischievous eye on Aurora.

After a moment, "It's caesar dimensions," she stopped, teasing, but Aurora waited, knowing Fortitude couldn't help herself. She was right.

"A few months after becoming bushtoe I changed the way I charged for taags, and I'm making a lot more, for exactly the same merchandise. It started when a customer wanted a thirty-centimetre caesar, which was not a problem since we have a couple; but it got me thinking. Now I charge for caesar mass, per half hour, minimum one and half hours. I've a minimum size available, eighteen centimetres long, ten centimetres around, or about three and half centimetres thick. This size dick has a base price, but for anyone who dreams of more, or is adventurous enough to try extra big, the fee is charged using simple multiplication, length-by-circumference; or it used to be. I had to adjust the formula because the customers began ordering the short but thick, and often I had to assign, say, a twenty-four- or five-centimetre caesar, just to fill the order for a thirteen-centimetre circumference.

"So now the basic price is calculated at 1 by 1.8 fee, which remains the same, but as the thickness grows, so does the loading, meaning a female ordering a fifteen-centimetre circumference but an eighteen-centimetre length, has a one hundred percent loading on thickness, making the fee 3 by 1.8, which is three times the basic fee; which is a bloody lot. Some are pleased to pay it. Of course, occasionally we are asked for the lot, seven thick and thirty deep, which is five times the base price. The biggest problem I now have, is a shortage of diameters, with demand exceeding supply."

Chapter 5
Home Visit

Expected but still arresting, the abrupt dismissal of silence as Enamour's tice announced Prudence's transporter was four minutes away, and as it would take her two minutes to walk out front, she had two minutes to leave the dresser. "Hardly needed the maths," she said talking to the mirror.

She stood up from her stool, ran her hands down each side of her body smoothing herself, then leaned into the mirror for a final close facial check. Today her presentation was modest, just ten minutes in the cavern for faint body colour in lilac no decoration, some highlight toner to the face, dark lilac lips, eyebrows and black lashes. It was to be a relaxing day, a family day, a day without pretence, and in the company of her nearest and dearest, being sisters, parents, grandparents, great-grandparents, niece, nephew and her son Justice. Her outfit was chosen for comfort and lounging, and she'd kick off her shoes as soon as she arrived at Mum and Dad's.

"Where are you Justice," she called, "it's time to go, come on, hurry up."

The freewheeling clatter of a ten-year-old running along the corridor arrived at her door, and the smiling face was eager to be underway.

"Let's go Justice," and she her hand went out to take her son's, but he was too impatient for that, and led the way down the stairs and out the front door.

As usual the tice had correctly forecast Affinity and Prudence's arrival by the kerbside, so the coordination worked well. From inside the transporter two jubilant faces and two pleased ones peered out, while Enamour and Justice waited for the door to slide open. Behind the control panel Prudence sat, while in the third row, were Affinity, her 15-year-old daughter Essence and twelve-year-old son Wraith. Justice slid into the middle row, to be joined immediately by Wraith climbing over from the back, while Enamour joined her young sister in the front.

With the ritual hellos, welcomings, and reaffirmation completed, Enamour found herself looking about Prudence's vehicle.

"This is a nice stretch extension to your transporter Pru. What is it now, an eight-seater? Enamour asked enquiringly, still perusing.

"We had the insert fitted a few weeks ago, and this is the first time it's been used. It seems like a good one, though, and only takes a minute to insert or remove, so it'll be handy for occasions like this."

"It's bigger than ours," Affinity called from the back

"Ours is old and junkie," Essence responded, her tone glib and taking the opportunity to reveal her embarrassment.

"That's for sure," Wraith confirmed.

"You can insert double stretch units now, which includes a second power pack, and that bumps the basic two seat model all the way up to a twelve-seater," Prudence informed her party as she turned to the vehicle's control panel.

"Quiet everyone, for a moment because the voice recognition's been giving some trouble lately. I've re-programmed my voice a couple of times but it keeps forgetting me," Prudence explained.

She touched the screen and it illuminated. "Proceed: Mum and Dad's" Prudence directed and the vehicle hummed to life, accelerating away.

Prudence turned to her passengers, "Good, it behaved. How big's our hurry?" she enquired.

"Not big, let's just relaxed," Affinity suggested.

"How does 150 sound?" and after a moment's silence, she interpreted that as general agreement. Prudence gave the final instructions, paused to verify they were being followed, then swivelled to face her passengers.

Normally it took about twenty minutes to passage all the city limits, the cross streets, bikeways, and footways and lock onto the 150kph zoomway vein. However today, according the transporter's information bank, the journey out of town would be three minutes slower than Utime, due to unusually high traffic flows on the crossbys but stopping anywhere would not be necessary. ETA, Red Hill Dunville was now 68 minutes.

Today the travel time was of little consequence, although their forebears would be anxious. It would be an afternoon for clustering, conversing, touching, advising, critiquing, debating, and idling with those who were slow to judge, quick to help, ready to comfort, and deaf to criticism. The sisters were keen to see their parents and grandparents, as they'd not seen then for over a month, and the youngins were too, more or less so.

As the sister's conversation circled catch up, and the boys giggled, presumably, about something inane, Essence found herself staring out the window, watching the passing structures of human enterprise and domesticity protruding from an ocean of city greenery. While an early lack of city foresight bequeathed a concentration of cloud piercing towers, the contemporary era ensured the architecture was surrounded by flora, and spaced so no shadow robbed another's sunlight. There were a multitude of shapes and intriguing innovations about modern designs but their external textures were identical.

"Hey everyone, look at her!" Essence exclaimed, her finger pointing at a five-storey building, its façade illuminated with the image of a swanning young female, her form unadulterated by any cavern work, and her natural features obvious but obliquely beneath fine fabric. The hologram smiled and swayed and came with a caption 'Obviously Melisma'.

"Not already," Affinity scowled, glancing at the scene, "we've just survived this year's election, and they've started already on next year's."

"Started what?" Wraith asked bemused by his mother's exclamation.

"She! wants to be next year's Now-Now," Affinity said also pointing a finger at the figure, then disgusted, dismissed the matter with a brushing off-handed wave.

Prudence glimpsed the disappearing figure while she could, and concluded, "She's not good enough."

"It's who you know, which counts," Affinity said, apathetically.

"I thought she was attractive," Enamour mused.

"So did I," came Essence.

"Me too," Wraith announced.

"Me too," Justice was not to be left out.

"What would you know Justice?" Essence demanded from her lofty five-year age advantage.

"Plenty," he snapped, undaunted.

The structure used to advertise Melisma's ambitions was of the contemporary and singular style. While building externals and internals were as diverse as temporal imaginations, the exteriors were all dressed in SAS (Solar Asset Surface) and thereby legally acquiescent. Three layers of microelectronic generating power cells converted sunshine, as well as insulating.

The passage out of the city did take three minutes longer than Utime, but no one noticed, although the breach into the countryside was course enough with some communal agreement and appreciation. The zoomway journey suffered a minor interruption when the control panel announced their vehicle was being moved aside allowing an ambulance to pass. They moved across and were immediately overtaken, then promptly returned to their vein and speed.

"That's something you don't see very often these days," Enamour commented casually watching the ambulance speed into the distance.

"No, I think they're only utilised when there's a shortage of skyvacs," Prudence suggested.

"I hope it's not for dad," Enamour thought allowed.

"Dad's condition is not that serious," Prudence opinioned.

"I'm not so confident," Affinity came in. "Ever since his heart dysfunction his PAHS (Permanently Attached Health Scanner) has been ordering increasingly stronger medication but I don't see any improvement in his condition. I think it's time for him to have a replacement heart. That seems the obvious answer to me."

"Sometimes they seem to fumble with patients, when the remedy appears simple. Surely that's what DAD (Diagnostic Assessment Determinator) would have found by now," Enamour observed, her inflection slightly despairing.

"We'd agree with that," Prudence mused. "Dad's not even seventy which means he has another sixty plus years, and with the quality of hearts being propagated these days, he's entitled to expect all of them."

"Maybe in sixty years, life expectancy will be 160, that's what I'm hoping for," Affinity mulled wistfully.

"We'll probably need almost total body part replacements by then, kidneys, livers, blood, blood vessels, pancreas, general plumbing etcetera, but the worry is what happens when our brains give up," Enamour wondered.

"When our brain goes, we won't know and won't care. Life can't go on for ever despite the technology," Affinity confirmed.

"Why not?" Wraith asked.

On approaching Red Hill the disparities between a dunville and a jot quickly become noticeable, some subtle, others immediately apparent. While dunville housing's external construction was of the same materials as jot apartments, internally they were smaller, lacked variety of design, amenities and capacity. The facades could not change colour or display images or graphics. The blocks did vary in colour but lacked lustre, and were in colours such as tired mustard, worried brick, exhausted green and navy-blue fatigue.

The feature of the streetscape was the landscape, which besieged the blocks with a comforting ground cover from which a variegation of well-suited trees and bushes regularly arose. With a considerable proportion of residents idle in retirement, or jobless, the greeneries were a venue for congregation, engagement and endeavour, where communal enthusiasm to further enhance their environment was a source of achievement and pride. The work fostered a good-natured rivalry between the blocks, and nourished a strong sense of community, for which dunvilles were gaining a reputation.

However, not so sociable was the struggle for societal standing, and since one's beauty was mostly irrelevant in the dunville, and consigned to conscious omittance, the ranking of caste was dictated principally by a person's residential address. Ground level domiciliates were the most prestigious, with the ground floor of a two-storey block considered preeminent. Second choice was the ground floor in any block, while the third preference was the top level in an eight-storey block, and so forth.

However, while physical rankings in the dunville were exacting, socially they were politically homogenised, though when it came to housing allocations, a person's historical beauty records remained a factor. When a new resident arrived, the formula for allocating available quarters, was a complex calculation of their jay rankings, the years they'd lived in each category, and the total of their jay years. Where there was a contest between two or more applicants with equal scores, the determination went to a count back.

Apartments could not be bought or sold, leaving all residents eligible to apply for any vacant apartment, in any block, in any dunville. Once again where there was a contest, the historical score was the determining element. Vigilant manoeuvring for improvement meant that in due course, most residents knew when their status had established them in the most prestigious address they could expect. No one could be evicted from their unit.

Agents were employed to keep a magnifying glass on apartments, their antennas tuned to detect signs of potential vacancies. Since many residents remained in their units till death or until physical incapacity forced them into special care, a successful agent's fingers infiltrated health records, special care assessments, even mortuary notifications. In addition, they employed spotters to eavesdrop on gossip and when possibilities presented, agents for those with high beauty credits and wealth, often resorted to the spectre of skulduggery to obtain advantage. Some aspects of human behaviour never change, seemingly.

Hardly had the family's transporter entered Red Hill than an excited voice yelled: "Look at those fatsos," Wraith's outstretch arm pointing, his eyes alight in astonishment. All heads turned to see a man and female hurrying along the footpath, followed by two early teenage males; a family group no doubt.

"They're not all fat," Prudence observed.

Certainly "mother" was way over weight, and as she strode along, every thumping step induced a severe ripple down her overhangs, while her boys bore meaningful lard reserves, the probable result of unnecessary eating, as well as unfortunately inheriting Mum's genes. But their dad, if in fact he was, was of another extraction, and seemingly ate from a meaner menu, since the shadow he cast was narrow. Mother, had on this day, made some effort to define her femineity, and while having spent little effort on facial elaboration, and refreshed the memory of an earlier hair styling, her sense of self-expression appeared in her abundant display of weathered cleavage. Dad on the other hand, looked to have made no effort to display masculinity, probably because he had little to bare. However, all were tidy and carefully dressed in the dunvillain way, and appeared to be making purposefully for a destination.

Affinity watched them for a moment, then reaching to gather in Wraith's pointing finger said, "Yes Wraith, they're unattractive, which is why they live here but we shouldn't be rude about them," she advised.

"I wouldn't hang out with them, that's for sure," was Essence's contribution to reassurance.

"We'd bashed 'em up at our school," Wraith announced shamelessly.

"Wraith!" Affinity exclaimed, "what did I just say about being rude, don't talk about people like that."

"Well, we would," he said protesting his mother's attempts to temper his attitude.

"Why are they fat, Mum," Justice asked looking at his mum.

"Because they ate too much when they were little, and grew up too fat," Enamour replied.

"I don't eat too much do I?"

"No Justice you're good."

Deeper into the dunville an old male and mid-aged female stood beside a mature spruce tree, engrossed with each other and in conversation. She stood straight, her hands clasp behind listening intently, while he leant with a shoulder against the tree, a walking stick hanging from his other elbow, and seemingly telling a fascinating story. Time had bent him but once he'd been tall, even statuesque, and now bowed and thin framed, he refused to concede to the eroding years, having dressed impeccably, and groomed himself carefully. She was another of the expansively chested type, with a waistline failing to delineate between her upper and lower portions, and was rather short legged. She was dressed for work, and before his interruption was probably occupied on one of the community's gardening projects. The old man was enthusiastically dramatizing a story, with the help of some gesturing and darting eyes, and he looked happy for the distraction, smiling, captivated and pleased for being listened to.

Walking peacefully along the footpath a featureless young female, heavily pregnant, strolled slightly uncomfortably, perhaps with little on her mind other than just enjoying the fine weather. She'd been born with few natural advantages, but had good height and a slender neck. Without her pregnancy she would likely lack shape or feature but her blessing lay with a pretty face. She was dressed casually, thoughtfully, and used colours tastefully. Her makeup was distinctive, and conveyed the particular information which guaranteed her certain privileges. Her pregnancy was surrogacy, and the thin 'warrior' stripes on her cheeks told her story. The blue line denoted surrogacy; yellow was for her first-time surrogate; and the red indicated she was within three months of delivery. The practice of females bearing this information was not statutory, but surrogates who did were afforded various concessions, including some visitation rights to the jot, although by the time they displayed the red stripe, these visits were no longer permitted.

She paused to joined the chatting couple which pleased them, the old man straightening off the tree and leant to kiss her cheek, while the gardening female stepped up and embraced her with both arms.

Affinity could not let the opportunity pass.

"Look at that poor girl En, is that what you want, all that discomfort and humbug? Think what it's doing to her poor body."

"Yes Affinity, it is, I can't wait," was her curt rebuff, hoping to stifle any evolution of the topic.

Affinity took the hint and looked outside again, where two middle aged men whose indulgence and/or indolence had taken indecent control of their midriffs; and between them walked a female whose figure seemed too well founded to belong in a dunville, Prudence thought.

"She looks too good to be here, and mum looks even better," Prudence said, frustratedly.

"Yes, Pru! We can see but she's probably a visitor, like us," Enamour snapped, wanting to kill another annoying, frustrating and pointless conversation.

"Still, it's bloody depressing visiting a dunville, and being confronted with our destiny," Prudence said, changing the subject.

"Of course, once upon a time the only inevitability in life was death. Now there's a another and it's the dunville, with its 'cemetery road' sign post," Enamour said uncharacteristically hosting pessimism.

"Just what I needed to hear," Affinity said with a shoulder shiver.

The transporter began to slow, eased towards the kerb and stopped abreast a waiting couple, who had stood from their bench at the sight of their family's approach.

The transporter spoke, "Prudence, we have arrived at the home of your forebears and I note they await you. Our transit time was four minutes more than Utime. My status is — power available 38 percent, which is sufficient for the return journey, however, should you wish to make diversions, without recharging, I have power available for the return trip plus another 85 kilometres at 150 kilometres per hour, or another 145 kilometres at 110 kilometres per hour or another 180 kilometres at 90 kilometres an hour. All systems are in good order. In the meantime, if you wish to cross the street immediately, the next passing vehicle is due in 85 seconds. Good day Prudence, and friends"

Sanguine and Sagacity had been anticipating the family gathering all morning, and as the bodies disgorged, they were greeted with hugs, kisses, welcomes and compliments. Enamour was the first to enquire into Sanguine's health.

"Dad, how are you?" she asked hugging him.

"Good today," he said, his unconvincing reassurance promptly registering with his daughters. Affinity reacted "So, what's really going on with you, Dad?" she demanded.

"Well, I've had some ups and downs lately but I'll fill you in later."

Three more smiling figures approached down the path in front of the apartment block, all eager to join the welcoming party. One male, two females, with an average age of 118, two of them family matriarchs and one patriarch, the missing patriarch, now immobile at 127 years, and sequestered in full time care. They were granddads, great granddads grandmothers, great grandmothers.

"Ah! Grandads, grandmas," and Enamour moved to embraced them, Prudence and Affinity close behind. For the great-grandchildren, the kinship bond was not as tight, the span of their generations wide enough for the seepage of remote disassociation, and their greetings prone to formality. As well, this was only half of the bygone brigade, as elsewhere there was still dad's tribe, with another four great-grandparents.

Sanguine hustled the multitude towards their apartment on the ground floor of an eight-storey block, a single bedroom abode with generous living areas, and all the facilities needed for comfortable living. Inside, Wraith found himself leaning against the arm of the chair seating his mother's grandfather. Not intimidated by the any indifference, he looked down at him and in his pragmatic style, asked the question which he had wanted to, ever since he could remember him.

"How old are you, Greatdad," he enquired earnestly. The reply was immediate, man to man.

"One hundred and nine Wraith, how old are you?"

"Twelve."

"Thought so."

Wraith turned to his great grandmother "How old are you, Greatgran."

Affinity intervened: "None of your business, Wraith."

The family never struggled for conversation be it idle chatter, gossip, sometimes solicited advice, others times unsolicited, but the afternoon always concluded happily, with issues off chests, frankness's appreciated, and irrelevancies abandoned. The three daughters had plenty for this gathering, with first on their list being Sanquine's heart condition.

"What's going on with your heart Dad, is the current medication helping," Affinity asked.

"It could be, a bit. I'm still going to work most days, but I had a couple of days off this week," he replied.

"Where's your latest medical report?" Enamour asked politely, pointedly.

Sanguine never wore his tice, and had to fetch it from the bench. He picked it up and waited while it identified his DNA, then he called up the report. Enamour, Prudence and Affinity huddled to read it together. After a minute Enamour looked up.

"That's unsatisfactory dad! It indicates your treatment is on course, your responses are in accordance with your prognosis, and there is no reason for re-examination or a change of treatment," her gaze flashing up at her father, "It's rubbish, Dad, rubbish!" she barked.

"It's," Affinity paused, "it's definitely rubbish, absolute rubbish."

"It's time we found a physician to reassess you Dad, and have your health parameters recalibrated because relying on your Bahs for monitoring, assessment, and diagnosis is clearly not working. The algorithm is obviously floored, which could kill you," Prudence concluded.

"Artificial intelligence has its limitations despite the boffins' insistence, and the problem with our digitally dependent lifestyle, is it's almost impossible to defy or argue with it. The system has a capacity to process large amounts of information, and make findings and determinations, but unfortunately, it's not infallible," explained Joss, Sagacity's father, who had spent his life working with AI processes and programs.

"We've endeavoured to eradicate human error, and guarantee outcomes using AI which is audited by AI, making AI responsible for maintaining AI, leading us to believe the system is fool proof, but it's not. Our expectations can be misplaced, as we forget the underpinning axiom of AI, is human," he said, turning to Sanguine.

"Your program, Sanguine, needs to be zeroed, re-sequenced with corrected data, reloaded and rebooted, as it appears your Bahs is missing important evidence. There are a couple of ways this can be accomplished; the first would be to feed some spurious and irrelevant facts into the current program, which will induce it to inform the monitoring technicians your scans are anomalous, and while achieving that will be difficult, it's not impossible. Better, would be to find a physician, who's accredited to interface the program, and make adjustments."

"Finding a physician is difficult these days as we believe too easily that sensors, scanners, computers, algorithms, nanotechnologies, robotics and technicians do the work better," Sagacity noted.

"I can find one," Affinity announced.

Sanguine appreciated their anxieties, and was beginning to appreciate his treatment was perhaps flawed, even damaging. "If you can find an appropriate way forward Affinity, I think I'd be grateful." He said somewhat sheepishly.

"Sure can."

Once again Affinity's demon was nagging, and her sisters' superficial and dismissive interest in her tiffanys had only served to heighten her irritation, and her desire to find some sincere sympathy and support. Mum and/or Dad were now the obvious targets. However, she'd overlook her mother's hardnose attitude to anything she considered frivolous, so expecting her sympathy, over her tale of deteriorating mammaries, only begot her mother's censure, and a reminder she was susceptible to a 'drama queen's' temperament.

Sanguine was more sympathetic, "You're right to worry about interventions Affinity, but sometimes you have to gamble, seize the positive and just do it. There are no guarantees in life, my dear daughter, but remaining optimistic and accepting challenges confidently are the things which makes life exciting and interesting," he advised.

Although the philosophy was mostly ignored Affinity found consolation in her father's oblique dismissal her mother's dismissal. She eased back into her lounge, internalising, and still felt somewhat alone despite being amid kith and kin.

Enamour's disclosure about becoming pregnancy was accorded far greater heed, and although she began by counselling her parents against criticism, it was Sagacity who again took the hard line and began Enamour's interrogation. However, she was quickly censored.

"Mum! Stop! I've had it from Maxim, and I've had little support from my sisters, I don't tell my friends, and I'm well aware, so I don't need you to repeat what I'm fed up with hearing. I'm sick and tired of it, and just want to get pregnant. I am going to get pregnant, and that's it!"

Enamour annexed her mother's gaze blinklessly, her inner palpitations longing for an approving smile from her mother. Sagacity smiled but it was the patriarch who had the sense of occasion.

"En, that's excellent if that's what you want. People will nag you because they believe your appearance is the most important thing in life; but it's not. If bearing a child will fulfil you, then do it, you've my blessing."

Sagacity looked at him, unsure if she agreed but decided against debate, and instead looked back at Enamour, and with babies the topic she suddenly began remembering what a beautiful child she had been, and how she'd been the joyous and easiest of her three. In reflection her maternal driver was unsurprising, but rather how had her passion lingered, frustrated for so long, when it now appeared motherhood for her seemed so becoming, even inevitable?

"En, you're a beautiful person, you have my support," she said and as she spoke warmth flowed through her daughter. Enamour jumped from her chair, and crossed to her mother for a hug, then to her father for more.

"I appreciate that dad, I love you both" she said quietly.

"Shit Mum, I'm a drama queen, and she's a beautiful person. Thanks a lot," Affinity scoffed but the sarcasm was flippant and inspired smiles all round.

The conga-line of revelations now brought Prudence to the fore with her news about reproduction planning. She was slightly hesitant in case she too would need to persuade her mother, unreasonably, that her plans were meritorious. She had nothing to worry about.

Sagacity turned to her grandchildren, firstly to Essence.

"So Essence, your alphaspection's coming up in a few months, how's it going?" she enquired.

"Aw," hesitation "Aw," "All right I think, yeah, good I suppose. It's only three months now; I'm a bit nervous though."

"There'd be something wrong if you weren't, I was petrified for weeks before mine, and I remember your mother didn't sleep for a week either," she divulged, "you've still to have your teeth veneered, when's that going to happen," she asked turning to Affinity for the answer.

"She's booked for the work to commence next week."

"What's her latest prelim saying," Sagacity asked.

"According to the Judco her prospects for jayone are negative sixty-forty, with some uncertainty about her torso/leg ratio, which is border line but her other measurements are good, so we can only wait and see," she said looking across to her daughter. Pointing, "Look at her. She beautiful, she's easily a jayone in my book."

All eyes turned to her. "Stop it Mum, you're embarrassing me," she said, although comforted by her mother's confidence.

"You'll make it through okay my dear. I did, and so did your mother and while the specifications are more rigorous these days, I'm confident for you too," Grandma reassured.

"So, what else has your Judco left to do for you," Prudence enquired.

"Nothing much, they're just careful with my diet and I'm still wearing a brace at night to help my shoulder-neck posture but I don't think it's doing much good, any more," Essence explained.

"However, the alphaspection isn't the only appointment she's anticipating. She wants an interview with a Pavs agent," Affinity's announcement, silenced the room for a jiffy.

Prudence had no doubts and move quickly to set the tenor, "I did it and have never regretted it," she said smiling at Essence.

"It wasn't really the thing to do in my day, but a few girls were doing," Sagacity offered dispassionately.

"I would have, but impatience scuttled my chances," Affinity admitted.

"Most girls do it these days, and if you're serious about it Essence you need an experienced and reputable agent, because there are pitfalls and you may not pocket all the benefits," was Enamour's warning.

"You're still a virgin then, Essence?" Sagacity queried.

"Of course, Grannie, of course I am," she said, indignant her condition needed verification.

"Well, you are almost sixteen, my dear; and at that age, lots aren't."

"Well, I am."

"Not for much longer, the way she's slumin' it," Wraith chortled, delighting in the opportunity to intrude into the cloud of adultish conversation.

"Shut up Wraith, what would you know?"

Sagacity decided enough was enough of the matter, and turned to Wraith, "so what's happening with you, young man?" she enquired.

Wraith stood up, pleased to take centre stage, raised his arms displaying his muscles, took a deep breath and rotated, "Muscle development Gran, triceps and pects, looking good, aren't they?" he lowered his display, "They're on my back all the time about my diet, but my numbers are still good," he said, anxious to have Sagacity sanction his self-confidence.

"You're growing into a fine young man Wraith, just keep up the good work, and stick to the food catalogue. What about your teeth?" she enquired.

Again, Affinity was the fountain, "Not for a couple of years yet Mum, they won't touch them until he's closer to his adult size. We'll probably have an adjustment to his nose about the same time."

"He needs a lot more than that." Essence announced.

Wraith looked at her, raised a finger and turned away.

Now it was ten-year-old Justice's turn to update grandma. "I'm having toning exercises and injections to make my hair stronger."

Sagacity turned a questioning eye to Enamour.

"His hair is not strong and without treatment they predict he'd be bald early, probably in his late thirties, so we don't want that," Enamour explained.

"No," Sagacity agreed.

"Listen Mum, there's a big night billed for the arena in a few weeks and we're going. Like to come?" Prudence asked, then added "it's a category one event, in red, with cloud."

She wanted to say yes but was reluctant since Sanguine's R-rating disqualified him from attending category one matches. With her hesitation apparent Sanguine chipped in, "You go Sars-dear, have a night with your girls. Stay the night up there, I'll be okay. You know I'm not keen on the arena anyway, it's mainly a girl thing."

Still, she paused, demurring, but the thought of a couple of hours of exuberance and adrenaline pumping savagery was beguiling.

"Come on Mum, you know you want to, so just say yes," Prudence implored jokily.

"Right, yes, I'm coming!"

Chapter 6
Disappointment

It was due, but for two days Enamour had ignored the familiar signals, reasoning optimistically, this month would be different, and while the sensations were habitual, they were merely the result of more than two decades of the monthly bother, she believed. But as her shower closed off, and the water drained away, she looked down. No! The watery red streaks running down her inside leg harpooned her dream. Breathless, she plunged into despair, but quickly a surge of anger swirled within, and in self-flagellation slapped her crotch repeatedly. She was not pregnant, and emotionally she was roller riding, her anger abruptly displaced by a wrenching melancholy. She looked down again, transfixed by the red vein wending across the marble to disappear down the drain.

If she'd had the test earlier it would have saved this distress but she wanted the suspense, extending the anticipation to enrich the exhilaration. She called for the shower seat and more water, and slumped into the chair, her head flopped back against the wall. "More," she called, and the flow became a torrent, flooding through her hair, over her face, spilling through her open mouth and down her body, but it's soothing could not wash away her quashing. She felt weak, drained, her head fell forward until her chin rested on her chest, her hands dangled on vesuvius.

As her mind began to clear, so dawned the reality of her predicament. Subconsciously she'd known for ten days or so she was empty, no cells multiplied in utero; but a blind dream had protected her desperation, until now. The evidence was dumbfounding. While her futile optimism now seemed unreasonable even masochistic, she told herself her behaviour was merely the product of her natural instincts, and there was much more to her driving forces than beauty, vivian, and self-indulgence. Further, she now saw the fading red streaks as confirmation of her femininity.

For years it had been nothing more than a monthly nuisance but the consequence of its arrival this month was a reminder of the fundamental human disposition to procreate. Now at thirty-nine she'd uncovered the fulfilment of feeling wholly female, and regretted the years lost to the erroneous indoctrination to ignore and forego what was natural, and for her, imperious.

It was Enamour's second failed pregnancy sortie, and while she had excused the first attempt as unlucky, this time her preparations had been meticulous, and the timing checked and re-checked. The failure was bewildering, her fertility had been confirmed, a scan had detected ovum in her uterus, and since she was in good physical and mental condition, there was no reason or incident, to believe she had aborted, unaware. There was only one creditable explanation. She'd been deceived by a dud impregnator, when she'd paid for what she believed to be quality.

Melancholic, she again raised her face into the stream, wanting to cry but not alone. She needed someone to comfort her distress, someone to cuddle, and a familiar voice of understanding in commiseration.

"Damn you Maxim!" she snarled, angry again, her fists clenching.

In self-pity she begrudged the absence of his comfort, leaving her to a lonesome duplicity, and while she felt some consternation about the secrecy and deception, there was no alternative. Maxim's outright refusal to consider, let alone negotiate with her, led her to proceed clandestinely, and she would only divulge her solution when an outcome was secure, and flourishing within. Her decision was final when he ridiculed her ambitions, and when her threats to use other covenants educed his indifference and sarcasm. While she believed her determination could menace their relation, she hoped it would not destroy it, though she was conscious of possible consequence.

She leaned forward resting her elbows on her knees, gazing once again but unseeing, at her dismay, and wondering if her sister posse would be consoling. However, the prospect for their earnest comfort was uncertain, since they'd both criticised her intentions, and while finally sympathetic, they had fallen short of avowing unreserved support. Affinity's objections still seemed to bubbled beneath her overt support, while Prudence, who was inclined to apathy rather than objection, might be the collaborator she needed.

Enamour looked into the mirror, and through half opened water douched eyes, she watched her blurred self, ran a hand over her stomach and saw the fantasy of herself pregnant. Her mania was becoming delinquent, and as she gazed, she wondered if she was delusionary. She had been strong enough to come this far alone but with yet another setback, did she want a baby enough to continue? Where had that thought come from? Her answer came instantly, along with the dismay of having had it at all. Forging on into a lonely future held no real fear, and her present dejection was merely a patch of gravel in her road, and an opportunity for reaffirmation. The cost benefit analysis was a simple sum.

Enamour's misery was waning, determination was in resurrection and standing alert, with forethought foremost. Two months had been lost, annoyingly, but in the context of her undertaking, she would log them as incidentals. However, two wasted months were a spur to guarantee they did not stretch to three, and since it was only eighteen days until she'd be estrus again, today was the day to launch anew.

As she dressed inattentively but methodically, her plans assembled, her ambitions schemed. and her feelings hardened against the deceptions to which she'd been subjected. There was no time for the cavern, the apparel hologram, or the printer. Her makeup would be a quick, old time and hand applied, which she'd put on while the hair capsule did its work. In a short time, she was prepared in a light green, once piece, string strapped, subterranean front, high backed, medium cut, and attuned to her mood. But her face and skin were to be plain, unenhanced, an uncommon demeanour which occasionally drew frowning disapproval in public, but Enamour's fondness for the natural, coalesced with her decision to ignore her sisters' qualms and the beautiful society's expectations.

The door to the offices of the Academy of Combative Sports — Male Division burst open, surprising the female receptionist, whose eyes flicked up from behind her desk, to see Enamour's long legs striding towards her. Arriving at the counter Enamour offered a formal smile, her eyes fixed and piercing. She was in no mood for pleasantries, or crap,

92

and no prisoners were to be taken.

"Good morning Enamor, how are you today?" came the greeting, immediately annoyed Enamour who was taken aback by the familiarity. It was normal to be identity scanned when entering most jot establishments, but still she was surprised, and momentarily paused to contemplate the female about to feel the brunt of her anger.

Enamour gazed into two bright green eyes, buoys in a silver face, atop a white and silver laced body with exposed and chrome tiffanys. Her crowning hair was short and frosted. There were jayones and there were jayones and this young female belonged with the elite. Enamour was not intimidated.

"You have me disadvantaged my dear, you know me but I don't know you. Good morning anyway. You asked me how I am. Well, I'm very unhappy, and hope you can put things right, without me spoiling your day or anybody else's."

Unperturbed, "Well Enamour, I'm Fable, and I know you since you've previously utilised the academy's taag services. If you've a complaint I assume it's about one of those visits. Though we rarely have unhappy customers."

Her manner was affable and her tone, heartening. Enamour relaxed somewhat, her body eased, reasoning an aggressive approach might not, initially at least, be her best tactic. A careful transit through this thistle might prove more successful than charging. She leaned over the counter closing into Fable's personal space.

"On two occasions I engaged taags from this institution but neither episode made me pregnant!" she announced, her gaze intensifying but only her lips moved. "This is despite clearly stating when I made the bookings what I required, and for which I paid a premium. Now I want to know what you're going to do about it."

Her blunt opening salvo showed no sign of ruffling Fable. Instead, she looked down and summoned Enamour's file. She glanced up.

"What did you book?" she enquired.

"Live shooters," Enamour snapped.

"We don't do live," came a curt response and an upward glance.

Enamour's annoyance surfaced.

"I know that, now! A costly and time-wasting discovery, but check my information anyway, and you'll see what I was promised," she said reaching over the desk and pointing at the information screen. "So now I want a live one this month, free, or my settlements refunded," she was snappy.

Fable looked up again and held Enamour's gaze. "I cannot speak for what you believe you were told, all I can say is that we don't do live, but if either of your episodes were unsatisfactory that's a matter, I can discuss with you. Here's your encounter summary, so we can see what your satisfaction indictors registered. This will determine if there is any reason for a refund. If it appears our taag failed to execute his obligation or fulfil your expectations, then we can review the liaison, and if your complaint has substance, we can work through how you'd like to be recompensed," her eyes went back to the screen.

"Liaison summary," she summonsed.

"Never mind that, I want to know why I was lied to, and by whom."

Her demand was ignored instead Fable now had Enamour's experience data on screen.

She stared at it for a few moments then looked up, expressionlessly but her glinting eyes betrayed delight., "You're a high-performance female Enamour," she announced, concerned her expression might betray her intrigue, so she looked back at the screen.

"Never mind that, as I said, I'm here to find out why I'm not pregnant, and hear what you're going to do about it.", but still she received no response, rather Fable continued to review the data.

"According to this, you've visited here twice in the last two months," she paused. "On the first occasion the event lasted nearly two hours. You were oralled for twenty-eight minutes, during which you experienced four highlights of varying intensity, caesar penetration took place five times with a total penetration time of sixty-eight minutes; which broke down into thirty-one minutes of strong participation on your part, and twenty-four minutes of passive reception," she looked up, "that means you just laid there."

"I know what it means!"

Fable looked back at her screen "For the remainder of the period you submitted to what we call theatre, which included tongueless kissing, and while you rejected anal play you still experienced two minor delights during this phase.

"The record shows you experienced six intense nefertities, ejaculating severely and flooding twice, and four others of fluctuating reward. Your last nefertiti lasted five minutes fifteen seconds, during which you attained uogasm for almost all of the continuum," she announced pleasingly, and looking up again, "Well done Enamour, I don't see many summaries this successful; it rules out any point of us discussing compensation."

"Nefertitis, uogasms! They were good but good was not what I paid for; I get plenty of them at home. I paid for live loads which were not delivered," her voice was hardening, but still she failed to solicit a reaction.

"On your second visit it appears your experience was even better, as it lasted almost three hours, with more than an hour of intercourse and once again you reached uogasm for an extended period. That's expected though, since once you've been here, we have a record of your sensitivities, response spots and preferences, so on your next visit we can brief the taag about your erogenous zones and capricious spheres. I think your visits here have been very satisfactory," she concluded confidentially.

"There was no outcome, that's the point! Hell, how do you people know all this stuff anyway?" Enamour demanded, suddenly tetchy about the way her intimate conduct had been monitored, analysed, assessed; and then recorded.

Still, Fable remained unruffled by Enamour's antagonism, and looked her in the eye. "All session pits are equipped with numerous censoring and movement tracking mediums. They follow your body's movements, and monitor nerve activity, physical responses, emotional status, and stress levels. They also record heart stress, body temperature, tracks blood flows, monitor brain activity, reads blood pressures, and detects inconsequential activity.

"Because females all differ, and therefore respond variously to the same stimuli, the sensors quickly discover the highly sensual provinces of your body. Some females have sensitive tiffanys, others sense little in that precinct, many cannot nefertiti without clitoral involvement, others can, some fancy anal contact, while others wince at it, some tingle when their toes are sucked, while others see it as time wasted, etcetera, etcetera.

"The pits are set for optimum environmental comfort level, regulating temperature and humidity, and it adjusts the aroma to stimulate glands with fragrances fluctuating from floral to fornication fluids, or a combination of them all. The music varies according to the mood and the tempo. Via ear chips, the taags receive continuous commentary on your status and respond accordingly, sometimes to their own volition, other times they follow the algorithm's suggestion. He knows when you're anxious for penetration, and when a nefertiti hovers, then following directions he'll regulate a tempo, and instigate any ploy which will drain your final reserve, and in euphoric anticipation will transport you to a voracious liberation, in the skies with nefertiti.

"And the taag is informed when his client is thirsty or would benefit from more lubrication. No female should leave here without an inner calm, totally relaxed, and expended. That's academy policy." Fable looked pleased with her explanation and expected Enamour to be pleased too.

"Now I understand why I enjoyed myself here, and it seems this place has nailed the copulation commerce business, having found the formula for fulfilling female fantasies but I'm not pregnant, and I'm sick of saying so."

Fable could see no point in explaining anything any further, besides she had something else in her mind. After a moment she looked up and smiled serenely.

"Enamour can I ask you about uogasms? Rarely do clients register them, but they seem almost normal for you. I thought I had good sex, and if I didn't work here, I'd be content, but I know now there's more."

Enamour looked at her, furtively, contemplating the girl's beauty, and although sceptical about being sympathetic, her preferred persona proved the palatable.

"I don't reach them every time Fable, in fact, it's only when my libido is in full flush, which is only a few days each month. However, there's a factor which is important. Do you have any idea of the difference between a nefertiti and a uogasm?

"No, except uogasms are better."

"I've no idea how your technology registers responses or what it assesses as a nefertiti, let alone a uogasm but female perceptions vary, and for those with demanding passions, their sexuality goes on maturing for years, while others, unfortunately, plateau earlier. One of two things happen with time, the first is the sex with a partner becomes familiar, hurried, boring, and consequently happens less, so refreshment is sometimes sought with strangers or new partners, or through experiment. There're sex parties, swappings, for a few sadism or masochism, taags and taafs, fantasy at the Couple's Callusionary Coop, and of course, drugs.

"Maintaining the adrenaline in these physical and emotionless escapades necessitates continued progress, usually towards the extreme, and while all of these diversions are rousing for a while, none will maintain a path to the total consumption, but will end, not euphorically, unfortunately. The answer lies in educating your sexual being, and working to graduate from the juvenile physical slog and its insipid routine, to a mental encounter, whereby your mind becomes your primary sexual organ, and takes control of your sensory mechanisms. In time Fable, even when multiple nefertities leave you exhausted but still feeling short changed, you're ready to move up."

Enamour leaned closer again unblinking, "Remember Fable; calisthenics and physical hijinks have a role in sex, especially for beginners but when you learn to nefertiti for ten minutes or more, while lying absolutely motionless, you've close to sensual liberation and the uogasm.

"I think I understand what you're saying and have an inkling, but how do I get there?"

Enamour straightened and looked around thoughtfully, then closing again, engaged her stare.

"Not easy, and impossible without the right partner, a rounded relationship established in mutual synergy, bonded by magnetism, and enunciated lustfully. Your partner must be intelligent and interested principally, even solely, in your journey and destination, not his own. And his touch should make you tremble with desire. The sexual relationship must, and I repeat must; function with him accepting the role as your servant while you must submit to your servant. Now, if he understands what it is he's attempting, the foreplay will commence with tactile bonding and reassurances. After a time, you must move to the mental phenomenon, meaning your imagination takes over, and the physical steps aside. Your partner's baton must skilfully orchestrate the lullaby from the prelude to a crescendo. His chief weapon should his tongue, not for licking, but for persuasion."

Enamour paused, "Got anyone in mind?"

"Yes." Fable smiled wistfully; she tingled inside, and embraced her thoughts.

"Your reproductive chemistry is critical when you're searching for this way forward. The time to venture is on those few days each month when your ovaries have remitted a consignment to your uterus, and your endorphins have reacted by wanting your egg fertilised." Enamour had been side tracked, and was now slightly irritated about it. Her tone changed.

"Well, that's you sorted Fable, but it hasn't solved the academy's deception, nor have you resolved what the academy's going to do, to make me pregnant."

"Enamour, Thanks for the dream, you've charmed my future and I'm impatient," she said reluctant to return to Enamour's problem.

"Another thing Fable. If you manage to reach this aspiration, you'll realise you won't want to go there every time. There's a time and mood for this bid, so don't be greedy, and go seeking out of season."

Fable smiled acknowledgingly, and accepted it was time to move on.

"As I said I don't know what you were told or were not told Enamour," she paused knowing she did know, "but I can only reiterate the academy can't supply active volleys," she looked down at her screen, "and since your log shows 32 percent euphoria, 58 percent gratification, and the last ten percent enjoyable. I'm sorry but there's no chance a refund would be approved," and she looked back at Enamour.

Silently annoyed by futility, Enamour admitted to herself she was wasting time in this hopeless cul-de-sac to nowhere, and accepting it was her only feasible option. But Fable had an option and it was her turn to lean into Enamour's personal space, "I can probably point you to someone who might fix you up. Give me your tice," she said putting her hand out as Enamour peeled it from her arm.

Fable keyed in some information and handed it back.

"Tice this guy, I believe he provides what you want, and being a jayone his physique should contribute excellent features, as well he's quite intelligent apparently. He's not cheap though, but has the requisite data guarantees with regard to DNA suitability, and gene purity, so as long as your DNA is compatible then you should expect a positive outcome. And I believe he'll be an improvement on our taags, who are a brainless lot of gonads."

"What else does he do?" she asked.

"Don't know, just fucks, as far as I know," came the cursory reply.

"Well, there are plenty of them."

"I think this one's doesn't care if you get pregnant, though."

"Sounds like, it's a full-time vocation for him?"

"I think so, I've referred a couple of others, and I'm probably not his only spotter."

Enamour sighed, "Hope he hasn't done too many!"

"I've no idea about that and it's not important with our DNA controls."

"I'm amazed there are so many fractious females flouting etiquette and want pregnancy, and I'm even more amazed so many need to resort to dobbin for the hors d'oeuvre. I thought mine was to be a lonesome defiance, but apparently, I've many more compatriots than the sanctimonious acknowledge."

"Well, Enamour, you're definitely in company, but I don't know if it's good."

For Enamour the visit to the academy may have borne fruit after all, but she'd had worthless expectations before, so she knew not to become too excited, too quickly.

Chapter 7
Surrogate Appointment

The day was over and at home Prudence was stretched out laying relaxed on her sacs (Sensual and Calming Sofa), her feet enjoying the massage pouches, while her arms and neck tingled to the fine vibrations of the cuddling rests, and electromagnetic waves relaxed her tension points. The sacs responded to vocal directives which controlled cushioning subtlety, and environmental factors including temperature and humidity, musical selection and the hologramer, for messages and/or entertainment. As woofs of perfume seduced her sensors and helped her day fade away, she chose to watch a 'gram'show.

At this time of the year, and with her team of designers winding down after completing the year's fashion collection, Prudence was looking forward to some time out, at work and at home. Arriving home, she'd hurried in, cast her bag aside on the passage table, kicked her shoes off in the hallway, and made a bee-line through the kitchen, destination bathroom. The door slid open as she approached and she began calling instructions straight away.

"Acast, I want number three disposal, at flow four, temperature five, for twelve minutes, with seven percent solution, then a five-minute rinse, with the three skin appreciations, all from two directions."

Understood Prudence, its sounds you've had a hectic day."

Prudence stepped into the mirrored cleansing zone, closed her eyes and promptly the sprays began. She stood astride with hands on her hips, turned her face up, arching her back. The draining water solution quickly coloured as it dissolved away her day's makeup, body presentation and hair style. That morning the cavern had outfitted her in stipes of alternate deep and faded lavender with a moderate outline, while her figure defining, seamless and glistening crop top, and almost knee length shorts were in classic blue. Her lavender hair, combed straight and hugging, swept around and over her right shoulder. Now it was all disappearing into the drain, rebirthing her ready for the morning's half hour in the cavern.

Now cleansed, naked and settled in the sacs, she felt reinvigorated and blissful, and was quickly disenfranchising from the day. Prudence enjoyed her work, and had been very successful, probably because as well as being gifted, she was conscientious and dedicated, responding to challenges with imagination and gusto. Her wake boiled with a litany of achievements, and her journey was a rapid rise to the upper echelons of the apparel and fashion industry. But, once home, and her front door was closed, it was to exclude the weather, strangers and work.

Despite her fancy for the stressless seclusion of home, her mind's inactivity had a tendency to seek another sucker, and sometimes it fanned the flames of her female on male fantasies, with exciting visions of exotic and erotic male subjugation. This evening her mind was inexorably drifting toward one of those occasions, and she began scouting through her 'gram' library for an old and familiar story, and one of which she never grew weary. Prudence could snuggle into reassurance as she watched glorious females winning the confrontation with males. The hologram's story was based loosely on events of years ago, when the battle of the sexes swung decidedly, expectedly, inexorably and permanently for females. The portrayal emphasised male weakness, in the face of female determination, when they surrendered their arrogant and presumptive pre-eminence, subliminally deluded, that power would remain in their hands.

Female's final struggle had had its ups and downs, and while at one time, early in the twenty-first century, females believed their dream was within reach, it had faded; due partly to stealthy and reactionary male push back, but more significantly, it was eroded from within. By and large females failed to resist the regression, and had stood aside for various reasons. Many were oblivious to the forces; some were content being subservient, finding it either convenient or believed it to be the natural order; some thought equality had progressed far enough and took their eyes off the main game; others were happy to shelter beneath a male umbrella, thereby abrogating responsibilities; some could not be bothered and/or their lives were too busy, or were too frazzled to be concerned; some succumbed to male propaganda contending differentials were not inequalities; while some prostituted themselves for the rewards accorded sexual pawns, and either ignored or were ignorant of their demeaning.

But as years past, the growing weight of re-subjugation re-ignited resistance, and voices calling for a new revolution gathered partisans. The mutiny began quietly, when a small cohort of energetic jap females recognised the screw of male cunning and scheming, had anaesthetized females back to near powerlessness. As the extent of this affliction came into focus, their passions maelstromed into a movement united in determination, with fellow females taking an oath of loyalty and secrecy, and pledging themselves to 'the fraternity fighting for females first', and promptly became known as the Fifes.

"No longer do we squat in caves, baby abreast, stoking the fire, awaiting food aid, hatching fornication avoidance plots; so, we must grasp the cudgel and use it to finally obliterate the remnants of males' delusory belief in their intrinsic superiority. It's time, it's over," was the contention.

Conclaved, Fife set about scrutinising, analysing and strategising, with the first assignment being to 'know your enemy'. Little external research was required, as there was a mountain of anecdotal evidence at hand, making it only a matter of collecting and collating the facts into a deducible format, from which conclusions could be drawn and a campaign concocted.

When the brain stormers' analysis was presented to fourteen females around a table, self-satisfying smiles and knowing glances exposed the unanimous delight of the group. A taut figured female, long necked, silver eyed, black flung haired, grey shaded body with scattered black outlined flowerings, slapped an outstretched hand onto the table, and opened the discussion, "Males! They're a simple bloody lot!" she said, and glared around at her audience "how have the bastards managed to laud it for so long, is the mystery."

"Because they're predacious with brains in their brothers, while we've deferred to their deceit and deceptions, that's how."

A feeling of 'this sounds good' swept around the table and was acknowledged with a round of clapping.

"We've only ourselves to blame, because we've put up with the intimidation, and been blinded by the charade of equality, despite the fact it's us females who have the purpose, the perseverance, and the pussies. The time has come to use these advantages."

"It's testosterone, which they can't deal with alone, resulting in their obsessive and unprincipled determination to share it, that's the issue, and always will be. However, females these days are just as amorous, enthusiastic, and demanding, and lucky, lucky males, we females are more amenable and accommodating for their outlets. The upshot means we females having more fun and satisfactions, while males absurdly take credit for their 'conquests' becoming easier, when it's been our choice all along. However, in their delusion they took their eyes off the ball, thus providing us with the opportunity to take advantage."

Their investigations concluded there were two categories of males; the old and the young. A core of old, shrewd and powerful men was the scourge. Along with their avarice, unscrupulousness, and relentless manoeuvrings for power, wealth and females, they have been, and would have continued to be a formidable force. Old men make wars and profits, while young men fight wars and die. Puerility was the outstanding characteristic of young men, who were libidinously obsessed, sometimes aggressive but fundamentally gullible, and often subject to single minded simplicity.

The Fifes' fathomed their way through a multitude of proposals and suggestions, deciding finally the answer was straight forward, though the pathway to success was not immediately obvious. Ultimately, they realised the only feasible route to change, lay in the hands of government and policy makers. Just being a noisy bystander had never cut the mustard. Fortunately, and increasingly through laziness, male influence in these institutions had slowly declined. Overturning the last vestiges of male majority in these institutions would open the gates to a female controlled society. Equality was no longer the goal, dominance was deserved and destined, they resolved.

Eventually, effective planning, tactical targeting, cunning, and hard work, saw their goal achieved, after gaining a majority on the Governing Council. Immediately the GC choreographed amendments to employment regulations and contracts, which gave females access to positions of authority, and management. This proved to be the decisive break through for Fifes. Equal opportunity had been a concept for ages, and while at the time, it was a step forward for females, in overtly stimulating some shift in cultural attitudes; the tangible advances were generally low grade and superficial. The glass ceiling was sustained by pillars of loopholes, excuses, and disguised and blatant chauvinism. Suddenly equality was no longer pertinent, instead it was 'access' which was going to change the cultural, the landscape, and the course of gender relationships, very quickly.

All employment positions above level two, were suddenly available and open, for challenge by any person who considered themself suitably ranked, qualified, more capable, or overall more appropriate, than the incumbent. If the challenger was assessed more accomplished than the incumbent, then the candidate took over. And human bias was deleted from the decision-making process, with an artificial intelligence algorithm assessing all challenges, and making determinations.

The genius of the approach lay in the fact it was not sexist, as its opportunities were available to males as well as females. It was a strategy founded in Fifes' conviction that females were more astute and competent than males, a contention which would become evident with the erosion of male hegemony. After millennia these female advantages had finally overcome and outsmarted male physicality and bullying.

However, for some Fifes the solution seemed too simple, their quandary being how to explain why, if females were more intelligent, etcetera, were they not already the dominant gender. They were concerned intelligence was not the only factor. Also, if females were undisputedly more responsible and trustworthy than males, what were the factors which had given males the control for so long

"How have we been subjugated, ever since evolution divided us for reproduction purposes?"

"According to Genesis, it's the penalty for Eve seducing Adam, while for succumbing, he was cursed with the incessant ejaculation affliction."

"That aside; while females are fundamentally conciliatory and creative, males are fundamentally predatory and belligerent; characteristics which go back eons when survivors were either the strongest and valuable. Males needed survival strength, while females were, fortunately or unfortunately, were valuable, for one reason or another Life's prime motivators were, and remain, food first and reproduction second, and while original sin may have been female inspired, females have carried a heavy burden, a burden, males soon identified, exploited and often abused.

"A pregnant female could collect and gather but could do little hunting, and there lay the rub. Once pregnant or nursing, primitive females trying to stay fed and warm, in a cave, or bush learn-to, relied on a social security system via the auspices of male contentment. A quid pro quo, would have been negotiated on the basis of a lump of mammoth and some firewood, in exchange for his sexual relief. Pregnancy would have been the female's nightmare, not only because of its demeaning constrictions, and itsthreat to her life, but because such an outcome would have caused (low I.Q.) males scant concern. Just what chicanery caused females to be pregnant in the first place, is probably not all that mysterious.

"As Homo sapiens spent countless millennia struggling from the mire; instincts, motivations and sensitivities evolved, and somewhere in this period, not only did foreheads stand up but sexual pleasure and especially nefertities materialised. The female nefertiti gave males the opportunity they needed for remittance, while deflecting the female's instinct to eject him. With his ejaculation standing by, her nerfertiti would have been his invitation: ho ho boyo, time to go, she won't say no, just now!"

"Despite this antiquity, females' eternal conundrum over pregnancy continued until the second half of the twentieth century when successful and pretty much guaranteeable contraception was developed. Finally, females were released from this infinity of sexual harassment, and leapt unabashed into a myriad of possibilities for self-expression and unrestrained gratification.

"No longer do we squat in caves, baby abreast, stoking the fire, awaiting food aid, hatching fornication avoidance plots; so, we must grasp the cudgel and use it to finally obliterate the remnants of males' delusory belief in their intrinsic superiority. It's time, it's over," was the contention.

Despite initially organising quietly, the Fifes leaders knew the operation required the resources and energies of many, and they needed female fidelity to spread the word, and recruited by word of mouth. There was no need for concerns, as the cause quickly became a topic where ever females met or congregated. Enthusiasm was fuelled by an instinctive perception the cause and the time were right, and many females, young and old eagerly joined the dash the endeavour.

In time the campaign burst into the public sphere, with a propaganda deluge, highlighting the advantages of instituting a competitive environment for middle and senior management positions. It would rid management of inefficiencies, and allow the cream to rise to influence faster than otherwise, an obvious benefit for society as a whole. However, a cohort of males quickly and correctly identified it as a ruse, and attempted to portray it as an irrelevant melee, staged by an insignificant group of failing jay class females. They claimed such a mechanism was unnecessary, and would destabilise a management forced to constantly watch their backs, when current accountability requirements monitored performances, and identified needed changes. The argument became a male/female matter, with the insinuation female wiles could see immaterial factors influencing changes.

When the debate became sexist females flocked to Fife, and while Fife did not deny the sexism, it continued to contend the change was necessary for a progressive society. Furtively, however, Fife began asking its members to individually refuse their annuments. No longer would they subject themselves to beauty assessments, as a way of holding public attention. Many females were keen operatives, for more than one reason, and assessment appointments shrunk. The Governing Council tied to intervene but threats from Nog-Nog and Now-Now about the danger defiance proposed to the beautiful society, were disregarded.

In the meantime, the uprising was motivation some proprietors, investors and others with pecuniary interests, to examine the fine print in the Fife manifesto, and when they did, they recognised opportunities in the proposals. They were sexless, being neither advantageous or disadvantageous to either gender. Unsurprisingly, female support was universal, while ambitious young males quickly appreciated the scenarios it afforded them. The change would be a mechanism to push aside the old encrusted class, while the oligarchy realised it would be an opportunity to identify, and weed out marginal management, jettison dead wood, and would amount to a permanent self-cleansing, and renewal mechanism.

The opposition was generally male, middle aged, middle management, who were justifiably worried about their capacity to survive challenges. Cruising along with their heads below the parapets would no longer be an option. In the end the movement had a conquering momentum, and when finally, the Governing Council could no longer ignore the issue, it went to a plebiscite, which resulted in 68 percent in favour.

The implementation of the momentous change began with defining the specifications for the assessment algorithm. It required detecting the factors which identified a person's assets and liabilities, and it became clear early in the process that females were going to have many advantages. The boxes they ticked included: they accepted responsibility willingly; were dedicated to their task, and persisted to conclusion, despite any setbacks or obstacles; had a capacity to operate effectively within guidelines; were not inclined to look for shortcuts or use deception; external troubles and disruptions were forgotten at work; they took pride in their person and their work; were always keen for further education, and improving their capability, and were usually loyal.

Their weaknesses were a vulnerability to become embroiled in workplace politics; did not adopt change easily; and had difficulty thinking 'outside the box'. While the politicking was assessed a minor matter, the other two aspects were not. Eventually, these two constraints made it difficult for females to replace the stratospheric oligarchs, who maintained their control, and were astute enough to realise it was them who should now keep their heads below the parapets.

In the meantime, however, the new era saw a rapid rate of challenge, which found females in many more middle, and senior management positions, far sooner than had been imagined. It was quickly apparent that the arteries of female penetration would eventually flow well beyond the hoped-for fifty percent. Fifers dream of female sovereignty was now reality.

It was all history now, and as the old hologram transfixing Prudence faded Now-Now appeared, "Good evening, Prudence."

"Bugger off." Prudence responded annoyed but she was ignored.

"Just interrupting to inform you, your tice has a message from the Pregnancy and Surrogacy Board, about your surrogate arrangements. Have a nice evening, Prudence. Good night," and she was gone.

The image disappeared, Prudence sprang upright, suddenly the evening's sombre dynamics had shattered, "Open the tice," she snapped, anticipatory excitement creeping across her face. The 'gram glowed with a written message, then the front door opened.

"That you Stone?" she called.

"You bet Pru!"

"Come here, hurry, look at this, we've got news," pause, reading, "I think."

Stone unhooked his earrings put them in his pocket, and arrived at Prudence's side to slumped down beside her, lingered on a soft kiss to her cheek, while cupping one of her bare tiffanys. Prudence allowed the kiss without being distracted from her tice message. When he was ignored his hand slithering down to hold vesuvius, and still with no response, broke off, straightened, and turned to read the message too.

An interview with a board assessor was booked for next Monday, at 11am, at the Pregnancy and Surrogacy Centre, and it was expected to take in excess of an hour.

"Damn a bloody assessor," Prudence protested, "What are we? Bloody kids! I've had enough of these people. Between having to answer a hundred questions for our propagation licence, then being told we can only have a male baby, now this nonsense of assessing us for compatibility with a surrogate! Is there any end to it?"

"It's all just part of making the whole affair flow smoothly as possible, and I agree there's some nonsense, but Pru, it's a small price, really."

"Yes, I know Stone but it's annoying, and it's such a big adventure, which will change our lives so I'm just tentative, I suppose"

"Are you sure we want this baby?"

There was silence for a moment, unexpectedly and suddenly Prudence had been jolted into reflection. She'd not confronted that question for quite a while, and now surprisingly, her mind was replaying the emotions and influences which had awoken her maternalism. Stone lay beside her on the sacs, then reached out pulling her close, propped up on an elbow, and leant over kissing her softly. With reality abruptly confronting her, the concept of having a baby drained her, leaving her susceptible top a cuddle and in his arms, she had not thought of turning back.

Her mind's replay didn't take long: "Yes, I do want this baby and I want the surrogate living with us, so I can be as much a part of our creation as possible, without the wreckage. And there's a few more reasons I want to keep a close eye on her. I need to watch her health, and a lot more."

"The surrogacy agency watches that with regular check-ups," Stone reminded her.

"Yes, well, I want to watch it as well, but that's only one of the things I need to monitor. If she's not here, how do we know what she's up to, she could be fucking half her neighbourhood, she might be drinking too much modco when she shouldn't be drinking any. I just wouldn't be able to relax unless I knew what she was doing."

"She's entitled to some private life, Prudence,"

"Not while I'm renting her uterus!" she declared.

Stone saw no point in arguing, and there was another matter of more importance needed resolving. But before confronting Prudence he needed to fathom an approach which would not ignite her paddy.

"I'm slipping into the shower," he announced, uncuddling her and standing up.

"Have you had something to eat?"

"Yeah, a couple of tats

"Fat controlled, I hope?"

"Of course," he said frowning.

Stone was back in a few minutes, clean skinned and relaxed, in undies. He'd been plotting, and was determined to challenge Prudence, once again about their offspring. Previously he'd failed to have his preferences accepted, not even appreciated, having wilted in the face of Prudence's insistences. Her mind was set on the structure and characteristics their son should annex, and so far, he had been unable to convince her, her dream was exaggerated

Developments in gene technology now allowed technicians to

culture outside DNA for infusion into embryos, thus allowing desirable characteristics from other body types to impact on a baby's final composition, while eliminating undesirable features. Embryos could be engineered to delivery specific characteristics in progeny. The procedure was available to anyone with a propagation licence but there were conditions and specifications to be followed. While these modifications were designed to encourage a gradual improvement in the community beauty standard, many applicants were still frustrated by the limit on the percentage of DNA which could be imported, that being 12.5 percent. The procedure was known as the Harlequin Program.

The technology had been embraced enthusiastically by both the jay and R Classes, both groups, naturally, wishing to upgrade their lineage. (R class parents producing lower jay class offspring was exacerbating the surrogate shortage.) However, the technology was not fool proof and unexpected and unwelcome features were occasionally discovered in pregnancy. If such faults as skin colour too dark, or poor skeletal ratios were developing, the veritable parents could elect to terminate the program. In such cases the surrogate was still entitled to her full entitlements, imbursement and benefits.

With a female embryo allocation, Caucasian parents often specified infusions of Asian DNA types, expecting such a modification to deliver a subtle olive skin, delayed skin aging, accompanied with a more refined graciousness. An Asian component was also expected to improve body conformation, with a reduced inclination towards such hazards as overweight, heavy legs, or over size tiffanys. One downside to Asian incorporation was the strength of the hair colour, being black, thereby drastically reducing the chances of their child inheriting the generally more desired fair hair.

When modifying a male embryo, parents also had a penchant for darker skin, but instead of the body refining elements of Asians, they chose Negroid DNA, expecting improved size, better skeletal ratios, height and strength.

On the other side of the colour spectrum dark skinned parents often wanted harlequins with Caucasian DNA adjustments, for lighter skin and in females some Asian refinement. Where the parents were predominantly Asian there was little enthusiasm for darker skin and in a son specified a bigger and stronger. This left them to gamble with DNA adjustment from a large Caucasian. Where the embryo is female, Asians usually ordered a little more height, otherwise sought only minor improvements, with technology still unable to do much to modify their hair colour. The final consequence of this parental meddling was that most Caucasians bore darker children, most Negroid types had lighter children, while Asians generally when growing a little taller or larger, often both in males.

The eagle's view of the Harlequin Program revealed two things; the first being society was evolving homogenously, and secondly, male and female physiques were diverging. While both genders were trending taller and olive coloured, males were growing considerably heavier, but females were becoming finer but taller. Desired facial features were scarcely a concern in harlequin configurations, as difficult to produce satisfactory results, and when such enhancements could be dealt with more exactingly, in childhood, surgically.

With the communal ambition being for beauty before brains, few designing parents considered intelligence to be sufficiently critical to supplant attractiveness. While some parents would allocate a percentage of intelligent DNA, if there was space to spare, only rarely would it be the primary grafting. Thankfully, however, some self-assured parents ordered intelligence, a very few wanting the full 12.5 percent modification devoted to improving this ambit.

Stone nudged Prudence aside and flopped back beside her again, then he kissed her again, softly, his lips moist.

"Prudence," he said quietly, "I'm still concerned about our harlequin decision. I can't see why you want such significant modifications when it's to be male anyway, and if you consider you and I, we look rather good anyway. We could have a natural boy, which even the finicky would appreciate."

Instantly Prudence's eyes flashed, her relaxed ambience vanished, and she angered his seductive kiss had been a ruse. She sat up and shrunk from him, her eyes glaring.

"We're not going there again Stone, I hope!" her contact with him withdrawn, now half-aliced on the edge of the sacs, her stare held, annoyed, her mind contriving. Stone returned the gaze, calm, determined not to be intimidated, and this time to have his position discussed before their escapade ventured any further. As they braced for battle, Prudence realised she was looking at an opponent who'd mustered munitions, something he resorted to rarely. A tactical about turn may the good manoeuvre at this point, as she felt her hardball style could strike a wall this time. Accordingly, she let her shoulders sink, her expression mellowed and she wriggled back to him. Her strategy this time would be 'yes, all right, but!'.

"Yes, all right Stone, if you want to talk it through again, but first can we agree the harlequin modelling is a good representation of what our boy will grow up to look like," she was hoping her tone was sufficiently fawning to imbue him with sympathetic compliance. He looked away, rolled his eyes, sighed quietly, looked back at her and let his head fall forward a hint. Prudence thought she had won the round and reached down to take her tice from the floor.

"Hang on Prudence! I haven't agreed yet. I know what the program can show, but I'm also know we share oodles of natural assets, and would produce a child with all the genes he'll ever need."

She ignored the comment, looked at him across her shoulder, eased a "fuck me please" smile and learnt over kissing him quickly, the tice already in her hand.

"Just let's have a quick look anyway Stone, it can't do any harm."

Stone was not too interested at gazing at parade of perfect physical specimens, with which he'd feel no empathy or kinship. However, in this game of 'blind man's bluff' which they were now playing he was wary of provoking Prudence's irritability. Prudence spoke to her tice, calling up the harlequin porotype program. The full-size hologram appeared on the 'gramer.

It was, Nog-Nog and Now-Now again scant and mauve toned.

Nog-Nog started, "Good evening, Prudence, how are you? I see Stone is with you, that's good. Welcome to Harlequin Modelling, the program designed to give you an indication of how you baby will grow up, if you decide on modifications. You can pick and choose DNA from the thirty-two sub-types but the program will not allow you to graft more than 12 and a half percent alien DNA."

Now-Now took over and spoke purposefully: "Good evening,

Prudence and Stone, before beginning, I'll mention that while we have faith in the accuracy of this modelling, remember the projections are not guaranteed, as anomalies can and do occur."

Nog-Nog returned, "The situation is this. Significant mishaps occur, about once in a thousand, however minor variations occur in approximately five percent of babies. For example, if you were to adjust for number three skin tone you might get number two or four, occasionally five. Another case would be if you decide to increase the height of child, there's is a small chance that additional height may not be evenly distributed over the torso so you get a skeleton outside jayone ratios."

Prudence didn't look at Stone but she was wanted to gauge his reaction to these warnings, which she chose to overlook. Her hesitation was momentary, then her head flicked to him.

"That's just one of the reasons why I'm not comfortable with this," he said calmly.

"Wait Stone," she said resolutely, and her attention returned to the hologram.

Now-Now continued, "The reasons for these discrepancies can be due to faulty DNA, or the foreign material may not integrate fully with the incumbent material. Despite this it is not our intention to dissuade you from embarking on a harlequin as 95 percent of outcomes are within four percent of the modelling. Less than one percent suffer significant slipups. Finally, if you decide to proceed, you'll be required to acknowledge the risks. For now though, we're off, so do your research and we hope all works out well, for you."

They were gone and the 'gramer awaited instructions.

Prudence looked to Stone, her eyes quizzical and her expression silently excited. He hesitated, gazing into hers, but his periphery was cruising, 'she's beautiful and I love her' he thought, then, "all right Pru let's look again! But I'm not conceding anything," his objection registered.

Prudence returned to the hologram and called "continue to harlequin modelling," and internally an excited anticipation was anxious to see her child. She flashed a wide-eyed grin at Stone, and her shoulders clenched in eagerness. Stone smiled and wanted to wrap his arms around her, squeeze her close, but under the circumstances it would be unwise to abandon his bridge head, when already she had him on the back foot.

A smiling female face materialised, "Hi, Prudence, Stone, welcome. First, I must confirm you are both to be the parents of this modelling."

"Sure are!" her head flicked another glance at her consort.

"It appears your details are current but I need you to scan your implants to be sure there's no confusion. I note that you both came out of alphaspection as jayones which you both retained for a considerable period, so we certainly have very strong foundations on which to build a beautiful boy. I hope the modelling gives you what you want. All images will be of your boy aged 16, that is, when he is due for the alphaspection."

Prudence swiped her tice over her upper left arm and handed it to Stone who did the same.

"Right, here we go. To start with, I'll put up a model of the boy you'd have naturally, that is, without any embryotic imputes. Then you can experiment with alterations but two images will remain, one of your natural son, and the other one will be with amendments."

The hologram was vacant briefly, then the apparition of a naked youth appeared, and began rotating. Prudence and Stone gazed silently, agog, the image and the solemnity of the confrontation, profound and dumbfounding.

"The argument's over as far as I'm concerned," he announced aloofly.

She turned to him slowly, her eyes still on the hologram "Not for me, it's not!"

The hologram proceeded to collate the specification of this person should he be born, "The analysis of this male person is: 92/128th caucasian 21/128th Polynesian and the remaining 15/128ths is mixed Negroid, and Indian."

Prudence was amusingly amazed, "You're certainly a fruit salad, my love," and turned to Stone, "Well, I'm claiming the Polynesian," she grinned.

"Why?" he asked, amused.

"They're the best lovers, didn't you know that?"

"Well, the negroid must be mine, then."

"Why?"

"Because they're the best studs."

The hologram was not finished, "This specimen would come through the alphaspection as a jayone, but it'd be difficult for him to retain that after age thirty. However, with suitable childhood growth management he could probably retain it for a few years more.

"What are your recommendations?" Prudence snapped, irritated.

"BAS2, which would be a seven percent infusion into the embryo. The DNA is of Semburu/Negroid type but with it comes an increase in the level of melanin, a skin darkening element, which is already present in the proposal. It would improve the torso proportions to a much safer level. BAS1, with a five percent infusion should create the hoped-for results. The tone would be closer to its base and the torso would be on a safer footing. However, a warning comes with BAS2. There's a three percent risk factor, which is the highest percentage permitted to go forward. The risk with BAS1 is considerably less, at one percent."

"Display both outcomes," Prudence instructed.

A third figure appeared. All rotated slowly and were watched silently for a few moments, Ston examining their structure closely.

"I can't see much difference between the harlequins," Stone commented, "there's about a two-centimetre height increase in them both, and the skin colour of the BAS2 is darker than BAS1 but not by much. I can't see either of them being worth risking an unfortunate outcome."

"I'm liking what I'm seeing," Prudence replied transfixed, a pleased expression escaping from the corners of her mouth.

"Is it worth the risk of something going wrong?" he reiterated, hoping she'd concede a little.

"Yes, Stone, it is, but it won't. Do they both solve the marginal torso problem?" she called

"Yes, Prudence they do, the BAS2 adjustment would give him an 18 percent margin for error, while the BAS1 would give him a 15 percent margin."

"What's his margin as a natural," Stone wanted to know.

"Less than ten."

Prudence was intrigued; "Is there a BAS3?" she asked

"There is, but your analyses, indicates the increased risk level is expediential, and would not be approved."

"Come into the sunlight Pru, be realistic," Stone urged, but the comment was not received kindly. Prudence let her eyes do the taking, to which Stone's eyes responded, rolling, then flashed in futility and he looked away.

"Display BAS3 anyway," she demanded indifferently, venturing solo.

The figure startled her, repulsed she jolted back, glancing at Stone to checked if he was similarly shocked. The boy was taller, very tall, which was okay but his colour had advanced to almost black and his features were poor composed, he was ugly. Stone concealed his self-satisfaction but when Prudence turned to him, astonished, his smile was oavarice. She burst into a giggle and grasp his shoulder.

"I don't think so," she said drooping her head on his neck, recuperating from the alarm of what was possible.

Stone said nothing.

However, Prudence was graduating from an academic excursion, to the excitement of engineering her very own male baby. A man from herself, a man for herself, a big man, a beautiful man, a man no female could completely pilfer, a jayone man. The apparition was morphing into flesh and blood in Prudence's glory-box, and with her heart excited by BAS2, he was excluding all other males for the moment. She turned to Stone, the glow of an guiltless youngster across her face, "What do you think of Phoenix as a name, Stone? It's just come to me. Look at him. Doesn't he look like a phoenix?" she was pointing.

Stone looked had her coolly, his insights into her personality and foibles warned him she was dreaming towards a let-down, and while her happiness pleased him, they were currently tasked with determining a life's destiny. That would best be achieved with gravity in control of the logic. But trying to guide her through a U-turn was fraught with peril, and could only be successfully executed, carefully, if at all.

"I like Phoenix" came his first 'but' step, "so let's put it on our list."

Her eyes' sparkle turned surly, "What list?"

The list of names to think about."

"Well, I like Phoenix!"

"So do I," Stone's manoeuvring was off to a rocky start, and it was beginning to annoy him. He'd been a reluctant though patient passenger on this journey, but the further they travelled, the less likely it seemed she had room for him up front. He decided to firm up, remove the pie from the sky, and be blunt.

"Prudence," he said solemnly and by omitting her affectionate appellation, signalled his new approach, which she noticed immediately, countering with another silent 'fuck me' diversion. Indifferently he batted aside her flanking manoeuvre.

"It seems you're purchasing a transporter, and deciding size, extensions, colour, which top lane versions you want, what off grid options can you afford," he paused. "But no, this is all about our boy, our baby, it's not about transporter extensions, it's about extending us, it should be about the manifestation of love into life, it's about the intangibles, love, loyalty, communion, instincts, and the human facets which cannot be catalogued, logged or ledgered."

Prudence wanted to dismiss his rational, as it threatened her vision, so she considered ignoring his criticism, but since her 'fuck me' ploy had twice failed, she attempted to retake the initiative, and peering into his eyes, she calmly said, "Stone, I can't see any comparison between creating a gorgeous son and buying a fucking transporter!"

"That's what I'm trying to explain to you Prudence. You're approaching this as if you are buying something," he tried to explain.

"Well I am. I am buying our boy, and I'm taking every opportunity to ensure he has all the available guarantees for a successful life, just as I would if I was buying a transporter. It's the natural thing to do, as well it's our obligation, plus, you seem to be forgetting we owe it to the beautiful society."

Stone found her reasoning difficult to counter, and off the cuff he couldn't think of an ancaesarm while Prudence was confident her argument and returned to the revolving images. However, there was a debate. The BAS2 harlequin was the boy she favoured, but the BAS1 was not significantly inferior and still quite attractive. As well, would she be happy with him if Stone proved too truculent, she wondered?

"Well, Stone, what do you think, I like BAS2?" she was looking at him, bright eyed this time with her 'cuddle me' enticement.

"He doesn't look much like either of us, and I see that as a drawback."

"Is that important? Have a close look at the natural one, he doesn't look much like either of us, either. He's just shorter than both harlequins."

"But he has a better alex and certain characteristics which are reminders of his heritage; besides, with him there's less chance of an embryonic cock up."

"Well, that's an exaggeration Stone, but would you be happy with ABS1?" she asked.

"I'll think about it but I'm still some way off."

"Think about it!" she straightened up, "For how long?" now irritated, the threads of her restraint were fraying. "You're leaving it bloody late to think about it Stone, I thought we'd agreed on a harlequin long ago," now a hint of despondency inflicted her emotional eddy. "All the information you need is in front of you," she said gesturing in the direction of the hologram, "what's the problem?"

"There's no point being aggressive Prudence, I'm entitled to think more about it," he said rolling forward on the sacs he stood up, and taking Prudence's hand with him as he rose. "Come to bed," he looked down to her, smiling.

She was unamused, and sulking somewhat, tugged her hand free.

Stone did not like her angry, and as he stared at her sensuality, he was determined not to depart without her, or leave her grumpy.

"You're magnificent Pru, and I love every ounce of you. Let's go to bed and end the day like we once did, every day," he suggested reaching his hand down, hoping she'd take it.

She glanced up briefly, then again, smiling privately, now aware the excitement of embarking on this baby odyssey had spiralled into a hunger for some corporeal nourishment. Her lover's resonance brimmed with a familiar implication, and infected her with an anxiety to succumb. There was a restless passion vorticing around her mind, and she could happily become his pawn, if a thorough mating session seemed probable. She looked up at Stone, her expression bland, but he sensed he needed only to reaffirm her irresistibility, and their next half hour was destined. Not that he had any doubt, anyway.

"Listen, you sultry bitch," and he paused to see if she was in that kind of mood. She held expressionless but she stopped blinking. Right!

He glanced at vesuvius, then at her tiffanys, then persuade her whole splendour, the sum of which produced a warm surge of appreciation in his mind, and a firming surge of libido in caesar. Prudence still disguised her rapidly spawning craving, knowing he liked the suspense; but she liked the tease even more. "Caesar's randy, ready and raring, while I'm itching to watch your nefertities and wondering how many times you'll cum, and if you'll squirt much, and how noisy you're going to be. All the while I'll love watching you, and admiring your beauty, and feeling the touch of silken skin, and delight of caesar at full stretch, at full depth."

When he reached out to her again, she took his hand, and waited to be drawn to her feet. As their skins came together temptation won and she conceded, wrapped her arms around his neck and hugged him. He slipped both hands around her waist, pulling them tightly together, his readiness easily felt. Stone leant back, lifting her off the ground, their embrace ending when she lay back in his arms, dropped her forehead onto his chest, and closed her eyes. His demonstration of strength was always evocative, and instilled the sensory security she sought.

Prudence lifted her head, clasp her hands behind his neck, and leant back at arm's length, "Take me by my alice Stone," she instructed. As soon as he did, she lifted her legs and wrapping them around his hips she arched her crotch into his lower stomach.

He peered down. Vesuvius, the ladies and vivian all leeched to his lower stomach, her virgin dewdropdewdrops alert for the occasion, while she felt caesar rummaging in ladies precinct, and she hoped he slither a path up to discover cleopatra. Her belly flexed, and she wriggled for the tingle, lowered her arm around his back, arched powerfully into him and wriggled some more, a memo that she was anxious to move on. Stone took one hand at a time from her alice, and slipped them under her inside legs, until they were outstretched either side of his hips, and vivian was poised eye to eye with caesar. Prudence held her breath as Stone directed caesar at vivian, and when they touched, he paused. Prudence waited while he teased, staring at him expectantly but when he just wagged caesar at vivian, smiling gallingly, her eyes frowned. She punched vivian at caesar but he withdrew further. Her glare went to war.

"You! You bastard Stone, you bastard!"

He was stirring her ire, something which would make her anxious, even desperate, which in turn would summon determination, physical enthusiasm, and sensual rage. For that she needed the top position, and after her first nefertiti would scarcely pause, before striking forward for another. And her second was unlikely to be her last. Stone grinned to himself. Everything was going to plan, but he needed her believe it was her plan.

"I've had enough of your BS Stone," she announced as she pushed herself away, she released her hold and put her feet back to the floor. "You've had your chance Stone, and you just chose to antagonise me, so now it's going to happen my way." She pointed at the sacs and he obeyed, flopping down on his back and stretched out caesar waiting. Still a little peeved at his reluctance to comply with her harlequin wishes, she stood astride his feet, staring down at her quarry. She looked at caesar's erection and decided it was too arrogant. "I'm not sure if I'm going start on your face or finish up on it."

He didn't care.

Chapter 8
The Arena

It was evening, and the sisters three stood circled in the terminal awaiting their mother, who was on the thirty-minute, high speed, hover track journey from Red Hill. They were early simply because they wanted to be, hyped in anticipation, and in the glow of the terminal's lights they chatted restlessly, giggled, laughed, stimulated by the prospect of a couple of hours of ruthlessness at the arena. It was an occasion for an outburst of fun and vulgarity, and the emancipation of inhibitions, and the trio had embraced the dress in red code whole heartedly. The accolade for the most outlandish was problematic but Prudence likely had the points over her big sisters. Affinity's time in the cavern had been for a quick toning in satin, medium red, sprinkled with silver flecks, her hair's silver streaks contrasted in the heavy red, flowing. Her high waisted, mid-length, bright red, self-adhesive, culottes peaked above her naval and behind swept low, exposing some cleft.

For tonight, Affinity's worries over her tiffanys had not dulled her presentation, with the dewdrops of her lovelies almost below the parapets. She was red petalled, with a petal sustaining each three-quarter tiffany; lower down three petals in front and two behind bore a modicum with modesty, while the cavern's masterpiece delivered her with a body of red flower clusters. Glowing red eyes might unnerve strangers, while her feet were heeled.

Enamour's display was bold, with sophistication lauding over crass, in a fine gold threaded satin falling off her shoulders in a deep vee to the waist, from where it clung tightly to her nether regions, revealingly. The red was subtle, and in some lights appeared nearly pink. The cavern laid a multi-red lace pattern from top to bottom.

When the capsule arrived, the canopy swung open, the seat raised Sagacity from the semi-reclined position, turned her outboard, and she stepped out. Red from head to toe, beginning with her feet being dark red but fading by her face, which displayed red lips and eyelids, then the hair resumed full red. She was in a one-piece, hugging dress with a stretched hem, and a daring, underarm V-neck. Aground, she stood erected and stretched out her arms awaiting embraces, which came in order of seniority, Affinity, Enamour and Prudence, as was custom.

"Mum, you're looking great!" Affinity exclaimed, easing back for the overview.

"It's good to be here. I've been looking forward to tonight for days. You said there's cloud, didn't you?"

"Sure is, mum."

She grinned, her shoulders shivered, a demon darted about her eyes, and she threw embracing arms over the shoulders of her closest two daughters.

"Can't wait," she said glancing around them.

"How's Dad?" Enamour enquired.

"He's had a good couple of weeks, health wise, and business seems busy, which makes him a bit grumpy at home. But he's good; says hello to you girls."

Affinity was impatient to move on, "Let's stop for a modco," she proposed.

Yes, was the consensus and Sagacity led off, her elbows expecting her brood to link up. Promptly the four were striding in unison, the pavement ringing to their clanking heels and swaggering rhythm.

On entering a suitable establishment, they found themselves far from alone in red.

"It's going to be big crowd tonight," Sagacity observed.

Already Prudence had her tice out ready to order. "What would you like Mum?"

Sagacity thought for a moment, "Caramel coffee, I think"

Affinity intruded, "Have a small modco with it Mum."

Again, Sagacity was thoughtful, "I don't think so." but she was unconvincing.

"Go for it Mum, you're here for fun, so have some," came Prudence's encouragement.

The incitement breached Sagacity's reservations and stirred her lynx, which the years, her age, and the dunville, had almost anesthetized, and the 'go for it mum' set her mind rewinding. It was nice to be back in the jot, and she wanted to have fun, exploit her jay status for a while, and she planned to jettison motherhood tonight. Of course, she wanted modco.

"Yes! I'll have a medium," she retorted, feeling the prickle of insurrection at the sound of her herself engaging impulse, or was it her real character?

"There's a condition tonight, girls. No Mum tonight, it's Sagacity. Understood?"

Broad grins lit their faces.

"Okay Sagacity," Prudence snapped eagerly.

"I'll have a full," Affinity announced.

"Yes, a medium for me," Prudence told the tice.

"Just coffee," Enamour announced purposely.

Enamour declining a modco was not too unusual but on an occasion like this night, it was more or less unexpected.

Sagacity reacted quickly, "You not pregnant are you Enamour?"

Enamour's expression soured almost imperceptivity, "No! Maxim still refuses to go positive, which makes it difficult,"

Unusually, this establishment still employed humans beings to serve tables, and the quality of this staff was a big reason it was crowded, especially with those in red. The physique and charm charged waiters, male and female, were all jayones, or pretty close.

"Welcome gorgeous girls, you're obviously off to the arena for some anonymous misbehaviour and fun," he said glancing around them all.

The patronising was too much for Prudence, whose initial infatuation fleeted, destroyed not only by his condescending tone, but also by his air of male superiority.

"We don't keep our misbehaviour anonymous!" she snapped, with enough inflection to extinguish his situational jurisdiction.

"He's just funning Prudence, and I'm okay with it," Sagacity chastened, with a supporting glance from Affinity.

Shortly, undaunted and still in rhythm, he returned with their orders. and asked if they required anything else, and when they did not, he wished them to "have an exuberant night, ladies. I believe the line-up includes a big female brute."

"That's our plan," Affinity responded, and as he turned away, she rubbed her hand over his alex.

"Changing the subject completely," Prudence said leaning into to the table, and looking around her compatriots grinning, "On Monday our new fashion range will be released, and there are exciting innovations, and some spectacular new concepts this season."

She had their attention: "That's the good news, the bad news is that if you want to take full advantage of the advances, this time, you'll probably need new printers, since some fabrics improvements can only be processed by the latest model.

"Another innovation allows you to coordinate the printer and the cavern, which will reduce cavern time since you'll only need to choose your clothes and makeup on the hologram, then the printer and the cavern will coordinate to produce a perfect match up. The cavern will advise you if it thinks any of your choices are incompatible with your dress.

"That's a worry," Enamour thought, and looked at Prudence to continue.

"And! If you wish to make adjustments to a garment, the new program will respond to verbal instruction, so the keyboard is gone; an improvement long overdue in this age. It's going to be easier, and more fun playing around with outfits."

"Pru, that sounds promising. What's in the range to be excited about?"

"For the first time we've divided the range into three categories, and you can purchase the catalogue separately, or all together. The categories are the FM range, the LM range and the GM range, with over a hundred designs in each."

"What do they mean?' Enamour snapped, a touch tetchy at having to ask the obvious.

"They're the Fuck Me range, the Love Me range, and the Gorgeous Me selection, and while all categories boast exciting new concepts, we've put a big effort into the GM, this year. The emphasis is more about the clothing, not the body, and it's about colour, shape, style, movement, glamour, femininity, even fantasy. There are frills, feathers, fluting, lace, layers, gatherings, gussets, puffing, piping, pleats, French knots and embroidery.

"The biggest conceptional change is to what is now the FM designs, with an increase in the area of skin exposure, which we're increased from 75 percent skin to 88 percent. You might think 88 percent skin is nearly naked, but it's a long way from it really. There is an optimum amount for exposed skin, and once exceeded the style becomes crass, and while that attracts some, going too far defeats the 'fuck me' look, and shouts 'slut me'. With 12 percent cover, we have delivered style but maybe not class, for now anyway.

"Another of the big innovations to this FM range, is the infusion of synthetic pheromones into the fabric, and that's one of the reasons for the new printer systems. These pheromones are generated naturally by females when they're on heat, and naturally, that's usually when they feel like dressing from this range. Our testing of this product indicates the effects will be positive. In a group of identically spec'ed females, half of them in FM, and mingling with a similar number of males; over 70 percent of males were attracted to females wearing pheromoned garments.

"We identified the increase in exposure skin as a crossover from sophisticated sexuality, or erotic seduction, and while blatant sexuality has always been part of our collection, never has it been separate and conspicuous. Market testing says buyer will respond to these trends, as they offer the wearer more scope to definite themselves. Of course they are not as flamboyant as the LMs, or as expensive as GM, but they do have a simple elegance, which creates splendour,"

"Sounds tantalising for some, but of no interest to me, my dear Prudence, it's your LM collection which sounds interesting," Enamour said.

"Would anyone else like another modco?" Affinity asked confidently.

"No, you don't, it's time we were going" Sagacity proclaimed and immediately stood up.

Outside the roller-path was collecting a mounting number of reddies, most spirited already, and the banter was abundant. Sagacity's contingent stepped into the column, of which the majority were female. It was female hegemonic fantasy which the producers used to attract large crowds.

In the crowd, the speculation was largely about the expectations for the monster female fight.

"I heard she's going up against an opponent with two Tom Thumbs," was one of the comments to emanate.

"You can't have two Tom Thumbs," came the abrupt response.

"Just what I heard, friend."

"Apparently, she's only fifteen," was another rumour disclosed.

"Where did you hear that?" Prudence asked the stranger politely.

"This week's Bullibill."

Ahead, the arena glowed brightly in the darkness, decorated with colourful light beams directed at its walls and dome, others probing the heavens. Around the base, bright white lights blazed from the entrances, where rows of reddies shuffled their way inside. As they drew closer, the thump of music could be heard pounding out a fornicating rhythm, and in the queues many patrons were already hyped and gyrated accordingly. On the roller-path the chatter volume was increasing, and bursts of raucous laughter rose above the hubbub.

The social segregation takes place at the entrance, with gates for each category, after which a short verification race must be navigated, where patrons must look directly ahead for the scanners to check identity implants, and an iris recognition corroborates the information. If a discrepancy is found the race diverts the culprit into an interrogation zone for warder investigation. Admission fees are collected by way of the scanners direct debiting accounts.

Should a spectator be entering through a race above their rank they are automatically gated into the correct zone but if they are entering below their designation a hologram at the end of the race advices them accordingly. And wouldn't you know it, it's Nog-Nog and Now-Now again. Sagacity and company entered via the jayfour lane, Affinity leading the way. Now-Now looked at her. "Welcomed Affinity, it's nice to see you here again. I note you're in the jok lane, but you're entitled to a Jar placing."

"I know," she snapped and strode on, irritated by the unsolicited advice.

Enamour and Prudence received identical advice and ignored it also.

To remain grouped, Sagacity's JOK rating obliged her daughters to accept a terrace further from the action than need be, but it was a tiny tally for matriarchal membership of their night's hijinks.

Once through the entry rigmarole, the arena opened into a cavernous, roofed, amphitheatre with the fighting pit in the centre, from which rows of circling stalls radiated upwards. It's standing space mainly, an innovation to encourage freewheeling exuberance, with rails dividing class zones, the highest ranked spectators at the front and the jayfours consigned to the upper echelons. For this event there was no allocation for dunvillians.

Once inside japs continued to ringside, or were diverted to confidential booths, private observation booths from which to watch the events through one way glass. The cubicles were expensive, were furnished for two, and being highly demanded, needed to be booked well in advance. Couples, sometimes threesomes, utilising "Confidentials" reckoned on the visual violence inflaming their 'flight, fight or fuck' instinct, assuming the 'fuck' factor to prevail, and expecting that surges of libidinous loaded, and substance fuelled adrenaline, would instigate a lust for copious carnal correlations.

The arena surround sound was engineered to enhanced the impact of the fight brutality, synchronising with every thump, crunch, punch, groan and moan emanating from the fighters.

By the time the quartet arrived, the stalls were already very much rendered in red, heaving red, oozing red, gyrating red, despite it still being almost an hour before program time. Affinity continued to lead having spied a likely spot, and they arrived happy with her choice, exchanged a round of high fives, howdied the neighbours, front, back and besides; bumped some hips, laughed and giggled oodles, and as the beating tempo permeated and the modco assisted, gusto kicked in, the girl's night out was well primed.

Prudence began to pitch to the arena's throbbing, and instantly and intuitively Affinity twinned, and in a moment, four were jiving. Sagacity's rhythmic enthusiasm suggested her daughters had inherited their inclination for abandonment.

High spirits and crowd numbers continued building until take off time, when abruptly the pulsing polyphony went silent, snuffing self-amusement and then ignited a reactionary roar of approval for the

127

impending. As the roar waned a subdued beat resumed, backgrounding a welcoming from enlarged holograms in pit centre "Good evening, good jot people, welcome" the voice was female and familiar.

"Tonight, it's a four-bout package, with the highlight being the first time appearance of our fifteen-year-old female demolition tyrant. Her name's Romance, but there's nothing else nice, pleasant or agreeable about her. She's over two metres tall, weighs two hundred and eight kilos, and she's too mean and ugly for a social rating, and too dangerous to be let out, so we keep her in a cage and her favourite food is raw beef."

Despite the dubious ballyhoo the audience's delusionary belief was willing, self-inflicted, and while the raw meat and the cage claims were likely bunkum, hopefully her capacity to crush opponents was not rumour. The thunder of delight rattled chests. Six and half metre Nog-Nog announced the first contest would be free style with males, no Tom Thumbs; the second would be males, ankle tethered, with a half metre separation, with Tom Thumbs; the third would be a four female all in, free for all, , with TTs; while the highlight match between Romance and a class A male would also be free style with TTs. As Nog-Nog finished and faded, the music resumed full volume, and thousands of hips, feet, shoulders, waists, heads and arms resumed their ardent anticipation. Sirens reverberated and the sea of red erupted into a cacophony of yelling, waving arms, air punching, feet stamping, clapping and cat whistles.

Affinity bounced on the balls of her feet, skyward arms swaying, while a bowed Prudence with two fingers to her teeth, dispensed piercing whistles, as her alice romped to the rhythm, as a watching and grinning Sagacity, resorted to the double shuffle and rhythmic clapping. Enamour stood straight, her eager expectancy more subtle, but she effervesced inside, and each waist-high jab was punched from a taut chest, braced shoulders and disciplined fists. Her knees bounced in time.

Suddenly geysers of white powder gushed from floor vents, and another reverberation of approval shook the arena but quickly subsided as the spectators sucked in the hanging cloud. The prescription further invigorated bodies, and amplified sensory perceptions, so sound was accentuated, light was brighter, colours were brighter, passions sensitized, while emotions magnified, and pit action perception exaggerated. The geysers would erupt three more times during the night. Enamour's breaths were shallow, slow, minimal, and unnoticed.

A real fleshed, long legged and tall female rose from the centre of the pit, g-stringed, alice rocking, in heels, and toned in shades of red which accentuated her erogenous zones, and her cropped hair, was the reddest of all. Audience approval intensified when she stretched her hands above her head, shook her three-quarters', and pirouetted for all to see.

"Suck it in beautiful people, it's fun time; time to let loose the leviathans, and see what mutilation the ugly and disgusting can inflict on each other."

Long Legs announced the arrival of two big brown fighting males, then stood aside as the prancing combatants bathed in the accolade, and acknowledged the acclamation. The dress code for fighters was a simple protection binding for their caesars; while their oiled bodies highlighted bulging physiques. They paraded the perimeter stirring crowd enthusiasm, and as it rose the fighters machine gunned the air with their fists.

There were no referees in the combat zone, neither were there brakes, as fights continued until one pugilist found themselves unable or unwilling struggle from the floor. However, an adjudicator watching remotely on a screen could penalize fighters or suspend an event for blatant breaches of the rules. This occurred rarely since audience response to any such intervention was always hostile, sometimes threatening.

With Long Legs departed a Tom Thumb tethered the combatants together at their ankles, with half a body length of chain, then departed. As the fighters confronted each other, their smiles snarled. While the first body shuddering blow refreshed the uproar, the appearance of blood produced even greater approval, as did the knock down. In the end the contested concluded with two blood splatted fighters, and an unconvincing winner, and the crowd was split between approval and disapproval.

Long Legs was back, this time her three-quarters swing naked, and in unison to her strutting She introduced the all-female contest, four combatants, no pairing, no partnerships, all in, each wanting to be the last female standing. The fighting four were all the same height, anatomically similar, slightly chubby, with heavy necks and low centres of gravity. They were painted identically, in black and white vertical stripes, neck to toe, white faced, and bald red headed. If they were clad at all, it was difficult to notice. Unpainted, maybe they'd be attractive, sort of.

And to add to the colour confusion, a Tom Thumb was assigned to each fighter. TTs were always painted white, female dwarfs, less than half the height of their principals, with the responsibility, in certain situations, for protecting their assigned fighter. If, for instance, their principal was grounded, their Tom Thumb would stand over them to fend off the opponent until their principal regained their footing. Assaulting a TT brought immediate disqualification. Also, if during a bout, the principal needed water or a revitalising substance the TT had the necessary at hand. These responsibilities ensured effective Tom Thumbs were in high demand, and commanded a healthy excise.

Amid circling TTs, the match promptly descended into an indistinguishable flurry of heaving and jabbering black and white jumble. However, a ruthless strategy soon emerged, when three set out annihilate one, and despite her undaunted TT, she could not rescue her unconscious victim. Then, quickly and summarily, two thrashed one, leaving two panting survivors to slug it out. The stripes plunged at each other grappling for the initiative eventually descending into a fists and knees melee on the floor. The TTs took a leg each and dragged the opponents apart. The fight did not inflict the requisite amount of damage to satisfy crowd lust, and when the pair mutually crawled to the edges and collapsed, the howls and hoots, infused the atmosphere menacingly.

"I find fighting females a tad disagreeable," Sagacity said learning into Enamour ear.

"I see it no difference to primitive brawling for sexual access, and genetic survival, so I always want the prettiest to win, be they male or female" she called back.

When Long Legs reappeared to announce the main event she was rowdily received, as she sauntered purposefully, in just a lonesome pussy patch; arms high, smiling, flaunting. The crowd seemed to want more of her, and renewed their shrieking cacophony each time her departure threatened.

"Look at her tits. They're fucking gorgeous," Affinity shouted to Prudence, cupping her own, agitating them.

Finally, Long Legs ended her announcement and stood aside, awaiting the combatants' appearance.

The sight of Romance hushed the crowd for a moment, except for a few disbelieving sighs and moans. She was big, very big, hairless, naked and slightly blue. Ever part of her was large, very large. Her shoulders were like thighs, her thighs were more than two arms lengths around, alice was her counter weight, her legs were worrying, her neck was of a waist, her arms sledge hammers, her tiffanys huge with inverted dewdrops, rested on a surging midriff of chest high muscle, verandaing her vesuvius hump. Surprising, was the apparent solidity and visible muscularity of what otherwise would have been a huge frame of shuddering flab. However, the 'pièce de résistance' to her absurdity, was the tender young face which bore no relationship to her body. High checked, full checked, small nose and mouth, her eyes lids and brows hung over her eyes, an average forehead, slightly double chinned, but all silky, unblemished and childish.

Long Legs moved up beside her, slipped her arm around her waist, and on tip toes stretched up kissing her on the cheek, "Isn't she fantastic, isn't she beautiful."

Romance brushed Long Legs aside, and began to strut.

"Well, she could be pretty but really, she's ugly." Affinity called to her neighbour, an early thirties, probably jil female.

. Despite this being her maiden public appearance, she appeared neither hesitant or trepidatious, and as she stomped around the pit, she moved easily, possibly graciously, was flexible, and was manifestly a powerhouse. Romance's Tom Thumb was fittingly oversize too, still a midget, but corpulent, square, nonetheless well experienced in the ways of the pit, and likely to be useful to her newbie. Romance ignored her, as she appeared to notice and enjoy the adulation, even smiling, albeit arrogantly.

Long Legs announced Romance's arrival and when a yellow tinged, category one, male appeared, it was the signal for an outburst of hooting, which he'd heard before, so he just waved. Fortitude and Aurora needed to ensure Romance's career launch ended successfully, and to this end had selected Hastings to fight her. Technically and publicly, he was still a prime specimen, ranked in the top echelon, but had managed to obscure the fact he was not quite the fighter he'd once been. While the doyens had identified his susceptibility, and were sure he would be beaten, Hastings had been around too long not to be aware of the skulduggery, and as a result had put considerable thought, into the fight and his tactics. For the occasion he'd been fitted with several disguised blood satchels, so expectantly he'd be a mass of blood in defeat, artificial and hopefully authentic. Romance's vulnerable body parts, particularly her eye brows, knuckles and knees had been layer with artificial skin, part of the scheme to see her pristine in victory. Two tom thumbs circled the boundary of the pit in opposite directions, grinningly accepting the accolades as their own. The start signal came with Long Legs's disappearance, and the pit door's closure, but neither contender advanced, rather their eyes went into bat. Romance saw just one thing, and it was ugly and contemptable, and while she was immediately impatient, she refused to concede to the need to take the initiative. Rather she'd been coached to wait for her opponent to walk into an early downfall.

Hastings knew his height and weight inferiority, up against her weight, youthful capacity for recovery and endurance, meant this big nasty, and brainless female needed to be regarded cautiously. She had a weakness though, being top heavy, substantially so.

Without hint or warning he attacked; charging, aiming for a low blow he fell to the floor at speed, skidding feet first at her knees. He struck before she dodged, one foot crunching her knee, the other crashing into an ankle, sending Romance's comprehensive alice walloping to the floor, the impact rippling a wave across her flesh. The surprise and speed of his attack shocked her, and silenced the crowd momently, before a howling dismay, of disappointment erupted.

Affinity loudly derided Romance for feebleness; Prudence was having second thoughts; Enamour felt sympathy for the big blue girl; while Sagacity was anxious for contest to get on. Hastings leapt to his feet, hoping to consolidate his advantage with another strike, before the Romance could haul herself to her feet. However, TT9 stood sentinel in defence, grimacing, angry eyed, and she was not about to relent.

Romance was flabbergasted, and glaring up at her tormentor her tongue raged, her teeth milled, revenge fumed, and her imagination saw the maggot a bloodied unconscious splash on the floor. Still sheltering behind her TT she rolled away, sat up, and with surprising dexterously stepped to her feet, threw her shoulders back, let her arms dangle low and glared at Hastings.

TT9 stepped aside, Romance stepped forward, deliberately, eyes bulging, one fist raised, the other lowered and primed, but Hastings was unphased, stood fast. Then he was in range, and her upper body spring detonated, dispatching a whipping fist on a roundhouse decapitation mission. Her target vanished, and as she attempted to recovered from her wayward follow-through, a counter punch came from her side, and careered to a concussional crunch to the side of her head. Romance was on the floor again, this time disorientated, while her arena support fell silent again, for longer this time.

Hastings readied again, to punt her in the midriff but TT9 was too quick again, and with a flying leap vaulted Romance and stood, spread eagled in defence. TT noticed Romance had been hurt, and worried she might not recover fully before her protection time expired, so disregarding the implications, charge head first at an unexpecting Hastings, driving testicles indoors.

He folded and collapsed, TT9 raised her arms, bounced around the pit on her toes soaking up resounding approval, and looked towards the adjudicators' port, with begging hands, pleading she'd only acted protectively, not maliciously. Her petitioning failed and Hastings was awarded two grams of mm and three minutes for recovery.

"Did you see that?" Prudence called to Affinity knowing of course she had but wanting to relive the delight.

"Incredible, what a piledriver, she's fantastic," Affinity marvelled with a little shadow boxing.

"Can Romance win, do you think?" Sagacity asked.

"Not sure, mm's a powerful stimulant, so Romance will need to come up with something new," Affinity mused, growing cynical and sceptical.

"If she can think," Prudence chipped.

Hastings was sitting head bowed, pain evident, while TT15 injected the mm, then she pushed his legs apart, lifted caesar and sprayed his brothers with anaesthetic. Romance sat too, thankful for the three minutes recovering, and for TT9's massaging of her shoulders and neck. TT9 leant into her ear, "Listen baby, try to whack his goolies. They'll be numb for a while, but another good hit to them could finish him. It doesn't matter about the aj, it's the crowd we must please," she instructed, straightening up and brutally massaging her under chin with both hands.

For Romance the advice and the vision roused a cynical smile, and abruptly jumping to her feet, to much acclaim, she was anxious to execute the suggestion; but Hastings, with his legs outstretched and apart and resting back on his elbows, just stared at her sauntering bulk. She was not interested in him, instead began punching her fist into her palm, and looked crowdwards. She spat on the floor towards her opponent, to much approval.

Hastings stood up feeling the mm was beginning to work, felt sharp, light on his feet, and with two successful strikes against the brute, was confidence a third would be enough. Unexpectedly he lunged towards her again but it was a feign and he propped, but Romance just dropped her guard arrogantly, and waited for him to move into range. Instead, he retreated, and when Romance thought he might charge again, she charged, expecting her weight, strength and momentum would be overwhelming.

Suddenly Hastings scheming was shattered when his view filled with her shuddering mass and two willing fists rushing at him, head down, her eyes glaring like headlights from beneath her brows. Not technically a text book tactic, and fraught but by the time he realised he'd been inattentive, it was too late, and the blind attack was about to prove a very viable tactic. His last moment and frantic attempted at an upper cut plunged feebly into her belly, as her forehead and coercive momentum smashed into his face. Her fists hammered his solar plexuses.

The feel of his face crunching was emphatic, and with her head now buried in his crumbling chest, she leaned and pushed hoping to lay him out in ignominy. She was conscious of the crowd roaring, cheering, and her enthusiasm to please them, fired her urge for a mighty victory. However, despite his setback Hastings managed to remain on his feet, albeit in a stumbling retreat, while at the same time managing some close range but harmless punches into her midriff. Oblivious to his counter attack Romance lifted her head grasped his neck with both hands and surged forward again, lifting him off his feet and throwing herself to the floor with him the meat in the sandwich.

Blood oozed from both fighters, from Romance's forehead it was genuine but under the lighting it was less obvious against her blueness, while from Hastings it was artificial but bright against his yellowness. The geysers spurted another dose of cloud but Enamour did not join the uproar, instead she reached for a filter with which to cover her nose.

"I've had enough of it," she said, responding to Sagacity's enquiring gaze.

Affinity was bouncing on her feet, her fists tight and shaking, her thumbs pointed down, she was anxious and wanted a quick conclusion to the match.

Prudence was subdued, convinced the baby beast was going to uphold her responsibility to female pre-eminence, and she punched the air again, in approval.

Romance straddled Hastings, sitting up on him, pinning his elbows to the floor, then she bent over his face to puff in his face. However, he was stronger than she'd reckoned, and it required all her weight and spread legs to restrain his arms, and prevent him squirming an escape. The cheering was being overhauled by a slow, cladding countdown.

Unnoticed TT15 approached and flung a beaker of oil over the bodies. Hasting promptly rolled, broke from her hold, flipped onto his stomach, pulled his knees up and arched up, sliding a fumbling Romance forward over his head. He sprang up, pounced at her, but she recovered too quickly, rolled aside and sprung to her feet, irate at forfeiting her winning position. Romance decided on another head first attack, but Hastings darted aside and began trotting around her in circles, enraging her, peeving the audience, and provoking almost unanimous hooting.

When the uproar showed little sign of abating Hastings succumbed, and turned to face his patrolling pursuer, whose intentions appeared set on snaring him in another rush. He was correct, and when she came, he dispatched an accurate and head shuddering uppercut, but Romance was possessed, relentless and impervious to its effect, and countered immediately, stepping back half a pace and unleashing a upper slingshot which caught Hastings under the jaw, lifting him off his feet, and sent him sprawling. He was on his hand and knees, shaking his head, glancing back up at Romance. Then she leapt again, airborne to a chorus of delighted screams, but she thumped onto an empty floor, her quarry gone, labouring to his feet.

Romance rolled up onto an elbow glaring at her escapee, when she reckoned his legs were within range, she committed every muscle to slinging a floor level sonic foot at his stumps. There was a oophing grunt, a swish, a crunch, a crash, a groan and Hastings was swept on an inverting transfer across the floor. The din was deafening. It was her most spectacular strike but it had been random, opportunistic, and luck could take much of the credit for its success. But the contemptable one was already back on his feet, seemingly ready to continue.

Romance decided the best way to turn him into a blood spot, was to stand toe to toe and break his arms. There were two considerations, however, firstly he was stronger than she'd anticipated, and secondly, how to corner him into a toe to toe knock out. She fixed her gaze on him, her mind seeing a large insect for swatting, "Stand and fight faggot," she snarled across the pit, her head protruding in a stalking demeanour.

Surprisingly he stood, motionless, staring, happy to contest the psychological encounter, knowing that battle he should easily win. Having flung her disparaging comment, she was no longer interested in a verbal skirmish, and was anxious for another attempt at a close quarter match. She stepped forward and when Hastings held his ground, and appeared unaffected by her advance, she was a tad unsettled. However undeterred, as she took the final forward step, and as she moved, her right fist broke loose. Her aim was for the side of his head, but an intercepting flashing fist deflected the blow, while his other fist came from below and drove deep into her belly, then furrowed a way through her flesh to her under chin.

This time, though, she'd braced, remained firm footed, and counter attacked with her most powerful weapon, the round house blow which crashed through his defences and struck the side of his head. It came unexpectedly and Hastings was thrown clear of the engagement, his consciousness wonky. Romance's confidence was suddenly superior and she moved across for the *beheading,* but a short, stout, white blob dashed into her path, hands raised, but she was in no mood to be delayed, and readied to sweep her aside.

TT9 screamed, "No baby girl, no," she pleaded rushing to intervene. Cloud filled the arena for the last time.

The audience chorused, "Yes, yes, yes."

TT9's scream gave Romance cause to hesitate, and with both hands in Romance's belly, she pushed her back.

"Don't be silly, baby girl, you can't touch his TT, you know that. You could be banned for a year, probably more," her warning an exaggeration.

Romance relented, turned and walked, 9's hand on her alice, encouraging her to move well away.

The crowd had found a new chant, "Go, baby girl, go. Go baby girl, go."

"There's no doubt about her being female but 'girl' is a bit aspirational," Enamour suggested, "and 'baby' is rathertenuous at least."

'Yes, brutal bloody bitch' would be the truth," Affinity thought, leaning to Prudence.

"Gorgeous, though," Prudence suggested.

"But can you imagine her in one of your FM outfits, because that's a vision which disturbs me?" Affinity asked.

"No, a rather gruesome thought I agree, but I can see her in a GM, pink, layered, easy fitting, frilled, drop shouldered, high necked behind, and in front, discreet tiffanys exposure, and dripping with pearls, would make seem erotic."

In the pit Romance had resumed her stalking, and would not be deterred, and remaining confident, was pushing forward again, prepared to walk through a hail of fists, if it meant entering her attack zone. Hastings, however, had other ideas and was on the trot again, his plot was for a gorilla war, staying out of range, await opportunities, then spring in to attack, then promptly retreat.

His tactic met congregational disapproval, and when his retreat broke into skipping, it seemed the reverberations threatened the building, while Romance's smile was cynical. TT9 went to Romance urging her to chase him even faster. Still backing away, Hastings allowed her closer, then abruptly stopped, leapt forward and stretching low, buried his fist deep into her midriff, once again. She flinched not and now he was within range, which inspired a rush of adrenaline some teeth grinning, and an urgency to attack mercilessly. Hastings had decided to stand his ground, striking her twice more to the body but it was his fatal mistake. Romance took a final half step into him, and brought her clench fists from high, crashing onto the top of his head. A micro second later Hastings' strength scarpered, his fists fell, darkness descended, and he sank to his knees, flopping face first to the floor. His body was smeared with blood.

Romance glared transfixed at the motionless body until TT9 rushed between them, fearing what she was considering, and again pushed her away. The relief of victory abruptly displaced her anger, and in ethereal elation she raised her arms to the crowd, and paraded around, not unscathed as planned, somewhat bloodied in fact.

"What a pisser," Affinity exclaimed as they turned to each other.

"How can a female, so ugly, be so gorgeous, I think the big bitch is fantastic," Prudence mused.

"She certainly stirs one's blood flow, and makes one eager to be abed," Sagacity vaunted, an observation which surprised her daughters, and saw them glancing at each other.

The final crescendo tapered off to clapping, the hubbub of conversation took over, and people began organising their departure.

The mass of red bodies funnelled towards the exists, while the music was beating a wind down.

Outside in the refreshing night air the four joined arms, and chose to walk rather than take the roller-path.

"That was one the better nights we've been too," Prudence mused. "I'd like to see more of Romance in action. Wasn't she awesome?"

"Can anyone tell me, or suggest, why the crowds at the arena are mainly females, probably more than seventy percent, I'd guess?" Enamour enquired.

"Well!" she exclaimed, looking around her compatriots.

"No idea," was Affinity's contribution.

"Males are being squeezed from societal prominence, and rather having that in their faces, they prefer to retire. Stay at home," Prudence suggested.

"I don't think it has anything to do with male ego," Sagacity pronounced. "I think males stay away simply because most of them don't appreciate the sport. Those that do are passionate, as you'd have noticed tonight, if you looked around. The increasing female affinity with brutality has grown in parallel with females' graduation from adjutant to general, and is the re-discovery and vitalisation of historically suppressed source of the adrenaline, something males have always held onto. When human relationships were the outcome of physical strength and stamina, we females were forced to ignore those forces and be meek, a status we accepted and eventually believed was normal. Now we are enthusiastic about the arena because it's simply a facility which facilitates the awakening and release from those historical constraints. It feels great! Bugger males! It's healthy!"

Prudence clapped.

Chapter 9
The Rendezvous

Eighteen days after her discussion with Fable, Enamour's fertility had been confirmed, her certified impregnator had been given the agreed twenty-four hours notification, and she was ready for servicing. She awaited him anxiously, in the deluxe apartment she'd reserved for the occasion. Her nerves boogied, nourished by an epinephrine stream pulsating through her mesolimbic pathway. She'd arrived early, pressed on by irritating impatient, as she couldn't find any useful way of filling the time until their midday rendezvous. Vainly she'd attempted to relax in the armchair, then up and then back seated, finally resigning herself to wandering the room, fidgeting. Even a Gideons could have helped, but there was none.

She checked the full-length mirror, admiring her figure, clearly visible beneath cream crepe. She moved closer, opened the crepe, and smiled at her femininity. She gazed slowly, her face, her lips, her chin and neck, and slowly hr eyes moved down, studying her every feature, pausing at those bits which made her female. She felt strong and confident about the day, convinced she'd end up pregnant, the pretext for her planned unmitigated indulgence, and unashamed exploitation of her secretive salacious self. Never had she been freed into such fenceless anonymity, and the effervescence was clouding out all things mundane. The irony lay in the fact, that she'd never considered being in the position, but when circumstances forced her hand, her imagination leapt her boundaries, and she could not wait.

Suddenly her tice sounded, and foreboding flooded her effervescent, engulfing her with an unsettling tingle, tip to toe. Was she apprehensive, startled or ecstatic? The tice announced the arrival of HFZer03, and despite her nervousness Enamour reacted according to plan, took her gold and purple embossed face mask from the dresser, and fitted it snuggly over her upper face, checked mirrorwards, curtsied to herself, and at the door instructed it to open. He stood tall, erect, expressionless, while Enamour's throat lumped, and a not so subliminal throbbing infected her.

If her splendour impressed him, he did not let on but she noticed a double-take when he looked at her mask. What a pleasing start, she thought, and in the flesh, he was at least as imposing as his hologram, maybe taller, larger in reality, an athletic face with a hint of rough. Groomed, long black curly hair hung to his shoulders, defined dark brows, penetrating black eyes and a slither of his porcelains gleamed. He wore one piece from the mid-thigh to wide open neck, in white, and otherwise he was unadorned, and was content to wait while Enamour contemplated him. Unembarrassed, she examined his lower midriff and fixed on the contour of his obviously acceptable caesar, a sight which produced a shiver of eager delight. She eased closer, and the back of her hand reached out, to politely stroked the delivery device she'd employed.

When he remained stoic, she turned her hand over and clutched caesar beneath the soft fabric. Its sum improved her private smile, and enthused, she pumped it gently with the heel of her hand but when his expressionless demeanour persisted, she was miffed. However, she felt that despite his apparent conceit, his libido was bubbling too hot for caesar to maintain its temerity, and would eventually betray his effrontery. Her grip firmed, her stroking increased and almost immediately the result was positive. She gazed into his eyes, and smiled, certain he was going to prove to be a bargain.

Suddenly she was thankful her first two impregnation excursions had failed. Providence often held sway for Enamour, and now buoyed by this promising prospect, she disengaged, straightened up, stood aside and beckoned him to enter.

"Glad you're here Zero-three," she welcomed, her enthusiasm conservative.

"Happy to oblige, my dear,"

He smiled formally, stepped inside, returned her look, and strode to sit in the chair she was pointing at. She sat in the chair opposite; he lay back, his hands behind his head, and for the first time his eyes began a steady persual of his client. Enamour felt buoyed by his examination, and wanted to open her crepe to display her entirety but since he'd refused to respond to her first provocation let propriety usurped her desire, this time. However, she only allowed her garment to gape enough to reveal a seam of her primary feminine features.

"Pleased to do business with you E," he said at last, lowering his elbows to his knees and leaning towards her, "Are you comfortable with our arrangement E, and ready proceed? Any second thoughts, or doubts, or questions?" he asked in a strong voice with a calming edge. His questions were merely courtesy, as all issues had been processed earlier, agreed and confirmed.

Enamour's sense of occasion was acute, believing that to bequeath her child's conception in ecstasy, would be an inheritance for positivity in life. And the moment she opened the door to Zer03, the last of her cautionary scepticism and instinctive conservatism evaporated, and now she was anxious for the agreement to materialise.

"Before we go any further E, I must say I'm not sure if you're titillating me, teasing, or irritating but I tending towards irritation," he said pointing at her face, and acknowledging her mask for the first time.

Enamour ignored the inferrence.

Unruffled Zero-three continued, "We need to verify identities E. I understand you're satisfied with the data my agent sent you, and happy our DNA projections and compatibility, as well as my genetic profile," another unnecessary comment since the facts were already established, "I've received your settlement which just leaves us to make sure we're who we say we are," there was scant cordiality in his voice, reminding Enamour, theirs' was an academic liaison. She chose to continue disregarding his manner, and besides, she didn't care who or what he was, since the visual validation was amble and she swiped her tice across his upper arm.

"This person previously identified as DNA compatible," the tice announced.

He took hold of her arm, swiped his tice over her, and released her.

"I can't see why my DNA is of any interest to you Zero-three," Enamour mused.

"It's okay?" he said curtly, stood up, reached for her hand and pulled her not gently to her feet, and towards the bed.

Enamour was ready for the transfer, but not for his raw manner, which needed curbing. Despite her initial audacity, she still sought some civilities and protocols, even if only token, and in spite of the liaison's contrivance.

"Is there a hurry?" she asked firmly and resisting.

"Yes E, our contract is for impregnation, not pleasure. And, no free return."

"Our contract stipulates an hour and a half, a provision I was insistent upon, for good reason."

"You need a taag then, I'm here until I deliver."

Enamour was determined to have her pleasures plentifully.

'Males! They keep trying to fight back', she thought. "If I just wanted impregnation, I would have had a syringe screw me, it would have been quicker, easier arranged and cheaper, but sadly steeped in stainless sterility, rather than in the sensuality of sweat, secretions, and soaked sheets," she said and refused to go any closer to the bed. When he stopped and turned back to her, she stepped against him, her tiffanys hugging his chest, and vesuvius against his leg. Unsurprisingly, he submitted.

"Zero3, I don't understand your reticence for a genial ninety minutes because I'm sure you'd enjoy pumping some pleasure, at your leisure, and love the burst of chauvinism which I've paid for. I want every minute of that hour and a half, and you wouldn't want me to make a default claim, which I will if you don't give me my due."

However, she sensed more could be achieved by seduction, than by insisting on contractual compliance. She would induce his surrender using charm, beauty, and overt sensuality.

She stepped back, opened her crepe fully this time, stood ajar, smiled and waited. When his gaze inextricably began another perusal, and a hint of avarice glinted in his eyes, she knew she was about to be victorious, surprisingly quickly. His expressionlessness had cracked, and unsurprisingly his dogma too had crumbled with his first involuntary phallic throb. It seemed, as expected in all males, his carnal culture was hostage to caesar's whims, while his meagre self-respect was sustained in arrogance. It was going to be easy from here, she thought, as she maintained the tactile tactic, allowing the effect of her estrogenic sights to trickled down from his eyes to his brothers. She glowed victoriously when he turned to her and moved back enough to gaze, particularly at her tiffanys and tummy, it was over. He leant down, his tongue tip circled her dewdrop, then the other. He looked up, "Goodness, they're enthusiastic."

Enamour smiled, still, still.

"I think they're a pair of nicest halves I've met," he said patronisingly cupping one in each hand.

"You know all about tits then, Zer03?" she replied deftly, refusing to concede to his puerile flattery or delusionary expertise.

But Enamour wanted to move on, "I find it disconcerting, calling you Zer03, Zer03, and while I don't want know your name, I'll call you Max. Is that okay?"

"I don't mind E. What say I call you Norks?"

"Corny, but okay, I don't care," she said, sliding an arm around his waist. She was in charge, and it felt right.

"Norks, your mask is cute, fascinating even but I'd like to see who I'm fucking. If you want fun, let me have mine too. Besides, your face is the barometer which tells me if I'm pleasing you."

"I think there's ample fun in mystery, Max."

She slipped her other arm around his waist clenching her hands together, pulling him harder into her crotch, then stretched up on her toes to taste his lips. Quickly though, her tongue went wondering and his enthusiasm for exchanging saps found them clutched full frontal, her head in his hands, while vivian hunted high on his thigh, seeking the tickle of cleopatra's chemistry. She felt caesar against her leg, and while it lazed on standby, she sensed idle potency steaming. After a few moments they eased from each other, and Enamour let vesuvius slip down his thigh, until she stood flat footed again.

"I'll keep it on Max, because behaving sleazily, secretly, in a surreptitious sanctuary, is more exhilarating, and better savoured in anonymity."

"Surely miscreance doesn't affect you Norks, either anonymously or honestly" he suggested.

He was wrong about that, but while she inwardly liked him thinking it, she felt his attitude was wrong, and had made an oblique attempted to control of their encounter, would be cut off again. "Certainly not, I've never been miscreant," she said indignantly, then smiled but moved away a little. He smiled back, and despite her token rejection, her mysterious self-confidence was beginning to fascinate him.

"Okay Norks, I'm happy to do it your way, for the moment"

While Zer03 had initially wanted to complete their transaction quickly, it was now Enamour with a short tapper on her lascivious fuse, albeit her motivation was quite different to his. She moved back to him, went up on her toes again, her tongue wondering, while her hand slipped inside his outfit, seeking to comfort caesar. Surprisingly it was drowsing but that was all right.

"Like me to rouse him Max, let him know it's action time?"

Of course, he would! But first.

He took her wrist, evicted her hand, and undressed quickly, thanks to some handy assistance. Enamour remained in her crepe, and was going to do so until an indeterminate moment disposed her to abandonment. Max flopped onto the bed, on his back, naked, his sprawling limbs stretching to the four corners, then he looked up at waiting and watching Enamour.

She gazed at him, contemplating the imminent. The urge to collapse on him was compelling but torn, she still wanted to relish his superb physique, and slumbering caesar. He was content to wait, happy to have his ego justified, and his offerings appreciated. Enamour's inner rumba was brief, and in the face of his allure she dropped onto the edge of the bed, nestling her backside into his waist, and looked into his eyes. When she took caesar in hand and began stroking, it responded promptly, awakening, stretching, swelling, solidifying, and finally throbbing softly.

It more than filled her hand, with about half protruding from her grip, and when she stroked it some more the word 'rock' rang in her mind. She bent over and took caesar in her mouth. It was more than a mouthful but she didn't mind, her caressing included inflicting teeth marks, since she couldn't help it.

"That's nice Norks!" Zer03 drooled.

Enamour's mouth and tongue were both devoted to persuading every molecule of caesar's estate to action stations. His erection committed its reserves and started pulsating at an increasing rate. Then it jerked threatening. Oophs! Hell! So soon! Too soon! No not yet, damn. What's his problem?! No wonder he wanted to settle as soon as he arrived, she thought. She abandoned caesar but it continued standing, log like and now lonely, and while certainly handsome, his strength of character might be lacking. Unthinking, she slapped it unkindly, her readiness to dish out discouragement, a demonstration of her determination to control the collaboration.

"Shit Norks, that hurt!" he complained, his head up off the pillow, eyes glaring.

'He's far too anxious, and deserved it," she explained unapologetically.

"Don't worry Norks, I'm in control, and you'll get what you want, where you want it, so don't fear the 'whim-wham, spam's gone, sorry mam'"

However, while Enamour thought he was probably trustworthy, intentions could not always be trusted, and she was not prepared to take him at his word, or risk having her affair conclude before her fantasy was a memory.

"Do you have any wofno?" she asked.

"No," he replied, disdainfully.

"No matter, I've some," she said, climbing off the bed, straightening her crepe, and going to her bag on the bench.

Zer03's gaze followed her, uncertain about going down this path, and inhaling wofno. When Enanour returned she noticed reluctance in his face.

She stood against the bed, looking down at him, with a petitioning smile, and holding out the nebulizer. "Please."

He did not answer promptly. Then, "I'm not sure our contract goes this far," he said raising himself onto one elbow.

"It doesn't Max. But I feel the contract doesn't matter any more, now we've drifted into the sphere of human emotion, and mutual gratification."

"I think the gratification will mainly be yours, Norks."

She paused, this time attempting a fawning pitch at winning his cooperation, "Please."

"I assume you have the antidote," he said finally, conceding.

"Well, it'd be pointlessly expensive, and a waste of my day if I didn't," Enamour said, showing him the second nebulizer. "But you mightn't need the antidote if we last long enough for it to degrade naturally."

"Two hours or more!" incredulity in his voice.

"Why not?"

It might have been a pointless discussion, but he'd spotted an opportunity, "Take your mask off, then," he instructed, though his tone entreated.

That was unexpected, and so was her reaction, because unexplainably she now wished to unmask, rid herself of the barrier between them, embrace the partnership fully, and free herself of any constriction to the abandonment she imagined.

Enamour stepped closer to his face until vivian was within kissing distance.

"Open your mouth then!" she directed,

He lifted his head, smiled, and opened his mouth.

"Breath in; deeply!"

He acquiesced then fell back on the bed while Enamour stepped back, dropped her crepe to the floor, whipped off the mask, flung it across the room, smiled, and postured seductively. She stepped her legs apart emphasising vesuvius, which inspired a somewhat sinister but smiling smirk from Zer03. There was a dash of danger in his devilment, and together with her liberation, and his longevity now guaranteed, their coalescence confirmed her unabridged intemperance was assured. And she was answerable to no one, especially herself.

She was concerned, however, that with his endurance now locked in for up to two hours, it would a shame if she finished in an hour or less. Maybe an hour, half an hour's rest, another half hour, might work. She dropped onto the bed seated at his side again, place the wofno on the floor, lay down beside him, pulling her legs up and rolled over to face him, her arm across his chest.

"Max, I'd like to spend some moments close to you, and the body which is going to seed me. And while it's only cursory and peripheral,

I'd like to sense of your contribution to my compassion, and while I'm anxious and looking forward to the erotic and carnal, you remain the answer to my desperation to fulfil the basic female function. I want lie, for a few moments in your aura; feel the ambience, and the security of believing you can deliver the physiology I need for my baby."

Zer03 was unsure what she was expecting, and neither was he sure, she was sure, but he had no desire to pry, or need to concern himself, after all his involvement would end this afternoon, and by next week she'd be irrelevant and forgotten.

"Norks, do you want to get on, we've only an hour and a half, remember?" he asked feeling her preamble might go on for too long.

"Time's not so important Max, is it? What else have you to do?" she asked, "I just don't want it to be over too quickly, Max, that's all. I've been wanting and planning for this occasion for a long time, and while in another place I mightn't mind hurrying, I'd like to absorb this for as long as possible."

He turned into her face and just looked at her.

However, her 'slowly' struggle was faltering.

She rolled onto her knees and turned about until she was gazing at caesar, and he had a close quarter confrontation with vesuvius, her ladies and vivian. She swung a leg over his face, her knees aside his head, then she spread her knees, lowering herself until his view became tactile and sensory. She dropped to her elbows, gather up caesar, and tip tongued its protrusion. She kissed its eye charitably, then again, and again, and when she grew impatient with its lack-lustre reaction her mouth took over, with her tongue's welcome a maypole dance. Enamour felt a fizzing invade her as his spasmodically pulsating caesar grew even harder, but while matters at his business end were progressing, at her end, Zero3 was ing slow from the blocks, much too slow, leaving her with no alternative but to lower vivian even further, this time onto his face.

"Norks, your pussy is gorgeous and the fragrance is very nice but what's the hurry?"

Enamour turned back, "Well Max I was hoping the licking jell I had infused this morning might be irrestible. Send your tongue in for a taste.," she demanded, "You could be surprised," she turned back to his erection, now filling both her hands. She licked its juice and rubbed her lips back and forth over the top. When the face in vivian moved, and a soft moist tentacle pushed through her ladies, a gulp shot through her body, and when his tongue began meandering around her jewels, her eyes closed, her body flexed slightly, and her nerves foamed. Her arms faltered and she sank onto him, holding caesar against her cheek. She parted her knees even further and jiggled a slight repositioning, hoping he'd attend more to cleopatra.

However, she was wanting too much, and his hands began slithering up between her legs, lifting her off his face, but not far. She waited, sensing she was not going to be disappointed. A finger crept into each side of her ladies, then two fingers a side and then three. He exposed her completely, giving his tongue full reign over vivian, and cleopatra's zones. Enamour released caesar, raised herself on her hands and arched, straining to wipe vivian over his face but he was too strong and held her off. When she surrendered, he pulled her down again an pushed his bottom lip into vivian. Fraught, she collapsed on him again, gathered caesar to her cheek again, and lay, content to absorb his tongue doing its best.

When his nose kneaded cleopatra, and his tongue went deep for more licking jell Enamour knew she could not last. She gathered her knees in, lifted herself from his face, rose up on her hands, kissed his erection, turned about, and fell onto her back, beside him. Post-coital nefertities would be okay but pre-coital climax, was an incident she was going to avoid, and now she waited motionlessly, gazing at the ceiling, one arm on his chest the other hanging over the bed edge, her knees wide, her presentation barefaced. She turned her head and smiled expectantly.

Zero3 rolled onto his stomach and clambered to his knees, turned about, pushed himself down the bed, until his close vision was again of vesuvius, etcetera. 'Gorgeous', he thought, and sat up enough, to admire her glory terrain, in the context of her full display.

This was first time he'd viewed the 'kept' version of vesuvius. It was magnificent, silky, neat, elegant, magnificence in marble, and the focal of female perfection. His eyes meandered, caesar grew anxious while Enamour lay charmed, loving his obvious and pleased admiration. For the moment Zer03 just imbibed her beauty, and sitting on his haunches reached out to run his fingertips across vesuvius, then again, then again. Her skin was fine and soft, lacking any hint of a pubic pelt, and then he had a stupid thought.

"You're not a virgin, are you?" he joshed.

Her head bobbed up to look at him, "Yes! Of course, I am, Max. So be kind," she quipped, wondering how he'd react if she encouraged the fantasy, and her head fell back to the bed.

He liked it, and decided to journey further into the innocence and invigorating world of early youth. "Well, I suppose as long as you're above the age of consent, it's okay"

After a pausing thought: "No! I'm not but that's okay, as long as you're gentle," she quipped again, but did not look up this time.

"Then we'd better keep our affair secret."

It was a fun moment but Enamour was not interested in encouraging r too much foolishness, even though she was not averse to some salacious titillation but, "That's certainly my intention."

Zero3 patient admiration had run its course, and the prospect of tasting vivian some more, had his knees sliding back out of the way, as his face found comfort between her thighs. His tongue was broad and flattened, and he laid it over cleopatra and thereabouts. The lightning consumed Enamour, but she remained motionless wanting it to delight her every nerve. For a while he massaged there abouts, and ran his tongue tip along the inside edges of her ladies, then he took cleopatra between his lips and sucked it into his mouth, all the while massaging it with his bottom lip and tongue.

From underneath, Zero3's up turned hand slid up his chest, under his chin and two fingers kept going, destination vivian. Vivian was well ready for them, and they slid in easily, until their tips turned up seeking gemma. Enamour's body flexed and Zero3 knew he was there. He couldn't do any more for her, and hoped she was pleased with his best oral effort. For Enamour matters had gone ahead more quickly than she'd wanted but suddenly she realise she was not the only one conducting this orchestra. It was pointless attempting to delay nefertiti any longer, as she'd lost that control, the moment gemma joined the party. But she'd not join in, and would lie motionlessly while nefertiti washed over her, once or twice.

When her restraint became rest, she lifted her head and looked into Zero3's eyes. "I wasn't ready for that," she complained.

He lifted his head, withdrew his fingers and grinned, self-satisfied, "Well, I can't take it back, as our contract specifies, no returns."

She smiled and let her head flop back on the bed, even thoughts of her agenda were absent for the moment, as she soaked up the enduring euphoria of the moment. Zero3 climbed back onto his knees and sat back on his heels, all the while admiring what he had just tendered, and was now anxious to make caesar's destination. He looked up at her as she looked down over her cheeks at him. She smiled.

"Okay?" he asked

"Surely!"

He leant forward, and with his hands on her inside thighs, gently began to ease her legs well apart. He didn't need to, since her inclination was ahead of his, and she was already eager for maximum exposure. He took her by the waist with both hands, and drew vivian to his erection. Caesar stood rigid at the vertical, and despite Zero3's lowering his angle of attack by bending over further, he took caesar in hand and directed his approach. She raised her head and shoulders and sat up on her elbows watching, smiling expectantly, but hoping he'd go slowly for a start. When caesar touched the ladies he paused for a masochistic suspense moment, then pressed in for a smooth and exhilarating admission to her well salivating enthusiasm. Vivian seethed the moment he arrived, and with every millimetre of his slow descent, her wish was for it to never stop. Her eyes surrendered; she expelled low groan; while his arrival at her bottom completed his rampant raid into her sensuality. As he withdrew it took her breath too, but she arched up so gemma could feel a full account. When he paused, she opened her eyes, and was reassured by the sight of the magnificence which was fucking her. When she knew his descent this time, was going to a plunge, she closed her eyes again, and readied for a hurricane to overwhelm her.

With his plungeis enthusiasm became impatient, and his deliveries began to morph into a pounding. When Enamour felt herself being pummelled she did not argue, instead she encouraged it to ignite her base notes, and subpoena another lusting resource, which normally she'd rejected. Today, maybe, too much testosterone is not enough. She was happy to ignore the quavers and didn't know or care, how long it was going to last. His grip of her waist was beginning to hurt, and he was plunging less and thumbing her more at caesar.

Thankfully he was tiring and slowing, weakening, and knew he'd contributed all he could for the moment. As he was obviously ready for some time out, Enamour thought, reluctantly though, she would also take a spell. But no, not now, no! Unexpectedly from her pit, a sparkle exploded, and she arched up seizing Zero3 by the hips, and began urgently pounding vesuvius at caesar. Despite still puffing he was keen to joined in, taking her by the shoulders, responding to her thrusts, at the same time straining to keep caesar up to his situational obligation. His occupation was total, and nefertiti took over, the electricity prolific, and for more than a few moments, time was irrelevant,

When her finishing breath drained, she subsided slowly and he lowered her to the bed. He gazed at her, her eyes closed, her interest only in recovery, but her beauty in collapse was poignant and desirable. Limp but puffing, she looked vulnerable, and shortly caesar began rising to take advantage.

Zero3's was a little surprised, and his ego took a boost, by the brief time it had taken to caesar to be ready for more activity. In fact, it was quite unusual.

"Norks! What else was in the wofnow," he asked, dubiously.

"Not complaining, are you Max?"

He'd guessed right, and no; he was not complaining. He looked her over again, and his enthusiasm for her was as acute as it was to begin with. And with all factors considered, it was likely his enthusiasm still had a long path to patter.

He picked up knees, parted them and held her waist again, and with his elbows pushed her knees wide. Enamour appeared to disregarded his intentions, but in her recuperation, she sensed his motivation, and was happy to submit to him preparing her for more. She had no intention of finishing up when more excursions and gratifications were her ambitions.

Still with closed eyes she shuffled her posterior into comfort and waited for caesar to begin powering into her grotto again. When it came it was consuming but again Enamour wanted to absorb the exhilaration in limbo, with her eyes closed, all in the physical, no visual. His pumping gained momentum but this time never became a pounding and for that she was happy.

Suddenly she needed to watch again and raised her head, then rose on her elbows. From determination his eyes flicked up a glance at her, and then returned to their business relationship. His shoulders bulged, his stomach flexed with each drive, the hairs on his chest rose, as his pects tensed, and his arms wrenched her in with each thrust. He was going so deep, cleopatra was being smacked, and gemma couldn't be more pleased with the wash-boarding of his every plunge.

For Enamour's the encounter was transporting her into a world of sensuality supremacy, where her body's only function, and need, was plentiful fornicating indulgence and ready exhilaration. It seemed today; too much was not going to be enough.

Zero3 had plunged into her a mere dozen times when nefertiti galloped in but this time it failed to frenzy or contort her. Instead, she lay serene, allowing the sparks to thunder about her being unhindered. It was going to last a long time, she knew that. Zero3 realised what was happening and understood. His tempo intensified and his rhythm quickened, but he was careful to keep it smooth, even gentle, hoping to help her cascades of ecstasy become an ultimate nefertiti.

When finally Enamour felt nefertiti drifting she let it go easily, happy to leave its ghost lingering. Zero3 rested, stretched back to sit but leaving his crotch slumped against her vivian, his mind working to maintain a strong erection inside her.

"Stay! There! Max!" she said now breathing deeply again, then lifting herself up to smile at him.

"Is it time for the antidote, do you think Norks?" he enquired, a hint of anxiousness in his voice.

"Not yet Max, one more time first."

"Are you sure?"

"Very! But relax Max, this one is on me."

"Righto," he smiled, withdrew caesar and lay down.

Enamour, looked at him, still enjoying the sight of his body. She straddled him or his stomach and looking down smiling, she began inching up her boy.

"Where are you going?" he asked, a touch of doubt in his voice.

"I think you can guess."

His smile faded but he didn't object, rather he came to accept she was a very demanding female.

When she arrived on his face, the residue from her already considerable stimulations and nefertities made for a wet and slippery arrival, but there was an obscure fascination about it, and he did not object. However, he was hesitated about consigning his tongue to vivian. Enamour fell forward on her hands and looked down, and began to gyrate slowly.

"Come on Max, you can do better than that."

He did, somewhat reluctantly but it quickly became obvious her abrupt pause was to fully absorb the feeling, and he was content to help her create a memory. She remained motionless for a time, because nefertiti was already circling yet again, and it was a delicate manoeuvre to ensure she remained in the wings and did not depart, as Enamour was not yet ready for her magic. Zero3's tongue was meandering around vivian, thankfully paying some attention to gemma, and was bypassing cleopatra all together. She twisted a little; oophs, no, don't move.

Enamour had to make a decision. Stay there and risk nefertiti crashing in before she was wished, or move onto to caesar and release her. When she imagined caesar filling her volume, and strumming her chords, the decision was easy. She lifted off Zero3 and shuffled her way down until vivian hovered above caesar, then she looked up, and grasp his pectorls. Zero3 took hold of her waist but she brushed his hands aside, and began to lower herself onto his mast of euphoria. Nefertiti had been hovering impatiently and Enamour's hope that she wait a while longer, was fruitless wish. It didn't matter much, and as Enamour began to slow rock so nefie began to tango. Her fingers were tightening their grip on Zero3's pecs, and as they tightened, so did the rate of her enthusiasm.

When nefertiti threatened departure, her grasp became intense. Zero3 took hold of her wrists and attempted to release her grip, but the hegemony of her fingers and nails biting into his flesh, released a flood from vivian, and he had to be content just to just hold on. She wanted to bite him so she fell onto his chest, and seized a mouthful of his flesh.

"Shit Norks," he exclaimed.

She ignored him, but bit no harder, and as vivian continued to flood, the sound of its splashing overflow encouraged more. She could feel his hands about her face, as he tried to ease her bite off, and as nefertiti faded, so did her grip of his flesh. He rolled her off and lay her on the bed beside him. It was several minutes before her day started up again.

"Like something to drink, Max?" she asked coolly, thinking a break would be nice before their final act.

He smiled. "Yeah, Norks, I'll get it, coffee?"

"Thanks Max."

"With anything."

"Maybe some cee. Just a drop."

"Done."

Zer03 climbed from the bed, went to the bench and ordered their drinks. He was having the same.

"Want it there, or are you getting up?"

"I'll have it at the table."

They sat opposite each other, sipping, and for a while in silence.

"You're a remarkable female Norks, and more exciting than I expected. I wish I'd met you under some other circumstances, circumstances which would made courting acceptable."

Enamour gazed at him cynically. "You're courting me now, simply because you're still to finish fucking me. You're still just contractor, who loves his work."

They had little to talk about since they had nothing in common outside the room, and Enamour wanted none.

After a while, "Come on Max, vivian's talking to me again, and I'm keen to have the deed done. She rose from the table and walked to the bed, to collapse in the ready position, and watched for Zer03's approach.

"Norks, I think it's time for the Woo For Now antidote, don't you?"

"I think so."

Done. Without comment he clambered onto the end of the bed, his hand pumping caesar back to life, while he knelt perusing his prey. He was somewhat impatient to finish, and felt she felt the same. As he began crawling towards vivian, Enamour pulled her knees up and opened her legs. With caesar commissioned and striking for the last time Enamour felt the bliss of her glass filling, and she opened as wide as she could, lifted her head to see, and as his rhythm built, she watched his shoulders bulge, his arms strain his stomach heave, his expression grimaced, while his long black swayed back and forth over his shoulders, and sweat began is dribble through the hairs of his chest. Enamour joined in thrusting to his tempo. Caesar felt different without wofno, stronger, astute, more enjoyable

"Keep going Max, it feels so good," she whimpered.

He did not reply but was encouraged to incite a little mercilessness, while her two fingers provoked cleopatra into joining in. The encounter lasted only a couple of minutes before a more demurring nefertiti approached. Noticing her begin to frown and press her lips, Zer03 paused, pulled his knees up, sat on his heels, gripped her waist, hoisted alice off the bed, and looking up at Enamour asked:

"Are you ready for me to finish, Norks?" he asked

"Any time Max," she muttered, and threw her arms back above her head, waiting. She'd had enough and wasn't going to watch the ending. It had been more than she'd expected, and now she'd had enough. Nefertiti could deal with the conclusion on her own, as she hoped she would welcome her impregnation.

Yes. All right."

"I'll give you all I've got, but let me know if it's too much," he said, determined to finish as powerfully as he could.

He gritted his teeth, flexed his shoulders, clenched his grip, as she waited closed eyed, her expression peaceful.

Despite a busy and exhausting time Nefertiti surprised Enamour with her ability to continue spontaneously and energetically, and from vivian shards of celebration ignited her body yet again. Zer03 paused deep inside her, shuddered, groaned, and as delivery commenced, he plunged powerfully several times more, then stopped yet again, to relish the final constituent of his everest.

Nefertiti's final say was perfectly timed, and took Enamour into the dancing never, never, and indelibled a memory she was likely to revisited often.

Zer03 stood up, her legs closed. "All right Norks. It's done."

Enamour lay motionless, breathing heavily, physically well spent but confronting her new reality. She wrapped her arms together, pulled her knees up until her heels comforted alice. Consciously, she closed vivian tightly, a pointless but a symbolic gesture to retain everything she had purchased. Now Zer03 was irrelevant, she didn't need him any more, and he was no longer of interest; in fact, he had abruptly become irritating.

"Thank you Zer03, can you go now" she announced curtly, but it was unmistakably an instruction. He was disappointed at being rejected so dismissively, having fallen prey to her allure, and striven to fulfil her wishes, he'd hoped for some fellowship, even expressions of appreciation before their separation. However, unflustered and without acknowledging her rejection, he rose, dressed, checked himself in the mirror, shook his hair into order and turned to her, "Good luck, Enamour, I hope this works for you, and your baby grows strong and healthy," he said turning to go.

"How do you know my name?" she demanded, shocked.

Zer03 felt slight satisfaction in revenge, but doubted revenge had been his true motivation.

"I know quite a few things about you Enamour, that's my business but it's private, so you've no need to worry."

She was unhappy with the development but had other important matters to ponder, and anxiety for his departure was an immediate one.

"I'd appreciate that Zer03!" she was angry. "I don't need others knowing about this."

"What happened to Max?" he asked slightly bemused she'd reverted so quickly to their commercial relationship.

"He's at home."

"Oh, I see. Anyway, as I said, good luck and be careful," he turned to leave.

Enamour ignored his departure, and when the door closed so did her annoyance, she rolled onto her side into a tight foetal curl, and was enveloped by introspection, secure though, in the feeling she would be pregnant any minute. She felt comfortable alone, indifferent about the dampness underneath, and wondered about the swimming race within. The fading echoes of the physical and erotic were being bartered, as she warmed to incarcerate and cuddle the sublime, and indulge in the triumphant of accomplishment. The reality of baring her own child was already an incredibly fulfilling experience, and being confident in almost being pregnant, hoped the winning swimmer through her cervix would deliver her a daughter.

Chapter 10
The Palace

Summit pushed back in his chair, ran his fingers of both hands through his hair and lowered his eyes contemplating his problem. The statistics screened in front of him were inescapable, damning and demanding, and hostaged him to find and orchestrate, a correction policy forthwith. There was nothing new or revealing in the latest data, as it was predicted, and he had watched the evidence accruing for several years. He was not totally unprepared for a critical change in the Pregnancy and Surrogacy Authority's operations, and had already broached options with fellow board members.

The latest reports had him wriggling in the seat though, and returned his thoughts to the possible solution lying in the establishment of a Surlace (Surrogates' Palace), an establishment offering a life style, personal and health support, education and remuneration, sufficiently extravagant to entice considerably more females into surrogacy. The project would recruit broadly for far more females from all three R categories, concentrate on specific strategies for more jayfours, and be alert to discover and coerce disadvantaged, desperate and vulnerable jaythrees into the program. Resource recruitment would be approached as an opportunity for surrogates to join a caring institution, interested, as well, in their wellbeing and guaranteeing them a secure future; whereas the authority's interest would remain principally in the production line, production figures, and ways of exploiting surrogates for optimum production.

Of several possibilities considered, the Surlace came up the most likely and practical way of overcoming the surrogate shortage, a predicament now critical for the authority since being served with an ultimatum by the Governing Council, to find a solution, quickly. Not only had the GC been compelled to step in, there was widespread conversations and concerns among the jay classes, one, two, and three.

Summit and his directors had accepted the Surlace concept readily and promptly commissioned a survey to ascertain if the initiative was feasible. The findings indicated a Surlace could increase the number of females opting for surrogacy by between twenty and thirty percent, with a considerably younger demographic responding to the opportunities. While these numbers would not solve the short term or even the long-term situation, a Surlace should resolve the impending impasse, at least on paper, and keep the authority's hounds leashed.

While the survey was encouraging, the latest statists nullified, to some extent, the Surlace's improvement. Even a thirty percent increase in surrogate availability, would not keep up with the predicted increased in demand, and in five years the waiting time for a surrogate was projected to be more than three years

However, Summit was uneasy about some of the survey's conclusions, and somewhat daunted by the practicalities of establishing and running such an institution. There were obstacles, pitfalls and avenues for failure, which had not been questioned in the survey, not least being the costs of establishing and operating, an establishment for 250 plus surrogates. The danger for the Surlance was it enlisted a significant number of females who would otherwise have become surrogates anyway, and while close management would, no doubt, boost baby production, a consequential increase in production obviously lay in drafting formerly improbable surrogates.

Once recruited, implanted, confirmed pregnant, and institutionalised, surrogate induction should commence. Wellbeing medication should start immediately, along with an inculcation program directed at instilling institutional addiction by cultivating dependence. The objective was simple and specific, and aimed principally at securing surrogate's long term untilisation.

Summit wondered if a Surlace full of overtly self-amused, pregnant zombies, would be publicly acceptable, for that is what he thought it would become. However, he expected the influential jay classes, would see nothing, hear nothing or say anything, out of self-interest, or they would justify it as a reasonable and a necessitous sacrifice, in maintaining the beautiful society. As well, the only persons entitled to close surrogate contact, and be in a position to notice any idiosyncrasies would be veritable parents, visiting their surrogates, and whose vested interest lay with silence. The health of their baby and not the surrogate would be their yardstick. Of course, some vertiable parents had no desire to contact their surrogate, and prohibiting parents visiting the Surlace totally, had been canvassed. As well, among the jay classes, conjecture would not constitute cultured conversation, ensuring anomalies did not become political. Still the issue nagged Summit.

More concerning, was the probable reactionary response of the jay classes, to mere meagre surrogates living luxuriously, maybe even in superior lifestyle. Already some animosity persisted over current surrogate privileges, which they had been granted, begrudgingly, in a fledgling attempt to entice more females into their ranks. But adverse comments circulating in elite circles, had so far been nothing more than vents for cynicism.

Suddenly, unannounced, the office door swung open, surprising Summit, and jolting him from his contemplation. He glanced up at Brilliance, 'what a big fuckable bitch', his mind flashed, as she stepped into the room, and strode up to his desk, stood straight, speechless for the moment, staring down, hoping her abrupt and unexpected presence would be disconcerting. She sensed it had worked, despite his casual and unresponsive body language. She was dressed from her high waist to her knees in glistening black, and in the cavern, she'd had a strawberry crazed applied to the remainder of her body. Her eyes were pink, with lips, brows and liner in red, above which short cropped black and pink striped hair completed her presentation.

"Good morning, Brilliance, what can I do for you?" his voice was matter of fact, his smile slight, and obvious was his failure to invite her to sit. She ignored the slight, glanced at the chair beside her, in time took a seat, and then stared at Summit. She smiled formally, and was pleased with herself, Summit thought, and he felt an underlying self-confidence and an omni presence, suggesting she was even more aggressively mooded than normal.

"What can I do for you?" he repeated.

She shuffled in her seat, sat forward but held a straight back.

"I've lodged a challenge for your position as Bustohe," she announced, her demeanour tensing noticeably. "I lodged the application with the Review Panel just now, and as required I am informing you that a copy of those informations will be available on your tice within an hour," she said.

It was not unexpected but now confronted with the fact, Summit was set aback more than he expected. He stared back at her unblinking eyes, and then when she scratched at her neck, he saw an opportunity.

"You can't do this job Brilliance, you're addicted to cocaine, most of which you obtain illegally, because you use far more than your monthly quota."

His dismissive arrogance prompted her disdain "How much I take, and where it comes from is none of your business, and it certainly doesn't interfere with my capacity to take your job. Neither will it prevent me solving the surrogacy problem, you have failed for years to remedy!" her retort was emphatic. "My claim will be determined not by my use cocaine or how much, but by my feasibility plan to engineer enough surrogate babies for the beautiful families."

Brilliance's response was a reprisal, and a red-flag Summit didn't need, since he already knew she was more than a formidable adversary. It was time step back from his notional superiority, and quietly watch her back and defend himself.

"All right Brilliance, give me an outline of your challenge," he asked demurely.

"It's simple; I'm claiming you've failed to provide leadership, or solve the surrogacy emergency."

"It's a shortage, not an emergency!" he retorted.

"It's an emergency all right Summit, and that's your Achilles heel. You haven't appreciated the gravity of problem, which is headlonging to catastrophe, and it's seriously jeopardising our beautiful society. There's a wave coming at us Summit, which unless we take major decisions and incisive actions, and implement effective solutions, is going to drown us. Well, I'm not going to idle in ignorance or ignominy, allowing your ruinous leadership to drag me down, or my society.

"You know as well as I do, that only sixteen percent of R females under 30 become surrogates, and only a quarter of those selfish bitches deliver more than once. Not only must both these figures need big increases, currently they are both getting worse. Certainly, the Surlace proposal offers good prospects, temporarily at least, and afford us some leeway, but you know, as I do, it is not the ultimate answer. Am I making sense to you," she enquired patronizingly, leaning closer and staring unblinking?

"Go on," he said nonchalantly, giving nothing, wary not to give her any munition. He eased a little deeper into his chair.

"Among other facts, you have failed to appreciate the negative effect improved embryo engineering, and refined growth management, is beginning to have on the increased number of jays graduating from their alphaspection. And almost forty percent of those graduates emerge as onejays. So, you don't need to be Einstein to see the beautiful society is ballooning, while the surrogate resource pool is; and will continue shrinking. Unless major programs are implemented now, in a generation the shortage of surrogates will be insurmountable, let alone the generation after them.

"Imagine the dilemma," she paused, and widened her gaze. "Imagine the dilemma; if jay females, through our negligence, are forced to get pregnant," she paused again. "One of two scenarios is obvious; either the beautiful society will collapse as we know it, or the population plummets. Probably both! I don't know if your morality could deal with that, but mine can't," her eyes remained fixed on her target, looking for some reaction but she was disappointed.

Summit kept his counsel, hoping she'd continue and expose flaws in her proposals. He left her to continue.

"And still on modern technology, the modern harlequin embryos are becoming so accurate and so reliable even R rebas are breeding jay kids. Rs should be refused access to the harlequin program, and this is one avenue which we can use to pressure the Governing Council to take some reasonability for the problem," Brilliance was gesturing enthusiastically with two upturned palms bouncing. "It's depressing Summit, even you must realise that! Beautiful females pregnant. What else can I say?"

Brilliance's dramatics were semantic, since her solutions didn't exist or were simplistically silly, but idealistic, was Summit's conclusion. Even so, he was circumspect enough not to dismiss her proposals out of hand. Considering the social and political environment, even the implausible should not be disregarded too quickly.

Brilliance was not finished, "However, one of the positive avenues in the Harlequin Program is the potential to breed and rear females suitable solely for surrogacy. There appears no reason why harlequin technology cannot concoct females highly motivated for pregnancy, whose bodies find pregnancy mostly trouble free, and deliver easily. It's an avenue I'm still investigating, and which I imagine will be the second phase of my SSS program."

Summit was beginning to appreciate he was contending with a lateral thinker, who threatened to discover solutions which could expose his flaws. He'd always known she was intelligent, but had disregarded her because of her questionable personal and habitual lifestyle habits, and her aggressive disruptive professional attitude. Suddenly his shallow insight and underestimation imperilled his future.

Brilliance went on. "All the proposals, ideas and programs so far promulgated, have the same scenario of failures. They're bogus, and inevitably guarantee a reduced jay society of elite males, and a clique of females, who'll live in an isolated and shrinking community. And once isolated, the diasporas' convictions will solidify, and their commitments will become compulsions, further corroding of pregnancy will continue. With a surrogate drought, the jay classes will ultimately comprise females who choose not to have children but who'll inveigle a remnant surrogate from a corrupt system; and the few who recuperate sufficiently from pregnancy, to maintain a jay rating."

Summit stirred from his detached calculations, "Already procedures can correct most physical defects, and they'll continue to improve, and if society approaches the collapse you're forecasting, the rewards offered surrogates will grow exponentially, even to the point where some jay females, even two and threes, will be seduced into service."

Brilliance was unmoved. "Even if beauty can be fully restored post pregnant, there's no reason why jay females should be forced to endure the trauma of pregnancy, the nausea, the discomfort, bloated bellies, restricted movement, denied social interaction, lose libido, or the final agony. And then undergo months if not years of recovery, and more discomfort and restrictions, etcetera, when we are in a position, now, to implement programs which can maintain an ample supply of surrogates. I have the strategies but you must give way," she shrugged, eyes closed

164

momentarily.

"If you have these proposals, why have you not put them forward at our meetings?" he asked.

"Because I need to be in a position to ensure they go forward, which I cannot do just sitting around a table. I need to be at the top table, and have the control to ensure they're implemented. The details are in my challenge submission. I've used that avenue to outline the proposals, and guarantee the credit for them remains with me, that is, pre-empting any plagiarism," she said in a tone and with a glare, which left Summit in no doubt who she had in mind.

She wanted a reaction, expecting him to prod for more information, but Summit just stared, unwilling to play her game, and knowing she could not tolerate silence for long or contain her proposals, in the face of an adversary. She succumbed.

My plan comes in two phases; phase one is to attack the short-term shortage, then the second phase is to implement a strategy for correcting the supply issue, long term. As I said, much of the long-term solution still roams my mind, and I've some things under consideration but my plans for the short term are defined and ready. The first step I propose, is to restrict surrogate availability, to one and twojay females."

Summit's eyes widened and his brows jigged, surprised.

"Then we lower the age of surrogates to fifteen," Summit's eyebrow was again surprised but he had a complicating contention.

"Does that include virgins?" he enquired casually, hoping to inject a herring.

"I can't see why not."

"It's happened at least once before," he remembered musingly, this time attempting to distract her with trivialisation.

Brilliance ignored it contemptuously, and continued delighting herself, demonstrating her superiority, "The nub of the solution lies in going ahead and establish the Surlace but larger than the one on the drawing board. My calculations show we need at least 400 surrogates immediately, and while that number will satisfy current demands within twelve months, the medium term will require more. Of course, a Surlace policy first needs the Governing Council's go ahead, then there's construction, fitting out, staffing, recruitment, and inauguration, before we even get started. While much of his organisation can be done concurrently, it's all still going to take more than a year, I suspect."

Summit thought he'd spotted a miscalculation. "We're troubled finding 150 surrogate presently, but you're suggesting double that plus 100. I think we'll be doing extremely well enticing 250 into a Surlace." Summit said, convinced her proposal was unrealistic.

"They're out there, and can be coerced with the right incentives."

"Which are; because we've been unable to lure anything like that number so far?"

Brilliance was dismissive, "Just take my word for it, means can be found," she was anxious to deliver her 'piece de resistance', "the major game changers will be multiple pregnancies, and shorter pregnancies. They're so simple and straight forward, I can't understand why they've not been thought of before," she said gazing unblinking.

Now she surely had Summit's attention, and he paused watching her as he straightened in his chair, learnt forward, and rest his elbows on the desk.

"What do you mean by multiple pregnancies," he enquired earnestly.

"Impregnate surrogates with twins, even triplets, if an assessment of their physique determines them suitable. They could be implanted simultaneously with embryos from two or three different parents and this would increase production by one hundred percent immediately, and by even more as the technique is refined. Naturally there's some uncertainties at the moment, the biggest one being how many surrogates would decline the option, even for double or triple the fee.

"However, for those ensconced in the Surlace and therefore servile to its influences, their successful persuasion rate would be very high, over 90 percent I would anticipate. And I'm speculating here, but I suspect that a surrogate, who delivers twins successfully, may easily be enticed to have triplets for her next indenture, especially having received her rewards for delivering two. If they are kept healthy and happy, as they should be, they could grow addicted to the rewards. The possibilities are promising, and I've other proposals which would make multiple birthing more attractive."

"The whole suggestion could be worth considering but at the moment it sounds very speculative," he said indifferently.

"It is why a Surlace is essential. Once surrogates are embedded in that environment and conditioned, they are at our behest, allowing us to manipulate them pretty much."

"You mean zombie surrogates"

"Nothing so crude Summit. It's diet control. Our charter is to supply surrogates, and I'm not aware of any controls, or guide lines, about how we achieve that," her eyes widened, "Production can be increased further, while making life easier for surrogates. It's a win-win, proposal," and she paused for Summit's attention.

"The pregnancy period can be condensed. Feasibly, it can be shortened from nine months to eight months, even to seven. It's probable the pregnancy period could be shortened even further, reliably, and we need a research department within the Surlace to investigate just how much more it can be shortened. In the brooding cycle we need to determine how long is human gestation essential, and at what stage the foetus can be transplanted to science for finishing incubation. Surrogates should be utilised for the essential primary stages only, and this could turn out to be six months, probably less, maybe even five months, or four. Not only would this relieve surrogates of the uncomfortable and fatiguing last couple of months of pregnancy, compounded by multiple carriages, it would leave them in better physical and mental condition, and so able to move onto their next pregnancy sooner. As well, if surrogate pregnancies can be reduced substantially, it'd be another inducement for surrogates to contract for more multiple births. I see no obstacle to surrogates producing three to five pieces a year, say for ten years, maybe longer. Those sorts of figures have the light of solution about them, don't you think."

Summit had a thought but he was not going to say so, preventing her adding it to her submission. Having shown her capacity to think through ideas, she may have already schemed it in, but anyway he was going to stay 'mum'. If pregnancy periods were reduced significantly, even to five months, it was possible some jay females would elect to become pregnant, especially if their body type suggested they would suffer no long-term detriments. A surrogate shortage could accelerate such a trend, ultimately reducing surrogate demand substantially.

"Yes Prudence, you've thought through your propositions well, but you haven't confronted the basic problem of the dwindling surrogacy pool, and where you're going to find your start up 400 surrogates. Long term your figures are plausible, but still the fundamental impasse remains. The answer to any problem can be resolved theoretically, even mathematically, but it can all finish up fictional."

Brilliance glared and waited a moment. "So, what's your answer!? At least I've the vision to develop a possibility, one which I know will work, and while there'll be teething difficulties, and will likely take longer to establish than expected, it only needs people's belief and the commitment, to make it happen. That's why, Summit, you're no use to me, the authority, or the beautiful society. You're a short sighted, lame duck, who, sad to say, is age decayed and I've no doubt you're finished Summit. I also have no doubt that as Bushtoe I'll have the strength, which through either grace or gall, will renovate this crumbling department," Brilliance was stabbing a pointed finger at the floor.

She paused hoping to elicit a reply and though Summit was struggling to stayoptimistic, he succeeded at least overtly, to appear unaffected by her well calculated strategy. Her presentation was calculated to induce a sycophantic inclination in him but that strategy, at least, would easily be disarmed. He stared at her, his eyes circled her head and face, and he was reminded that she was certainly beautiful; then they rested on her tiffanys.

"How old are you, Brilliance? You must be getting on, or are your tits beginning to sag prematurely? My reba has the same problem," he concluded, hoping to disrupt her line of thought, and have her return to type, or at least to the female he knew.

He had known where it hurt, and although a flush of spite surged through her, she quickly and astutely realised he had been defeated, and had sunk into desperation, so from aloft she'd ignore his childish goading. She smiled, slightly, ostensibly privately but cunningly enough for him to notice.

"Would you be expecting a position with the authority, when I'm the Bushtoe?" she countered, her tone official. Touché.

He had been mistaken reasoning she was always distracted, swimming to the mood of her addictions, and now the more she outlined her ideas, the more Summit's mind began calculating a defence. She had a number of advantages, including her jayone rating, the probable support of the majority of her co-directors, her substantial academic achievements, and her personality profile was reassuring. He would find succumbing to her challenge demeaning, on a number of levels, including the victory of beauty and arrogance, over experience and reliability; dreaming over investigation; and ambition over evidence.

"So where in your plans is the next generation of surrogates coming from," he asked again, attacking the only vulnerable aspect he could find, for now. But he was not interested in her ideas, rather in testing the limits of her imagination, hoping it had reached the realm of pomposity.

"As I said, there is no quick fix to that but I've some speculative suggestions of a fringe and irregular nature, and which would require some blinkered outlooks, but for the moment I won't disclose them. My long-term proposal for super surrogates will necessitate finding and indoctrinating females who are physically capable, mentally sound, and emotionally vulnerable to accepting their purpose in life is to breed; and live a special life, producing and raising surrogates, like themselves. As well, they will possess instinctive breeding inclinations, an affable disposition, be compliant and fatalistic. These surrogates would live separated from the mainstream, and be encouraged to bond with their offspring, raising them for surrogacy.

"We must start securing these super surrogates now, and implant them as soon as the harlequin can assure us it can supply the embryo specification required, even before a Surlace is available, and even if it's never available. If they produce two to three babies a season and they raise them as well, that should be a permanent solution to requirement.

"The figures are surprising. Statistically if a surrogate in this program produces three pieces a year, for ten years, the first intake needs to be fifteen and allowing for some losses, the average production for the year would be forty to forty-two pieces a year. I know drawing fifteen surrogates from the present primary production line, will further strain the already desperate situation, but I see no alternative."

As Summit listened to Brilliance's proposals, they were clearly substantial, even feasible but he was not about to strengthen her position with constructive criticisms, or reinforce her self-confidence. Instead, this time he'd try to flippantly attack her soft underbelly.

"What about you Brilliance, are you ready to become a surrogate when you sink to a jayfour or even a jaythree, maybe you'll consider twins? That'd be a real contribution you could make to society," he asked, cynically.

"Try not to be childish Summit."

He was exposed and looking for security in unsettling her, but again she was not going to rouse. Rather she was enjoying the high ground and gazed down, happily watching him ponder. However, she took a moment to consider this well aimed cuff. "My ambition is to save beautiful females from pregnancy, and just how I go about achieving that is for me to justify. Certainly Summit, anything you say will have no influence on my actions."

Summit stood up, "Thanks for coming Brilliance, and for informing me of your challenge. If you've nothing else, I'm busy and would ask you to leave," he was abrupt.

Brilliance swivelled around, stood, and elegantly strode from the office, while Summit watched her rear appreciatively.

As the door slid closed, he felt a wave of 'thank goodness' and slumped in his chair, his head back against the rest, then he wiped his hands down his face. Her not unsurprising but unexpected display of brazen ambition was unforeseen, while her uncanny acumen and amorous aura, had struck him hard. The power and potential of her policies were taxing his mental digestion, and he needed some time to replay and comprehend what had just happened. His vision was of her leaving his office, his thoughts were struggling to concentrate, while despondency infiltrated, as he accepted he was no longer dealing with a facetious bimbo but a formidable foe. In fact, her challenge was more than threatening, it was menacing; the outcome more than a possibility, rather a probability.

Summit closed his eyes pondering his past and present, the years he had spent at the authority, his position, his place in the beautiful society, his peer standing, his social status. He had seen other males toppled by smart jayone and two females, and they were not pretty sights. Determination was stirring in his depth, and if this female wanted a fight, she had found the right bushtoe for one. His dejection was short lived though, and since his masculinity had just been raped, his gloves were coming off, the rule book was going in the trash, and his scheming was stepping outside his courtesy zone. It was time to call in some favours.

Chapter 11
The Allocation

It was a comforting room, well lit, in soft and varying shades of cream, with vibrant arts work in tones of blues and greys hanging on walls, the desk white, the chairs in cushioned leather bound in subtle off-white. The floor was polished bleached timber with scattered heavy pile fawn carpets. From behind the desk, dark blue lensed eyes peered from a powder white face crowned with swirling mousey hair, with white traces. The grey lips and eyes were outlined in purple. The powdered white skin continued down and over wide bare shoulders and fell to the waist on either side. The fitted halter necked cream with white swirls outfit hinted at her body's idiosyncrasies, textures and movements, and were intentional and subliminal.

Stone and Prudence had barely acknowledged the welcoming Nog-Nog and Now-Now as they hurried through the foyer of the Pregnancy and Surrogacy Authority building, and now sat in the leather-bound chairs. Stone was calm, there'd been no foreboding or anxiety but the waiting had triggered a tinge of excitement. On the other hand, Prudence's blood pressure and heart rate had increased on entering the offices, not out of excitement or anticipation, rather out of animosity towards the authority and its jurisdiction over her plans for a child, a matter she believed personal and private.

"Good morning, Prudence, Stone, my name is Nemasos, and I'm here to get your baby underway," her voice was reassuring, lacked palaver and was devoid of any aggravating tone, "welcome to the Arrangements Office. Her smiling white face garnered a polite response from Stone but Prudence saw an inquisitor, and she had no intention of being congeniality.

Nemasos continued, unaffected, "I've all the results and information we need to progress with your surrogate allocation, that is, as long as you are satisfied with the amendments to your harlequin application."

"What kind of child are you offering us, then?" Prudence demanded; her antagonism barely camouflaged. Nemasos glanced at her screen but she didn't need to, being well aware of what was displayed. She looked at Prudence with resolute but sympathetic eyes.

"The appraisal committee has permitted a BAS Harlequin," she looked back to her screen but detecting Prudence's prickliness, hurried on before she could interject, "of course, as you are aware it's to be male, and while a BAS is a diminution from the 2BAS in your application, he will still be a very niece child, who as an adult is expected to be two to three centimetres taller than his unamended embryotic figure. He will be slightly bigger boned and have a natural weight of six to eight kilos above the unimproved expectation. Further, the BAS adjustment means there should only be a marginal alteration to the skin or hair colour.

"So what was wrong with the two-bas," Prudence challenged, staring at Nemasos.

"The projections for a 2BAS harlequin unfortunately showed an adult bearing little resemblance to either of you. Almost all the critical features were extended beyond permissible limits, skeletal ratios, facial structure, skin colour, and other minor alterations. It's board policy that harlequin children should retain a discernible physical connection to its parents, and I'm sorry to say the two-bas harlequin was outside allowable parameters, by a considerable percentage. The two features well outside allowances were the facial structure and skin colour.

Prudence was angry but she was at a loss as to how to respond, knowing the Pregnancy Authority's decisions were final, there being no grounds of appeal. She was confronted with two choices; firstly, she could wait two years and reapply for the child she wanted, but run the gauntlet of the same probable outcome; or, she could accept this exacerbating predicament, and give the go ahead to what was on offer. She turned to Stone hoping from some consoling support, but he looked happy and just smiled at her.

"Can you show us his hologram again?" Prudence asked, a sense of resignation in her voice.

"Certainly Prudence, do you want the baby, at ten years old, at 15," she was interrupted.

"As a young man," Prudence snapped.

"I was coming to that. Hologram file SPJ2HABJ," Nemasos instructed and a half size figure appeared on the desk.

"That's no good, make him 100 percent," Prudence ordered.

On instruction the full-size adult figure appeared standing out from the side wall frame, and Stone smiled to himself. Prudence glanced for a moment, then turned to Stone, stone faced.

"He's going to bloody well look like you," she said her eyes alight but frowning, unsure if that was good or bad, and adding to hervacillation, was Stone's obvious satisfaction. If he was happy, did that mean she should be, also? Stone could see she was reluctant to accepted the inevitable, and he was going to let stew in her own disquiet until she accepted the reality. He just smiled his acceptance of the situation, but she still wanted to quibble.

"His caesar is going to be bigger than yours," she noted, with some satisfaction in her voice.

Stone was unperturbed, but "that's good, isn't," he mused, self-satisfied, while reaching out to stroke her thigh. His touch was annoying.

"It's no laughing matter Stone," and she brushed his hand away.

Stone's manner sombred, "Be happy with Prudence, look!" he pleaded gesturing towards the hologram, "I can't wait to have him as my son, he's more than enough man for me, and it's him or nothing," he said looking away and lowering is hand.

Reluctantly Prudence accepted her inclination to persisted with the rear-guard aggravation was pointless, and although she was not prepared for unconditional surrender, she was beginning to bond with the harlequin she was examining.

"Give me a look at the baby," she asked, calmly.

"Day one," Nemasos instructed.

Their man vanished and a baby appeared on the desk. Suddenly Prudence needed no further conversion, her only disappointment now was her baby was just imagery.

Nemasos decided to move forward.

"If you're satisfied with what has been approved, we'll green light the harlequin to go ahead, and I would expect the embryo to be ready for implantation in about a fortnight. I note we have all the core materials from you both and the adjustment DNA is also all in stock."

"We've not even met or approved the surrogate yet. Let's start at the beginning," Prudence interrupted, her truce threatening to be short lived.

"Yes Prudence, I realise that but we won't select or vet a surrogate until you've accepted the harlequin, because if you refuse it, we've wasted everyone's time and arrangements."

"Let's get out of here for a while, Stone. Let's go for a drink and some stimulation," Prudence suggested, hoping she'd feel more accommodating if she calmed and found some positivity. She turned to Nemasos, "give us an hour to talk this over, okay?"

"There's no hurry, take the time you need. You both need to be happy with your decision, so take all the time it takes. If you decide to go ahead the next matter which needs negotiating is the surrogate's fee," she said.

"You're happy with this baby, aren't you Stone?" Prudence asked softly, looking into his eyes across the café table, the ambience of acceptance about her.

"Yes, I am, Prudence. At least half happy, my other half would be happy if you were," he said, treading carefully.

"Bastards," she splurted, her composure vaporising momentarily, "who do these people think they are, we live in a free world, supposedly, what gives them the right to tell me what sort of child I can have?"

"We don't live in a free society Prudence. When we're ugly we're consigned to the dunville, whether we like it or not, so that's not freedom. As well, no society can function without rules, and we've chosen a society in which beauty makes our life good, and these controls are the price of that life style. I'm happy with it and don't understand why you're not."

"I would have thought that was obvious," she said dismissively, looking passed him into the street.

Stone knew Prudence had no alternative but to accept the situation, and he also knew that when she eventually accepted the new harlequin, it needed to be her own decision. There was no profit in trying to convince her; firstly, because it would probably annoy her; and secondly, he was not prepared to risk of ever being accused of influencing her to accept something she did not want.

Prudence also knew it had to be her decision, and with the image of her baby brightly drifting into her mind, she knew where her path would end. While the obvious was compelling, her resentment was fighting a stubborn rear guard. Stone was well familiar with her style, and as he watched her, he noticed an easiness settling upon her, albeit slowly, and he sensed it was the moment to arouse their partnership.

"Tell me what you're thinking, Pru," he asked, knowing.

"He's a beautiful baby, don't you think Stone?"

"He is that, and he'll grow into a handsome man."

"You're right, and I know my attitude has been overwrought, but I still resent the dictates of a faceless bureaucracy, which has indoctrinated us with the belief they work for our wellbeing, and the prosperity of the beautiful society. Well, there's a dunghill of bullshit in their propaganda," she moaned, in a final volley of frustration before capitulating.

It was less than an hour when they were returned to the whitish room and the whitish operative who was unsurprised by news that they were ready to go ahead, as soon as possible. Nemasos smiled perceptively, as she'd seen it all before, and had not concerned herself about the outcome.

"That's good news, I'm sure you'll be happy with the product. Now, you need to make an offer to the available surrogate, and if she agrees we'll make final arrangements. If she does not agree we can negotiate some more, and if that fails, we can try to find a surrogate prepared to accept your terms. However, it's a sellers' market, and their fee has steadily increased for several years."

"So you have a surrogate available?" Prudence asked, a ring of excitement in her voice.

"Yes, you've come to the head of the queue finally and an A class surrogate became available several days ago. If, for some reason, you're not happy with this one, you're entitled to select again, but it will mean a delay, probably of several months. However, if you will accept a B or C class surrogate, the waiting time would be considerably shorter."

Prudence's wariness warning alerted, "So has the one ready for us, been rejected before?"

Nemasos looked at Prudence momentarily, "That's confidential information," she was curt.

Prudence was stymied by another brick wall but she bit her tongue knowing there was no gain in verbalising her thoughts, but Nemasos moved quickly to short circuit her annoyance.

"I'm sorry Prudence but I can't tell you any more, firstly because it's against the rules, secondly, I don't have that information anyway, and it wouldn't be fair to the surrogate."

Stone chipped in, "It doesn't matter Pru what other people decide, we'll meet the surrogate and make our own decision." Again, Prudence had nowhere to go, and Nemasos again decided to push ahead regardless.

"The figure which I believe would secure you this class A surrogate, is 1.9 Sye," she announced, glancing between her clients.

Stone looked at Prudence surprised by the high price, though her return gazed implied the amount was inconsequential, but Stone wanted more information.

"So how much would a B class surrogate cost?' he asked, avoiding Prudence's gaze.

Nemasos paused "Somewhere between 1.3 and 1.5 Sye."

"What about a C class?" Stone continued.

"Come on Stone, be bloody serious," Prudence said feigning jocularity, but unsuccessfully concealing her distain, with the fact he'd even enquire

Stone did not acknowledge her or the implications but continued to explore the system, so awaited the answer to his question.

"Somewhere between 1.2 and 1.4."

"So there's little price difference between classes B and C but there's a considerable difference between A and B, so if we were to consider a class B surrogate what are their type differences?" Stone asked but his sentence had scarcely finished before Prudence pounced. She'd put up with this long enough.

"We're not destitute or bankrupt, and Stone, we're not interested, in any surrogate except a class A girl. I don't understand you sometimes," she said, shocked he'd even considered it, let alone want the details.

But Stone was not to be shot down so quickly or so contemptuously, and he turned to her casually, let his look linger briefly, and casually turned back to Nemasos, wanting his query answered. She understood the silent message.

Nemasos wriggled in her chair, straightened and looked hard at Stone "Classifying candidates is complicated due the large number of variables which are often intangibles as well, and finding the balance between the pluses and the minuses is not easy. The best we can do is give each characteristic a ranking, then plot the average. Even then the outcome can sometimes be misleading. Just the same, an experienced surrogate can be more easily classified, since her performance information is recorded, along with her stress and fatigue levels, physical adaptability and age.

"For first time surrogates, one of the initial matters we addressed is her disposition for stress, anxiety, depression, her propensity for panic attacks, and blood pressure stability, all factors which can be detrimental to a foetus, and have consequences into adulthood. While these conditions can often be medicated, still they remain influencing elements. Mental stability, obviously, is critical as females embarking on this undertaking for the first time, must be cable of conceptualising the commitment, and maturely assume the responsibility. Next, her physical structure, physical condition, and age are assessed.

"For instance, a fit female may indicate for depression as a symptom of pregnancy, which would mark her down but she would remain suitable under medication. On the other hand, a female who had proved a good surrogate, with two previous pregnancies, may then loose points for fatigued, but out of financial or other interests, offers herself for another pregnancy anyway, rather than taking a lay-off. Fatigue can aggravate undesirables such as anxiety and depression. There are 12 categories in the assessment schedule with points available totalling 120. Those scoring in excess of 100 are class A, those over 85 are class B, while those below 70 are unsuitable for surrogacy."

Stone spied an argument, "So a class B surrogate with a score of 99 is virtually the same as a class A female with a 100 but the 99er is a half Sye cheaper."

From the corner of his eye, he noticed Prudence lithely readjusting herself in her chair, and hoped his contention had caused her to consider his logic, but instead suspected she was irritated. Surprisingly she did not comment, so he turned to her with raised and quizzical eye brows, waiting.

She let him wait several moments, "Not interested Stone!" she said curtly, calmly, but contemptuous of being consulted.

Nemasos intervened, "It's a pointless asking me as that information is also confidential." She pushed on. "The price I mentioned does not include her medical or living expenses, for which you'd be responsible. The end cost to you would be around two Sye for an A class female."

"We can resolve the living costs issue forthwith, as I need to have her ensconced with us," Prudence announced.

"That does not always work out," Nemasos warned.

"We'll cross that bridge if it crops up, but in the meantime, I'm determined to bond with my boy from the beginning, and I want to watch her belly grow, and I want to run my hands over it, and put my ear to it to listen for his heart, and see him moving, and I want to be there for his arrival. And we'll pay her a living allowance, as well," she said turning to a slightly surprised Stone.

"Well, we can only hope the surrogate assigned to you will appreciate that much attention. She may not, of course," Nemasos cautioned.

"Don't worry about that Nemasos, she'll feel at ease with us," then her optimistic conviviality succumbed to practicality, "Hell, what more could she want? It's an escape from her dunville for nine months, she gets to live with the beautiful, has medical care handy, and she'd have the best of everything," it seemed simple and obvious to Prudence.

Stone shrugged and turned to Prudence, "Seems fair but instead of living in the Jay society where her movements will be restricted, she might be happier in her dunville, among friends and family."

There were other reasons Prudence wanted her surrogate at home, but had been reluctant to say, for fear of being offensive, but it was time to be frank and explain why she was not prepared to concede on this matter.

"I'll have the surrogate at home, and that's an end to the matter. Have you thought what might happen if, once she's impregnated and returned to her dunville, or whatever warren from which she hails? I understand alcohol can be found in dunvilles so what happens to our baby if she's drunk? How can we control her intake of illegal stimulants and hallucinates? What's her sexual appetite, is she going to want fucking, and by who and how often? Does she have an abusive boyfriend, etcetera?"

She looked Stone straight in the eye, "do want some hobo fucking on top of your son!?"

Stone was surprised by her outburst, but found no argument, "You leave me with little to disagree with this time, Pru."

Nemasos intervened, "while we can't monitor every aspect of a surrogate's behaviour, we test regularly for things like alcohol consumption, which while illegal it is about particularly in dunvilles, so we check for it, as we do for legal substances which are forbidden during pregnancy. Close monitoring of their physical condition can give us some indication of life style but it's not very satisfactory. If we are suspicious about a surrogate's behaviour, we can conduct clandestine observations but generally speaking most surrogates are conscientious and give parents very little course for concern."

"All right, let's just go ahead, say yes to everything except alternative living arrangements, let's meet the surrogate and unless she's totally unsuitable, get on with having her impregnated," Prudence was impatient.

Nemasos looked up, "Woo! There is one more matter to deal with, and that's fee's due in the event of an incomplete pregnancy. Miscarriages still occur, albeit very occasionally, and abortions can become necessary in the cse of foetal deformity, which are even rarer. I'll outline the normal scale of fees, should such an unfortunate eventuality eventuate.

"For a class A surrogate on impregnation.05 Sye is due for a stable embryo, then .02 daily for the next 90 days.006 per day for 105 days, and for the final 75 odd days.008 per day. In the case of a premature live birth the full-term fee is payable, while for a late delivery, which is also rare, the daily rate continues. When a birth fails to occur on the scheduled, it is up to you to negotiate with the surrogate, whether to await nature, or to intervene, but the surrogate has the final say."

Prudence turned to Stone again.

"Happy."

"Yep."

With the master plan, the intricacies and the fine print sorted, Prudence put the academic aside and her mind turned to the palpable, the physical and the practical.

"Can you give us some information about our surrogate, and show us her hologram?" she asked.

Nemasos didn't look up, just summoned the information, "Surrogate ATS Clarity, presentation, full size."

When she appeared from the wall frame, Stone gawked for a moment surprised, then turned to Prudence with a wry smile. She too was surprised, and after brief exchange of consensus, they turned back to the hologram.

"What does ATS stand for," Prudence asked.

Nemasos looked up, paused, "A class, Teenage, Second."

"Second what?"

"Second surrogacy."

"Shit," Stone contributed.

"Well, she's almost nineteen," Nemasos informed him.

"Come on," Prudence urged, flicking a 'get going' hand.

"Proceed Clarity."

"Hello mum and dad hopefuls, I'm Clarity, and I understand you're seeking a surrogate and I'm looking for an engagement, so I'd like to see if we can come to some agreeable arrangement. Since this introduction is not interactive, I'll just tell you a few things about myself, and give you some indication if I am the type of surrogate you're wanting. I'm 18, an Rthree, which is probably a lower rating than I need to be but it's automatic for anyone who never had the alphaspection, which I haven't. My family have been dunvillians for generations, and happy to remain there. We're a surrogate family, with my next pregnancy being my second, and I've two older sisters presently pregnant on assignment. My oldest sister, who is quite a bit older than me, had her own daughter before becoming a surrogate and is now on her third contract. My other sister did not take a contract until she was twenty-two and is now almost due to deliver it.

"My mum had three daughters of her own, then she threw out our father while I was young, and then she undertook two surrogacies," she paused, "so I think it's obvious, pregnancy is a way of life for us. If my first undertaking is an indication, then you can expect me to suffer a little nausea in the beginning, other than that I will comply with the dietary schedule, be punctual for progress evaluations, adhere to any and all medical interventions and deliver easily. I am not annoyed by the close attention of the veritable parents, but dislike being expected to answer to friends and relatives, etcetera. So that's me in brief, and I hope to see you shortly. Goodbye for now," and she was gone.

Stone and Prudence looked approvingly at each other, then she turned to Nemasos, "Well it's a big yes from me, at this point, but what's a female like her doing in dunville with an Rthree rating?" Stone asked.

"I can't explain that, but I've had some personal contact with those females, and I can tell you they're a close-knit family who live very well-off surrogacies. They are comfortable with being pregnant, and probably know more about the condition than most medical professionals. Personally, I think you've hit the jackpot with Clarity."

Prudence was pleased, "Well, she's not a jayone but neither is she an R. She'd come through an alphaspection easily as a Jag, probably even a Jok; but be that as it may, she's ticked all my boxes."

Stone was not quite so convinced, "There's probably an issue or two which she's not disclosed, as there's something about her which concerns me. However, for now I'm happy to take her at face value, and agree she's the type we want," he paused, "One thing though; because her first pregnancy went smoothly is that a true guide to the next time? Stone asked Nemasos.

"Yes, we find it's the best guide we have, although sometimes the second confinement can trigger emotional disturbances, usually close to delivery when they recall the trauma of their first delivery. Then we resort to mild sedatives which contain the problem. Clarity at 19, maybe on the tender side of emotional stability but physically she's ideal and with her family environment, we're quite relaxed with her class A classification," she explained, glancing between them, set for more questions.

For Stone the waters suddenly muddied. "If she's so reliant on family support where does that leave us, wanting her to live with us."

"We'll make adjustments," Prudence snapped, wanting the subject cruelled. "When can we meet her?"

"She's available anytime, so you give me a date and time and I'll arranged it."

"Tomorrow, 10am," Prudence said, turning to Stone. It seemed to suit him.

"Ten tomorrow morning," she confirmed.

Chapter 12
The Interview

That night Prudence lay awake, thinking, tossing, turning, naked, the image of her baby boy inescapable, thrilling her with promise, until finally wishing he'd leave her in peace for a while, while slovenly Stone snored, having fallen asleep soon after going to bed. She'd attempted to capture him in conversation but he had avoided any discussion with the potential for disharmony. She looked at his bulk silhouetted against the night sky window, and in frustration reached out and took hold of limp, and lifeless caesar. A few strokes of gentle inducement failed to elicit any response, and his heavy breathing continued its steady cadence, aggravating her restlessness, and although now impatient she persisted softly, but not for long. She took a firm grip, and started some serious stroking, striving to stiffen that which she hoped might turn her thoughts, sap her strength and finally, seduce sleep.

Initially she had not considered a corporeal encounter, but in tedious sleeplessness, she'd grasp caesar as a simple fondling amusement, but soon the thought of it deep in vivian roused a tingle which needed entertaining. She didn't care if he awoke or not, as long as caesar stood tall, as she knew it would; then she'd happily help herself, not for the first time She envisioned a brief rough rump with some buzz, on otherwise likely listless anatomy, but now as she worked on the uprising, an inner gush stirred a craving for a committed carnal companion. Frustration yielded to a familiar desire, and a love which sought closeness, cuddles and quiet conversation in her ear. A moment ago, she didn't care if he awoke or not, and if he did, it mattered not if his mood would be carnal or cranky but now, she wished to arouse him in an affectionate way.

Her sudden mood swing was surprising, since only hours ago she'd been thoroughly slaked, on the edge of the kitchen table, one of gemma and cleopatra's favourite places, and Stone liked delivering with both feet grounded. While her goal, a few minutes ago, had been for a sip of a vigorous fornication, ending with at least a forgettable nefertiti, but exhausting her enough to want sleep; now her ambition was far more desirous.

When Stone showed signs of stirring, she employed oral encouragement hoping he'd wake. After a minute his eyes squinted across at the clock, "Hell Pru, it's bloody three o'clock. I thought we fixed this up earlier tonight." He squirmed, turned onto his back, making himself more accessible but seemingly ignored caesar's movement. Despite her hopes Prudence sensed he was not disposed to helping her, though caesar was providing different indicators.

Bugger him! Prudence released caesar and lifted her head. "Just lie there, Stone, go back to sleep, I'll help myself," she said, surrendering her hope of inveigling his enthusiasm. Slowly she pulled up her knees, rolled over, and straddled him, over the tops of his legs.

Without argument he lay listless, feigning sleep but blood flows beyond his control were urging him to muster some enthusiasm. Prudence's hands cruised his chest and waist; her ankles rubbed against his, and she felt sure the innate strength slouched underneath her, was brooding. Caesar was firming nicely, while Prudence's patience was pressing, inspiring her to slide down his legs, and bend over to tongue more incentive. She lifted her head, when she thought his erection was enough, and gazed at it standing silently in the dimness, then pulled vesuvius slowly up his body, notifying vivian of the impending. When caesar flicked, she lifted until the ladies kissed him, then lowered herself, descending surprisingly easily onto him. Her passion's fountain had been more forthcoming than she'd realised.

She bent down kissed his lips lightly, then his nose, his still closed eyes, but a mounting feeling of dominance, spawned by his vulnerability, was empowering, adding another tingle to her anticipation, and unleashing a dose of abuse was tempting. While he persisted in ignoring her, ostensibly being sleepy, he was content to sanction his erection's independence, and Prudence smiled at the thought it was to be just caesar and herself. On this occasion that would be ample.

With her hands gripping the bedding beside his chest she began sweeping vesuvius and company back and forth, delighting gemma, while Prudence arched, straining to invite cleopatra's participation. However, expecting his lifelessness to engage gemma and cleopatra simultaneously was a forlorn hope, so she sat up and handed the responsibility for commissioning cleopatra to her fingers. A sudden flood of unexpected, enigmatic and exuberant delight ignited a passionate drive for euphoria.

"Bloody hell Prudence!" Stone exclaimed conceding, opening his eyes, "Ease up."

The outburst drained her as quickly as it had arrived, and nefertiti which been so desperate for a few moments, now lingered stubbornly on the periphery abandoning Prudence to a steady rhythm, stroking vesuvius and company back and forth over caesar. She was fatigued and was beginning to puff, but her determination for the destination was compelling. Stone was tiring of being banged about, and decided to participate. He reached up took her waist and began synchronising with her tempo. Prudence paused, straightened again, then flopped forward on her palms.

"Stone, I'm doing it myself this time, and I'm enjoying it, so just lie back, caesar's all I need," she said dispassionately, her inclination having flipped from compassion, to mutinous selfishness, and a desire to orchestrate this episode the way I liked."

And she did, for a while, leaving Stone to concentrate on maintaining caesar's condition. Suddenly, with little warning, Nefertiti burst in, propelling Prudence into a moment's frantic flurry, but didn't stay long, symptomatic of her fatigue. She collapsed, breathless, beside Stone, heaviness invading her body, while her mind, at last, lazed thankfully, in sleep's now inexorable onset.

It was still early when Prudence woke but Stone was missing, though it was of minor consequence, since he wouldn't be far, and she wasn't thinking of him, anyway. She had only a few hours' sleep, still felt lethargic, and wished just to pull her knees up, lie foetal, and snuggled into the halcyon contentment which still imbued her. She felt confident about the day expecting that by its end, their baby realisation arrangements will have been completed and a surrogate will have been launched on their journey.

The bedroom door slid open to reveal Stone standing naked with a cup in his hand, but she was facing the other direction.

"Good morning Pru gorgeous, like a coffee?"

She rolled over and stared for a moment. "Put something on, for goodness' sake, Stone" she said, a touch annoyed at been disturbed.

"You were keen on it a few hours ago, I seem to remember."

"Yeah well, that was a few hours ago but now I'm comfortable, though a bit bruised."

Barely were they inside the Pregnancy and Surrogacy Authority building, ten minutes ahead of schedule, then Prudence reacted. "Bugger them," her splurted aroused again by the necessity to submit to the system, the holograms her target.

"I going to miss this Now-Now, when the new one is appointed," Stone commented, turning to look at her as they walked.

"No, you won't Stone! Fresh female flesh, feeds your fantasies."

He grinned sarcastically, and she grinned back, their exchange bawdy.

On entering the off-white office, with the black and blue art works, and the wall frame, Nemasos already sat behind her desk smiling, and at the end of the desk sat a young female, plainly dressed, shoulders to knees in a one piece, in wide diagonal stripes in aqua and cream, with short blonde hair unenhanced though facially carefully prepared in aqua, lids, and nails, cream lips outline in aqua, but completely without body work. She stood and motioned a half pace towards the arrivees.

Prudence instantly checked her structure. Body ratios, legs torso, the horizontals, in a moment all appeared acceptable, alice nice, tiffanys three-quarters, overall more than acceptable, to be honest. She certainly had the statistics to escape her dunville. Stone didn't do the analysis but knew in a glance she was a polished stone.

"This is Clarity," Nemasos announced, her hand indicating.

Prudence moved to her quickly wanting to formally embrace her, but for now decided hand contact was neutral, and the correct protocol, while Clarity's hand extended discreetly waiting. Prudence took her hand, and with their touch her restraint debunked, and she stretched both arms out to embrace the girl, pecking her on the cheek. Clarity was surprised but acceded, lifting a hand to Prudence's shoulder, holding it politely until

Prudence finished, which was not long.

"I've waited a long time to meet the girl who's to have my baby. It's wonderful, and I hope you're excited about it too."

Clarity wanted to dampen Prudence's enthusiasm and deal with business, "Yes Prudence, it's a big moment for you, I see that, and it's weighty for me too, but in the end it's just an agreement. I've done it before, rather well I believe, and I'll do as good as I can for you too, if we agree on a contract," she said.

Prudence's display of emotion surprised Stone too, and sensing Clarity's caution, he stepped up, took her hand firmly, smiling broadly, "Pleased to meet you, Clarity. We've been anxious to learn about you, and know you, and trust we'll have no trouble finalising our contract," he said, reminding Prudence all was not yet done and dusted.

"I hope so too," she added.

Nemasos looked at Stone, pointed to the two cream leather chairs, "Pull them in closer, Stone, please" she suggested.

Stone responded without comment, dragging them up to the desk, glancing at Clarity as he did. She noticed him looking and smiled privately. Prudence and Stone sat.

Prudence was keen to commence fashioning cordiality with her surrogate, and discover a strategy most likely to securer her cooperation and compliance.

"Clarity can I ask you a personal question, one which has nothing to do with your surrogacy," and an approving nod gave the go ahead, "I understand you've never submitted to the alphaspection. I'm sure if you took it, you'd have a jay rating because you're an attractive young female."

Clarity appeared unsurprised by the question, and was quickly ready with her answer. "Our family doesn't do that, we're happy with the more relaxed dunville life style, and see no advantage in the struggle for status in a jot. We think dunville folks are genuine, especially those who've never lived anywhere else."

"I can understand that Clarity, and while I'm in no hurry, I not too worried about the day I move there," she said, feeling her first foray had fallen flat.

But a petite smile crept across Clarity's face, and Prudence was pleased.

Nemasos took over. "I've already given you, Prudence and Stone, some details of Clarity's background but I'll just fill you in on her recent history. Clarity undertook her first surrogacy at the age of seventeen and six months, delivered at eighteen and three months, nearly a year ago. Her pregnancy was almost trouble free, with health issues arising only twice, when there was a small increase in her blood pressure, for which she was prescribed a mild medication. And there was an increase in tooth decay, again not significant, and certainly divorced from any foetal implications. Both are common in pregnancy and of no serious consequence.

"She delivered in three hours without the need for any interventions, the baby being born in good health and undamaged. Health checks on Clarity since she delivered have shown her to have made a full recovery, and is presently assessed as being in excellent condition, and suitable for another implant.

"Now; I have run through your offer with Clarity and as it stands, she is agreeable.

"However, there are still a couple of matters we need to settle," Prudence announced, "and the first is living arrangements," she glanced at Stone and then at Clarity, "Clarity, we, well me in particular, need you to live with us for the duration, I want to be close to you, watch my baby grow, and feel him moving inside your tummy," she implored her tone poignant.

Clarity silently looked her in the eyes, then flicked her gaze at Stone. All eyes were on her, which allowed her to possess the situation for a moment, then she fixed on Prudence.

"What would be those arrangements?"

"Your own bedroom, bathroom and living room, with prepared meals which you can eat alone or in our company, visitors would be welcome in your personal areas as long as they comply with jot regulations, and you'd have use of a transporter when regulations allowed," she explained, "Of course if you passed the alphaspection you'd have more freedoms to move about."

Again, Clarity looked at Stone before answering Prudence, "Yes, I could be happy with that, provided I could visit home from time to time, and it doesn't reduce my fee."

"No; it would not change the financial arrangements but how often would you want to go home," Prudence asked, concerned.

"Not often, but as I said we're a close family, and I'd need to visit them occasionally, just to catch up."

"We could arrange for them to visit you with us," Prudence countered.

"I'd still like to go home some times."

Stone decided his views were needed. "I think we could live with that," he suggested firmly.

Still Prudence was unhappy, "Do you have a boyfriend, Clarity?" she asked

Clarity understood the reason for the question, and thought it relevant, but her smile balked, not in fear of aspersions, but it could be opening a can she wanted to keep closed.

"Yes, I am nineteen."

Prudence's mind was racing, "Will you need to see him once you're pregnant?" she asked leaning forward in her chair.

"Not later on anyway, not alone."

The conversation was moving into dangerous territory, and Stone moved again to intervene. He sensed trouble brewing if the issue morphed into a discussion about Clarity's private and personal habits and behaviours.

"Clarity," he said looking into her eyes, "I will be frank with you, and I hope you won't be offended by anything I say but Prudence and I are just concerned for the welfare of our baby, and I hope you agree that if we need some reassurance about your lifestyle, that's legitimate."

She thought for a moment before replying. "I will look after your baby properly, I assure you. I think my record shows that," she said hoping not to be pressed for firm undertakings which she'd be obliged to refuse.

Nemasos picked the moment to intervene, "I suggest you consider leaving the accommodation agreement out of the contract for now, because I think, in time, you'll come to a mutual agreement, which will be flexible and satisfactory."

There was an exchange of glances with no one giving any indication of wanting to pursue the issue. Prudence had picked up on the potential for friction but had consoled herself with facts her surrogate's record was exemplary, and she looked decent, and sounded sensible. "All right, I feel Clarity understands our concerns, and I feel she's sympathetic, so I'm happy to leave it at that, for now," Prudence said, glancing at Stone.

Her anxiety was gone, she had surrendered to the process, and was prepared to forge ahead accepting that not everything could be resolved. That's life!

Nemasos was keen to move on, "We have another matter; Prudence you've expressed an interest in having you baby breast feed for a period," she said and paused for the subject to be considered.

But Prudence needed no thinking time, "I would like you to feed our boy for a period," she said looking at Clarity.

Clarity was thinking. The subject had been one of numerous discussions at home, with her mum believing it was worth the financial return, as well as it being physically helpful, while her sisters argued it was better to promptly escape the emotional perils, and recover relaxed and obligation free. She hadn't been asked to provide lactation for her first surrogacy, neither had she considered offering to contract it, content to avoid the subject. Her delay worried Prudence.

"It's important to us, Clarity," Prudence pressed, "We don't want to use the artificial substitute, because we don't believe it can provide the same sense of sanctuary and security, which comes with snuggling into warm tiffanys, nor can it foster the compassion which comes from suckling to the rhythm of a beating heart."

Clarity continued to return gaze, thoughtfully. The word 'compassion' stood the hairs on the back of her neck, and her sisters' warnings were not to be taken lightly.

"Even for two months. We're happy to pay you well," Prudence implored.

Clarity thought for a few more moments, her considerations mercantilel

"Three feeds a day, in daylight hours, for two months and you use a roby for the other feeds, as I'm not prepared to express. And I'll only have the baby for feeding, he arrives when it's due, and you take him again, as soon as he's finished. How much are you offering?" Clarity asked.

"Would you continue to live with us for that time?" Stone asked.

Again, Clarity paused in thought. "No," she said finally, and then, "I will have been away from home for about eight months, and I know by then I will be quite homesick, and not prepared to be away for another two months. As well, I wouldn't want be in the same premises where I could hear your baby."

"Would you consider for the first month," Prudence asked.

"No, Prudence when the pregnancy's over, I'll go home."

Stone and Prudence looked at each other, their exchanges unspoken but understood they were dealing with a strong and independent female, who was capable and prepared to negotiate as long a is it was within her ambit. And already they seemed to have come up against her non-negotiable position. However, it did not mean a way around the impasse could not be found, with a little more time than was available, at the moment.

"Let's assume that some way can be find a way for Clarity to feed our boy for two months, with an arrangement which suits her, and on that basis, we can still go ahead and agree a fee," Stone suggested.

Clarity smiled approvingly.

Nemasos knew the going rate for such an engagement, "One and a half times the final daily pregnancy rate, is a fee often settled upon," she revealed.

Clarity wasn't sure how much that would be, "So what does that amount to?" she asked.

"For the final 75 days of a regulation pregnancy you receive point, zero, zero, eight sty; so for the feeding you'd be paid point zero, one four sty, which for two months or 62 days, would total, point eight six eight sty; say point nine," figures she quoted without reference.

"Yes, I'll do it," Clarity agreed before Prudence or Stone could consider or reconsider. "That'll leave another three or four feeds a day you'll need to arrange," she pointed out.

"We're happy with that Clarity, thank you," Stone replied, since Clarity was looking to him.

"The Gamro is probably the best of the robys," Nemasos advised. "It's the one we recommend based on consumer surveys and test results.

For the baby it's technically identical a human mother, with a teat and breast structurally identical a human breast, while the holding pouch mimics natural human features and attributes. For a baby, still oblivious to its life, we believe the Gamro fulfils all its needs," she explained.

"But it cannot radiate the ambient aura of the human spirit," Prudence complained, "Even a new born knows the difference between a human and a Good As Mum Robot."

Nemasos had an alternative. "There are a few wet nurses which could help but they are scarce, and the ones which are available are usually spent surrogates focused on a final financial sortie before retiring. Despite this they're highly demanded, expensive, and with a long list, you've probably left it too late to be bothered joining the queue," she said.

Prudence looked harshly at Stone, as if it was his mistake, they'd missed the opportunity.

"It's not my fault Prudence," he exclaimed, wide eyed, "Anyway Clarity has agreed to give us two months," he glanced at their surrogate and smiled, then turned back to Prudence, "so be happy lovie."

"What about a part time nurse," Prudence asked desperately looking at Nemasos.

"I think the same would apply, Prudence but I'll give you the agency details and you can inquire."

"Right, I've had enough for today. We've resolved all the critical issues, so now it's just a matter of the contract and its verification," Stone announced, standing up, looking down at Prudence, over at Clarity and across at Nemasos.

Nemasos was anxious to wind up as well, "I believe we've ticked all the boxes, and done well to reach agreement on all the important matters. The contract will also include all the statutory conditions regarding such matters as dispute resolution, and non-completion provisions, etcetera. The contract will be on your tice, in around two hours, which, if it's what you agreed to, and remain happy with, just scan your iris and attach it to the contract and tice it back to the authority."

Prudence grinned coyly, a prickle ran up her back and suddenly her world was happy, her baby was approved, a surrogate found, the contract all but settled, insemination due in six days, implantation the following morning, and now all the planning, anxiety, and debate, were behind, them and the highway to her baby stretched adorably ahead. For Stone he was grateful to finally close his book on the debate and frustration.

Shoulders together aboard the hover transporter homeward bound, the gravity of their achievement had them quietly reviewing their commitments, while all the implications and realities of such a significant redirection to their lives, still awaited their full appreciation. Stone turned to Prudence as she turned to him, and when their smiling eyes met, he filled with a fuzzing warmth, charmed at a serenity which had transformed his reba from a single-minded empress, into an inspiring and beautiful female whom he loved. She knew what he was thinking.

"I like it too, Stone," she said and looked away, then with her business expression returned, she looked back. "All that's left now is to convince the girl she must live with us!"

"That's not necessary Prudence, she's already agreed to it. The only problem is your fear of her private and personal behaviour, and while I'd prefer she not indulge in some activities for the next nine months, but we can't extinguish human instincts, or dictate, or scrutinise her personal conduct, all the time."

Prudence grunted and looked away again.

Chapter 13
The Results

Once again Affinity was transfixed by her mirror, naked, motionless gazing at her tiffanys. After weeks, they had been unwrapped yesterday, and in the privacy of her bathroom it was time to again study the results of the moulding treatment. She was pleased. The promise had been delivered, and now she wondered why she had spent weeks deciding whether to undergo old style surgery, or have injections, or risk the latest moulding sensation. Once committed, Affinity found the procedure exciting, especially the time spent holograming herself, selecting the tiffanys she wanted.

It had been three months since the clinician assessed her tiffanys, concluding their reformation would be straight forward, and she was given several computer designed tiffanys, from which she could select. Certainly, the most attractive and provocative, not surprisingly, were the 'virgin's', but on her, disappointing, were simply unsuitable. Quarter pluses, spherically perfect, dewdrops petite and 45/55.

Regrettably she accepted her maturity but, and in doing so found the most appealing necessitated larger tiffanys, enlarging from minus three-quarters, to three-quarter-plus. She found her final selection titillating, and were a smiling improvement to the spherical, with 15 percent separation, high carriage. and while the position of her dewdrops would be moved, they would remain at 50/50, which while not perfect were satisfactory.

Affinity bounced on her heels and smiled. Gone was the sagging, no longer were her dewdrops contemplating a sorrowful attitude, and the hint of stretch marks at their sides were gone. She took them in her hands. They were not as sensitive as before, in fact they were insensitive but she cupped them anyway, feeling their weight, stroked them, tickled them with her nail tips, and wished for the company of someone to share her pleasure.

Once the treatment commenced it had taken two months, she had worn the moulds and three times a week attended the clinic for particle magnetic beam manipulation for tissue restructuring. These treatments were adjusted at each visit. Each time the clinician had smiled and reassured Affinity he was happy with progress, and progress was according to expectations.

She clasped her hands behind her back, arched, thrust her tiffanys up and out, and the sight was stimulating. She caressed them again, from the top her hands slowly slithered down, over her dewdrops onto her midriff and then she did it again. Affinity did not notice the slight swelling on the underside of her left tiffany.

It was only a week later when her joy frowned a little, and she noticed a slight distortion of her port tiffany. In front of the mirror, her examination was close, precise and assessed from all angles. Concern was pulling at her spirit, as she could not dismiss the fact her corrective treatment may not have been as successful as she'd celebrated, and in fact something was amiss.

"Summit, can you come here?" she called calmly.

"What do you want, I'm still in bed."

"I know you're still in bed, you always are at this time of day. So, get up and come here I want you to look at something," she said maintaining a congenial tone.

"It's not your tits again, after all this, is it?" he enquired frustratingly.

"Yes, it is!" her impatience had arrived.

Summit succumbed, and was on his way, and once at her side he leaned forward to look at her chest.

"What am I looking at" he demanded.

"Rub your hands over my tits, and especially feeling them underneath" she said quietly, turning them towards him, and pushing her chest out.

"What for?"

Just do it!"

He obliged, but rather hurriedly he stroked each from the top to under the dewdrops.

"Do is slowly Summit and see if you can feel anything."

Summit tried again, this time more deliberately, hoping this would satisfy her.

"They're gorgeous Affy dear, there are plenty of younger females who'd be happy to have them."

"Can't you feel anything Summit? Feel them again, properly, start underneath this time," her emphasis on the adverb.

He complied this time, being even more deliberate, and following her directive.

"There seems to be a little bit of unevenness but that's probably normal at this stage," he summarised then turned away.

"I don't know why I bother talking to you Summit; it always seems to end up a waste of time."

"Essence! Essence honey, got a minute," she yelled

"What do you want?" came a muffled and distance reply.

"Come here for a moment, I want you to look at something and tell me what you think."

"It's not your tits again, is it?"

"Just come on Essence, please."

A few moments later the bathroom door swung open and Essence, in uniform, appeared.

"It is your tits again, isn't it? For goodness' sake, Mum, I thought they were fixed."

"Just run your hands over them honey, and tell me if you can feel anything."

"Mum!" she exclaimed "Get dad to do that, I don't want to feel your tiffanys."

"Do it please, I'm worried about the treatment, and I can't get any cooperation from your father."

Essence looked at the floor, hovered for a few moments searching for an escape route but unable to find one, looked up at her mother, and moved towards her, her hands coming up.

"You could have put some nickers on before calling me," she snapped, as she confronted her mother. Affinity ignored the comment.

"Just do it for her Essence," came a called from the bedroom.

"It's your job dad, not mine."

"Do it anyway."

"I am," she said as her hands began high on Affinity's chest and slowly worked their way down, over and under. Suddenly her nonchalant expression changed, no longer was she dismissive of her mother's mania.

"There's lumps there, Mum," she was looking into her mother's eyes concerningly.

"I know, that's what I'm worried about, also they've lost a lot more feeling, and I don't like things at all."

Summit's reappeared, this time heading for the shower.

"Dad! Mum naked was more than enough, but you're a step too far."

She was ignored, looked back at her mother and realising her hands still rested on her tiffanys withdrew them, looked aside and eased away. She was in no mood to enter the world of her mother's obsession, and while her tiffanys obviously needed investigation, she wished to avoid the probable drama at all costs. Besides, she had concerns of her own.

"Just go and see about them," she was flippant "I've worries of my own, and you don't seem the least interested in me. My birthday is coming up, and then my alphaspection, and I'd like to talk to you about them but you're not interested," she concluded, sulkily.

Jolted, Affinity's attention wheeled to her daughter for the first time in months. In fact, she'd not thought about any of the family much recently, instead her mind had circled her tiffanys and herself. Any thoughts about the family had been her disappointment in their lack of any real concern for her problem. Essence's outburst was not only surprising, it was alarming as well, and promptly filled Affinity with guilt, leaving her scrambling an appropriate response. Essence realised her wide eyed and gazing mother was shaken, and defensively she moved back a touch, anxiously for her mother's reaction. For Affinity the moment was defining, and her guilt was beset by the creature of beauty afore her, the rising phoenix of a gorgeous and stunning daughter. She stared; where had her girl gone, when did she leave? How had she graduated unnoticed?

For Affinity the moment was significant for several reasons; the one at the forefront of her mind was the abrupt realisation her self-obsession had blinded her to aspects of her family, and life, which ultimately should have shadowed her problems. Two things were suddenly obvious; the first, she had missed or avoided the daily niravans of family life and second, she was beginning to understand why her family was not very sympathetic to her self-centred plight. There seemed a correlation there.

She reached out for her daughter and took her shoulders, smiling. "You're very beautiful Essence, what can you be worried about; there's no need? Your alphaspection will be straight forward, I'm sure of it. You'll make one, and so you should, since you were born gorgeous and as you grew, we were meticulous to correct even your slightest imperfection," was her rapid-fire response

"I know Mum, but Mum; I'm nervous and can't wait until it's over, and in the meanwhile, I'd like you to be interested enough to talk to me about it."

Affinity gathered her gown from the floor, pulled it on, took a final glance in the mirror; put an arm around Essence's shoulders, and looking into her eyes suggested they have breakfast together, a long-foregone habit. As they entered the kitchen Affinity called for two number seven breakfast, and promptly a nearby hum reassured them the order was underway. They sat adjacent, at the table's corner, comfortable enough to exchange chosen glances at each other, without the effrontery of sitting opposite each other. A ping signalled breakfast's readiness, and both females motioned to collect them, then seeing the other's move both plonked back into their chair. They laughed, exchanged smiles but it was Affinity who failed to make another gesture, so Essence did the honours, and during the few moments she was gone Affinity felt her tiffanys again.

Essence's concerns had been the least of her worries, but now shamed she would pay her heed, and give her the advice to which she was entitled. The contradiction in their circumstances was stark, with Essence in ascendency, and on the footplate of a jay life, where she'll revel in the privileges of her beauty and status; while Affinity in descent, is struggling frantically in the waning wake of her glory days, desperate not to end up wallowing in the stagnant waters of a dunville.

Essence placed the meals on the table and sat.

The emerging cordiality was momentarily interrupted when school ready and energetically overloaded Wraith busted into the kitchen on his way through.

"Don't worry sis, with your short legs and big alice it's a dunville for you, but that's not too bad. Granddad and grandma, are happy enough there, so you'll be okay." He was gone.

Neither mother or daughter reacted but as they paused for the trailing vortice to fade, another door swung open, and Summit entered, also making for the exit.

"No breakfast then," Affinity mused.

"I'm in a hurry so I'll grab something at work; I'll probably be late tonight, got something on."

"Love you ear rings dad, are they new?"

Summit looked at her and managed a quick smile, "Had them for a while, but this the first time I've worn them."

Affinity glanced at him, moaned apathetically, not interested in 'something on' could mean; then he too was out the door. Affinity looked back at Essence, reached out, gathered a hand full of her daughter's hair, pulled it forward over her shoulder, spread her fingers around the back of her head, and with her other hand, took Essence's hand. The distant front door closed.

"The truth is, my dear daughter, I'm probably jealous. You're so pretty, with so much good life and fun ahead, while I'm sinking into the mire, seemingly alone. I know I've had my turn, and I've had a healthy share of life's fun, which probably makes the future seem even more miserable than it should be, but that's the way I feel. I'm not going to apologise for it but, Essence, I am sorry if you've felt ignored, very sorry."

"Knowing you are jealous makes me feel better, Mum; it tells me you see me, and like what you see, and that's satisfying and cuddly. You might not be as young as you used to be, but you're still very attractive, and spunky, with oodles of pulling power. You've got many jay years to go."

"You're a very sensible girl for fifteen, Essence, you make me proud."

"Sixteen really Mum, well, soon anyway."

"Yes, I know! Sadly."

"Tell me about your alphaspection, Mum."

Affinity withdrew her tactile affection, looked blankly at the opposite wall, and felt hollow when she remembered how long ago it was. The occasion was one of life's mentally etched events, and as she started recounting her experience, she struggled to maintain a positive tone. She succeeded thanks to the helpful smile on Essence's face, and the brightening excitement in her eyes. In fact, for Affinity her story telling graduated from a begrudging retrieval of history, to the revival of her youth. Her enthusiasm grew as she relived the nervousness of the inspection waiting room, the desperation of her hope, the anxiety of the wait for the outcome, and her huge relief with the result. She finished by conceding that many things had probably changed since she endured the alphaspection, but she had enjoyed resurrecting the memories.

Essence had never been admitted to her mother's youth like this before, and eagerly absorbed her tales, and was elated by a sense of equality with her mother. She was about to join her mother on her side of the alphaspection but she wished a wish, to step over her alphaspection and discuss her subsequent ambitions.

"There's something else I'd like to talk about, Mum," Essence said a little shrinkingly.

Her tone forewarned Affinity that maybe the real reason for this mother-daughter heart-to-heart was still to come, and she was intrigued, but suspecting. When Essence vacillated, she knew she would not be surprised to be unsurprised.

"Well come on lovie, what is it?"

Essence lowered her gaze, she wanted this conversation, and knew she was committed to her plan but she didn't know how to start. Finally, she looked up: "It's about my virginity."

Affinity smiled knowingly, she had the inkling since this had been mentioned nonchalantly previously, and she knew Essence well enough to know her thoughts usually flowered. But deep inside she did not really want to confront what her baby girl planned, so she was not going encourage disclosure, rather she would feign naivety, and let Essence possess the conversation.

"What about it?" Affinity enquired after a moment, politely.

"I want to commercialise it!" she snapped.

Affinity paused, her jaw sagged, shamming surprise, her widening eyes effervesced, and she smiled broadly, impishly, "You want to what!?" she asked resolutely but failed to hide her amusement at the terminology, or the titillation. But Essence was not ready to have the subject subjected to inconsequence, frivolity, or the devilment, to which her mother seemed attracted.

"You know what I'm talking about! That's the term used these days, but if you want to make fun of it, then forget it," she barked.

Affinity closed her smile, and with chastened eyes looked at Essence solemnly: "I'm sorry Essie, the last thing I want to do is make fun of such a serious matter. I know exactly what you're talking about but maybe you're rushing me. You're only fifteen."

"Sixteen."

"Not quite yet, lovie."

Essence's forgiveness did not come immediately, rather she took a moment to stare at her mother, and only when she concluded she was sincere did she continue.

"I want to make an appointment with a Pavs (Post alphaspection virginity sales) negotiator," she explained.

Affinity abandoned femalehood in favour of motherhood "Are you sure you're ready for that Essence, it doesn't follow that just because you have your alphaspection, you need to lose your virginity. They are not related, really. I still see you as my baby, and I think I'd like you to stay there a little longer. While you may think you are ready for this, I'm not sure I am."

Essence sprang up from her chair, pushed it away with the back of her legs, and stood statuesque staring down at her mother, her point poignant, her posture a highlighting of her post puberty features.

"There's not much baby left Mum," she proclaimed, her voice exuding confidence, as her hands sweeping down her body, her eyes fixed on Affinity making sure she was acknowledging her.

Affinity had to agree, there was no baby girl in sight, she was full female, a fact she had previously and unconsciously chosen to overlook, but Essence's audacity had swept away the mist of denial. She had ignored her daughter's post alphaspection dreams as girlish fantasy, and should not now be nonplussed by the facts, but she was struggling.

From mineshaft of her past, she gazed at the horoscope of the tall glyphic displaying figure, radiating sexuality and eroticism; and the discernible delight in herself suggested seductress would be an amusement for her future. Affinity also saw a young female wanting to appropriate her cavern, use her fashion programs, and commandeer her printer. Unexpectedly, abruptly, there was to be another sensual being in the house, and the new one would undoubtedly shadow the old one; and there'd be more colour and presentation, more exposed skin, longer legs, cleavage and more, and goodness knows what else.

While the vision of Essence at barely sixteen sent a shudder of apprehension through her, she could not deny the memory of her own sixteenth birthday or of the water which had already flown under her bridge by that age. It left her without an argument, and now after the years, and an ocean, she found no reason to regret her history, so surely her role now was to shepherd Essence into the delights of maturity, while pointing out the potholes and hazards.

"I'll agree Essence there's no baby left in what I'm seeing, but you probably can't see all the implications of what you've about to become, and I doubt you fully realise just what it is you're to deal with in the next few years. There's two ways of learning about it, the first is the hard way, alone, but the second is easier, and you'll find that route by heeding good advice," she said.

"What do you mean?" Essence enquired as she resumed her seat at the table, thankful she was now being taken seriously, and keen for the conversation. She looked at her mother expectantly.

"Your body, with which you're beginning a love affair, will transmit signals which will spark different receptors in the adult world, and particularly the adult male world. On one hand your beauty will attract danger, serious dangers sometimes, but mostly you'll lure a cavalcade of people, from whom you'll find acquaintances, select friends and beguile lovers. Some of those associations will be mistakes but the effect of those mistakes on you, will depend on how astute you are, how quickly you learn, how quickly you can abandon wreckage, and how well you recover.

"Your body is so important at your age, and in this society, its quality will decree not only where you live, but how successful you'll be. But what I hope you understand is that society regards your body subjectively, and reacts and dictates according to its assessments of your beauty; however, that's only one street down which you must journey. As far as society is concerned you may as well be a statue; but being human the secret to happiness means learning to live with what you have."

"Why then mum, are you so afraid of the dunville?" Essence asked.

"I don't know, to be honest Essence, but I think probably it's not the dunville which frightens me, but if I lose my jay rating it means I've lost my life's struggle, I suppose. The end of my journey is in sight, and it's not pretty." she said, unsure if that was true.

"However, for you and I, we're blessed, or dammed, for being female, as our bodies are persistently the source of male fascination, even obsession and formally subjugation. The point I'm making is, while your body can deliver you incredible pleasure and fun, it can also subject you to pain and suffering, even worse, and it can condemn you to considerably more pain than pleasure, unless you're careful. Males can be major dispensers of pain and/or pleasure. The other aspect, with which you're familiar, is your body can be a tool for advancement," she looked at Essence who smiled.

"Commercialise it," Essence chipped in, but Affinity had intended something more intuitive.

"Well Essence, you've certainly identified that opportunity but it's only the beginning of your potential for exploitations, if you chose to utilise that asset. Deploying the asset between your legs, might be okay but remember your greatest asset is between your ears. Your female anatomy will generally only be advantageous in the base male world, but remember it's now us females, who control society and its upper echelons. Pussy and pleasure on our terms is necessary, but it's beauty and brains which has given us the advantage and you must strive, on behalf of all females, to preserve it.

"I suppose exploiting both is the way ahead," Essence thought was the answer.

Her mother ignored the comment and went on. "Since you need to deal with both females and males throughout life, it's important you know how to distinguish between the way you deal with males and the way you deal with females. When males look to take advantage of you, they will mostly sniff for your feminine vulnerabilities, be they sexual or their perceived fragility of female weakness. On the other hand, when females look to for advantage, they will rummage for your faults, with which to disparage you.

"Essence, males are rather simple beings but can be, and usually are, devious, particularly when targeting young, vulnerable females, like you. If you show any propensity for carnal generosity they will swarm, their little brains frantic to find your susceptibility. You must assume every comment made, or question asked of you by a male, is part of a scheme, which is okay if you want nothing more.

"However, if your expectation is for something more substantial, then you risk being disappointed. While many approaches will come from descent well intentioned males, learning to identify the difference is something which usually comes, finally, with experience, and I can't explain how to tell the difference."

"Mum, are you telling me not to have boyfriends," her smile was gone, the hint of a frown showing. She'd never seen the male world as the enemy, and she was not sure if her mother's attitude and unexpected warnings were unbiased, and the product of her own disappointments.

"No Essence, just while you're adventuring, I'm advising you to be wary and vigilant when interacting with males, and make sure you control the situation at all times; you must always be mindful of being in charge. Don't ever let a male prevail, because that fight back is fraught, in some instances even dangerous."

"I've found boys can be pretty pushy, and difficult to piss off," Essence agreed, thoughtfully, and beginning to think mum's warnings could have some foundation.

"That's why the female struggle has been so important. You'll find the director-general of a man's life hangs from the bottom of his stomach, and his unrelenting struggle is to emancipate its savings by either co-opting or coercing your comforts. Never let a male take anything from you, it must always be your decision to give, if you want to but don't hesitate to take from him."

"Is that the kind of relationship you have with Dad?" Essence perceived some contradiction between what she was being told, and what she had seen.

"Interplay will change if you finally commit to a partner or reba, and it can mean adjusting to the give and take precepts, however, the female must establish her integrity in a partnership, and begin the relationship preferably with superiority but with equality if necessary. Never mind the chemistry, it will percolate best trickling down."

News of Essence's commercialisation plans were not revealed to her father until the following night's meal, as he had been absent until then. His reappearance after 24 hours brought down a familiar veil of tension between he and Affinity, their wall a familiar one, one these days contested silently. They'd both had accepted that demanding explanations, telling lies, making demands and yelling insults, always ended inconclusively and achieved nothing. Despite the verbal armistice, the battle's silence was always palpable, claustrophobic, and for Essence and Wraith their muted exchanges used to be of anxiety but now they were just tedious.

Affinity was in the facilities cluster fingering the keypad, ordering the evening meals when Summit entered. Her inclination to glare beams of disgust were spoilt when his tice sounded. However, while her glare went unreceived, just looking at him renewed her resolved to remain tetchy, and she dialled in one of his less favoured meals. Summit took the tice from his arm, glanced at the ID, and uneasy, left the room to answer it. There was no hologram attached.

The eating precinct was dedicated, of polished timber, round, programmed, calibrated, old fashioned in style but discernibly modern, the four electronic place settings, the giveaway.

Wraith, under instruction, laid the meal trays, then was first to sit at his dedicated, programmed and calibrated chair, then Essence, and as Affinity sat and readied to eat, Summit re-entered the room. She watched him sit opposite, her expression expecting. His response was a fleeting peek at her and "just work," he muttered as he sat. Affinity didn't believe him because she didn't believe much of what he told her any more, and while he knew she thought she knew, he knew that whatever she thought she knew, this time she was wrong.

As they each sat, a digital screen flipped up in front of the meal, with a welcoming message, hoping their day had been pleasant and prosperous. A red light on the upper right-hand corner turned green, indicating the food had been weighed, the ingredients assessed and outcomes configured. Lines of information appeared recommending what meal adjustments should be made to ensure their correct calorie consumption. Affinity looked at Essence:

"Well Essence, you're the one about to have the alphaspection, let's hear how you're going."

Essence didn't mind, being happy to be the centre of family interest, so she leaned forward and touched her screen, causing life's everywhere synthetic voice to begin delivering details.

"Essence, you had a quiet day using only 24 percent of your available energy, while your intake of calories was seven percent above recommendation, the result being an indiscernible increase in body fat but a 45gram increase in body weight. The consequences of these shortcomings are minor, and your recommended calorie intake for this meal is 1750. The meal you have selected for this sitting contains 1900 calories so you should leave 150 calories. Since your taste responses indicate your least liked foods are those in category C, it's suggested you reject item C3. Thank you and enjoy your meal."

"Well, that sound rather satisfactory," Affinity said casually.

"Sounds to me like you should have done bit more work," Summit said just as casually, looking down at his meal.

"Sounds to me like you're getting even fatter," Wraith blurted from his fooded mouth.

"What's yours say Summit," Affinity demanded, her tone of an inquisitor, hoping for an indication of his mischief of the last 24 hours.

Summit had already perused his details and thought twice about being honest, but decided instead to stay snik (silence now is key). He was severely dehydrated, his fat level had fallen five percent, weight loss was 650 grams, energy consumption in the last 24 hours had been 107 percent, and his fatigue register was in the red. The screen offered a list of remedial intakes to restore his health but considering his age it would take several days before he could expect acceptable indicators. It also warned him, that to continue functioning under current stress levels could permanently damage his health. For the moment Summit decided to ignore the directive.

"Well!" her eyes bulged.

He looked up at her, his pained expression suggesting she 'get lost' but her stare was challenging.

He gave in. "I'm a bit dehydrated, I've used an average amount of energy and I've lost 50 grams," he lied and turning to Wraith hoped to change the tone of the gathering, "How'd you go today, son," enquired.

Wraith's disinterest in reviewing his details had nothing to do with keeping secrets, instead the figures were of little interest, and he couldn't be bothered. But he looked at his father and the 'help me' frown was enough to produce his begrudging response. He gazed at his screen for a moment.

"I used 82 percent available energy and gained about 30 grams, everything else is the same," he said flashing a glance from under his eyebrows at his father, and satisfied his intervention had been enough, he returned to his meal. Affinity knew there was more, having glimpsed the red light on his screen.

"What's the alarm for Wraith," she demanded.

Wrath looked, humbugged and huffed: "The thing wants me to measure my height again."

"Well, measure yourself then enterer it, it's not a big deal. You're still growing so of course it needs updates, otherwise it can't monitor you properly."

"Right," but his tone conveyed no confidence he'd comply, and he'd need further nagging.

There was little interest in Affinity's readings, as it was taken, they'd be within parameters, as usual, but she was not to be denied her stage, if for no other reason than to remind the family just how disciplined she was, the insinuation being, they too should aspire to wellbeing virtuosity.

"My indicators are all rather satisfactory, with no weight gain, and the energy consumption reckoned at 52 percent. I can eat my normal meal without concerns," her announcement seeming of interest to Essence only.

"That's good Mum," she intoned, without disturbing the rhythm of her eating, her thoughts more about her father.

Affinity's thinking meandered, one moment about Summit, the next about her tiffanys, then about Essence; while Summit's mind was glued to the tice call he'd received from the warders; and Wraith's deliberations were about which morsel to consume next. The silence didn't last long, with Essence deciding to stride the gap of hesitation, and tell her father what she planned. She swallowed the last of her mouth full, rested her forearms on the table and looked at him.

"Dad," she said cautiously, wishing he was more approachable, and when he promptly looked up, there was no alternative or escape, she was committed.

"I'm making an appointment with a Pavs agent," she declared quickly, then stopped abruptly.

Affinity smiled at Summit, the gestured designed to demonstrate her awareness of, and support for Essence in the matter. Summit lowered his eating utensils, looked into his daughter's eyes, thoughtfully. Her announcement brought Wraith to halt too, not because he was flummoxed but because he guessed what his sister was referring, was adultish.

"Are you sure you understand all the implications of that venture?" Summit finally asked.

Now the matter had been broached, and her father's response had been dispassionate, Essence's self-confidence grew.

"Well, it's got to happen sometime, so it makes sense to commercialise it," she could hear herself being repetitive

"Yeah, but. There's a vast difference between losing it with someone you like, possibly love, and you like being with, then losing it to some rich, probably old bastard, whose lecherously and addled brain lacks the slightest respectful thought. No doubt he'll be ugly, even obese, who'll need a permit to enter the jot, and who'll climb from his gutter to find some polluted pleasure, in penetrating a jayone virgin."

Affinity felt Summit was still not finished and was compelled to intervene. "Essence doesn't deserve that Summit," she snapped "There's a right way and a wrong way, to go about enlightening her, and positioning her to make an educated decision about going ahead, or not."

Summit stared at for a moment, glanced at Essence, and returned to his meal. He could do without this at the moment.

"What are yous talking about," Wraith splurted, his eyes flashing around the table.

"Essence wants to sell her virginity," a consolatory Affinity said.

Wraith, like all twelve-year-old boys knew the theory but the reality had him guessing, "What's it worth?" he demanded before anyone could short circuit his participation in the conversation.

"Quarter kilo of gold," Essence said expecting that card to trump all qualms and objections.

"Sugar sis! Sell it!" She now had her brother and her mother on side.

"Who said it must be a rich old bastard, it could easily be a handsome young rich bastard," Affinity suggested.

"Handsome young rich bastards don't have to pay, nothing like quarter kilo of gold anyway," Summit countered.

"Well, there's not many free virgins any more, if you want one you've pretty much to pay these days," Essence said, drawing on peeral conversation.

Summit, however, was still fathoming, and while Essence appeared to have adopted a immature and academic view of natural human evolution, he could only see an unsavoury grub sordidly interfering with her; and making the ultimate intrusion into his daughter. He gazed at her; the image he pictured was not nice.

"It's not a matter of a rich old bastard or a young one, but any man who's prepared to pay that kind of sum for a virgin, is warped; because it's not about the sex, since a virgin is a tentative and innocuous thing, whose inexperienced means she lacks the capacity to contribute anything exhilarating to a sexual interlude. So it's about something else."

Affinity had had enough, already, again. "Summit! Don't you understand Essence doesn't need to hear your version of what goes through the male brain, and if you can't give her good, sensible, balanced, untainted advice, bloody well shut up, until you can. Her event will be closely supervised, and while some of her pre-conceived images will turn out to be mistaken, a balanced preparation will ensure any adverse effects will be minimal, and easily dismissed."

Essence felt the discussion was becoming a parental affair, and she wanted to stop that.

"I know what goes on, I've seen holograms, not animations, I've watched holograms of virgins being screwed by older men. I'm not afraid, I can deal with it," she announced looking between her parents.

Essence had leached the impetus from the discussion, for the moment at least, as Summit looked at Affinity and gave the hopeless shoulder shrug of surrender. He leaned back in his chair and when Affinity appeared to agree, he turned to his daughter again. "All right Essence if you've made up mind, okay, but I want to be kept up to date with what you're up to, and if you've any worries or hesitations, you must promise to talk to me."

"Thanks Dad, I will."

"Can I sell my virginity?" Wraith demanded, his wide eyes darting about.

"Maybe, one day," Affinity mused.

"Not until you're big and strong and grown a lot more hair, by which time you'll probably have no virginity to sell, anyway" was his father's summary.

Chapter 14
The Confrontation

Enamour strode towards her front door, staring at the red and green terrazzo, her mind circling her intentions to confront Maxim, and resolve the stalemate which had set-in after he learnt of her pregnancy; while she had responded by retreating into the comforting cocoon of her pregnancy. Uncharacteristically she'd found lassitude a source of bliss, not wanting tomorrow bothering today. Finally, her sisters had helped convinced her there was only disadvantage awaiting Maxim's initiative, as it would likely undermine her negotiating position.

She looked up as the front door swished aside, and she stepped indoors. Normally it was reassuring to be at home, hers' and Maxim's private space, the nexus of their love but now with their relationship threatened, tension hung in the air. As she walked through the house her resolve stiffened, though she still had no clear vision how best to broach the issue. She'd defined some ground rules, and she'd not resort to criticism or blame Maxim for refusing to fecundate her desperation, but neither would she abide criticism, suggestion or insinuation she bore any guilt. Her conscience was fine, and she'd castrate any attempt to disparage her morality. She would not raise her voice nor retort in kind.

For all her planning and determination, her approach to the lounge room found her balking, thinking another time could be better. At the last moment she was apprehensive, but why? Could her subconscious be undermining her after all, was she vulnerable and sensitive to criticism; had she dismissed Maxim's uncooperativeness prematurely; perhaps she'd not accepted her baby's furtive paternity? No, none of the above, she had simply avoided the inevitable discussion, until common sense could no longer be circumvented. She loved owning her pregnancy, and felt no hurry to share it but had awakened slowly from that refuge, knowing her baby needed a family. That would include a father figure, and obviously Maxim was the overwhelmingly and favoured, and maybe only, candidate. She could see her little girl at the centre of the family, adored and loved. If only it was to be a daughter but she wasn't going to know until its birth.

Maxim would be home already, likely reclined in his usual chair, so when the door opened, he was there as expected. She paused in the doorway; Maxim looked up, stood up, and after a moment, moved towards her. Enamour recognised the look on his eyes, and her apprehension drained. They both, it seemed, had the same plan for the evening, and there was to be no frustrated or fatigued lovers' spat, but a mature parley, between intimates wanting a resolution. Her tactic had been the right one, and now with Maxim's brooding ostensibly over, all was to be all right.

Enamour leant against the doorway, relaxed, a private smile spreading from her lips, excited by a swelling reassurance and remembering why she loved him. Because he loved her! She wanted to dash the last steps to him and sink into his arms but she was enjoying the expectation too much. He arrived but paused before reaching her, failing to gather her into the embrace for which she now longed.

His face was stone but his eyes gems, Enamour surrendered, and the instant she stepped forward his arms opened and she fell onto his chest, to be clutched tightly. The sound of his breathing by her ear, the touch of his day's whiskers on her forehead, and his familiar scent, all in the cradle of his strength, rendered her wanting, precious, and feminine. Then his grip slid down around her waist, he leant back to gaze at her, and still without a word kissed her lightly on the lips. Enamour took the back of his head, her passion inflamed, and they bonded in an exchange of erotic essences in a tongue tango.

Her abrupt emancipation from segregation was the touch paper to her pent aspiration. It was more than a month since their last intimate tryst, and almost two months since she'd expeditioned. That event she recalled daily, and although the memory remained vivid, its ghost was unable to fend off her accruing hunger. She had wondered if pregnancy and desire were bedfellows, and while probably not later on, her incessant but suppressed yearning now flowed, and in his arms, she longed to be submitting abed. Instead, Maxim loosened his hold, eased away, then taking her hand led her to the couch, to sit. He sat beside her without touching her, while Enamour lay back on her elbows, her legs provocatively enticing him to take advantage.

"No Enamour! I'm anxious too, but first we need to talk about us."

"I know Maxim but let's talk later, let's do first things first," she urged.

"No En, I've been mulling over our relationship for weeks, and I've come to some decisions which we need to discuss. To start with, I have to say I had no idea you needed this so badly, nor did I appreciate that at your core, having a baby was fundamental and absolute, as apparently it is for some females. As we know hind sight's only usefulness lies in its capacity to benefit the future, and while this outcome has disappointments for me, I now know you even better, and love you even more than before; I think.

"I'm awfully sorry for ignoring your desperation until it was too late, although I did not ignore you as much as I failed to recognise the irresistible force which drove you to have a baby. I think probably I wasn't listening, because the prospect of a female as beautiful as you getting pregnant was crazy. Now you're pregnant elsewhere because I was blind to the truth, and the only excuse I have, is that jot females use surrogates, and I thought no further.

"When you told me you were pregnant, I was bewildered, and I can't remember much about my thoughts. I don't think I was angry; I certainly wasn't pleased, neither was I dismayed, or even disheartened. I didn't hate you or resent you or feel betrayed, just stunned and desolate, lonely and bewildered.

"Inevitably, when the truth settled, I felt wounded and hemmed in by the cheating I perceived, but still I couldn't imagine life without you En, and I knew from the outset, I'd end up accepting it. However, I deserted you to suspense far too long, maybe because I wanted to hurt you, and that's probably another truth, but I know now there's no gain in fretting. Sometimes dispirited lovers hurt each other but it's tragic if revenge poisons their misunderstanding. In empathy love will survive suffering, but revenge is fatal, and I didn't want that."

Maxim bent down and kissed her knee, then looked up. "I'm sorry if I've hurt you, Enamour, my love."

Enamour sat up beside him and put an arm around his neck. "I wasn't hurt too much Max, as I was happy being pregnant, and I'm glad you've accepted it because I want our little family united and growing together, and when we added to it in a few months it will even more complete."

Maxim wasn't sure about the collective noun 'we' and wondered if 'more complete' was a tautology. "There are still some subjects and sensitivities I'd like us to consider, to help me to adjust, before I'm lured to rethink or reassess."

What! Enamour had assumed too quickly Maxim was ready to resume their relationship and their formal life, but abruptly her eagerness was called to account, and she was desperate to keep afloat, what had been launched only minutes ago.

"Well, I don't want you rethinking or reassessing Maxim," her voice echoed disaffection.

"I know En, and it will be okay but I'd need a few emotions put to bed

"I'd like you to love me first Maxim, the taste of your lips moistened me, and I can feel you inside. It's been too long," she said, hoping quenching her thirst, and his, would not only divert his thoughts, but would move his mood to amenability.

"En!" he said firmly, "you're not listening. I think I'm entitled, and I know your game

"And what game's that?" she demanded.

He smiled knowingly, "You're hoping after half an hour's seduction, I will have been blinded to your duplicity," he explained unconvincingly.

He knew her well but unperturbed she decided to leave his deduction dangling. "Half an hour!" she exclaimed, her eyebrows feigned surprised, feeling he was in retreat, "I'll barely have warmed by then. My mind's more on two hours."

He smiled, her ambition amusing, but he was not to be waylaid.

Neither was Enamour to be corralled. "Where's Justice, when will he be home?" she enquired, wanting to know how much time was available for inducement, manoeuvring and for the jaunt, for which she was impatient.

"He's at Disoso Park with friends; they booked a spot a week ago; I thought he told you."

"No."

213

"That's probably because you haven't been a part of this family for a while, my dear Enamour; he must have been uneasy about telling you."

"So, you told him he could go, without talking to me."

"As I said," he said, with a slight shoulder shrug.

"What are they doing there?" Enamour turned more towards him, her eyes demanding.

"Digging a hole, what else can they do there."

"How big?"

"One by one by one point, I think."

"Nearly two metres deep. Maxim, that's ridiculous."

"It might sound big but they'll probably not dig that far, since there's only four of them, and they've only booked for two hours."

"What is it about boys and digging holes, I don't understand it."

"It's not only boys; there are always some girls there too."

"Not many, and they're the ones who want to be boys, anyway."

"Why would any girl want to be male these days, especially those growing up in the jot? And with the age limit at the Disoso (Dig some soil) being fourteen, the girls mostly disappear well before that age anyway. Between ten and twelve and puberty's advent, sees most girls gone but an odd one or two keep digging a bit longer."

"And they're the ones who grow into ballsie females, and of whom we'll always need a few," Enamour conceded. "It amazing though just how popular digging dirt is, because whenever I pass the park it's a hive of heads of youngsters and holes and heaps and hoes, all hueing a hollow, which is filled-in overnight," Enamour observed.

"I like it, it's important developing adolescents' interaction with nature, especially the earth. In an age when almost everything is manufactured, artificial, imitated, governed, manipulated and predictable, and our environment excludes most things natural, by covering, coating, plastering, concreting, painting, laminating, plating, sheeting, mining or shrouded agriculture; digging dirt is wholesome. When the young are able to grab handfuls of earth, have dirt grounded into their knees, and have thrown dirt in their hair, they are happy, and it often releases them from shyness, inversion, and can help instil confidence, Maxim maintained.

"And when the remnant geneses are only found in few garden parks,

214

they regarded so valuably that human activity within them, is all but prohibited. Where can a child or youth climb a tree? Our evolutionary circumstances, explains why the Disoso's escape from egotism and pretention, is so popular with formative aged adolescents."

"You're overrating its importance Max but I know they seem to have fun."

It occurred to Enamour, however, her pregnancy will position Justice much closer to reality, than will any hole digging. He'll discover babies are not ordered, and when ready for delivery would be, picked up from a clinic; and instead, he was going to watch his sibling grow in his mother's belly, and although he'd probably be denied the visual trauma of birth, that decision will be made closer to the time. As well, he'll discover the source of a baby's first sustenance, before its synthetization and mechanical delivery.

She wondered if he'd want his friends to see his pregnant mother, or would he believe her apparent eccentricity needed privacy, or would she become a learning experience for the local youngsters? Would her familiarity in the neighbourhood cause any dissention, and if so, how much; and at what stage would her pregnancy stir silent whispers at social tat-a-tats; would the whispers foster confrontations? They were all considerations Enamour had contemplated before the event, and none bothered her, especially as she mindfully ticked off all those folks who had a relevance in her life. She felt inferior to none, was intimidated by none, nor felt the shadow of any.

"And Justice and his friends are practising for a competition," Maxim continued.

"They're what?" she enquired unsurprised.

"There's a competition at the end of each month. They are entering the four-boy section, for the quickest team to dig a hole two by one by two."

Enamour felt overloaded with extraneous information but accepted she did not quite understand, nor wanted to understand, Maxim's contention.

"Did you let him take the transporter?" she asked.

"Yes, why not?" Maxim was curt.

Enamour's shoulders drooped noticeably, and she looked at Maxim painfully, "He's only ten Maxim and you know I'm not happy about him driving himself at that age. It might be legal but he's still too young. I think twelve, even thirteen is young enough," she complained.

"Nothing can go wrong En, you know that, his tice ignition authority restricts the transporter to juvenile lanes and those lanes go where he's gone."

Enamour ignored the reasoning, "I don't like him being so independent at his age, I suppose. Not for a while anyway."

"I don't think he's too young to nurture some independence. It's not as though he's about to leave us or anything."

Enamour's urge to argue faded when she realised there was already amble potential for conflict between them, without introducing this issue.

"Enamour, your pregnancy's made me to examine our relationship as never before, since it's never been assailed like this before. I know I opposed your pregnancy but going external and arranging an alternative without warning me was unnecessary, probably underhanded, and undoubtedly unethical."

Enamour sat up straight and listened guiltlessly but she was not about to argue, even though she believed he was, or should have been, aware of her determination, despite his claims of being hoodwinked.

More, there were further reactionary feelings he needed to exorcise. "Emotionally, morally, academically, theoretically, technically and any other 'ally' you can think of, I should be incensed, hurt and disappointed; I should feel betrayed, deceived and cheated. Logic says I should have scoured my recollections for all your defects and assembled a tally of flaws sufficient to have inspired revenge," he said gazing at her for a moment.

A sense of obligation persuaded Enamour to continue patiently but she stared not seeing, hearing but not listening, prepared to accede to Maxim's need, and perhaps deserved to have his price acknowledged. She hoped his expressions of grievance, and self-ingratiation, was his release and the preamble to their re-bonding.

"However, every time I wanted to hate you, or leave you, my mind froze and the vision of emptiness frustrated my deliberations. For a while I wanted to hate you, I wanted revenge but it never made headway as an option because it kept striking a wall of affection. In the end En, fear of life without you is the axe you wield. I just love you, it's that simple."

"I'm not sure about your metaphor Maxim but you're making me very happy," she said smiling, still transfixed but leaning back in the lounge again.

Maxim looked down and shrugged a little uncomfortably; Enamour was quick to react, siting up again, she took his face in her hands and kissed him on the lips.

"I love you too Maxim, and thank you, I don't know what I've done if you'd taken the other option. I love you too."

Maxim was relieved and happier now she'd listened to him, freed from asphyxiating melancholy, he was delighted too, to let bygones be bygones, and already he sensed the driftwood floating out of sight.

"I'd never appreciated I loved you so much En, or knew you were so fundamental to my life, or that the threat of losing you could be so frightening. So now I'm happy to, accept your child into our family, but don't be upset if from time to time I show some fragility towards your expanding figure." He paused, then continued tentatively, "unless you'd consider starting again with our child."

Lightning struck, Enamour was incredulous.

"What do you mean?" she demanded, her gaze piercing, he'd startled her again.

"Start again with my baby?" his voice lacked conviction, even apologetic but he had to ask.

Of all the possibilities to cross her mind, this had not been one of them. The suggestion was quaking and alien, the implications repulsive and the aftermath distressing. The only entity which was ever going to passage her birth canal was already ensconced to her uterus and nestling in her heart, and there was no conceivable circumstance or claim, which could bring that under review or discussion, or consideration, let alone, fact. Maxim knew from Enamour's expression his piteous hope was hopeless, and his best strategy now was to close the damper on her irritation.

"No, Maxim, under no circumstances!" her voice was clear, the message unambiguous.

He was peeved slightly and was not going to be dismissed so adamantly without commenting, "It was just a suggestion En, and I don't think it was unreasonable since I am your reba, and a partner in this family."

For the first time in their discussions Enamour was seriously annoyed, and felt a warm flush rise from her neck. After weeks spent fruitlessly trying to convince him to contribute his half to her pregnancy, he now belatedly sought to have her surrender the success of her struggle and start again. She glared at him but only briefly before falling victim to his obvious disappointment, and her anger melted. She wished conviviality's return, and while she'd appease him, she'd not expose her flanks.

"Maxim, I believe what you've said about your feelings for me. You've been lovely considering everything, and while I love you too, I want you to know, my pregnancy and this baby gazumps everything else," she said touching her stomach. "I hope very much you can live with it."

"Yes, I realise that En but there was no loss in asking, and if we are going to have another child you cannot blame me, even at this late stage, for wanting it to be mine," he said, "Nothing ventured, you know that. I'll accept the situation though honestly, I've still some animosity but since your position is non-negotiable, I've no alternative but to consign my miscalculation, to the amnesia of time."

He was still a little unstable but Enamour shrugged it off, content to wait, confident he'd emerge from his tunnel of doubts and confusion, into the light of reality and would become accustomed to it. Besides, she felt his trough was about drained, and this could be the moment to turn his thoughts to her earlier postulations, and consummate their reunion.

"Forgetting about it could be a strategy which works for you Maxim, but it won't work unless you first accept it. I hope you can do that." she said, eager to sign off on the subject. "What time will Justice be home?" she asked, her tone humdrum.

"He's been gone nearly an hour, so another hour, I suppose," he said glancing at the HIP (Household Information Panel).

"Set your tice Maxim to alert us when he encodes the transporter for home, and to warn us when he's five minutes away."

Maxim too, had had enough of the bog, and although relieved of the torment, some unease lingered. If he had thought about it, he would have realised Enamour had given him nothing, not even an expression of disappointment, he'd unfortunately missed out. The concedings had all been his, and ultimately the victim of her beauty and charm, and his love.

However, having emerged from their bunkers Maxim felt refreshed, and found himself gazing admiringly at his creature of beauty, but seeing her now in a brand-new light. There was more to her now, more than the gentle female of delicate purity he had adored for so long. Their affection now had a guttural edge, her pedestal was gone, her fragility immaterial, and her mischief had abruptly emancipated his obligation to propriety, and roused his excitement at the vision of fucking a wench. Her capacity to impersonally fall pregnant to a stranger revealed an unforeseen, and surprising dynamic he wanted to taste. The situation was rejuvenating, and surprised him by how quickly his perception of her could change. Even more bothering was how much he still felt for her. Bizarrely, she was now a more complete female, and his imagination was scheming a pathway to her salacious euphoria, and his libidinous grandeur.

"I've never fucked a pregnant female," he announced jovially, their strains seemingly securely stored.

Enamour stood up, tall, and looking down, "Haven't you? We'll correct that anomaly right away but I'm only just pregnant, not enough to make any difference, does that matter?"

"Not at all, we'll get there in a few months" he replied with a smirk, while it occurred to her, he might be kinky after all. Okay!

Although Maxim had spent a solitary month, now in retrospect, his rather easy modification should not have surprised her, and what was potentially a chasm, had been merely a rut.

"Maxim, I need you to make love to me, or I'll settle for a rollicking, as long as you hold out until I've finished, which might be quickly or maybe take a while, but definitely more than once"

She continued to surprise him, this time with her blunt options. She had always been exciting and often a mysterious fornicatrix, sometimes a princess, sometimes cute, a lassie, wanton, luscious, even vixen, most often lover, but until now, never a strumpet, or republican.

Enamour stood, stepped around in front of Maxim and took his head in her hands pulling his face into vesuvius. He took hold of her waist, opened his mouth wide, mouthed vesuvius, and poked his tongue into the light fabric. Without regard for his intrusions, she dragged the fabric clear, up to her midriff to which Maxim's tongue darted into the vacancy, while wrapping his hands around her backside and pressing his face into her ladies. Still holding his head, she lay back against his grip, shuffled her feet further apart, and arched vesuvius at his tongue.

Enamour felt her weeks of seclusion had been a positive period for pregnancy awareness, interrupted only by minor bouts of nausea, but unconsciously they had left her sensually insolvent. As a result, her initial ambitions had been perfunctory but now with Maxim's tongue igniting genuine petitions, she began to appreciate just how rapacious she'd become. She felt a rapidly rising current of impulses and imperatives advocating for a vigorous excursion into an emotional discharge, with bursts of euphoria, sufficient to leave her depleted, and in the comfort of calm contentment.

She lurched involuntarily at his face, then again, this time deliberately, and again, and cleopatra alerted for the impending journey. Enamour's eagerness escalated each time cleo was reached but then his tongue was missing and she looked down frowning. Maxim sensed her urgency, and knew it was time to be more than just a face in her belly, so he stood gliding his fingers over her pussy as he rose. They stared at each other talking silently, a moment spent acknowledging each other's expectations. He pressed caesar against her.

"Well, you can't do much with him in there Max, better get him out," she suggested, not too concerned.

"I won't be needing him until later," he countered.

"Good," she replied knowingly. "It's nice the way you always know me and do the right thing. Don't hurry", she said softly, the smiling stage of their encounter was passed.

When Justice arrived home Enamour was refreshed, and when he entered the room, he looked at his mother relaxing in the chair, and dashed towards her. "You look happy, mum," he smiled wrapping his arms around her neck, and sitting across her knees.

He was gritty and grubby and smelt rather but for Enamour his enthusiasm for her was the only reassurance she needed to end her day securely embedded in her family unit again. While her psychic absence seemed not to have effected Justice, and with Maxim consummated, the joy now, was in the prospect of her family being four.

"Did you dig to the bottom of your hole," she asked releasing him to look into his face.

"Nope. But we will next time."

Enamour pulled him back to her chest, her arms around his back.

"Easy Mum," he complained, attempting to wriggle lose.

She freed him enough until they looked at each other again.

"Justice I've some news for you, which I hope will make you happy," she announced firmly, her eyes smiling.

His expression eager, his patience fleeting.

"What mum?!" he demanded.

Enamour patted the seat beside herself, wanting to sit. He did, quickly without looking away.

"What is it mum?!"

"It's good news Justice, and I'm very happy and I think you will be happy too."

"Well?"

"We are going to get a baby, Justice," she paused watching his face which turned curious, "which means you'll have a brother or maybe a sister when it comes."

More information was Justice's reactionary thought. "Which one, a brother or sister?" he sounded urgent, his gaze enquiring, the totality of the announcement needed downsizing.

"We won't know until it arrives."

With the reality registering, his thoughts were beginning to enquire, his mother's news was inspiring, but returning to the question of gender was his focus. "Why don't you know if it's a boy or a girl?" he asked.

"Because we won't find out until it's born, then we'll know."

"But everybody knows what they're getting, don't they?"

"Not everybody Justice, some families don't, and we don't want to know."

Now he was confused, since whenever his friends were told about a future addition to the family, they all knew its gender straight away, so why didn't they.

"Can't you find out?" seemed the obvious next question.

"We don't want to, Justice. Aren't you happy about it?" Enamour understood his confusion, and was wondering how best to explain the difference.

However, Justice wasn't struggling as much as Mum thought, and as he began to appreciate the practicality, and realised his line of enquiry was revealing nothing, so he'd change track.

"Does your surrogate know?" he asked, looking enquiringly at his mother.

"We don't have a surrogate; we don't need one." Enamour had decided to answer his questions as directly as it had been asked.

"Then how are we getting a baby."

"Because I'm having the baby, I'm our surrogate."

Justice knew there was something unusual about that, it wasn't normal, because he'd never heard of mothers having babies, it was the surrogates who had the babies.

Enamour pulled him into her chest again.

"Don't worry Justice dear, you'll understand. At the moment the baby is very tiny and growing in my tummy, so there's lots of things for us all to see, and learn, in the coming months."

Justice pushed himself away far enough to look down at her tummy. He couldn't see any difference and looked back at her. "How do you know there's a baby there," he asked, acute curiosity now dominating his mind.

Enamour knew where this question-and-answer session was leading, and was unsure how to answer the ultimate question.

"Because I went to the clinic and was tested for a baby," she lied. "You must be hungry Justice, let me order your meal," she said, easing him off her lap and standing up.

Chapter 15
Caught

Summit's anxiety had merit, his subconscious the source, but glib denial justified his wondering, why the warders wanted him. The previous evening's tice call had been brusque and despite asking, he was given no inkling as to the reason, or allowed any manoeuvring room. Instinctively he wanted a delay, allowing him time to make surreptitious inquiries about the matter, as he sensed a need to discover if he should be bothered, should devise some explanation, or require an alibi. There were associates in the Division whom he could rely on for information but the demeanour and tone of the caller left no doubt the appointment was concreted and compulsory. It had unsettled him but he'd comply, since he certainly did not want warders calling at the office, thereby risking his directors becoming aware of the matter, be it serious or spurious.

For the interview he had dressed down somewhat, both in attire and makeup, choosing to restrict his presentation to enhancing his natural colours, rings only for jewellery, and he donned a casual fitting blue and yellow striped one-piece set, with high collar.

As Summit walked towards the Warders Division Building his gait was a sturdy amble, and his air of nonchalance was self-persuading he had nothing to worry about. He looked up at the three-storey building, the one of his destination. Almost at the entrance he paused still gazing up, at its four, glistening blood-coloured pillars spaced across the frontage. Between them, rising glass facades continuously screened a meandering and fraternising display of chrome colours. It was appealing, Summit thought but the distraction was fleeting as the weight of the moment began descending, and he understood what Julius Caesar felt beside the Rubicon. Neither Caesar nor he, knew what the future held, but the difference lay in the fact the Roman crossed voluntarily, whereas his crossing was compulsory. He stared into the entrance, shrugged, straightened, and strode through the entrance of shimmering blue vapor, into the foyer.

Once inside, the outside hubbub faded, and the energising light of the morning sun was supplanted by the sterile and shadowless glow from concealed sources. The ambience was insidious, even menacing, and suddenly his dragooned self-confidence became a cryptic rear-guard. His suspicions were foreboding, and a reality was jolting him from irrational pretence, into accepting the inevitable. He was well aware of an occasion, an incident, and an endeavour gone awry, which could probably explain his his attendance, this morning. Although he had thoroughly researched and planned the incident, and been aware of the potential for accidents, he had foolishly pursued his goal, even when he knew it was foolish.

Mentally shaking down the plausible, Summit strode deeper into the foyer, aware two hologram figures were primed to come alive and annoy him, so as usual he gazed steadfastly ahead, determined to ignore them. For a moment, it seemed the couple might be inanimate today but no, having almost drawn abreast, they suddenly came to life, with Now-Now breaking into a smile, "Good morning, Summit, welcome to Protection Division 7B and thanks for being on time."

Summit increased his pace but her eyes followed him, "Summit we note that you have not responded to the survey with regards to amendments to the beauty specifications. Can you attend to it shortly?" she asked.

Summit stopped, then turned slowly to the couple and lifted his eyes, looked at them and snapped. "What survey?"

Now Nog-Nog came in, "Summit, it's disappointing you have failed to cooperate with the survey. It's not helpful to fail to have an input, and then complain if you dislike an outcome."

"The one about caesars being measured and classified, you mean."

"Yes," she came in again.

Summit paused, "Well if you start making caesar size an item for assessment, then by the same measure, vivians should be appraised too."

"What's the correlation?" Now-Now demanded.

"Simple, females want long thick dicks, while males like bottomless, tight vivians. I would've thought even you'd realised that! And, what's the circumference of cocks or the cosiness of pussies got to do with beauty. They might be important physical attributes, but they have nothing to do with beauty, unless you're considering allowing ugly pricks, with big dicks, into jots."

"Please respond to the survey Summit, where your viewpoint counts," Nog-Nog said closing the matter.

"You are expected in interview room 13, which you'll find by turning right at the end of the foyer. Investigators PW1 and PW 17 will join you there when the room notifies them you've arrived," Now-Now informed him.

Summit turned from the holograms, still annoyed but privately grinning about his suggestion, for which even the artificial intelligence did not have an appropriate come back.

The back of the foyer was another glass wall also oozing with chrome colours but it was the side hallway and the sign above it, "interview-assessment-interrogation," which revived Summit's unease.

Now well inside the snake's mouth, he decided that before venturing further into its viscera he'd cast aside his recent trepidation, subpoena an assertive stride, and regain his unassuming demeanour. His walk to Room 13 was along a stark white hallway with engineered silence, but no signage, another unsettling and designed tactic. Doubtless he was being scanned by several types of monitors, which would have detected his anxiety.

Without warning there was a whiz, a blue light doorway appeared in the white wall just ahead, and a voice abruptly announced he had reached Room 13, "please enter and take a seat," but Summit was not to be rushed. He looked into the blue light entrance but could not see through, then he glanced from whence he'd come, and then to the other end of the hallway, the delay allowing him a few moments to ground his confidence. Satisfied, and with a sudden urge to confront the threatening, and have the matter resolved, he stepped through the blue light.

Once in the room than the blue light vanished, leaving him uncomfortably vulnerable and at the disposal of protection warders. The room was more white, stark. Almost immediately another blue light entrance happened on the opposite wall but Summit remained indifferent, looking at the empty desk, the two chairs on one side, and on the other side a lonely third chair, which he assumed was his. Two warders materialise through the light, gazed unsmiling at Summit, but at least their expressions seemed passive.

The dress code for the Division warders was conservative, even old fashion, these two in grey with fine yellow stripes, sheer fabric, shapeless, two-piece, mid-sleeved, broad collars and neck lines open to mid-chest; blemish concealing makeup, and jewellery only earrings and finger rings. Their hair, short cut, of natural colour, one of them with it curled, the other slicked down. Both bore tices on their arms. They said nothing, rather signalled Summit to sit in the lonely chair, while they moved to the other side of the desk and made themselves comfortable.

By the time they were comfortable Summit was well seated and scrutinising his adversaries. The chap with the short curly hair sat back, puzzling Summit as to whether his role was to sit back and supervisor, or sit back and learn. He was the younger one but his superior body language, and detached ruse suggested he could be the man to watch, and of whom to be wary. He looked at Summit cavalierly, with unfocussed eyes, and when his companion learnt onto the table squaring to Summit, he looked distractedly at the far wall.

The match was set, the antagonists ready, and Summit stared across the table at a pair large brown eyes rigid in their sockets, quizzical and seemingly with a plan. His eyes were tactical, and Summit was ready, returning his gaze with equal obstinacy.

"Thanks for coming in Summit, I'm PW1 and my partner is PW17. The matter we need to explore is a serious one but we hope it can be settled promptly. Information has come to our notice which requires us to discover if you are in any way responsible for wilfully injuring another person. It's a significant offence which could have severe consequences" he said, and paused hoping the atmospheric gravity of his words would be coercive, and help expose Summit's albatross, if there was one

Suddenly his cerebral choreography cleared, his suspicions vanished, the incident was vivid, only the upshot remained mysterious, and he felt insecure. For the moment he contemplated the two enemy faces on the other side of the table. Furtively he scorned them for not identifying themselves by name, and decided to correct that insult by bestowing them names. They came quickly, Snail and Slug, he decided suited them. Snail was the older one, with curly hair who was leading the questioning; while Slug still laid back in his chair, and was likely mulling for his vulnerabilities. Summit worried his covert hostility would have been detected by now, and programmed by the scanners, so he tried to relax.

Slug nonchalantly turned and duly fixed his gaze Summit, a device employed ineffectively, Summit thought, but still, his scrutiny was palpable.

"This is how your interrogation will work," he announced inoffensively. "We will ask you questions, and while your verbal answers will be recorded, your physiological responses will also be monitored by the scanners. This will allow the assessment algorithm to signpost lies, fabrications and other deceptions, as well as record your emotional reactions. Deciding whether or not you're guilty, will be determined by the Judgement Academically Determined and Penalty Specified algorithm, commonly referred to as Jadaps.

Slug paused, looked down, rested his elbows on the desk, looked up and fixed his gaze again on Summit again. "There are three ways of proceeding from here. The first, is you can submit to a full contact dynamic interrogation; or second, you answer questions without the tactile recordings, when you'll be scanned remotely; the third option, is you to say nothing but we'll still ask our questions, and your physical, emotional and physic reactions will be metered remotely and assessed. Do you understand?"

Summit was not to be hurried into agreeing to anything so early in the encounter, certainly not until the accusations were detailed, and not until his mind processed his predicament. He needed to position himself so he could levy some influence over the interview.

"Before I say anything, or commit to anything, I'm entitled to know why I'm here," he said aggressively and self-righteously.

Their glares flinched not, nor did their expressions falter.

"One, YCFM Brilliance, lies unconscious in hospital suffering from what was apparently an overdose of a mind-altering substance."

"Shit."

"No, poison. And we need to discover if you were instrumental in administering it, or partly responsible."

Snail stared mutely, neither he nor Slug budged for the moment, a pause Summit took to reset his composure. He needed to, since his fears were materialising. Summit ignored the accusation. "How is she?" his enquiry genuinely but his interest was mainly of self.

"We don't have a prognosis, just a condition report, and at the moment she's stable."

"Good," he said deciding any further enquiry could be reckless.

Snail continued: "Now you've been briefed on the situation, I expect you to cooperate, so the matter can be determined quickly and simply. We need to discover the extent, if any, of your culpability for the female's poisoning, and to this end, you'll need to explain how traces of your DNA are connected to her disorder.

So, this is the process: now, we are required to outline the interview options. Second, we'll explain how the algorithm will process the interview, decide if you have a case to answer, and if you do, it will decide if your guilty or innocent, and if so, then it will specify a penalty. When it's all over you will be provided with a tice transcript of proceedings, as Jadcaps recorded it but it will not detail how the decision was reached, but it will give a certainty factor, which can be important. Neither will it reveal what factors determined the penalty.

Slug took over "So which interview method will you agree to," his tone hinting at impatience.

Summit glanced at the ceiling his deliberations overt. However, he realised he was being asked to make a decision about something of which he still knew very little. Sure, he had a rudimentary understanding of the system, of law enforcement and the humanless judiciary but with Brilliance unconscious in an infirmary, he needed to measure and calculated every step, and needed more information.

"I need to know more about the process, because presently I have only a sketchy concept of the differences, and I have no idea of the implications associated with the different interview methods."

Snail attempted to mask his frustration but when he eased back in his chair Slug saw his cue to come forward.

"This is the situation," he announced.

"The program initially records your answers to questions with either a plus or minus but then adjusts its readings according to your physical, mental and emotional reactions. In other words, if it deduces you have lied, either blatantly, or given an honest but incomplete answer, or your answered is tainted with a diversionary emphasis, it will amend the score.

"It also divides the questions into three rating; critical, important and periphery, and as you would expect each category has a different influence on Jadaps' final result," he paused and looked at Summit questioningly.

"Go on, so what bearing do the three types of interviews have on the outcome." Summit asked beginning to grasp the modus operandi.

"Jadaps is not the final arbiter in deciding a verdict, nor are its penalties binding. Anyone with considered good cause can appeal Jadaps ruling, and petition the social court to review it. To have a Jadaps' decision overruled, the litigant must show that Jadaps misread, or mis categorised an answer, or misinterpreted a question. There are no other grounds for appeal. Jadaps' readings of physiological reactions cannot be disputed, except in rare circumstances," Slug paused but before he could continue Snail moved forward to continue.

"The point of the three types of interview, is to allow the interviewee some discretion to choose which ever they feel most comfortable with, however, the system is designed to encourage potential defendants to undergo the most intensive process, the one which requires you to be physically connected Jadaps.

"If you are found guilty using the first method, and you unsuccessfully appeal that verdict, you are then liable for an increase in penalty. When Jadaps deliveries a finding it will also give a percentage of certainty.

"If the certainty factor is, say, 95 percent guilty, and you decide to appeal, then a second guilty verdict would see a 50 percent increase of the penalty. The lowest certainty it can give for a guilty is 85 percent and a Jadaps decision this low, if appealed, would only incur an increased penalty of five percent, for a second guilty verdict. Any certainty factor below 85 percent always comes back as a not guilty.

"Without going into all the details of the other two interviewing methods, if you were to mount an unsuccessful appeal against a 95 percent guilty decision following a remote scanning interview, the penalty would be doubled, etc. The big difference with these less efficient techniques is that we, the warders, can appeal a not guilty verdict. Admitting an offence reduces the penalty and Jadaps considers mitigation, provided you submitted to a questions and answers algorithm under scanning.

"The procedure is designed, firstly, to encourage your fullest involvement and secondly, acceptance of Jadaps decision. It has proved an efficient way of establishing the truth, and very rarely does the social court overrule Jadaps.

Slug continued. "The program is a big leap forward from the old jury system, which regularly fell victim to to human foibles and eccentricities and peer pressure, returning incorrect verdicts. Juries were suspectable to a hypnotic and silken voice championing a convincing but conniving case. Flashy talk, fancy clothes, kindly faces, agreeable manner, ignorance, prejudice, simple mindedness, and failing concentration, often had more sway on juries, than did facts.

"If a guilty verdict was delivered, be it dubious or dependable, the sentencing was blighted by inconsistency, sometimes bias, the artefact of a sanctimonious judiciary, who are comatose in a conviction of their superiority and intellectual infallibility. Preeminent and above government, this self-endearing, aged clique, found justification in high bench pontification, and their perceived responsibility to preserve societal order, and morality. Unfortunately, often their aspirations for society were not aligned with their constituent, but being infallible believe; 'If you don't know what's good for you, we do!'. Thankfully artificial intelligence is immune from these bogus notions, distractions and persuasion, and with its meticulously researched and carefully crafted parameters, it produces just justice.

Summit wasn't confused but neither was he confident he'd understood all the implications but still, he had a sense of the objective.

It was Snail's, now you see me, now you don't turn, "What we are required to do at this point is to read you the State Law. There's only one law and it's very simple, leaving no opportunity for argument or debate, and in my experience it well and truly covers all contingencies.

"It states: 'It is an offence to: do, or allow to happen, or negligently cause to happen: any damage, potential damage, or loss, or potential loss, to any living being, property, organisation or institution. Do you want me to repeat it?"

"No."

"The law now is very simple, there's no reams of gobbledygook, no discriminatory palaver or hierarchical jargon, and no loop holes for the vanity of the semi-intellectual legal mercenaries to exploit, or with which to extort clients. This law finally includes the one thing which has been missing from our justice system for time immemorial. Common sense!"

"As we said each question we ask is ranked, according to pertinence, and are either critical, important or periphery. For example, if I asked you your name that is periphery, because while it is information we need, it's not relevant to the outcome or findings. An important question would go like; 'did you see the male attacked', which renders you a witness, not a person of interest; while a critical question would be something like; 'did you send a threatening message to the victim', which means we want to know if there is a direct connection between you and the incident.

"While Jadaps leaves little wriggle room when dispensing justice, the ranking of questions is one area where disagreements sometime occur, and an inappropriate ranking can affect a verdict. Most successful appeals alleged incorrect question rankings."

"Seems straight sailing," Summit said though his thoughts had strayed to other matters.

Suddenly it was all over, for now. Snail sat up and announced, "That's as far as we go for now. You have been informed of your situation, and been briefed on the procedures and processes involved. Now we must allow you five days to consider all matter relevant to your position, and prepare any submission you consider relevant and or helpful. We'll see you next week, same time, same office, when we'll seek the truth"

Summit had not expected it to end so abruptly, certainly not before he had been quizzed. He had not even nominated an interrogation method. The announcement filled him with relief, fresh air rushed into his mind, and ignoring Slug and Snail, he unconsciously sprang to his feet, paused a moment, then defiantly walked from office 13. While he was relieved to have escaped the inquisition, his disposition was decidedly more dejected than the ominous mood he had borne into the building an hour earlier. When he arrived, he had been circumspect, now he felt surrounded, and the view ahead was equivocal and depressing. Anxious to escape the building's oppressive ambience, he scarcely heard, and blatantly ignored his farewell. "Thank you for attending Summit, we'll see you next week, same time. Please respond to the survey."

Now he was angry but kept striding towards the shimmering blue light doorway, aware any retort would be unsavoury. He stepped through the blue light into the late morning sunlight, and suddenly nature's warmth, and the open sky began eroding his depression, the radiance causing him to stop and face to the sun. The sounds of the everyday clamour helped the soothing.

Stilled, he let the ultra-violet do its work, restoring his sense of normality. While superficially his stress waned, beneath his sorry circumstance a White Pointer lurked, and then there was his family, which comprised a rotisserie of neurosis, flowering sexuality, and annoying adventurism. Plus, there's the extended family and in-laws, likely to indulge in a flow of innuendo, insinuation, patronisation and cynicism. Summit knew his dilemma would have a significant effect on his family's lives, and life style.

Chapter 16
Essence Acts

By the time the gang gathered for the evening's meal Summit had made arrangements for the following week, and now his thoughts circled the quandary, wondering whether to break the news to his cohort now or fob it off until later. Some other time would be a dodge but in view of his day so far, it was a comforting alternative. However, his duty was probably to enlighten them forthwith, plus instinctively he liked difficulties confronted sooner rather than later. This evening he'd confess all, well probably; not all!

That evening a premonition hung in the air, and only Summit thought it was his sensibilities which were the root of the phenomenon. Conversation was sparce and when Essence's call announced the meal and they sat to popping up screens, no one seemed too interested in the day's data.

While Wraith was the least perceptive to something impending, he was astute in detecting the evening's cheerless vein, and characteristically let all and sundry know he'd noticed.

"All right, what's going on, why isn't anyone talking," he demanded.

All eyes went to Wraith briefly, then glanced at each other, only Wraith lacked a tale to tell. Essence wriggled in her chair, rested her arms on the table, straightened her back and eyeballed her family briefly, one at a time.

"I made an appointment with a Pavs lady this afternoon," there was the hint of apprehension in her voice, and as she glanced around seeking approval.

She had Wraith's full attention, his face eager in anticipation, Summit, otherwise distracted was unsure how to react, and preferred to avoided the issue, if possible, while Affinity suppressed the urge to divulge her calamity, and responded appropriately.

"Good on you, Ess, tell us about it," she said smiling broadly at her daughter.

"Well, I was pretty nervous about going in, so I asked Pensee to come with me."

Affinity interrupted. "Why didn't you ask me to come with you?"

"I don't know, I just decided to do it, and since I was talking to Pensee about it, she just ended up coming. Anyway, it was rather simple, she asked me about my alphaspection, wanted to know if I'd talked you guys about it, and she told me to bring a parent to my next appointment, in two weeks."

Summit's paternal instincts overcame his reticence, and he looked at her with an accepting smile; Wraith's unquenched fascination wanted to know, "Is that all?'; while Affinity stretched over and stroked her daughter's cheek with the back of her hand.

"That's good sweetie; just remember if you have second thoughts you can back out at any time, don't be afraid of that."

"Yes, I know Mum but that won't happen."

Silence descended momentarily while the four delivered some sustenance to their digestive systems.

Affinity rested her hands on the table, leant back in her chair, flicked unnoticed glances around the family. She stopped and stared at the middle of the table.

"My news is not so happy. I went to the clinic this morning about these bloody tits of mine, and they are not happy with them. Neither am I. The lumping is not normal which I could have told them that; but any way they did a biopsy, the result of which will be available tomorrow. Also, a skin scraping was taken so I don't know what's going on. I wasn't told very much but I'm sure they're worried the situation is serious. I just feel like crying."

"Let's not worry too much Affinity, at least not until the test results come back. I've never heard of a breast disorder which can't be corrected," Summit felt duty bound to say.

"Summit," she snapped staring at him, "I'm sick of you telling me not to worry, as everything can be fixed, because sometimes it can't, and it doesn't make me feel any better you nagging me with that all the time."

He was in no mood to respond, fed up with her, he returned to his meal and let the matter pass. He'd never before felt anxious in front of his family but he was now, as he prepared to unfurl something significant, which unfortunately his family needed to worry about. Wraith, however, saw an opportunity to contribute.

"It'll be okay Mum; they'll fix you up."

"I hope you're right, buddy," she consoled optimistically.

Essence could not think of anything constructive or encouraging to say, so silence prevailed but Affinity knew something was going on with Summit, and she sensed a revelation of discord was coming. Impatient to have it out, she stared at him unblinking, a tactic she used to niggle him and coax a reaction. Without acknowledging her gaze, he felt her reproach, and the volley of arrows being pitched at his guilt. He swallowed the food in his mouth, wiped his hands in the serviette, quietly drew a full breath, grasped his knees, sat up and looked up.

"I have a situation," he announced.

Satisfied she'd silently inveigle him into disclosure Affinity relaxed, feigning disinterest, and looked down at her meal. Knowing her suspicions were confirmed, she would remain silent but brace herself for whatever it was, which was to hurt her.

"What situation," Essence asked anxiously.

A few nights ago, when I was at the club there was an incident when someone was injured, rather badly as it turns out, and since I was present the protection warders have interviewed me about the matter."

Affinity's disguised apathy had a heart attack, and a familiar trepidation invaded her.

"Was it a descent female or just another slut?" she demanded resolutely, despite the presence of her children, her composure only just managing to contain vulgar disgust.

Summit looked at her, then glanced at Essence and Wraith. He preferred not to go into detail, especially now but Affinity's motionless set, and her obvious potential to explode, left him few alternatives.

"Yes," he said off handily, his tenor couched to infer his guiltless position, and therefore no apologetic or defensive inference was required.

"Yes, what? Slut or not," she spat, her eyes widening.

Essence and Wraith shrunk into their seats, glancing at each other and exchanging knowing smirks. Affinity needed no more information, her experiences and their history meant she could fill in the details. Now, for the sake of her children, and her own sanity, she allowed her surging rage, and the vitriol poised on her tongue's tip, to drain away.

"Whatever trouble or problems you have, keep them to yourself Summit. We're not interested, so don't bring them home to this family," her response was measured.

Summit fell thoughtful, he didn't want the problem brought home either but it had a momentum which inevitably would knock at their door. He looked at Affinity, hoping at least for a touch tolerance but her unblinking signal clearly indicated there was none on offer.

"I don't want to bring my problems home either Affinity, but this one will come home anyway, so I think you all should be forewarned," he said gesturing with up turned hands, his idiom for eventualities beyond his control.

"I attended and initial interview with the warders today, when I was given details of their interest in me, and the procedures to be followed and next week I'm to undergo a full interrogation to determine my part, if any, in the incident."

Affinity realised her antagonism was pointless, something she'd known from the beginning but after all their years, she still found it difficult not to react angrily to his betrayalor delinquency. She calmed, let her feelings sink but was still annoyed by the humbug and embarrassment she foresaw. "It's a shame we don't have jails any more," she said, but Summit aped disinterest, even nonchalance.

By the time Summit passed through the blue light door again he had accepted he was in serious trouble, theorising the warders would not be conducting such a thorough interrogation if they did not have substantial incriminating evidence. Everything about the previous interview suggested they were comfortable with his culpability, and there had been no indication they considered him a mere witness.

As he passed through the foyer, he was again given instructions but he just turned to them "Bloody DNA," he splurted, having concluded the warders had located some somewhere implicating. The holograms were unaffected, and kept delivering their instructions, finishing by reminding him he had still not completed the survey.

The investigators were the same pair as before, as expected. Summit was pleased about that since their assigned pseudonyms imbued him with a sense of seniority. He wanted to call them 'Snail' and 'Slug' but knew there was only detriment in antagonising them.

He sat in the same chair and Slug sat opposite him while Snail began taking leads from the black box at the end of the table. "Have you decided on a tactile interview or remote scanning," Slug asked.

"Tactile, since it puts me in the best position, should I need to appeal," he said hoping to make it clear he was not going to be easy, whatever the finding.

Slug acknowledged with a head nod and turned to his screen to prepare, while Snail attached a transmission contact pads to Summit's temple, and another to his inner arm. He handed Summit an old fashion card on which a phrase was written.

"Just read this, it allows Jadaps to calibrate a number of aspects of your physiology including voice cadence variations, variations in blood pressure and body temperature and activity in the body's neurological pathways, as well as some other features which I don't really understand."

Summit took the card, read the text to himself, glanced at Slug then Snail, bemused, turned back to the card and read aloud, "Attempts to deceive Jadaps are readily identified and will registered all negative aspect to your answers. No guilty interviewees undergoing this inquisition have avoided the temptation to deceive or mislead. Delilah managed it."

Slug watched the control panel for green lights, "It's happy," he announced.

He went to his chair and sat, joining Slug, fingered his tice to life, opening the case notes.

"Now, all we need to do before we delve into the incident proper, is for you to identify yourself, we need your code and name."

"BGTGM Summit."

Slug began outlining the details of the matter under investigation. One YCFM Brilliance, was unconscious in hospital, having allegedly been poisoned with what has been found to be ERG29F, a drug which is normally very difficult to obtain. It is a tightly controlled, mind-altering concoction, used exclusively by Jadaps to administer corrective sentences to criminals, convicted for violence. Never had a convict sentenced to a dose of ERG29F be known to re-offend, rather they go on led a quiet life in a dunville. However, it was a sensitive drug which required patient analysis, and careful calculations before use. Any quantity destroyed brain cells and change personalities, and in this case the warders wanted to establish what damage the administrator of the drug was expecting, who did the administrating, what was their objective, and was the outcome as expected.

It was illegal for anyone outside the judicial regulatory regime to dabble with the substance. It seemed likely that whoever had administered the drug to Brilliance, had made a miscalculation, and while a motive for her assault was a mystery, there was no doubting a third party was involved.

Summit could come up with no other tactic than to try to stay calm, remain stress free and answer all questions honestly, as an innocent person would. However, he was tethered to an instinct to examine possibilities, strategies and find a way through the predicaments, which was going to be difficult. He tried to relax anyway, letting his shoulders sink slightly, and thinking about how to stop thinking, in the end only coming up with 'what the hell?' as a solution. Surprisingly that thought relaxed him a little.

It was Snail's turn: "Can you tell us where you were eight nights ago, and detail your movements from dusk until two a.m.?" the grave issue, was at hand.

"At the Jayrave Cudgel, in a private room, from about mid evening."

"Apart from yourself who else was there?"

"One of my fellow board members of the Pregnancy and Surrogate Board, YCMM Arrant, two office managers both YCOMs, Raft and Craft, and Brilliance another board colleague."

Slug and Snail looked at each other, "Raft and Craft?" Slug exclaimed.

"That's right," Summit confirmed, poker faced. The matter was closed.

"That's only five people in a room at Jayrave, it sounds extravagant for so few people."

"Yeah well, I wanted to turn it on for the night."

"Why so?"

"Well," he paused in contemplation. "I don't know about this. But Brilliance and I have never got on, and we've often been at loggerheads, and recently she lodged a challenge for my position as Bustohe of the Pregnancy and Surrogacy Authority While I believe I will ward off her sortie, there is always a chance I may not. With this in mind I decided to approach her with a view to establishing an improved rapport and negotiate a mutely beneficial arrangement, which, I was hoping would leave me in situ for a couple more years, at least. In return I was going to offer to hand over to her at some point in the future without her having to mount the challenge. Knowing her weakness for a certain type of indulgence I used that bribe to entice her out for the evening, to discuss her challenge but unrealistically as it turned out, the hope was in vain."

"Why would she agree to a night with you?"

"It was not just with me, she wouldn't have agreed to that but because she uses more cocaine than she's legally entitled, she found the invitation to a night out with associates and coke supplied, too enticing to refuse. I knew that at the end of the month she'd be looking for more, so I timed my approach accordingly"

"Did you exploit her vulnerability, then?"

Summit thought about that for a moment, either answer had pitfalls.

"In as much as I expected an opportunity to negotiate with her, I suppose I did. But certainly, in no other way."

"Did you have that discussion with her?"

"No, it became obvious very early in the evening my plan was flawed, and I had little or no opportunity to achieve anything."

"Why not?"

"Because initially she was interested in cocaine only but soon after her appetite for carnal hijinks ignited and her appetite was substantial. She just wanted to snort and screw."

"Did you join in?"

He paused, "Yes, everyone did."

"How long did this activity go on for?"

"Which activity, the snorting or the screwing?"

"Both."

"It started and stopped but overall, about three hours or a bit longer, I'd guess."

"That's a long time for one female, did YCFM Brilliance object to any of the attention being paid to her," Snail asked.

"Drop the YCFM and just called her Brilliance. But no, it wasn't continuous I said that. She was keen, and she set the pace and kept encouraging everyone to join in, and I kept her fuelled."

"What do you mean?"

"Cocaine. That was her fuel."

"When did it end?"

"When she fell, asleep."

"Well, was it sleep, or did she fall unconscious?"

"Well, she laid down; I thought asleep but I can't say, I suppose."

"Laid down. From what you've been telling us she spent the evening lying down, what was different about the way she laid down to go to sleep?"

"Most of her fun was not horizontal, in fact hardly any was."

His risqué insinuation was ignored.

"I can assure you Summit, she may have been asleep for a period but she was unconscious when her Bahs raised the alarm and summoned an ambulance, just after one a.m.

"Okay."

"Her Bahs reveals she had been asleep for seventeen minutes, before she was poisoned and the poisoning which triggered her alarm. Now, what we need to know is what happened between the time she fell asleep and the time her Bahs was triggered."

"Nothing, the others left when she collapsed. They'd all had enough and needed no encouragement from me, but I waited awhile to make sure she was all right. I must admit I was a little concerned for her, especially after everything which had happened during the evening, particularly the amount of cocaine she's had."

"That is interesting because whoever administered the ERG we know did so between her falling asleep, and becoming unconscious. You're either lying or omitting Summit, which makes no difference to us, because Jadaps knows the truth. Honesty is the only thing which can help you now," Slug pointed out.

Summit wriggled in his chair, Slug and Snail in contemplation had fallen silent, a tactic he suspected was a deliberate unsettling ploy, before confronting him with an inexorable scenario. The double act continued this time with Slug coming forward, while Snail eased back in his chair.

"Summit," Slug started solemnly, and paused looking at him closely, "An admission of responsibility in this affair would curry some benefit for you in sentencing; as Jadaps is programmed for sentence reductions for admissions," again he paused hoping a moment of reflection would encourage Summit to confess, what otherwise was expected to eventuate anyway.

Summit took the moment to reflect, and while the suggestion made sense, he was not yet quite ready to surrender, not at least until he knew how much they knew.

"What's your next question?" he questioned. The pauses between questions and answered continued, then Slug presented an opinion

"I don't believe you had any intention of having a discussion with Brilliance that night, because it's an unlikely venue for a business meeting, and of those people partaking in the degeneracy, you would be the only one, with the influence and contacts to source ERG.

"I believe the episode was a well-planned contrivance of yours, calculated to immobilise Brilliance, and eliminate her as a threat to your position. It's apparent your plan did not turn out how you schemed, with the damage to Brilliance ending far worse than you expected. We think you sought to impair her IQ to below 100, but you ended up reducing her to 58, causing her mental retardation. It appears her copious intake of cocaine aggravated the poison, something you probably failed to calculate, causing her collapse into unconsciousness Would you like to comment on any of that?"

"If I'd asked for a business meeting it would not have happened, as I said, that's why my inducement had to be something different," he chose not to comment on the accusation or his responsibility.

Slug chose not to pursue it, instead he changed tac.

Snail took over in an apparent change in questioning, "Did anyone have anal sex with her?" he asked casually, then looked up from his tice.

A fresh flush of apprehension caused Summit to pause, while his mind struggled in a haze of thoughts. with the one becoming prominent suggesting his troubles were about to worsen.

"I don't know," which was not the truth but was the only strategy he could devise.

"Did you?"

Summit had come to the end of the blind alley and there was no escape.

"No," he snapped, and his resistance drained.

"We know that, because an examination of the victim shows that sodomy was not part of the evening's indulgences, but!" he hesitated to allow their eye contact to refresh, ""However, her anus was interfered with, was it not, Summit." Snail eased back confidently, pleased he was about to deliver the final blow.

"How do you know that?" Summit muttered, caged.

"The medical examination of her revealed, two foreign elements in her rectum. First, there were remnants of the capsule used to introduce the ERG into her, and the second was a trace of DNA, your DNA. You Summit inserted a capsule of ERG into her rectum, causing her the degradation, and we believe you did so after the others left the room. Do you have any comment?"

Suddenly Summit saw a ray of light, or was he a drowning man clutching at straws. "How can you be sure her damage was the result of the ERG and not the cocaine? She'd taken so much, it could have easily been the coke," there was no spring in his voice.

Slug's eyes narrowed and his stare hardened. "Let me assure you Summit the examination and diagnosis of YCFM Brilliance was thorough and conclusive. Do you think this interview would be taking place if there was any suggestion cocaine may be responsible for her condition?"

"No," he snapped.

Summit had felt the narrowing conduit of inevitability all interview, and now all which was left, was for the trap's door to slam shut. The thud was jolting. After several days of apprehension, thinking about what he should have done, scheming rationally and irrationally, hoping for an alternative explanation, cursing, regretting the absence of a soul mate's consolation, and occasionally realising he had little chance of hoodwinking Jadaps; he was not unhappy this part was over. There was relief and an opportunity to sluice his head of the accumulated dead brain cells, an absolution he'd enjoy by allowing his mind to hover in blankness.

Now a transcript of the interview would go to Summit's lere who had 48 hours to examine it, negotiate with the warders if he considers any of the questions incorrectly ranked and if a satisfactory resolution could not be agreed with them, they would apply for arbitration by a social court mediator. In the meantime, the final draught would be submitted to Jadaps to determine if he caused, or negligently caused, or allowed to cause, any damage or loss to person/s or property. If the determination is in the affirmative Summit will be assessed again by Jadaps which will adjust his sentence according to the credits or debits found in his character.

Some one hundred questions are asked on a screen to which he will answer verbally, and once again his physical reactions will be monitored and recorded and assessed by Jadaps. Jadaps will want to know such facts as: was Summit ever oneJay; how long did he hold that level; what rating is he now, how long has he held that, was his reba ever a oneJay, how long did she hold it; what is she now; does he still expect to have a jay rating in five years, ten: what programs is he undertaking to maintain his jay rating, what about his reba; what ages are his children; are they in the hands of justjays; if his parents were ever jays are they still jays; if not how old were they when they moved to dunville; what avenues have you pursued to remain a jay?

Other bracket of questions asks such questions as: do you believe the specification for onejay is too low, do you believe there are jayfour people who should have an r-rating, should r-raters be allowed into the jot with a work permit, should pregnant females still be allowed in public after dark, do you believe Nog-Nog and Now-Now play an important part in maintaining beauty standards, do you listen to their advice, do you think their advice is good advice, do you act on their advice?

Jadaps also wanted details of his work and its contribution to the beautiful society, and in what other ways does he contribute to society?

When Summit completed the character analysis questionnaire he relaxed back in his chair, and having allowed a blasé attitude to infect him, had come to two decisions; firstly, the assessment was bollocks, and whatever sentence Jadaps had determined so far, he had now effectively seen to its doubling.

Chapter 17
The Folly

Summit lolled back on the wide footpath bench, then slid down until his outstretched arms rested along the back rail, as his gaze slowly swept the buildings on the opposite side of the street, from whence he'd just walked. It was the Warders Divisional Headquarters the hour he'd spent there was destroying. He looked up, and let his head fall back until he stared into the tree tops spreading from the park behind. The sight snared his attention. It had been a long time since he had stepped aside from the contrived, to appreciate the organic, and in melancholy his mind drifted to his mortality. It dawned on him these trees would still be swaying to the breeze, when he'd be dust beneath. At least then his troubles would be ended but why wait until then, fuck, snap out of it; he sat up, learnt forward until his elbows rested on his knees and gazing aimlessly at the ground, he brooded, wondering if there was a path from gloom to pragmatism.

His predicament, like most human plights, was the result of either ignoring an inconvenient obvious, and/or dismissing adverse potential, and irrationally assuming a desired outcome. It was always the result of inaptitude, or foolishness or selfishness; which were never quickly or easily overcome, rarely resolved reasonably, equitably or happily. He had succumbed to inaptitude and vanity.

Lifting his head, leaning back again he took a deep breath this time gazing at the pedestrians on the opposite footpath, some ambling some hurrying; he watched the transporters scooting along the thoroughfare. On the footpath some folks strutted, displaying, the jayones exchanging acknowledgements while ignoring those considered lesser. He noticed that while most pedestrians appeared destined, there were a salutary few merely enjoying life, admiring the park, absorbing the scenery and the fresh air, and were drilling their coronary and vascular systems, while appreciating their environment and of being members of humanity.

However, the scene began to annoy him. The jot was pompous, the class distinctions were exaggerated, and the codifying was isolating. He realised quickly his new prospective was probably the product his dilemma and imminent exile.

Disillusioned, he slid to the end of bench, swivelled and dangled his legs over the end, and again considered the trees. Spring was well embarked and while the virgin greenery promised the youthful joy of the new season, Summit failed to appreciate the message, but he did hear the strains bird chatter. He watched a pair for a while, remembering how as a boy he would have thrown stones at them, then they were gone, one either escaping or teasing.

Out of the blue, Summit's life had been cast deeply into shadow, leaving his contemplations circling his downfall, and rummaging through the debris of his self-inflicted disarray, the result of a struggling hope of maintaining his status in the jot.

"So, this is the bloody beautiful society!" he said quietly to himself, sarcasm infiltrating his dejection, but he moved on quickly seeking fresh light, to a fresh life. He was only now beginning to grasp the gravity of his situation, and understand how his blinkered effort to preserve his status, had brought his downfall. It had been a testosterone fuelled exploit, which had been his stairway to the gallows, and now society had its hand on the trapdoor leaver. At the time, not only did his mercenary and regardless approach to protecting his position seem rational, but he believed his intentions were just an extension of a normal business strategy. This illumination may not yet become his 'Road to Damascus' but the upshot of the morning's sentencing left no debate or doubt about his destiny.

Now, from atop jot's scaffold the horizon was ill defined and smoky, and he grieved his exile from the life into which he'd been indoctrinated; the lifestyle he'd stridently pursued, and remembered how he'd seize all opportunities, avoided pointless endeavours, and goalless undertakings. Until now he'd been a master of minions.

However, regret was counterintuitive, and with another mood swing threatening, he took a deep breath of positivity, determined to bypass pessimism. He sat up, straightened, crossed his legs, and stretched his arms out again, resting them along the back of the of the bench again, then casually glanced up and down the street. This time he noticed people differed significantly, when not viewed with an eye for their rating or social stratus. Their differences became obvious; their presentations, body language and mannerisms, social and generational divisions, dressing statements, fashionable colours, hair styles.

An obviously onejay female bearing down caught his attention, and while she was still some way off, he stared, blatantly, academically, and as she drew closer, he studied her colours, her flashing chrome eyes, her exposures, her life within, her self-pride, and he wondered if she was happy. She oozed confidence, though Summit saw opulent decorum. She possessed all the features which would normally have alerted his libido but today he saw a discerning female, he hoped would look at him. Maybe he should think about Affinity in the same way. The onejay's security radar detected his incursion, and she looked up, logging him as either benign, or did he stirred her pagan impulses, since she smiled? His mind filled with a vision of Essence, who he thought was as beautiful, and who he hoped would finish as sophisticated as this female.

Another approaching figure caught his eye, this time not one of beauty, rather an outsider, an interloper a dunvillain, and male. Despite his impeccable presentation, his portliness, and disappearing chin, were a couple of features which suggested he had never been a jay, but his short legs and unfortunate torso ratio, were his most discernible faults. Dunvillains were permitted to work in jots with restrictions, but then only if they possessed attributes otherwise unavailable. Summit usually ignored them or when confronted, ceded a dismissive grunt; now though he was interested in dunvilles and dunvillains. His insight into dunville life was confined by insinuation and rumour, as well by some sheltered visits to parents and grandparents in their quarters.

R-raters in jots normally kept their elbows tucked, and proceeded defensively hoping to avoid discrimination, and while the approaching dunvillian strode a positive gait, his lowered gaze was a scrutiny shield. He was almost abreast of Summit before he realised he was under watch, and surprised, his head jerked up. Before he could pass, Summit interposed.

"Excuse me friend, apologies for staring," Summit said aware he had surprised the fellow, and with an indifferent gaze, he turned enough to engage Summit.

"I see you're dunvillian, which is okay," his hand flicked dismissively, "and I'm wondering if you've a moment to talk about dunvillains working in a jot?" he asked.

While the chap, corralled unexpectedly, he seemed to recognise the angst of a worried individual, and was sympathetic That was until he noticed Summit's stainless wrist band. The sight of a convict band was a cautionary warning, and his faint smile faded. Summit reacted by raising the incriminating wrist.

"Yes friend, I'm dammed, and my days in the jot are numbered. I might even end up your neighbour. But I hope to continue working in the jot, at least for some time."

Summit held out his hand, "I'm Summit, at the moment a bustohe."

The stranger hesitated for the moment, then responded, "I'm Adieu."

The stranger relaxed, and looking into Summit's expression saw a compatriot in waiting, while a whiff of compassion induced a smile, and incited some affiliation. He joined Summit on the bench but at a stranger's distance.

"Growing into adulthood it took me some time to accept I was a guppy in a goldfish bowl but when I discovered goldfish are, by enlarge, festooned wankers, it became easier," was his opening salvo, and taking the opportunity to tell a jay, albeit an expiring one, what he thought of his society.

"They might have the legs measurements, the tits, the six packs, the ratios and the specified density readings but there're countless skulls of inert grey matter, while some are just vacuums. Unless you jays use less of your harlequin quota breeding colour and shape, and more on intelligence, it's going to be dunvillians running this world in another generation."

Too late, Summit had provoked a parochial outburst, even a diatribe of criticism about his life. However, he'd listen tolerantly, hopeful of some helpful tips.

"But that aside, once you grasp the fact that jays are in many ways inferior, then it's just a case of ignoring their pretentious bulldust, and concentrate on your job." he said, his conviction almost convincing. "It's always a relief to leave this place and return to the common sense, and common folk of the dunville," he said.

"So, what are some of the day-to-day pitfalls you experience working with jays, Summit asked, again.

The stranger looked at Summit wondering if his enquiry was genuine or just befuddled crackling. Or was he just taking the mickey for the hell of it? But accepting that it was serious, "There are good folk and good intentioned folk here, but there's too much flaccid macaroni in the soup, stodgy and of lean value."

It rang true to Summit "Yes, but on a personal level, as a dunvillian do you encounter disrespect, discrimination, demeaning sneers or jeers while you're at work," Summit was disinterested in a point of view, he wanted facts, specifics, anecdotes, incidents, outcomes.

"Yes, well! I'm subjected to the random derogatory slight but not at work, where I'm a research technician in a team setting, and we've all goal orientated, interested primarily in each other as colleagues. I'm a team leader and regarded for my contribution and leadership but I suspect though, in a social setting the interface could be different."

It was another opportunity to expound his prejudice, "Outside the laboratory I find the jot is full of air-heads! The male cranial cortex has roots in their triceps and testicles, while female brains drink from the nectar of their tits and twats," he paused, wondering if his exaggeration was excessive, while Summit accepted the stranger had an attitude difficulty. Unrattled though, he hoped a modicum of flattery might persuade the stranger to be more objective.

"So, you must have special qualifications or some valuable experience which can't be found elsewhere in the jot."

"I suppose so," he conceded, Summit's salutation having achieved little.

"Is your work interesting, or secretive?"

A hesitating stare, "Yes, interesting but not secretive. It's research into bacterial mutation stimuli," he said quickly.

"Right," Summit replied, not comprehending or caring but he felt his stranger was moving into an amenable mood, "are you making progress."

"Yes! I'd like to think so, but for decades the bacteria battle has been protracted, and it will probably go on infinitum, since every time we get ahead, it fires another round of grape shot, sending us back to basics. After all these years, there are still lethal bacteria lurking and mutating."

Summit hoped he'd oiled the stranger's ego enough to escort him back to his anxieties, "I'm been sentenced to a dunville, and it'll probably end up being terminal," he said earnestly and looking intently at the stranger, who smiled wryly, and glanced back at the wrist band.

Summit raised his incriminating wrist again, "Yes, seven years I've been given," he dropped his hand to his lap, "and this band stays on until I've been transferred. My family doesn't know yet, and I've no idea how I'm going to tell them, or how they're react. Not well, of that I'm sure. Especially my reba."

"No, won't be easy, I'd imagine, but as far as living in a dunville and working in a jot goes, while there'll be the odd hiccup in the jot, there's no need to stress, but you'll be surprised by the pleasures you'll discover in the dunville. Of course you know the jot life from the inside, which give you an advantage over the likes of me."

Summit was not ready to dismiss a life time of faith, without some reaction, "Don't mind me being blunt, but, dunvilles are for the old, the decrepit and the ugly," he took a breath.

"And the criminal," Adieu interjected pointedly."

Summit ignored the comment. "Not that I'm saying you're any of them but you don't have the shape for a jot. Surely you must feel, at least occasionally, slightly jealous of those who live here."

"Look about you," The stranger straightened, and swept a casting arm, inviting Summit to behold his jot vista. Transporters hurried, pedestrians obviously moved to various refrains, opposite three warders stood together in conversation, and for Summit the scene was normal, nothing new, nor of notoriety, or even particularly noticeable. He watched closely.

"Take a look Summit," he reiterated, "at all your jays. Don't you notice anything?" he asked.

Summit was bemused, about what it was, he supposed to see, or look for, but in the interest of their casual affiliation, he searched some more. Everything was normal, and everyone seemed about their business He looked at the stranger he'd invited into his day, but was now feeling usurped, and thought their conversation could end pointlessly.

"Come on Summit, tell me what you see, just pick on anything and comment on it?" he implored impatiently.

"Just people going about their lives," was the best Summit could contend.

"Yes, but what about those people?"

Summit's heckles were on the move, and annoyance was brewing, "Just people friend, as I said, just people."

Undeterred and ignoring the implications in the tone, the stranger persisted.

"Look at these people;" again his arm swept the scene, "It's a world of stereotypes, a monoculture of prescribed beauty, individuality sought auspices of caverns. Where's the variety? There's no curiosity in walking these streets, because people are only individualised by the colour of their sprays and stains, and their intimate displays. Look! They're all the bloody same," he said passionately.

Summit had never perceived his world was so tiresome, and although presently feeling endangered, and susceptible to suggestions, he was not ready to truck with this impression.

"Can you see any variety anywhere, male or female? If you have a close look, you might detect those struggling to hold their place in your jot but the pageant is of homogeny, leaving the people struggling for identity. Since uniqueness and eccentricity are stultified by statutory common factors, personality is smudged with exaggeration," he concluded.

Offended by the insults, Summit stepped up to dispute his hyperbole, "All peoples have emphasised their beauty, it's primeval, and mainly it's been on the demands of females. It has included all kinds of perversions for females including: obesity, stretched necks, bound feet, bound waists, white skin, tan skin, large breasts, piercing, small waists, hairlessness; while males have used bravado, sometimes associated with piercings, tattoos and design scaring, to tempt females.

"Historically for both sexes' beauty has required physical modifications and decoration, and that has fluctuated and evolved with eons and cultures. Any beauty, all beauty is only a metaphysical point of view, translated into a mindset, which is instilled, not instinctive. However, instinct plays a part in beauty perceptions, with a female's ability to reproduce, a factor; while males as protectors, and the perceived ability to seed strong progeny, makes them attractive. Since our society imagines, arrogantly, it has attained beauty's zenith, it has entrenched the conviction by specifying, codifying and regulating it. And of course, we've gone a step further by creating jots and dunvilles, separating the beautiful from the ugly."

Adieu had had enough. "When you arrive in your dunville my friend, one of the benefits will be your induction into the world of variation, and a true appreciation of the gorgeous, and hopefully you'll learn to savour authenticity. You might discover delight or amusement in the sight of a wobbling alice, or in a pair of spilling tiffanys. I do. And you might be surprised when interacting with the portly or aged by their stimulating and intelligent conversation, and their convivial company. I'd be disappointed if you failed to find pleasure in disparity, and the absence of the social stresses you live with now."

Summit was finding the discussion off putting, since it was probably highlighting some truths, he'd preferred not to accept. He was losing interest in the topic and the stranger. However, the stranger was astute and sensed Summit's mood change, but he was still intrigued, and wanted to know more about his demise.

"Why have you been banished to the dunville," he asked firmly.

Summit glanced at the chap, initially not wanting to talk but his burdened was increasingly oppressive, and suddenly he wanted to share his anguish, escape his battered self-esteem, accept his guilt, and his blackened prospects, with someone else. 'A problem shared, is a problem halved'. Probably untrue but he related to the sentiment. If anyone was to be the recipient of his spleenal discharge, a stranger was sensibly the target. At least with his insecurities and confessions in a stranger's hands they would disappear with him, and become no more than inconsequential tittle-tattle among strangers. Alternatively, if he sought consultation and relief from friends, his predicament would remain ghosts of his world, in perpetuity.

"I've just been found guilty of maliciously injuring a person, and sentenced to seven years in a dunville, which for a person my age, is for life," he explained matter-of-factly.

"Seven years! When were you sentenced, when are you to be

transferred?" he queried.

"Just now, this morning," came with a resigned sigh, "Yes, Jadaps calculated seven years was appropriate but I've heard of lesser sentences for worse offence."

"You can appeal to the Social Court, you know."

"Unfortunately, jadaps returned a certainty factor of ninety-five percent, which makes the chances of a successful appeal highly improbable, and that would only increase the sentence."

"Well, if seven years is a life sentence, there's nothing to be lost in an appeal," seemed the logical extension, "You don't know, it might be reduced to five years, or so."

"Wouldn't help, it'd still be a life sentence," Summit said dejectedly.

He was keen for more details, "So, what of this person you harmed."

"Bitch challenged my position!" he snapped, but as he spoke an enigmatic feeling gripped him. He felt a gush of remorse, and his description of her as a bitch, tasted bitter.

"It was a female then? She must have been a genuine threat."

"Yes, her challenge was serious, and could well have succeeded, so I took precautionary action but unintentionally it went wrong, not only because of the harmed it caused her but even if it had worked, it would have still been immoral. That's clear to me now."

"What are you going to do about it?"

"What can I do about it?"

"Have you thought about confronting her even apologising? Admitting your culpability, and acknowledging her situation could square you up, and help you come to terms with yourself."

Out of the blue the stranger had turned from obnoxious to obliging, and from being antagonistic to empathetic. His suggestion lit the light on Summit's oversight, and it dawned, he had scarcely considered Brilliance since the incident. Not unnaturally his predicament had been preeminent, and his impulse, had been first and foremost for self-preservation. Now reflective, he looked away musing on his culpability, his mind turning to an unconscious Brilliance, and his senses swelled sympathetically, for her undeserving fate.

He looked up, "It would be the right thing to do, wouldn't it?"

"Yes, it could help you both."

Summit took off his tice and asked for Brilliance's whereabouts. She was at home and her medical profile said she'd been home for two days; her physical condition was improved but her mental impairment remained significant. He turned to the consoling stranger, "Thanks my friend for the talk, I'm going to call my victim to see if I can help her, and good luck with the bacteria."

Chapter 18

Summit vacillated for a week before plucking up the nerve to approach Brilliance. He could not understand why he was hesitant or why he'd picked up his tice a dozen time to contact her, but never finished dialling. Surely, he wasn't frightened of her, or was he frightened of facing the consequences of his idiocy and inaptitude? Was his new found regard for her, and her predicament, a matter of sympathy, or were more sinister motivations sneaking about his cranial cavities? Her reputation was difficult, no impossible, to ignore and her present misfortune may have dulled her moral judgement even further. That was a national socialist thought, which is why he was afraid of it, or should have been. When he called her, she'd been remote, and her conversation estranged, but she had responded positively to his desire to meet her, without hesitation.

As Summit approached Brilliance's door on the top floor of her apartment block, he was nervous, even trepidatious, and especially tentative about the greeting he'd receive. She had been a strong female, a formidable opponent, rancorous if inclined, all characteristics and excuses he'd used to justify his deed. But what of her now? Had the warders exaggerated her condition, had her acrimonious traits dissipated, or worsened, or was she an incoherent simpleton; and while he had no idea, at least now he'd embarked on his mission of conscience, and was hopeful he'd find her better than had been suggested.

"Summit; you've come to see me, how nice," came an unseen voice while he was still some distance from her door.

He recognised Brilliance's voice but it was different, the sharp, self-confident authoritarianism was gone, so was the arrogance and the intensity. Soft, simple and sweet was the new chord and Summit felt some relief. The door slid aside and standing there, waiting, smiling, was Brilliance, causing Summit to pause gazing. She'd retained her splendour, the statuesque full-figured female of before remained but her piercing eyes had changed, their absent virulence replaced with charm, so he thought, or wanted to think.

She looked immaculate, presumably she'd been in the cavern for some time this morning; her body sandstone tinted, overlaid with a soft grey lace patterning. Her tumble weed hair of sandstone was laced with swirls of gold, which was also her colour for her facial. Her outfit was identical in colour as her body patterning and was high collared, with a neck line to her waist but with dewdrop coverage. Summit had always surreptitiously admired her legs, and now they compelled his glimpses again. The familiar adversary of old was missing, instead he saw a warm, even innocuous female, who just seemed cheery, jovial. His guilt burden was easing.

She stepped out to greet him, wrapped her arms around his waist, and pulling him close, and softly kissed on the lips.

"It's been ages since you kissed me Summit, and so long since we've been together," she said, surprising him, since they had never touched, or even been close to kissing, but it seemed the truth about the currency between them was no longer remembered. There had never been any overt, covert or repressed affection between them, although Brilliance imagined some now apparently, and was now anxious to resume. For a few moments he was indecisive, but with his arms automatically about her, her overt passion, and her firm figure firmly against his, she was igniting a new dynamic.

He eased from her embrace, "How are you, Brilliance? I've been anxious to know how you're you are, are you feeling okay? I've been worried about you," he enquired, looking into her eyes fathoming for the extent of her changed.

"They told me you've been a fuckin' arsehole to me Summie," she said assuredly, looking at him with a flickering gaze, "but I don't care 'cause I love you, just the same," she said. She reached for his head and pulled him to her lips again, then broke off and took his hand.

"Come in Summie'. Wanta drink, or somethin'?" she asked impatiently leading the way.

"That'd be nice."

Inside her colourful and immaculate unit, she looked back at him, "Sit there," she instructed in a tgone with whichy he was familiar, and pointing at her couch, while she moved to the food control centre, pushed keys on the control panel and stood back glancing at Summit.

"Wanta modco," she called.

"Not for me Brilliance, just plain coffee will be fine."

"I'm havin' a double," she said, and ordered them.

Summit watched her, enjoying her familiar figure but the female within was a stranger, bizarrely infatuated with him. However, he understood there was an explanation, and the incongruity of the circumstances had his thoughts bouncing about what to do next. He knew what the right thing was but he knew he wasn't going anywhere, for now.

"Sorry Brilliance, I didn't understand, please repeat," the food dispenser called. She repeated the order, her tone exaggerated and aggravated.

"Fuckin' ting, it's always doin' that," she exploded, turning to Summit, "you said ya' wanta jus' coffee, didn't you?" she confirmed, wide eyed.

"Yes. Please, Bril."

She repeated the order and waited a moment to be sure her instructions had been understood, then turned to Summit again.

"I'm havin' trouble lately gettin' tings to work properly. This outfit I'm in," she said lifting her arms in display, "is not what I wanted but it's what th' fuckin' cavern and th' printa giv me," she complained.

"You look very nice, Brilliance," he said, as the dispenser announced one coffee and the double modco were ready.

She looked at him for a moment with messaging eyes, then turned to retrieved their drinks, walked over to hand him one, then stood above him, rapidly sipping hers. Summit was studying her, aware she'd degenerated substantially from the driven and ambitious antagonist she once was, and he supposed he should be pleased. But her persona had suffered severely, and it was saddening. However, it appeared her cravings and drivers remained, albethey, directed differently.

Her modco was gone, its container cast into the nearby trash extractor, she looked down at Summit then dropped onto the lounge leaning into him. Her face was almost against his cheek, and her hand slid around his midriff.

"Hurry n drink ya coffee, Summie."

He took a gulp.

"Got any cee," she asked, poking her tongue into his ear.

"No, Brilliance, I haven't."

Her tongue was gone, so was her arm from his midriff, and she jerked away, "I want some Summit, that was the last of m' modco, which is shite anyway. I need some cee."

"I'm sorry Brilliance, I don't have any."

She sprang upright to the edge of the lounge, her eyes seething, "Well, get me some!" the old rancour was back.

But it was encouraging; she might not be as vulnerable as he first thought, since feeding her addiction was still her price, for the use of.

"How about, if I get you more modco?" he suggested, taking her shoulder and squeezing it lightly.

She grasped his wrist and placed his hand on her tiffany, her demurring eyes smiling, and she fell back into the lounge, "Well, fuck me t'en. Get me more cee later."

Abruptly she was confounding, unsurprisingly considering her behaviour so far, but there were contradictions. His ethical dilemma had a simple solution, but there were oblique perplexities he couldn't identify, not honestly anyway. While the threat she once posed was clearly nullified, was there now any immorality in his talking advantage of what previously would have been impossible? Would it offend his conscience to partake of her offering, knowing it only had an immoral dividend? The thought process was a formality, certainly only academic, since Summit's underlining motivations were characteristically decadent. While he gazed into her eyes, his peripherals were appreciating the rest of her.

"Come on Summie, I wanta fuck! What's w'ong, you' mojo broke!" she barked, and smiled despite her aggressive demand.

Summit surrendered willingly, and without even the pretence of hesitancy, he happily flayed like a fly in her web, devoid of any impulse, inclination or ambition to escape. Any internal righteousness debate had evaporated, as his conscience versus ardour conflict, sank into its final and dissolute phase. He had approached her abode speculatively, superficially sympathetic, and had braced for frost at best but with hostility probable. He had planned, somehow, to couch an apology, then see if he could help her, but the almost unimaginable was now promised.

Had the dark inner sanctum of his disgust been toying hopefully, all along, that her intemperate carnal style had survived.

With his guilt dismissed more or less painlessly, and the prospect of any consequences ignored, his gazing appreciation of her features and allure, was a matter of infatuation. It did not bothe him that his behaviour was unacceptable, inappropriate, and unseemly. Happily, hijacked by her sullied virtue and mysterious appeal, he was ready to step forward and capitalise on the opportunity. His otherwise predicament, and the dunville prospect were in another world, and was going to remain there until this consolation was consummated.

Holding his wrist and watching him Brilliance stood, and with her amble strength hauled him to his feet; and ushered him towards her boudoir, where she cast him adrift in the direction of her cradle. He sat on the edge of the bed awaiting her.

"That's good, Summie," Brilliance said smiling, and kneeling in front of him, eagerly setting about locating caesar, which she examined for a moment, "You've wanta t' fuck me for a long time Summie, now you can," she confided, surprisingly. Obviously, she had a good recollection of segments of their past, contrary to her reminisces about their loving past.

"I was hopin' it'd be bigga, Summie," Brilliance complained, studying the top of caesar's erection, peeping from her fist, "but I can git off, on it 'cause I love you," she said.

Her disappointing discovery could have been deflating but Summit felt he had nothing to be ashamed about, and was sure he could establish his bona fides through performance. But her initial response to caesar made him think. What size did she consider acceptable; how big would be impressive; what was she used to; or was it just her dream; maybe a side effect of her defect? She released caesar and stood up, hooked her thumbs under her shoulders-straps, pulled them down, slipped out of her outfit, and flicked it away with a toe, stood upright with vesuvius in close focus, teasingly hoping Summit would drool. He was too old for that, at least overtly, but internally she succeeded, and caesar too, was pleased.

She leant over, grasp his shoulders, pushed him back onto the bed, then impatiently disposed of his foot wear, dragged off his lower attire, casting it aside. She stood up again gazing at caesar, perhaps frowning, and hoping to promote some improvement, she bent over and with one hand gasp caesar firmly, and pumped briskly. Glancing up at Summit she asked; "isn't there any more, Summie." She quickly assumed there was not, gave up and climbed up, straddling him, and shuffling into position lowered herself, watching her ladies welcome caesar. When vivian felt his arrival Brilliance anxiousness took control, and fell heavily to full depth, paused, closed her eyes and waited for the bliss. Then hoping for more, she stretched her legs wider until the straining hurt but the dividend was too small.

"What the fuck, Summie! How am I s'posed to cum on that?" she sounded angry.

Her dissatisfaction with his caesar was annoying but more so, it was baffling, since when she plunged onto caesar he had touched her ceiling, so length couldn't be the problem. And there was no reason to think his circumference was an issue, as the fit was tight enough, so he thought. Was her natural penchant for antagonism emerging, meaning the ginger of the encounter was the real problem, not caesar? Was she masochistic or sadistic, or was it just characteristic? Were the fumes of anger her pathway to nefertiti? Summit wondered if this had always been her way or if it was new. He decided on another approach, and went to roll her off and over, planning to have her on her knees, then to angrily punch a pounding into her from behind. The instinct was typically his response to her old-time antipathy, and in this situation it felt invigorating. However, when he took her by the shoulders and went to roll her, she countered immediately, sweeping his hands aside.

"No, ya don't, Summie!" she asserted.

She sat on his stomach for a moment, staring.

"Righto," then he lifted her legs, and swung them around until she sat starring at caesar.

But caesar was no longer interesting, and she learnt over, took hold of his leg with both hands, and lifted it up until she held it tightly between her tiffanys. She stepped over his other leg, wrapped her ankles together and arched vesuvius into the base of his leg. If caesar was not big enough, his leg was the right size for her ladies and cleopatra, and she was impatient for her libido to lubricate the fornication. . She pulled his leg up tighter, hoping for even more contact

"T'ats better, Summie," she announced, and she wiggled her ladies well open, until cleopatra was the main game. Caesar and his brothers were irrelevant for now, and it concerned her not, of their whereabouts, or if her enthusiasm injured them or not.

She began thrusting urgently, whipping cleopatra up and down his quad, all the while griping his leg with both hands, straining for more leverage, better spread and maximum sensual connexion. If her eyes were open, they stared unseeing at the opposite wall. Caesar and the brothers had lost interest in the episode, were relaxed, and had taken shelter way below.

Obviously, Brilliance's desperation was grave, and she needed an outcome as soon as possible. It didn't take long, and when the sun of her ecstasy began to flare even her lungs stepped aside to make way. . She tossed her head back, and began raucously enlightening everyone within earshot she was euphoric.

"Fucking, yes!" she yelled "Yes, yes"

Summit watched her back and shoulders flexing, toiling, straining; continuing to lash alice, vivian and company back and forth. He wanted to reach and hold her around the waist but sensed he was not a factor in this event, and any interference would be rejected, likely angrily. His leg was the only anatomy which interested her, so he'd just watched and waited.

Reluctantly and frantically, and too soon, her finale was consuming her, and when the prolonged and all devouring nefertiti began retiring, having fulfilled her physiology, Brilliance's mysticism echoed with hollowness. Although spent and grasping for breath, she continued to thrust, somewhat meekly, at his leg despairing for some sensory ignition.

"Come on, please, come on, come on!" she groaned, straining,. "Come on," then her mania began to build a rhythm again. Her juices and strength flowed back, her core filled with confidence and she recognised there was no hurry. This time there was a journey to be enjoyed. When the vision of her finale usurped the journey's leisure hertempo grew quickly, and she wanted it straight away. Then her flood burst, her head fell back, her legs clamped onto his, and again, she needed to inform the world.

"Yeees, yeees!" and her vocal elation morphed into a series of groans and calls. She pulled his quad higher again, and for a moment froze. Then her head went forward again, the thrusting resumed a wind down, as as a goodbye thank you. Finally, she'd surrendered, slowed, dropped his leg, rested her head on his knee, and paused for some recovery.

Summit was anxious for his turn. While she may have lost interest in caesar, he was beginning to show interest in vivian again. He attempted to rolled her off but at his touch her head sprang up and around.

"I'm not finished," she declared

Back together on the lounge Brilliance took his hand, and held it against her inside thigh, then abruptly made demands.

"You've gotta come and see me everyday, Summie and bring me cee."

"I'd like you to come in to work again, Brilliance, we need your ideas," he suggested hoping to change the subject.

"I don't like t'at fuckin' place no more."

"We need you Brilliance, and I'm missing you," he lied.

Brilliance reacted, sat forward and turned to peer into Summit's eyes, her message understood even before she spoke.

"No! No, Summie, I hate you there. You've gotta come here every day and bring cee when I'm out, and you can fuck me, while I'm happy. Do you promise?" she asked mellowing and resting a conciliatory hand on his chest.

With Summit's testosterone reserve depleted, the light of another truth managed to penetrated his reasoning. His mind went to the threats her irrational and irresponsible honey trap posed, to him, his family, and his career. He needed to excuse away the bothering fact she remained a mine field, but now an unstable and unreliable mine field. Plainly she was neurotic and temperamental, and with her old tenacity intact, the combination was dangerous.

"Well, Summit," she demanded, "are you comin' to see me every day?"

"Brilliance," he paused and looked closely into her eyes, "I'd like to but I can't, not every day, but I could come every few days if you like, and I could probably bring some cee," he said and eased back defensively into the lounge.

She gazed at him from under a frown with her celebrated calculating stare, then she smiled ominously, "Every day's what I want Summit. And you'll come," she said, her hand reaching for caesar, squeezing it painfully.

She was becoming an enigma and potentially a hazard, most of them stressful, all of them fraught, as any contact with her could suffer from her unpredictable mood swings. As well, despite her difficulties it was apparent she could not easily be outflanked.

"Brilliance I'm just too busy," he reiterated, "You can understand that can't you."

Her eyes were talking again, bulging, and locked on Summit, her cheeks rippled to her clenched teeth, and rage wrinkled her forehead. Her fist rose, and her rigid finger pressed into his chin. Through angry teeth, and with a guttural resonance, she served her next volley, "I 'member tings which makes me 'ate you, and I still don't like you Summie, even ya dick's too small," her finger poked deeper into his chin, "If you leave me I'll make you a miserable life."

"I'm not going to leave you Brilliance, I like you too much, but we can only come to together when I've the time," he said, hoping his plea would dissolve her resentment, and taking hold of her poking finger he kissed it.

Her face relaxed slightly, her eyes eased to a squinted, and Summit thought he might be gaining some control of the situation.

"So, you'a gonna turn up, to fuck me up, when you'a 'ard up, with a 'ard on?" she surmised, with surprising insight.

Chapter 19
The Outcome

Chit-chat around the evening meal table had been sparce. Affinity had just received her mastectomy appointment due in two weeks and was mediative; Summit's was scheming to delay his transfer to the dunville and needed to update the family on his situation; Essence wanted a family discussion; while Wraith devoid of any interactive stimulus, focused as normal, on his food. The table information screens were up but no one was inclined to discuss the day's statistics. As the eating began to finish up Summit brushed aside his amenities with a back hand, leaned on the table and looked at his daughter. She felt his eyes immediately and returned gaze, expectantly.

"Essence, you've been fidgeting and shuffling all meal. Either someone's died, or you've something you want to talk about."

She was pleased to be noticed at last, and glanced around to see if the others were paying attention as well. Well, her mother at least.

"I spent an hour with Vestal, my Pavs agent this afternoon and I've all the information about going ahead with it," she announced, looking at her mother slightly guiltily. "I know I was meant to take a parent for this interview but dad was unavailable and you've a lot on your mind with your operation and everything. Vestal agreed to explain the procedure to me, but will go no further until you and dad understand the implications and approve the final arrangements," she explained a little apologetically.

Affinity was not amused, not obviously anyway, "I know that, but even so, I'm sorry you went ahead without me there, I'm your mother and this is a meaningful affair in your life. For me some things are going backwards at the moment, and it would be nice to be part of your life which is moving forward," Affinity explained.

Essence did not want to prolong the conversation since what had been done, had been done. "Yeah, I know Mum. The next meeting will be after I decide when and how it's to happen, and for now that means I need you and dad to help me."

"What's about me?" Wraith protested.

"You're not invited," Essence snapped, without glancing at her brother.

"When's your alphaspection," Summit asked.

"A month tomorrow."

"Shouldn't that be the thing to concentrate on for now?" was his escape route.

"Dad! It was only last week you got my final assessment from Judco, which found I'm definitely jaytwo, with a good chance of a one. So, what else do you expect?"

"Shouldn't you use this last month working on the fine details, the ones which might make the difference between a one and a two. "

Essence was exasperated; the alphaspection had been a major topic most of her life, and thankfully it was soon to end. With her hazy adolescent horizon fading, promising her exciting formative years, the last things she needed, was pointless persistence. Her yearning to escape childhood was compelling, and the frown on father's face was frustrating. She sighed and dropped her hands to the table.

"Dad! I don't know what you expect. I'm doing my exercises, I'm sticking to my eating program," she said pointing to her screen, "nothing can be done in the next month to add a centimetre to my legs or two millimetres to my middle fingers, or bring my shoulders a midge forward, so what do you think I should do. I very much want to become a jap and think I might make it if I'm close enough to be sent for the OBA, but if I only make jil there's nothing I can do to change that in the next few weeks."

Summit had been watching her, off and on, since he arrived home and now opposite him at the table, her regulation dress code had plainly been abandoned, and that too was irritating. She was displaying beyond her age, with too much of her female fleshly features featuring; and seemingly she had spent an hour, or so, in her mother's cavern enhancing her presentation. The only consolation was it revealed her artistic bent and good sense of colour and coordination.

Her long fair hair, streaked with olive and gold swept around the back of her head and returned around her neck and under her chin. Her face colour remained natural with highlighted eyes and lips in olive and gold. She wore dark green lenses. Her body was in a familiar design with the base colour in olive, shaded dark at her feet and fading as it rose up her body. There was some variation in the shading to highlight her femininity, while her whole body was covered with a fine gold lace scrolling. And she must have been at her mother's designer program and printer since her attire did not even hint at being part of the junior dress code. Her stark white seamless shorts, waisted below her midriff from which shoulder straps rose narrowly over her tiffanys before descending down her back to cleavage revealing rear waist.

"Essence the way you're dressed is not only illegal for your age, but if you are discovered it could mean deductions at your alphspection, you know that, and you're taking a big risk not abiding by the code."

There was a second's silence and Affinity joined Essence in staring at Summit, so Wraith thought he'd better too, not to be left out. Affinity was quick to detect her reba's annoyed disquiet but suspected it had nothing to do with Essence, but before she commented Summit was also aware.

"I know," he growled and she looked away accepting his implied apology, their unspoken communication and resolution, the product of their recent armistice.

Wraith was bemused but Essence was not going to let his comments pass uncontested.

"Hell dad, what's your problem tonight?" she demanded, the flush of self-confidence surprising and inspiring, and immediately she ensconced the faculty into her growing catalogue of learnt adult behaviours. "One minute it's my diet or some other thing, now it's the way I dress. I'm in the house, not out in public, which doesn't count. What are you going to say in a month when I dress like this legally and in public? Besides, what's wrong with it, some of my friends are wearing outfits better than this," she said spreading her arms displaying her upper half.

"All right Essence, you're right, I apologise," he said looking down and waving an open hand across his face.

His concession defused Essence's irritation and quickly she seized the opportunity to take the high ground and further test her self-confidence, "I understand Dad, that losing your little girl could be disappointing but I'd prefer you admired the female you've raised, and who'll make you proud."

Summit accepted he'd been out of step but was not going to feel sorry for failing to evolve with her but now he realised he'd been stroking upstream, when it was time to float downstream. Having apparently come to terms with each other they exchanged empathetic gazes for a moment, while Affinity just wanted to guide the conversation back on course.

"So Essence what did the agent have to say, what did you find out?" she asked.

Essence rose from the table and disappeared for a minute, returning with her tice. Pushing aside her mealtime evidence, she placed the tice on the table, and demanded "display pavs info," and she looked up at her audience.

"The thing about it is, the amount being paid for virginities, depends on the girl's rating. Naturally jayones are paid the most. Based on two-quarter stye, they receive 100 percent, jils are paid ninety percent, joks get 75 percent, and jags receive 60 percent. There's no recommended price for Rs who want to sell, Vestal said sometimes Rs can negotiate even higher fees than jayones because they attract clients who want physical characteristics outside jay specifications, weirdos, she said.

"Just great!" Summit spat.

"Shut up Summit," Affinity snapped.

"Like what?" Wraith wanted to know.

"I don't know! Oversize tiffanys, hairy bodies, that sort of thing, I think," she revealed hesitantly. "Of course, anyone can negotiate, so, even if a jayone is unhappy with the standard fee she can ask for more.

"The base price is just for the starter package, where the virgin is available to her client for half an hour, she's naked, only needs to lie down until her virginity's gone, and then it's done."

"Shit," Summit dropped his head; his reactionary instincts abandoning his recent conciliation, his thoughts disgusted by the vision of a stranger on his daughter.

"Shut up Summit," Affinity snapped, fearing another pointless outburst.

Summit grappled for a positive, "It's a bloody good reward for few minutes I guess, and I suppose it's no worse than some skinny, foul mouthed, dickhead kid in the back of a transporter, or in his putrid bedroom," he surmised, his tone resigned.

"You should have more regard for my intelligence and self-respect Dad," she regressed somewhat to the defensive.

Affinity chipped in turning to Essence, "So if that's the basic price, what are extras?"

Essence looked at the list above her tice, "there's a lot of them. The first is an extension to the initial half hour. I can choose to sell further half hours at the rate of point O-five stye or point one-five stye per hour. After their initial foray clients are allowed a second penetration after half an hour, and again after another half hour, but no more than three times altogether. As well as paying for the extra time, the extra sex costs point one stye. So, it's pretty good, because if you sell three hours, which is the most permitted, and I've been screwed three times I've earned a stye. And there's still; more extras which boosts the earn further."

"Jees's."

"Shut up Wraith." Affinity turned an anxious expression to her daughter, "Essence, I hope your agent is outlining the full implications of these commitments, because after your first penetration you might have pain and discomfort, but you're considering having another two, when you might not be in any condition for it. Depending on the caesar size and the pounding you'll almost certainly receive, meaning you'll be bruised, maybe even lacerated, and you could have stomach cramps. These consequences are likely, and even more assuredly when the customer believes he's paid for, and entitled to treat you as a commodity."

"And I guarantee that's exactly the type you'll encounter," Summit chipped in.

"That's why I'm talking about it to yous. However, if I'm hurting at any point and in pain, I can stop it. I'm paid up until I stop."

"And how does that work Essee, because if your client has certain expectations and you cut him short, that's a recipe for trouble?" Summit wanted to know.

"The rules and controls are fully explained to the client before the agreement is finalised, then the whole event is monitored by a chaperone who is responsible for my welfare and will intervene if necessary."

"I'll do it," Summit splurted, imprudently.

"No! you will not!" Affinity flared, "That's the last thing she'd want."

Summit knew as soon as he spoke, he didn't wish that responsibility to haunt the rest of his days. "I know Affinity!" he retorted

"There's nothing to worry about Mum. Parents aren't allowed to anyway, so my agent said." Summit was happy consoling himself in the hope the safety guarantees, worked.

Essence had more, of what she hoped was comforting information, "As well, the agency supplies a mild sedative she which relaxes, makes me happy and dulls any discomfort."

Being drugged before being fucked, made a certain sense to Summit but he kept the thought to himself.

"I'm told the client may want me to pump his caesar, maybe before his first time but especially after the first time, if I decide to offer the extension. That's worth point 0-two stye, so I'll probably agree to that but I've already said definitely no, to having it in my mouth, even though it's worth point two stye. If he wants me to go the full way and give caesar a wank I've no problem with that, since I've done it to a boy already, and it doesn't bother me, but definitely no oral, thanks very much."

"When have you done that Essence?" a surprised Affinity wanted to know.

"Just for a boyfriend," she said dismissively.

"When did that start?"

"I don't remember, a while ago. One thing led to another, and it just happened. I found it amusing, so I'm pretty good at it now, and besides, boys can be insistent sometimes," again she was still dismissive.

"Don't ever let your Auntie Prudence know boys tell you what to do," Affinity said, while Summit kept his ribald thoughts to himself.

Essence was not fussed about detailing her habits to her parents, especially not within her little brother's ear shot, and wanting to move on, "I think I'll agree to kissing, on the condition that if I dislike it, it stops. Again, I've kissed boys and it's okay, but older men might be different."

Feeling isolated in the caesar wanking discussion Wraith saw an opportunity to re-join the conversation. "What's kissin' worth?" he demanded.

"Not much, only point 0-five."

"You could negotiate for more," Summit suggested.

"It's not that important, to me."

"All the same, you're doing this for income, may as well maximise it," his comment cursory, inconsequential.

Essence was uninterested.

Summit slumped deeper into his chair, feeling left behind, out of depth, cumbersome, almost foreign, leaving him uneasy, but still, he knew he needed to remain inside the ambit of fatherly and family participation.

"You're not doing this just for the income, are you Essence? There's something more intriguing which must be driving you," Summit suggested, after listening to her impartial, academic and surprisingly mature approach to her devirgining.

She looked at her father thinking, while Affinity, having been alerted by the question, was interested as well and awaited her response too.

"Yes Dad, you're could be right," she conceded, and fell thoughtful.

Then, "Turning sixteen is a major event in my life as it is for everyone, and after spending my childhood and youth obsessed with the alphaspection, I know it's my graduation and fanfare into a new world. I want to do something outrageous, which is fanciful, becoming customary, even common and doubtlessly memorable, and I see part of my induction including the destruction of my hymen.

I've fought strong temptations, in my bed and against male fuelled palpitations, and preserved my virginity, so now I'm ready for the reward. I think I feel like a beautiful caged tiger or leopard, anxiously pacing, waiting and watching for the gate to open, and after my alphaspection I will dress the way I wish, visit any venue I choose, and indulge any adult substance I want, and I plan to burst into that world well announced."

Affinity jumped in before Summit could be gratuitous, "Well I hope this introduction to your sex life doesn't damage its future," she said casually but her thoughts moved on, "Essence you shouldn't forget you've parents, and the post alphaspection autonomy you're imagining will still be subject to our influence, for another two years."

"Yes Mum, you know, but still everything happening at once. I turn sixteen, have the alphasepction and I'll be free to do all sorts things I can't do now."

"Not totally free," Summit reinforced his reba's advice.

Essence glanced at her father then continued unabated "I will still need you all of course, and I'm still yours, and expect to be influenced by you but you must stop treating me like child."

The conversation had strayed from the one she wanted and was unhappy being reminded that even after her alphaspection her parents retained some control of her behaviour. However, she would press on, "Dad, I know what you're on about, and where you're coming from, I do. While I could lose my virginity ignominiously in a dark corner, and I've escaped a couple of dark corners, thankfully, I want a heralded event, privately of course, and if it takes something different to make it momentous, in attractive surroundings, and for which I'm being paid ridiculously, so be it.

"It's certainly better than having it happen with some quivering, pent up testicle stressed sixteen- or seventeen-year-old, whose sudden and surprising success means he lasts for six frenzied strokes and five seconds to your introduction; up against a wall, his trousers around his knees and your knickers dangling around an ankle," Affinity said, her advice rooted in regret.

"Can't argue with that," Wraith appreciated innocently.

Again, Essence wanted to move on, "There are more add-ons, worth quite a lot if I select them."

"Go on." Summit snapped impatiently.

"If I agree to have the spectacle hologramed the reward is substantial and comes in two price categories, the first is point one-five stye if my face is masked, but if I'm identifiable the price doubles to point three."

"Sick." Summit grumbled.

"If you're going to do it, use the masked," Affinity advised.

"Makes one wonder what sort of male pays this amount for a virgin, when half an hour with a whore, at a fraction of the price, is ten times the

270

fun, than a day with a virgin. And what's the hologram for anyway? Bragging evidence with his equally insipid friends, or will he just keep it for jerking off?"

"Thanks dad!"

Summit brushed a calming hand at his daughter, "No, No, Essence, it's not a reflection on you, you're a beautiful and exciting young person, and I'd be happier if your virginity was lost in company with a nice strong young male, with some experience, who you like a lot, instead of some dottering old fart with a complex problem and riven insecurities."

Essence had a reply, "Yes, age is a consideration but I have choices. If I insist on a male under the age of thirty, the base price is discounted by seven percent, but if he's over forty then it increases by seven percent, so the base price is only for males between the age of thirty and forty."

"What if they're over sixty, or even a mind stupefying, seventy plus?" Affinity asked.

"Not sure, because I wasn't interested, but I think it's almost double."

"Go for it," advised Wraith but his contribution was ignored as usual.

"I've said yes to being licked, because I like it and it pays point 0-five," she said looking again at her tice, "The two positions I must agree to are missionary and doggie, while others can be negotiated, if I'm willing."

"Do you understand everything you're being told?" Affinity wondered, aware of some positions, males can attempt.

"Hell Mum, of course, I've watched it all on holograms, you keep forgetting that."

Affinity did know, and while nothing her daughter had outlined, had been too disquieting, the emerging picture was losing its lustre.

"What else have you got for us?" Summit enquired.

Essence looked back at her tice.

"Ah, anal. That's out."

"What's that?" Wraith was ignored.

"Vestal says some agents sell it because it worth about point three stye, but she's reluctant, and I'm not interested either," she continued studying her tice.

"I can be asked to shower with the customer if the assignment is for at least an hour, and it's worth point zero-eight if I agree to being washed and dried. That's without digital penetration, but fingering pays one-sixth."

"Tell him to bugger off, besides washing and drying are mechanised," Summit grunted.

"I'll agree to makeup and dressing the way the client's wants, and occasionally some clients supply their own cavern program for the work. This does not pay any extra but is just an expression of goodwill, I'm told. However, most clients want us to be natural since makeup detracts from the naivety and the innocence, so Vestal said. Also, the customer can select a venue but the agency will inspect and assess it for operational suitability and security, but the agency prefers using its own venue.

"So, where to now?" Affinity asked.

"There're a few things I must do. The first is a physical examination, to ensure my virginity, but also to assess that once ruptured the hymen will produce bleeding, since in some cases it may not. It seems it's hard to convince a client he's had a virgin if there's no blood, so while any complication can be rectified; it takes a month for the healing.

"While I can have these checks now, I must wait for my alphaspection before contracting potential clients, and finally on the day of the event I must have another examination to guarantee there's been no change to my condition."

"Sounds like it's a couple of months away," Affinity summed.

"Could be. Vestal said lots of virgins are commercialising at present, and it can mean a wait for customers. But if I'm jayone I will sell quickly, as a jil it could take a little longer. It's the lower jays who have to wait longest, while any R happy to sell cheaply go quickest, it seems. However, some Rs have unusual physical features and wanted by males with fetishes, and while they might have to wait for the right customer, the fee can be very high."

"There's Rs and there's Rs, I suppose," Summit observed, pointlessly.

"Yes. It doesn't take much, hairy bodies especially of vesuvius and underarm fetch a good fee, the hairier the high the fee apparently; tiffanys large enough to be consigned to the dunville are in demand, as well as extended dewdrops and large areolas; and fat females, the fatter the

272

better."

Summit "What checks are done on the, so called, clients?"

"He's scanned for disease, also for personality defects, such as mental instability and violent inclinations. As well, he must give permission for his Bahs to be accessed and monitored. I don't understand exactly how it works, but somehow changes in his serotonin, dopamine and other brain chemicals are indicators of a person's demeanour and the potential for sudden personality changes, which is one of the reasons for a competent chaperon's presence."

"How do you safeguard yourself from an abusive buffeting, or being lied on unduly?"

"That too, is a job for the chaperon."

"Have you worked through what you're going to offer?"

Essence paused for a moment, the question had her pondering. Until now it had been a menu, adjectives, options, prices, preferences, possibilities, the approved and the prohibited but now she realised she still had a way to go before accepting the existential implications of her intentions.

"Well," she paused and turned to her tice, "show pav selection."

"You've worked it out already?" Summit asked, surprised.

"No, not really, I've highlighted some ideas but I haven't made choices," she said straightening up, her eyes on the tice display, "Naturally the first thing I'll agree to is that my virginity goes, then maybe I'll agree to two hours, with a second penetration. I'm happy to massage caesar, I'll will try kissing, I'll agree to holograming with a mask, but I might still agree to full exposure."

"I bloody hope not," Summit interjected.

"I'm happy to be licked, and shower with some surface fingering, but I might change my mind about that too."

"I bloody hope so."

"I can't see any point in wanting a client under the age of thirty, since that means giving up a seven percent, and I could be interested in going over forty for the premium. I can't see why age should make any difference. Body shape is of some concern, since too fat, I think I'd reject."

"You'll only get fat if he's an R, and you should rule them out straight away, even jags you should refuse," was Affinity's advice.

Essence was thoughtful for a moment, "Yes, you're right Mum," she paused again, "Now if I come out of the alphaspection a jap, the offerings I'm thinking of accepting amount to one point five-three stye, above the base rate but if I was to agree to an over sixty, I could increase that further."

Summit groaned turning away from the table, "For goodness' sake Essence! You had me on side but you're making it hard."

"You can't be serious about an old bloke, surely," Affinity said disbelieving.

"Why not?" her outstretch hands and wide eyes begged a reason. "A male's a male, a body' a body, a dick's a dick. Why would an old one be any worse than a young one, and maybe an old one would be softer and his energy diminished," she retorted, her self-confidence slightly arrogant.

"Have you thought this through Essence, and realised if he's over sixty he'll be an ugly R-category male, and your first sexual experience could be in the hands of a skeleton, who'd certainly be energy diminished," Summit warned.

"Hell!" Wraith was aghast, sympathising with his father's tone.

"There are many, probably most, over sixty males who look fit and active," Essence said defensively.

"What if he's seventy?" Affinity asked.

"I probably wouldn't accept him, I don't have to take anyone I don't like," she said, growing a touch annoyed.

Affinity turned to Summit, her expression questioning. "Well," she said and paused hoping he would open the discussion they needed to have. "Well Summit, are you happy with what she wants."

He looked into his reba's eyes, thinking, then he glanced at Essence, then back at Affinity. Essence was watching him intently.

"There are two aspects which still concern me. First, what are the chances of it having a detrimental effect on her emotionally; and two, what physical harm is possible? I'm assured, neither threats are real, and since her holograms have familiarised her with the whole affair, and there'll be a chaperon, competent hopefully; so I suppose that allays most of my doubts."

Essence smiled, "Thanks dad," and she turned to her mother for her comments.

"I see no difficulty, dear daughter. I'm sure you're ready for it and since we've talked about it before, you know the biggest problem you'll have with males is not their appendage but their testosterone infused culture, and their caesar-imbued personalities."

Summit looked quizzically at her, where did that come from, why now, and although he accepted her bias, he was surprised she was nurturing it in her daughter.

"We're talking about one incident here Affinity, not the lifetime joyride of sexual delights, misdemeanours, and disappointments, or how they mesh with strangers, friendships, lovers and rebas."

"It's no good looking at me like that, Summit," Affinity quipped, "you know what I'm talking about, as well as I do, and know how quickly males react to the sniff of any perceived female vulnerable or available, legitimate or not. I've warned her, hoping to short cut her journey to the truth about you lot. The very fact that old males, and some not so old, will pay handsomely for virginity, unmasks the gross indecency that infects the decaying mind of some males. It's obvious when males whose licentiousness hovers in their frontal cortex are prepared to pay a premium to pillage a pretty fledgling female."

"Aren't you afraid of inflicting your daughter with a warped attitude, which could affect her capacity to have a fulfilling and rewarding relationship in the future?" Summit asked.

"If Mr Right comes along, she'll know. I'm trying to make her think and assess first, to be sceptical initially, and I see no harm in instilling some precautionary habits in her style."

"Don't worry Mum, I've seen some of their seedy side, and have more than an idea or two about what goes on in their minds. As for the blokes buying virginities, we virgins have the last laugh really, all that money for taking what we're anxious to lose of anyway.

"Essence, it seems you've done your homework, you seem aware of what you're committing to, and you've surprised me with your insight into male incongruity," her father said.

"Maybe I haven't thought of everything and that's why I wanted to talk. I don't want it to finish badly, so I'm listening.," she said, turning to her mother for her approval too.

"Keep your father and me up to date with your thinking and planning, and give me a good warning when your final Pavs appointment is due."

"Can I sell my virginity too, after my alphaspection," Wraith wanted to know.

"If you're still a virgin then, I suppose, but I'm sure you'll lose it to either desperation or temptation, before then," Affinity said wanting an end to the subject.

She straightened, looked around, then at the table, cleared her throat and looked up again. "The decision has been made," she said and stopped, suddenly stressed.

Three pairs of eyes gazed at her, all sensing something serious, and immediately realised it was about her tiffanys, they were to hear. They waited, no one was tempted to prompt or encourage her.

"The decision has been made," she repeated, "and diagnosis is that my tiffanys have an untreatable bacterial infection, and I'm to have a mastectomy quite soon."

Silence stifled the round table ambience as reba, daughter and son were shaken from the tree of Affinity's dramatics, and lay grounded, disturbed by the news, and uncomfortable at having dismissed the matter so often, and even ignored her hysterics.

Essence was first to acknowledge the repercussions. "Does that mean you'll fail your next annulment!"

"Yes, it probably puts me in the dunville."

"What about us!" Wraith exclaimed.

"Well, there's several things which will need sorting," was the extend of Affinity's reply.

Summit realised he could sit back no longer, the inevitable was nigh. "And there's another predicament to be taken in consideration," he announced calmly, and silence descended again, as his reba, daughter and son sensed his warning of several days ago, had become bad news.

Affinity seethed, the goodwill they had been fostering evaporated. Her eyes blazed and she wanted to express her disgust in anticipation of what she was expecting. "What is it," she roared.

"I've been sentence to the dunville for seven years," He announced bruptly. His gaze flashing around the table.

Essence and Wraith looked at each other silently, Affinity's stare frozen and Summit glanced around their faces again, waiting for their reactions. While Affinity's mind raced, her tongue stupefied; long enough for her to close the door on her furnace, and open her safety valve. "Summit, my dear alex," she said quietly, and paused. "While I need a mastectomy, you need a vasectomy, but you'd need a full castration to curb your behaviour.

Essence was uninterested in their dispute; her future was paramount. "So, you're both moving to the dunville?" her question rhetorical, and she required no time to consider her future. "Fine, but I won't be coming." She looked down and shook her head. "Pass my alphaspection and move to the dunville! Not likely."

Chapter 20
The Despair

Affinity was holed-up, brooding solo, in the Couple's Callusionary Coop, and having almost finished her first modco, didn't want to wait for her second, so she ordered in advance. Her simmering anger, and ill humour made it likely there were a few more to come, as she fought a rear guard to the news her tiffanys could not be saved. The door swished open and a pretty young female, probably a jaytwo, stepped in. Affinity arrested, stiffened, glared, her heart faltered, and sunlight glowed amid the drudger in which she chosen to wait. She was captivated, and filled with relief and affection as she watched her attendant, and the lithe subtlety of her walk. Her presentation was minimal but the result of meticulous shading and pattering in mauves, her finest assets tastefully displayed.

Affinity watched her approach unblinking and unashamed. "Affinity," came the girl politely, her voice reaching into Affinity, "You appear to be alone, are you waiting for someone, or would you like me to summon a consort for you? We've certified males and females available. Almost any type you'd fancy, from seducers to rapists."

Affinity was surprised by the mature assurance in someone so young, especially when plying a trade in which her experience could only be brief. But she was a touch irritated by the assumption she might need mercantile companionship, and was tempted to reply bruskly but the impulse was transitory, as the poise, the smile, and the beauty before her was ample antivenin to her antagonism. In a moment she recalibrated, and forwent any gratuitous invective which could have spoilt the girl's day.

"No sweetie but thanks anyway, my reba will be here soon; just bring me another one of these," she replied holding out her empty vessel.

She took it, "Do you have children?" she asked, as a matter of conversation, while watching her from the corners of her eyes.

"A daughter nearly sixteen, and a 12-year-old son," Affinity replied curtly.

"That's nice." She began to leave but Affinity's demanding gaze caused her to hesitate, then a beckoning finger summoned her closer. She did.

"What's you name love," Affinity asked her.

"Amity, Affinity."

Affinity's scrutiny focused finally, as expected, on her tiffanys; could be minus halves, maybe plus quarters, she guessed.

"You don't look very old Amity but I assume since you're working here, you've had the alphaspection. How long ago did you have it?"

"Almost three years ago."

"You've very nice tiffanys Amity, what size are they."

"They're plus quarters," she replied tentatively.

"And what density are they?"

"Nine point eight," she said turning away again but Affinity's heavy gaze persisted and again she paused.

"You're a lucky little flapper," Affinity said light heartedly but with a begrudging undertone, "at alphaspection mine were under eight and I'm paying the price now. My daughter, Essence, is to have her alphaspection soon, and her Jadco's testing reckons hers are nearly nine, which she's happy about," Affinity revealed, but her thoughts were with her eyes, and they were transfixed; as her hand reached for Amity's maiden breasts

"Do you mind?" she asked as her fingers touched the nineteen years old's soft as silks, "I'd just like to know what tens feel like," she claimed.

Amity was bemused but didn't flinch, or show any disbelief or embarrassment, but took only a moment to realise she didn't mind at all. "They're only nine point eights, Affinity," she responded calmly.

When Amity exhibited no discomfort or hurry, Affinity adventured a further liberty, spread her hand, and gently began running her questioning finger tips, supposedly feeling for texture and density. Affinity glanced up at Amity's bright eyes, and noticing she stood submissively, she lifted her other hand and cupped a tiffany in each. The touch was very pleasing, the scene alluring, but when she wanted to tickle her petite dewdrops with the tip of her tongue, and take them between

279

her lips, she accepted her foray was no longer academic, and withdrew her hands slowly, before the teenager detected her sensory curiosity.

"Thank you for not being offended, and letting me feel them Amity, I appreciate it. I just wanted to know what tens feel like since I've never known before. They're so nice compared to the seven point threes, which mine have been for my last two allments, and which have given me so much trouble. Despite my marginal tits I've managed to hold onto jaythree for a few years now, with the help of exercise and care but its stopped working, and now I've lost the struggle altogether, and I'm destined for the dunville without my tiffanys." she shrugged, smiling faintly.

Amity looked startled but remained demure. "That's depressing Affinity because you're still very beautiful," she said reassuringly. She wanted to enquiry further but decided that would be too intrusive.

"Thanks Amity. But what about your backsides, what density did your alice make?" she asked, as she stretched around to look.

"Not as good, they're only eight point four."

Only a close observer would have noticed Affinity's droll grin, "I made nine one, and it's still eight four, and a reason to smile, I suppose. What about your biceps?" she asked her hand sliding down her outside leg.

"Nine one."

Unbelievable, Affinity thought, and she yearned to reach out and touch her some more; but again, resisted the urge to intruded further into the girl's personal dominion, for now.

"Fetch that modco Amity, and with some extra cee, please."

But Amity placed the empty cup on the table, sat down beside Affinity, stretched an arm around her shoulders, leant over and kissed her gently on the cheek. Now it was Affinity didn't flush, or flinch; instead, she just stayed still, and warmed to the tenderness, and the infusion of youthful vibrance. Instead of alarm, foreboding or misgiving she hoped it would last. More than that, she had been bewitched more than slightly, and while a few minutes ago she'd felt empty, now there was a flow of wellbeing, wending its way through her fatigue. It was not the first occasion another female had inspired flutter in her roots, but no other had felt quite like the touch of this girl.

With exhilarating but unexpected possibilities having whetted her hopes, she didn't want it to end. But it did, and when Amity broke away, she stood up, gathered up the empty cup and smiled, leaving Affinity saddened. Amity saw it, and bent back down, kissed her slowly again, this time on the lips. She straightened and departed.

Alone again, she fell back in the couch, scanning the coop. She had chosen one the facility's more morbid scenarios, a reflection of her suddenly returned dejection, and recently discovered masochistic bent. For all intents and purposes, she was sitting in the corner of a dungeon cell in the coop's panoramic hologram. She'd chosen the dungeon from the menu of fantasy settings, and this one included a prisoner writhing in chains, while sweaty, hairless giants and goblin guards aggravated prisoners. The room smelt of human derogation and when Affinity's amusement descended into self-pity, depression and pensive self-abuse, knew it was time for some uplifting female domination.

She called for the beginning, and promptly chains rattled, heavy boots stomped, a whip swished and thudded, and in the distance, there was a cry of male agony.

"Hey, bitch," she yelled and one of the torturers turned and walked towards her. What a beautiful beast, she thought, a big tall female; wild, especially in the eyes; glistening teeth; muscular but lithe; four quarter tiffanys; uncontrolled lush black hair; brown skinned; naked; glistening and bare footed, and ringed pierced dewdrops. In one hand she carried a coiled whip, in the other she dragged a chain.

"Stop that screaming, back there," Affinity demanded. The jailer bowed, kowtowed with a fawning sweep of her whip hand, "Yes, your ladyship, immediately. Is there anything else your ladyship desires?"

"No," and the hologram turned back and disappeared down the passageway.

As the shrieks ceased the coop door slid open and Amity arrived with the modco, on this occasion she showed no surprise at Affinity's chosen environment. She placed the cup on the table and when Affinity looked up at her, "you're not happy Affinity, are you?"

Again, her maturity surprised Affinity, "We used to come here once but I never fucked to sadism, but today I could, I think. I feel that in my present misery it could be pleasantly scary, even invigorating, possibly aphrodisiacal I think that's what I need, and I've a tingle which suggests it could explode years of frustration, and revenge my waning self-esteem. It would be energy sapping and exhausting, I'm certain, maybe purging"

Amity's intrigue had piqued, and while she knew the services provided at the coop, were contrived to facilitate and enhance the expression of a huge range of fantasies, she wanted to know more about what had brought Affinity here.

"So which ones have you tried?" she asked enthusiastically, unfazed by the private and probably delicate nature of Affinity's past, and which she thought would be very titillating. She sat down beside Affinity again. Affinity turned to her and gazed unblinking messages, and Amity knew she was being beckoned. Affinity closed her eyes and waited, only briefly until moist lips touched hers. A thrill quivered all the way to her toes. Amity withdrew after a few moments, "Let me bring you someone Affinity," she offered, again, "I'm working and can't join you on this journey at present, but I can get you someone who can."

"No thanks Amity, and yes, I realise I'm old enough to be your mother, which is perturbing but I'm okay, there's no need for anyone else. I'm expecting my reba anyway."

"It's not your age Affinity, because I think you're very attractive, and the sun's still shines on your jay days. It's just, this is my work place and I'm not qualified to accommodate you. Maybe later, some time. Anyway, you were going to tell me which illusions you've enjoyed."

Affinity produced her tice, "I want the Callusionary menu!" she demanded and placed the tice on the table. There was a considerable list to choose from. Affinity examined it for a moment.

"Here's one we used to like, it's a beach on a tropical island and we have sex in the sand, with the waves crashing in the background, birds in the trees, the smell of salt, and people casually walking past, some stopping to watch us. We liked being watched, and did it in the street, on aeroplanes, in a football crowd, and other places. And there were orgies, but you couldn't share it around since all the others were just holograms.

"If you have self-holograms, then you can watch your partner screwing someone else, or watch yourself being screwed by anything you fancy. I've always had a thing about a line of males waiting their turn for me."

Affinity glanced at Amity and saw she was enjoying her tales but that was enough for the present. "You're not a virgin any more are you Amity?" she asked, wanting to build on the bond she already felt for her.

"No."

Not wanting the intricacies Affinity decided to enquire no further but it was too late.

"I commercialised it, about two years ago," she announced. That word, again, Affinity cursed silently.

"My daughter's doing the same," she commented, disinterested and returned to the fantasies, "here's one we liked. Play seven-three," she called. "As I said, doing it in public was common for us."

A street hologram appeared, high buildings on either side, transporters rushing in both directions, the footpath crowded with pedestrians.

"I like standing up and being pinned against the wall, and as soon as he started fucking me, people gathered, watching, offering advice, egging us on, and when my nefertiti arrives, I become quite vocal and cheering erupts. The crowd participation intensifies, which prolongs the experience, and when your partner finishes, the crowd applauds him, then drifts away."

"This one's a doozy," Affinity explained, glancing blithely at Amity, "It's for anyone drawn to the extreme and the sadistic. It's called The Revolution, and it delivers an experience which doesn't appeal to many females, and I've never tried it either. It's being fucked from behind while watching from a window, at an historical scene. There's a public square below, a baying crowd in uproar every few minutes, and it's the French revolution in full swing, with the guillotine hard at work rearranging society. On the scaffold the headsmen are huge, phallically gross, who in overture, delight in sexual sadism, while in the crowd intercourse, is willing and rampant.

"I have a friend who's the only female I know who regularly exploits this experience, and she's normally such an amenable and gentle female, who's always eager to be part of life's fun. She's a jaytwo, in her mid-thirties with a couple of kids, and is bushtoe with a development company, and obviously is very competent. Similarly, her rebas is a polite and pleasant guy, whose most obvious feature is harmlessness, but one visit to The Revolution was evidently, one too many for him, since never went a second time.

"But Grace too is reluctant, but unfortunately, she's addicted to the explosions it gives her, and while she always finishes drained, morose and vowing never again, the phantom of those oxygen sapping nefertities, inextricably erodes her resistance. A licentious lust awakens in her after a few weeks, and lamentably she slinks back with a taag, sometimes two, unable to defy her gravity any longer. She spends the following day at home in bed, I think not so much from physical reduction but rather in reflective despondency.

"Quietly, she explained her addiction to me. Repeated nefertities, every time the crowd cheers, she says, so extensive her knees fail her every time. I'll admit being tempted, and in some of my darker, angry moods, I've come close to trying it but I've always balked at the last minute. I don't know if that shows good common sense, or a lack of courage. Just the same, the way my life is going at the present there's every chance I could test it, but I worry I'm addiction prone, and I don't need that cargo. I know two females who were goaded by the extremely erogenous potential but they both abandoned it after one session, even though they are fervent buccaneers."

Having introduced her neophyte to some scenery pages of the coop's fantasies Affinity switched to its natural setting and looked at Amity, concerned the array may have been a fictional overload.

"I hope it hasn't surprised you too much Amity?" she said.

"No." she replied easily. "I've seen some weird and repulsive stuff on the hologrammer, and nothing's surprising any more. Actually, I've probably spent too much time watching it, and thinking about them. Since losing my virginity I've been unsure, probably confused about sex. I've had sex with a few males but I'm still using my Visene (virginity secured nefertities) fairly often, even though I'm not a virgin. I thought once I started having sex, I'd forget about it but it's the only thing I find at all enjoyable. It makes me wet, but when it's over I usually feel the nefertiti was a let-down. Even after three or four times, sometimes more, I didn't feel the way I think I should Even so, it's been more fun than the boys' I've fucked. So far, I think my best experiences have been while I'm asleep and free to let my imagination dream."

"Dreams are natural Amity, and as long as you wake up happy, then they're good." Amity's pickle had snared Affinity's interest.

"How long ago did you start with the Visene, Amity?" she asked with a mothering inflection.

"I used to borrow a girl friend's when I was twelve, but when I was thirteen Mum found it and bought me my own."

"How often do you use it?" Affinity asked carefully, sensitive to prying too deeply.

"Most nights. Sometimes I didn't turn it off, and fall asleep with it going."

Not surprising Affinity thought, and her eyebrows jumped approvingly, and while she chuckled internally, she could not suppress a wry grin. "O' Amity, you're delightful; you've made my day. I was miserable but now I just want to soak up whatever it is which makes you exciting. However, thinking about your disheartening affairs with males, have you wondered if commercialising your virginity may have launched you into mating sex, on a bad footing? Or have you been too impatient, expecting too much, too soon, from your intercourse and nefertities? Complete sexual satisfaction comes with time, and practise. The more time, and the more practise, the more the pleasure. As long as you don't lose hope, and keep wanting sex, you'll be all right," was Affdinity's advice.

Amity thought for a moment, "Losing my virginity was not an experience I wish to repeat, but there was nothing about it which was horrific. It hurt to start with, but the injection did its job, and I didn't feel much after a while. I'd seen all the previews, and been schooled about what to expect, etcetera, but what I did find upsetting was his grunting and his puffing in my face, and his refusal to hardly even acknowledge me. Even before he started on me, he barely looked at me, and said little more than hello. I'd thought, probably hoped, he'd looked at me and admired me even flatter me, shown me some respect, and been happy. But there was none of that, just have me naked and have his way as roughly as he could.

"When he rolled me over and entered me from behind, I was happier but it still it was an unpleasant experience. I hoped it would happen pretty quickly, but no, he kept pounding for ages. While it was not a happy event for me, at least I was paid very well, but for goodness' sake, I can't see how he got his money's worth. After that I expected normal sexual relationships would be a different thing, but now the sound of any puffing in my face, or grunting, or even a groan, is a big put off, I'm afraid, I suppose, that's a result of my virginity sale."

Affinity was a little stuck for advice, while her suspicions about the girl's problem and been right, she didn't know she had the answers.

The fact that you know things aren't evolving he way you had hoped or envisioned, means you are aware of your sexual demands, and that's a good start. Whether or not your virginity experience is a major factor, or not, in your dilemma, is hard to say. It maybe, it maybe not. However, I believe you're ready to leap into erotic whoopee, just as soon as you to discover your syrup," she said as she reached out, fingertip tickling her tiffany But just a word of advice. Your Visene is reliable and dependable, lovers, especially male lovers, often aren't."

Amity smiled, "I know somethings about males, Affinity. I'm studying the Triple B course, and it's been good," she said, some reticence persisting.

"I'm aware of it Amity, but I don't know much about it."

"It teaches us to promote our position in society, by identifying and capitalising on male foibles and stupidities, while stressing the importance ofengaging our female fraternity. The curriculum is not tainted with a male odium, rather it is meticulous in detecting the weaknesses in male culture. It doesn't endear me to males.

"The Triple B Institute has a record of successes, and many of our ranking females are graduates. The name is an anagram for Being Bitch is Best, and it's fundamentally an insight into male stupidity, unreliability, untrustworthiness and lechery," a learnt description, she liked to remember.

"Shit Amity, I agree males can be troublesome, and we females must remain alert, but that's a bit too hardcore. They're handy, if handled properly," she advised, but conscious she'd not achieved that very well.

"I've been told that, which is why I don't believe everything but I've memorised the list of warning signs and recommended reactions, so for now I'm more hopeful. However, I'm still unsure, as I know the theory, and I've seen a male make Mum miserable, but when I'm close to a certain young male, I recognise the desire to be held close, even submissive."

Affinity sighed to herself, this female was surely confused about her sexuality which was a shame, since it seemed her ardour was substantial, and her appetite plentiful. And it was evident she suffered from some inherited instincts, even considering sanctuary under a male umbrella, even disposed to their philanthropy.

"You have a male in mind, to steal you from your visene, do you?" she asked.

"Not really."

Amity stood up, kissed Affinity on her forehead, straightened, smiled, raised a thumb from her clenched fist, "Up the sisterhood, sister."

She was gone. The interlude had lifted Affinity's spirits, but her abrupt solitude unveiled her persisting emotional instability, and melancholy moved stealthily to repossess her. She took up her tice to call up a more encouraging scenery, selecting a mountain top view, with open skies, bright sunlight, and the horizon of jagged mountain tops. A breeze disturbed the stray threads of her hanging hair. However, despite the attempted obfuscation, the ambience could not dissuade her from gently clutching her tiffanys. She did not look down to them, preferring to gaze lazily at the illusionary hazy horizon, while her fingers examined her undulating and swelling problems, and her mind tried to fathom why it had to be hers, which had gone so wrong. However, the months of angry frustration were over, submerged beneath self-pity.

Her sisters, Enamour in particular, and Mum Sagacity all advised her against undertaking the reformation therapy, emphasising it was new technology, and while supposedly proven, new procedures sometimes spawned unforeseen and serious side effects, even failures. Past decades had succeeded in eliminating most debilitating aliments but bacteria continued mutating out manoeuvring science, one such mutation now the scapegoat for Affinity's fiasco.

The procedure had infused her tiffanys with a malleable molecular constituent, which would be stabilised in a pre-configured position and shape, using a cold laser process, all the while retaining some subtlety.

When complete Affinity expected a pair of perfect positioned, three-quarter tiffanys, riding high with a density rating around nine, with a prognosis for about twenty more years of tiffany glory. It had been a four-hour procedure, under the influence of a time warping and hallucinogenic antiesthetic, the principal after affect being euphoria. However, within a fortnight Affinity's elation began to dissipate, and her concerns were disquieting. After the fortnight, she returned to the clinic complaining, convinced something was amiss, but had succumb to the contention her worries were premature and unfounded.

After another fortnight, the technicians admitted something was awry and the subsequent testing confirmed a major problem, needing a major intervention to save her from a life-threatening infection. Apparently, bacteria had attacked the infused material which required prompt removal, for fear it would mutate further, and contaminate her natural tissue. Unfortunately, the infusion was now an integral part of the tiffany tissue and could not be surgically separately. Her tiffanys had to go. Artificial replacements could not be considered for at least a year, if ever, and was dependent on an assurance no trace elements of the bacteria endured.

"Fucking idiots," she shrieked just as the booth door opened and Amity entered with the next round of modco with double cee.

Affinity kept holding her tiffanys and watched Amity's every elegant stride, until the cup was on the table and she looked at Affinity, smiling broadly.

"Do I look like I'm ready for the dunville?" Affinity yelped.

"No Affinity," she said nonplussed by the question, her tiffany clasping, and was wondered where the conversation was headed, "You're a long way from the dunville, Affinity"

"Well, I'm about a fortnight away," she announced indignantly.

Amity felt she was on wonky ground, and thought it was time to escape.

"I'm sorry for you Affinity, I hope it's not too bad for you," she said, not wanting to enquire, fearing it could enmesh her in a conversation, requiring understanding and sympathy, something she wanted to avoid. "Is there anything else I can get for you, Affinity?" she asked sincerely, while easing away.

Affinity was hurt. The bond she felt had formed between them, was gone. "No thanks, thanks."

She exited briskly but politely.

However, she had been gone only a minute when she reappeared in the doorway, stepped in and then aside to usher Summit's arrival. She was smiling, Summit was not, Affinity's hands fell to her lap and though she smiled not, she was pleased to see him, even relieved.

In the past Summit's appearance would normally have annoyed her but today her battered, and long reclusive love for him was standing, and she wanted to go to him, put her arms around his neck, hugged him and be hugged but the years of drift and distrust, were an albatross too big. For now, some positive exploratory posturing would have to suffice, so she stood and smiled in the old adoring way, hoping he'd respond accordingly. Summit's eyes fixed on her, and after two days of avoiding her and their imminent discussion, he too was being moved by an attitude from the past. Instead of dodging the sentencing issue and the inevitable invective which would surely follow, he suddenly wanted her understanding and sympathy. He wanted to vault their wall of separation but since explaining his jot eviction would enrage her, he chose to continue with their accrued detachment, for the moment anyway

"Can I bring you something Summit," Amity asked.

"A double modco," Affinity snapped.

Summit, surprised, stared at her for a moment, then turned to Amity and nodded in affirmation.

Affinity's abrupt intervention was a step over their years of detachment, but a missive note in her voice, told Summit he was not alone in melancholy. They shared a sense that this encounter was to be different, and not mired in mutual apprehension. The decimation which had overwhelmed them both, and the consequential gloom clouding their futures, had doused some of the pig-headed behaviours they usually indulged in.

As he walked to her, their eyes whispered to each other, she stood waiting, her poignant smile warming, and Summit kept coming until he took her by the shoulders and kissed her softly on the lips. She wished it to last but a niggle amid her chaos, would not be dismissed. She put a hand to his chest and gently broke their embrace.

"Where have you been, you were supposed to be here over an hour ago?" she asked but her tone lacked rancour, rather it was of concern.

"I was held up and just couldn't get away," he explained and Affinity's eyes hinted a squint, as his words resonated of a familiar fibbing flavour. Today though she craved his comfort not confrontation, so she pretended not to notice.

"Can I get back to where I was?" Summit asked affectionately, still holding her shoulders, and wanting to escape any further interrogation.

"Where were you?" Affinity persisted.

He ignored the question, instead he wrapped his arms around her, and pulled her to his lips but this time with less tenderness and more passion. Her moist lips were a tingling reminder of how agreeable their intimacy once was; while Affinity basked in the moment and felt the luxury of old companionship. Stirring within them both, was an urge to climb from their mire but neither had the courage or the certainty to discard the past, just yet. Summit particularly, was cognisant and somewhat hesitant, his conscience suggesting emotionally inspired commitments could falter in the face of other factors.

Summit broke from their embrace, took Affinity's arm and beckoned her to sit, then he plonked into the seat opposite, her smile fading.

"Affinity, what on earth made you want our meeting here. Couldn't it have waited until we were home this evening."

"There was no guarantee Summit, you'd be home this evening, and I wanted this meeting alone, with you. This place is a return to happier days, to a time when we just wanted to be together, and where we found a lot of fun. I'm hoping the atmosphere here will rekindle some of our old rapport. I had some devastating news and thought this would be a very personal place to talk to you about it."

It made sense to Summit considering his predicament. "I've just had some devastating news, Summit, I don't know what's going to happen to me," she said looking him straight in the eyes, her voice a simile of the message.

Summit shuffled in his seat, uneasy even suspicious; he glanced around, then back at Affinity.

"Well, Affy, I've some bloody bad news too, so it seems it's to be a bad news day all round. You go first," he said, a flippancy in his manner.

Her heart skipped, and the moment inveigled nervousness to accompany her depression. "I don't know how to start," she stuttered, staring into the face of the male, who was once her confidant but had long been little more than an effigy. He should have been aware of her dilemma if he'd been interested, she thought, but his bad news she could not guess at, but she knew it would be 'bad'.

Summit seemed to peer beyond her eyes, and into the pain of her soul. A swelling of sympathy prompted him to reach out and let her know that in the stillness below their waves, he did care. He moved to sit beside her, took her hands and she turned to gaze at him, and in their silent exchange he felt her shivering.

"Ease up Affinity, just tell me what's happened."

"I've got to have my fucking tits off!" she blurted, anger breaking through again.

Summit blinked, glanced away momentarily then looked back at her, speechless, momentarily. He had no inkling this was brewing despite months of her tiffany dramatics. He knew all about her cosmetic adjustments but he'd believed it was routine, even mundane, and had worked out He was dumbfounded now, although he'd been told there was a slight problem.

"You're what?" he exclaimed.

"Got to have a double mastectomy," she said sombrely this time, relieved to have shared it, and desperate for comfort.

"Is that final Affinity? Have you had a second opinion? Are you sure you're not exaggerating?" he asked recognising immediately his query was a blunder.

"I'm not fucking exaggerating, Summit, and no, I've not had a second fucking opinion and yes, it's fucking final," her erratic anger spiked again, but promptly simmered, when Summit put out his hand, and held her around the neck.

"Yes, Affy, I know, sorry, I'm in shock, that's all."

"A flesh-eating bacteria, has infected my tits and the technicians tell me there is no alternative but to cut it out," she announced with finely veiled stoicism.

Summit understood some of the ramifications, particularly the emotional ones, and with an obligation to tend Affinity for a while, his mess would be remitted to the back stalls for the moment. Despite appreciating her situation, he struggled to find the appropriate response, whether to enquiry after more details, express sorrow, or just console.

"Damn, Affinity. Hell," he said, the words not his voice expressing incomprehension, "isn't there an alternative."

"No. Summit!" she exclaimed glaring, "what don't you understand? Would I be having them off if there was another way? Talk sense, for goodness' sake!" she exclaimed, then her head drooped with tears seeped down her cheeks.

Summit took his hand from around her neck, and wiped away her tears with the back of his hand.

"Can they reconstruct new ones for you?" he asked, searching for constructivity, his first sensible question.

"Not now, later on maybe, in a year or so."

"Are you in any pain?" he asked, came his second sensible query.

"No. They've both gone lumpy," she said and abruptly stood up. "Look," she instructed as her hands grasp the neck line of her cream and beige patterned chemises, and with a grunting surge ripped it open, fully exposing her chest. She startled him, and he could only stare.

"Well, Affy, it's so disappointing because they look fine to me."

"Feel them, then!" she ordered, thrusting her chest forward.

His response was not quick enough for her.

"Gone on Summit, fucking feel them. You couldn't keep your hands off them once."

He stood, and took one in each hand.

"Not like that! Gently glide your hands over the surface and feel the lumps," she directed calmly.

After a moment, he looked at her, "Yes, Affinity, I can feel it, and it's a bloody shame because they're as beautiful as ever."

"Bullshit," she spat.

He cupped them in his hands, leant over kissing one, then the other, then he wrapped his arms around her, hugging her tightly.

"It seems we're going to end up in a dunville together," he forecast casually. There was a pregnant pause. Oops! He'd just trashed his plans for a tactful introduction to his mess, and the soft landing he'd hoped for her. Affinity burst from his arms, open mouthed, her eyes demanding, and quickly sweeping aside her residual tears. She knew it. Hints, suspicions and his behaviours, had been accumulating, and slushing around her head for some time, now suddenly, unexpectedly, but not surprisingly he was about to unmask.

"What! What did you say, what are you talking about?" she demanded, alarm overriding despondency.

"Yeah, well Affinity," he stopped, staring blankly at her, while he scrambled to conjure the soft landing, for both their sakes. Delay was not helping so he grasped the nettle, "I was involved in an unfortunate incident some weeks ago, which resulted in another person being injured I've already told you that. but I had no idea it would end the way it has; and the upshot is; it was my fault according to the court, and I've received a heavy penalty. I've been exiled to a dunville for seven years."

Silence descended with a crash, Affinity fell back into her seat, her stomach fuming, her eyes ice, her world white, and the ambience electrifying. Summit returned her stare and felt her seething. The anger which had been patrolling near her surface for ages, had burst.

"So you are guilty then, you fucking arsehole Summit," she shouted, leaning into his face, "what the fuck have you done? What was it, another female? What fucking debauchery got you into this bloody mess? And you got caught," she paused and her eyes globed, "you stupid bastard, serve you right," she paused again, "I'd sentenced you to life," she said flagged, and looked aside, the outburst over, and gloom shouldered its way back to pre-eminence.

Her conjecture was, unsurprisingly accurate. He looked at her but her eyes persisted elsewhere, and she sat slouched, as if avoiding any more painful disclosures. Summit eased away a tad but took her hand, leaving her to private thoughts, while hoping her emotional roller-coaster would berth. Like it or not, they were embarked on the same boat and while they boarded over different jetties, they needed to stroke together if they were to arrive somewhere tolerable. For the moment though Affinity showed no inclination to re-join their conversation.

Summit was watching a lonely figure, who a few minutes ago seemed open to an improved relationship, although he hoped his latest tomfoolery, would not be a ravine too wide. He noticed the untouched modco on the table.

"What's in that?" he asked pointing at the cup.

"Double cee," came a concessional reply, along with a benign glance.

It was a moment for reflection and overview, with an ambition to dismiss bygone mistakes, and allow perspective to influence a sensible decision. One of them needed to take control and begin plotting a course for their lives, as subconsciously they had both accepted the truth, that despite their turbulent and ragged relationship, they were destined to remain together. He took the cup from the table and held it toward her.

"Someone went to the trouble of making this, and you'll feel better if you drink it," he suggested.

She looked at him, reasoning, but for the moment she was only going to respond with humourless levity, "No one went to any trouble, other than to tell a bloody stainless panel to make it. And I've had fair bit already," but she took the cup.

"I think I'll have one too," Summit said, took the tice from his arm and order a cup, no extras.

After a couple of sips Affinity's spirits began recuperating, the lights seemed brighter, and an impulse to step from her claustrophobic misery was precipitating. Summit noticed her expression brighten, and hoped their sparring might be over, for the day, anyway. Could she be at a corner? Where would that leave him?

Affinity held still, gazed poker faced and unblinking at him, until he ceded and smiled. "What, Affy?" he questioned with an upturned hand.

She made him wait a moment. "We both know you're a bastard Summit, but I remember loving you, and I'd like your help to rediscover that person."

This was unexpected and surprising, and while his first thought was positive, his second was scheming an extradition from the boxed box he felt. Suddenly he felt the walls closing in and for now, his best option was a diversionary tact.

"Remember the afternoon we met Affinity, and how we felt so right together," he said seeking to stimulate her sentimental sentinels, and exhume her youthful excitement.

Affinity placed the empty cup on the table, then looked around at him.

Summit's tice lit up and announced his modco was ready for

delivery. "Did you seal the room," Affinity demanded.

"Yes," Summit stretched to the panel on the table, and the door swung allowing Amity in. She noticed Affinity's bare chest, and her chemises hanging from her shoulders in shreds. She placed the cup beside Summit and smiled, "Is there anything else you would like," she enquired, her eyes flicking between them.

"I'll have another, with double cee," Affinity announced.

Amity hesitated, "I'm sorry Affinity, but you've already had more than your quota," she said firmly but politely. Affinity's lowered her frown but peered up.

"Amity, my dear and beautiful girl, just work it out. I want another one!" the severity of her demand increased as she spoke.

Summit chipped in, "Get it for her and put down to me. I don't want any more after this one."

That defused the situation, and although not happy, it was an escape for Amity but a foreboding for Summit.

Happy, Affinity had other sparks zipping about her mind, and she turned to consider the father of her children, which sparked a throb in her stomach.

"I do remember out first meeting Summit, I couldn't take my eyes off you, you were beautiful, a jayone, in blues, with captivating eyes and a gorgeous charm, and we made love the very next day."

He smiled and nodded a yes. "You're still handsome but you don't fuck me much any more," she said glumly, the comment rekindling a familiar refrain, "So who are you fucking at the present?"

"Neither of us should start down that path again Affy, because neither of us can be sure where it will end, so there's no good there."

"None of my partners breathe, bleed or have nefertities," Affinity countered sarcastically.

"That's a pity Affinity, if true."

Conveniently the door swung open, clipping their conversation again, and Amity delivered Affinity's modco. Affinity and Summit watched each other silently, anxious for their privacy back. Amity was aware; made her delivery quickly, and left.

Affinity took a temperature testing sip, then tossed her head back swallowing half the cup's contents. She sank back into the chair watching Summit, while cultivating a spawning assertiveness.

She'd had enough of their whirlpool exchanges. She stood up, lifted her arms high, arched her back, stretched strongly, and lingered enjoying the feel of nerves coming alive. After a moment she looked down.

"Summit! Are you going to tell me exactly what you did to get seven years in the dunville?" she asked, choosing at the last moment to omit the expletives, and the insults.

Summit looked up at her and decided to tell all, "I attempted to nullify a female who'd challenged my position as bustoe but the venture got out of control. I was out of my depth, and she's ended up with brain damage, for which I've been convicted."

He looked at her, not pleased or displeased, rather hoping to seem indifferent. She clapped his cheeks.

"Well?" she demanded.

"Not now Affinity," he said casually.

Despite his pretentious nonchalance Affinity knew he was annoyed, and for now that was enough, since she didn't really want any more details anyway. She flopped back into her chair, her backside on its edge, her legs stretched out and open, her back sinking into the cushioning, her chin resting on her chest, her vesuvius apparent and messaging silently. Affinity looked down her nose at her dewdrop then reached a finger to tickle them, looked at Summit and smiled an encouragement he understood.

When he failed to respond she snapped. "Well!" her fingers spread to cup her tiffanys. Resigned to not gazumping their reconciliation, at least not until its potential it was further explored, he stood up and stepped between her knees. He knelt down, looked into her expected eyes and smiling face, and stirred with an urge to reignite a past indulgence.

"Tice the High Street Summit, and see if we can both be happy."

The suggestion was appealing, and in a moment the sounds of traffic and walking feet were distinct, then passers-by glanced at them, a number pausing hoping to view something interesting. Summit took hold of her outfit's waist, opened the front, then leaning away pulled the garment off. He looked at her pussy, then into her eyes, then at pussy, then into her eyes, and smiled. His hand went forward cupping vesuvius, while his other hand stroked the top of her leg.

"Go on Summit," she urged, her expression animated.

Summit took hold of her knees, eased them well apart the bent over until his face rested on her ladies, and his tongue began roaming her foyer. Cleopatra responded straightaway and in moments was erect. Summit's tongue continued, slowly circling cleopatra, then some soft flicking up and down, then he pushed his mouth deep until his lips captured cleopatra and he sucked her in between his lips and massaged her gently with his lips and tongue.

The contrast was stark between this experience and the last time, when he'd pushed her against the bathroom wall, and hurriedly fucked her, his self-interest devoid of the slightest sympathy or sensitivity for her. This reawakening was more stimulating than anything she'd imagined likely for the day, or for any other, for years. Their half dozen onlookers huddling around, cheering and clapping when her face grimaced to her overwhelming nefertiti their encouragement stimulating her to keep cumming until she reached an exhilaration she'd forgotten. Summit had rediscovered excitement with his reba, which enthused him to drive for her the ultimate gratification.

Chapter 21
Sister Chat

It was Sunday again, five days since Affinity and Summit, through misadventure and miscalculation, were cuffed together in a cage of grief labelled for the dunville. For Summit there was no escape, while for Affinity the chance of returning to the jot was not impossible but complicated and fraught. She'd arrived early at Green Gardens, and was standing by her transporter anxious for her sisters' arrival for their customary lunch, some companionship and their perspectives on her predicament. She had dressed smartly, as usual, although her commanding use of red suggested suppressed resentment, and her missing cleavage was a veiled message, which doubtless would quickly be noticed.

Prudence's transporter pulled in, and parked close by, the door slid open, and out stepped a smiling and sashaying sister, eager to embrace her. Affinity tingled at her approach, feeling blessed to have such a wonderful sister, sentimental despite a little underlying cynicism. Pru's multi-layered outfit, in multi-shades of blue, seemed from her new 'Gorgeous Me' range, with its refreshing swirls, colours and fabric achieving gorgeous entitlement. From her bare shoulders, her long neck and face continued with the shaded colourings but simple, with the lips and eyes in severe blue. Her pale blue/heavy blue striped hair curled and pulled behind her ears which were edged in heavy blue stones on descenders. But the diamonds in her beauty were her eyes.

Their embrace released some of Affinity's nervous uncertainty. Prudence's swathing arms, her sweet aroma and her affection were the painkillers for Affinity but too quickly Prudence broke off to look Affinity in the eyes.

"There something wrong Affy, what is it?" she asked, concerned.

"I've an issue or two but let's wait for En," she suggested politely.

They did not wait long as Enamour's transporter was already

parking. When she stepped out Prudence immediately recognised her outfit being from her new 'Love Me' range, with greys the theme. The three moved to meet but they'd gone just a step when Prudence's smile sank in open mouthed surprise, and before they came together, she gasped, "En, you're showing!"

Enamour's grin broadened, she paused, and keen to emphasise her condition, posed with an arched back, then circled her only just babied tummy with a swirling index finger, "Great isn't it," she boasted, "but I'm surprised you noticed, nobody else has, not even Maxim."

"I'm happy for you En," Affinity conceded.

With the welcoming ritual consigned, the trio strode indoors and found themselves queued behind a late twenties couple in discussion with the maître de. Prudence was pleased to notice another female outfitted from her new collection and was surprised how quickly it was being accepted. This outfit, with a permeating lime-coloured undertone, was from the FM range and on this tall female looked stunning, even from behind. The graded organic polymer fabric meant the outfit clung to the body in places and hung evenly in others. Prudence knew the view from the front and the almost full tiffany exposure, then clung to the midriff before falling short above the knees.

The sisters stood back chatting quietly, waiting, when Affinity leaned to Enamour and asked when was she due.

"Seven months, fifteen days," she replied.

The tall lime figure spun around, her swinging three-quarter tiffanys in faded lime shuddered to rest, above which two piercing black eyes, with green outlines, glared.

"Are you pregnant?" she demanded, glaring first into Enamour's face, then lowering her gaze looking for the evidentiary zone.

"Thanks for asking pet," Enamour replied politely. "Nice dress pet, nice titties! And yes, I am pregnant, can't you tell? I know there's not much to see yet but in a few more months there'll be a lot more; with luck."

Lime Female was a little disconcerted by the patronising impudence, but in aloof disbelief, had no intention of dropping the matter.

"You've no business being pregnant in public. You're the last type we need in our community, fucking shameless! Why do pregnant females flaunt themselves? I saw another one a few days ago, it was nauseating. Go home and stay there until you've dumped the embarrassment, and are packed for the dunville," she was jabbing a finger towards Enamour's stomach.

Seeming to have startled or embarrassed herself, Lime female promptly turned about, and glanced at her companion, who gazed at her wide eyed and bewildered.

"What's funny?" she snapped, but annoyed she'd broken off prematurely, she wheeled back to confront Enamour again, but Prudence was there leaning forward between her sisters, her grin tittering, "Listen, miss mammaries," she said feeling it was her turn to wag a finger at Lime's pretentious pair, "You've enough to worry about with tits like yours, they're already looking at the floor."

But Prudence was ignored, Lime's irritation remained with Enamour, "Why haven't you used a surrogate, like respectable jay females do?" she demanded.

"Because, pet, I have a uterus, and the nefertities are better when you're getting pregnant," she continued in her polite way.

Lime girl was nonplussed, and with the nefertiti red herring scotching her assault, she went onto the defensive. "I'm more than happy with this," she said, turning back to her partner and reaching to stroke the outline of his obviously fulsome endowment. "He's a plus four by two, and knows how to use it," she bragged.

Prudence was pushing forward again, this time waving a dismissing back hand, "Take your tits and his dick, and move on," she instructed, and being more upset by Enamour's patronising, than Prudence's insults Limegirl turned away huffy, reluctantly acceding that sometimes recalcitrants survive in jots.

Once settled at their table Enamour showed indifference to the incident, but inside she relished being noticed, even if the compliment was intended as a crude insult. For Affinity the incident faded quickly, but for Prudence one comment was echoing around her mind. She stared at Enamour thoughtfully until she was noticed.

"What is it Pru?" Enamour asked finally.

Still her thoughts lingered, then, "You said nefertities are better when you're getting pregnant."

Enamour smiled sisterly, not at all surprised by the enquiry, especially that it came from Prudence. "Well, Pru, they are; definitely better," she reiterated, and teasingly failed to elaborate.

It annoyed Prudence, "Don't play funny buggers En. Are you going to explain or not?"

Enamour looked at Prudence, her face easing to a knowing smile. As well, the question compelled recollection, and that induced a smile deep within, as well. She was thinking.

"Well, Prudence," she paused, "if it's the personal intricacies you want."

"I suppose I do."

"Then, I suppose. The sex is no different, there's no secrets, it's one's state of mind which differs. I craved absolutely for invasion, and I wanted his plunges deeper than ever, because I supposed I hoped that might get the seed closer to its destination. Sometimes I'd watch, but not often, I preferred the closed eye sea of colour, and the mystical symphony of my nefertiti vacuuming his amalgam.

"I always wanted to make memories, and whenever my body and mind were in harmony, my instincts and desires were eager to rhumba. And they always did. Even when I felt my first nefertiti stirring, I wouldn't hurry it, rather I enjoyed its roaming independence. I liked it threatening, and when it finally flooded me, the imagery of the intricacies' fascinated me. The dynamic just added an extra edge to the endeavour and the excitement. You can't imagine my disappointment whenever I didn't end up pregnant," she said after a moment.

"Sounds like you shouldn't have been too disappointed, knowing you'd have to do it again," Affinity noted, illuminating the obvious, but the residue of her objection to her sisters' situation was still detectable in her voice.

"How long did it take you to get pregnant," Affinity asked casually,

"Four months," came the answer immediately.

Prudence smiled, her shoulders wagged, "sounds like it should have taken years."

"Or, I could keep getting pregnant," Enamour mused.

"You could what?" Affinity exclaimed.

Enamour flicked a hand at her big sister. "Don't worry Affy, I'll be happy with just this one."

"Could try pregnancy, myself, if it's more fun," Prudence mulled, her eyes wishful, her smile mischievous.

Affinity glared at her for a moment, "Don't talk rubbish Pru, even as a joke, you know she's exaggerating," her eyes glanced at Enamour, who just winked.

In a semi-serious, but serious moment, Prudence decided to do the cost/benefit equation on getting pregnant, but the promise did not equate to the sacrifice, it was an improper fraction.

Enamour had the solution. "Prudence, just pretend you're getting pregnant. It might work. That's where I started, and while I was predisposed anyway, the pretence reinforced my determination to go all the way," Enamour said.

"Just stay well away from the whole subject," Affinity directed, staring at Prudence.

Enamour reached across the table and stroked her sister's resting forearm, "It's simple Pru, there's two facets to fornication. There's pleasure and there's procreation, and when you combine them, the way nature intended, the passion provokes appetites, which journey's you to unexpected peaks. I feel sorry for females who fudge the fun, the experience, unitising surrogates."

Another thought nagged Prudence, and although she thought it might annoy her sisters, she'd have her say

"Just the same En, it seems we all just lie back and cop it too often, giving males the impression we're his implements. I hope you realise you need to take control of your sexual activity," Prudence said.

Enamour's expression soured slightly but swiftly she dismissed the aggravation, and regarded Prudence's political opportunism, as normal.

"I've nothing against 'copping it' Prudence, the more the better sometimes, particularly if I'm amorous but tired, which can happen. I have days when nothing's gone right, and I've arrived home subconsciously lusting and wanting release from tedium, then copping it becomes alluring, knowing ultimately my listlessness is merely chicanery by cynicism.

"However, I find some very satisfying sex comes with brazen resolve, and exaggerated participation; then when I'm spent, finished, strewn breathless, I can still twinkle if I'm still being pumped. Occasionally, it's a tryst which spawns illusions of a leviathan at me, and I'm beguiled by the beast which overpowers my imagination. Outwardly I remain tranquil, but within, the exhilaration of the creature's form and strength permeates my core, and my nefertities geysers with its every thrust. The peace which settles after such an affair lasts a long time."

"Enamour, I always saw you as a gentle, and demure person, refined and proper, but at the same time I've suspected that behind your façade, a sensual but carefully controlled dynamo resided. Now though it seems you're far more tempestuous than I thought," Prudence summarised, rather academically.

Affinity was still thinking, but Enamour wished to move away from the fanciful.

"The thing is, En," Prudence said looking at Affinity, "while you could be right about the emotions when trying for pregnancy, it's the other ninety-nine, point nine nine plus percent, which needs considering."

Prudence worried Enamour's extra sexual delights were, unfortunately, retrogressive, as they implied male pre-eminence, and while she accepted male enthusiasm often aided female euphoria, she felt the politics of fornication needed daylighting, again.

"Enamour you must keep sex in perspective. We females have successfully taken charge of society. We have fought our way to political, social and commercial supremacy. Just look at the society we have built but we remain exposed to male dependency, if we continue to submit to their sexual ambitions. What you seem to be describing, means the best sex comes when we're submissive, and that's bothering.

"So, what's the problem Pru?" Affinity enquired, slightly interested, and indulging Prudence to continue.

"I'm not sure, but I know the only time I feel the empress of my sex, is when I'm face fucking him. Sure, I have my fun on top, and even from underneath or doggie, I can influence the rhythm if I insist, but my libidinous ravishings only ride rampant, when vivian engulfs his face. And talking about fantasies, I tremble at the malevolent vision of suffocating him, or drowning him, and wonder what nefertitic outflowing would that incite."

Enamour didn't smile, "I think my fantasy's probably deviant, though not depraved but yours' Pru, is sadistic."

"I know, but that's all right, it's fantasy," Prudence was unapologetically

While their confessions surprised Affinity, they did not ring alien, nor even seem out of character. In fact, she could see how their aberrations were a bridge to their dreams, and the world of unfathomable logic, where unconstrained life inhabits the cryptic side of consciousness. Dreams know more about ourselves, than does our conscious. It's under the auspices of sleep, where nothing hides, and where we wander pointlessly, usually confounded, occasionally excitingly, that nothing advantageous goes on to our consciousness, when sleep takes flight at the slightest sight of light.

Does fantasy betray a second life? Seems reasonable. Do we wish to privatise our fantasies because they are personal, fanciful, immoral, disgusting, illogical, irrational and therefore secret property? Not necessarily. Or does that life embarrass our ordinary life? More than likely. Is there truth in fantasy, is fantasy's reality welcome? In hatred, yes; in sensuality, probably.

"What it boils down to, you two, is; Enamour; you use bestiality as a turn on, while Prudence your fancy's necrophiliac. I'm worried for you both, as there's nothing positive about either hallucinations," she said, her tone a confusion of scornful jest.

"No, Affinity, they're just fantasies, that's all, and surely, my dear, you must have had them too," Prudence said defensively.

"Yes, I suppose I do, but they're not menacing or unnatural. It seems I don't have the imagination of you two, but the Callusionary Coop has supplied my fantasies from time to time, but never innocuous," she claimed.

However, Affinity was not comfortable with the conversation, nervous about any secrets she might accidently exposed, and wished to swing in another direction. Prudence had set out, once again, to espouse her current theories on female sexual patronage, and she thought a return to the subject could be ideal at this juncture.

"Well Prudence, how do you suppose female sexual status can be improved, when the real problem is that many females are happy with the status quo, particularly now we reign in most other fields? I'm content with the hierarchical sexual structure, and see no difficulties with the gender divide. It's personality which is important.

Prudence needed to press her point. "Affinity, this is last realm of male hegemony, and while I think we suffer from faulty anatomical design, males must understand the performances and techniques choices aren't theirs' to make. Males still expect to have sex whenever they've the urge, and I'll admit, I've even surrendered, because I still have some curbed sense of duty to his brothers, which keep manufacturing his stuff."

"That's why they have madam palm, and her five daughters," Affinity explained.

Enamour turned to Affinity, "So when you're not too interested but pressured Affy, how do you deal with it?"

"Well, it's not an issue any more but in the past, if I've submitted, it was usually I found doggy style. It's the quickest way to have him done. That is, unless I feel two hands seize my hips, and the piledriver takes over, then I'll tell him to bugger off. If he makes it so obvious that all he wants is to jerk off, then he can use madam palm, not my cunt," her sentiments unambiguous.

"And as far as the grope is concerned, and his impudence in thinking a meddling finger's going ignite anything except rejection, makes me wonder about male intelligence. Obviously, there's a kinked connection between their brains and their brothers," Affinity surmised.

Enamour had a different point of view, "I know the midnight wandering hand can be a wet blanket, but whatever the hour I can generally be cajoled, since I'm easy prey to the sensual kiss to the middle of my back, or a meandering tongue tip up my spine. The ascent from slumber to sensuality can come easily, even quickly. And I don't need to be trying for pregnancy to have the beast visit."

Affinity and Prudence exchanged cheeky glances, acknowledging in titillation, there was a classified dimension to their sister's prim and proper ways. Prudence continued campaigning, "What we all must admit is we are still sexual servants, and while you, Affinity, claim to dictate the conditions of the midnight grope, I think your fantasies must be masochistic," she pronounced looking at her, "while it sounds like you, Enamour; you'll submit to just a hint of pandering, which makes you of little value to our campaign."

Enamour had more. "I think you're pushing a chain, Pru. What's our loss leaving males with a sense of sexual influence. It probably gives them the impression of still having ultimate control, anesthetising them to the truth; and you're overlooking the fact there's fornicating, then there's love making. I believe most females still aspire to love making; that's the critical issue, and male's trump card. As well, most females are comforted by a feeling of love beneath an umbrella of strength and security." she suggested.

"I'm not sure love making is that important in this era, especially for jot females. While males have always sought beautiful females, other considerations have traditionally influenced female choices, however, these days their sexual gratifications are more often found in the physical and the practical, as much are the emotional. Despite that, and despite usually taking the initiative and having turns in command, I usually end up submissive," Prudence complained.

"That's because you're lucky enough to finish first Pru, which is the way it needs to work, and besides it's a nice place to end up," Enamour suggested.

Affinity had had enough, and after a sleepless week mired in a vortex of worry and self-pity, she was anxious for some indulgent and empathetic communion. She felt she had contributed enough to Prudence's campaign for now, and wanted to move to her predicament, "I've had some devastating news, you two!" her face sank, "and I need to share it, so you can reassure me, my trauma is not as traumatic as I'm finding it," Affinity announced, then paused.

"Come on sis, out with it, what's wrong?"

"I'm to have both tiffanys removed, urgently."

Enamour stiffened, Prudence's face came across the table, "What!".

"And as well, Summit has been sentenced to seven years in a dunville."

Echoing silence stunned the scene, after their time together, where did this come from? Suddenly sickened, her sisters stilled and stared unblinking, as the full implications of the news unfurled in their minds. Prudence and Enamour exchanged wordless horrors, while Affinity relieved at liberating the leprechaun, relaxed, her shoulders sinking Dolefully.

As the impact of her news depressed Prudence, she again swung uncontrollably into campaign mode. "Why Affy, have you ended in this position? You might think it's because of your tits. Well, it's not; it's because you were taught young that a certain type of tiffany made us beautiful but have you ever wondered why that shape and size is attractive. I'll tell you why; it's because that's what males like. So, Affy, even though you've always been beautiful, your obsession for male pleasing tiffanys, is going to cost you dearly."

"Shut up Prudence!" Affinity wanted understanding, not a lecture.

Enamour had had enough of Prudence's prolongation too, and turned to Affinity. "How did matters reach this point Affy."

"My tiffany restoration procedure was an absolute failure, and now my tits are septic, and I'm to have them removed in a few days," she explained.

"I'm not often stuck for words Affy but at the moment I not sure what to say. I want to ask if there's any alternative, or a way around this but obviously, there's not. Tell me though," Prudence glanced at Enamour, "Were you warned or given any indication the procedure could go so wrong?" she asked

"Yes, and no. I was ticed an excessive amount of data, about how well it had been tested, how effective it would be, how good I'd look and how happy I'd be, but at the end there's always the escape clauses, the fine print, warning that all medical procedures have risks. Of course, having enthusiastically absorbed the hype, it's convenient to dismiss the warnings as mere formality."

"So, can they reconstruct them?" Prudence asked.

Affinity had to go through the explanation again.

"So, does this mean you ending up in a dunville," Enamour asked quietly

"Probably and that's what Summit and I are expecting."

"Well at least you'll be close to Mum and Dad, which will be a silver lining of sorts," Prudence observed.

Dunvilles don't worry me too much," Enamour announced dismissively. She'd wanted to sway the conversation from emotion to reality. "Affy, sis, just stand back from it, look beyond the jot, and the jays and the conformity, and there's another world out there which is probably not all that bad," she tried to sound convincing.

Affinity glared at her, "How do you know that En, you've spent your life in the jot, and I don't know about you but a jot is where I wanted to remain for another twenty years, at least."

"Well, that's probably unrealistic En; ten years; yes," Prudence suggested.

"Mum and Dad are happy where they are, even though Mum's still a Jok," Enamour pointed out.

"What about Essence and Wraith?" Prudence enquired.

"Essence is booked in for her alphaspection shortly, and wants to make arrangements to sell her virginity a couple of days later. However, we haven't thought about it much yet, though Essence sees the alphaspection as her ticket to freedom, and says she's adamant about staying in the jot, while Wraith will suffer with us, I suppose, as there's no feasible alternative," she said.

Silence interrupted the conversation.

Prudence looked at her sisters, and they both seemed to be telling her to say something. Affinity felt she needed to direct proceedings.

"It's okay, I've given you my news and it feels better off my chest. Now it finished for now, so what's happening at your place Pru."

"So! Everything is good for us, with our surrogate underway," Prudence announced, sensing the hiatus was an opportunity to deliver her update.

"The news is all positive, the only set back being the down grading of our harlequin application. However, we've accepted the revisions as the prognosis is still handsome, and we had no alternative. When Stone and I met our surrogate Clarity, she impressed; she looks fit and healthy, is intelligent, seems happy, and is surprisingly attractive for a dunvillian.

Affinity's eyebrows alerted.

"Attractive! Are you still planning to have her live with you?" she stopped, looking into Prudence's eyes.

"Yes Affy, I want that, and I think the girl will agree."

"And she's attractive?" she questioned again, sceptically. "I've tried to warn you against having the surrogate at home," Affinity said, turning on her big sister's dogma, and looking to Enamour "What do you think En?"

"I think the arrangement is risky," she said casually, hoping her disinterested tone would discourage the conversation.

But Affinity was not finished, "All I'll say is, if you bring another female, to live in your house, you're asking for trouble. She's bait you don't need."

Disappointed her warning seeming to float into the never never, Affinity surrendered, "All right then, just remember my warning."

"All right Affy. In the meantime, she was implanted two weeks ago, and a verification and stability test will be carried out in seven more days, then we'll bring her home."

While the luncheon discussions had updated the affairs of two sisters, there were still Enamour's intrigues to come, and it was being anticipated.

"Well En, I sense a veil of serenity about you, making me think you and pregnancy are journeying along contentedly, but what's happening between you and Maxim. Is the communications still remote and superficial?" Affinity asked.

"Well girls, the battle is over, the war is won, and I must say I'm very pleased with the result."

Prudence raised her thumb, "That's my Enamour, power to the proletariat," she exclaimed, grinning broadly at her sister. There was hope for her, after all.

"Hardly the proletariat," Enamour mused. "Yes, Maxim and I had an agreeable reconciliation, and I believe he has genuinely accepted my situation and my baby, and he's also accepted he'd made a mistake. While he'll accept my baby as part of our family, he did ask me if I'd like to start again, with our baby. I was appalled by his suggestion and ruled it out immediately. I've been through too much to start again. The one I've got is the one I'm going to have."

Prudence could not help herself, "But getting pregnant has benefits En, why did you say no?"

Enamour just stared at her blankly, and failed to reply.

"When Maxim refused you pregnancy you did the gutsy thing, and dealt with the situation the only way you could. Thankfully it's worked for you," Affinity said, seemingly having finally accepted her sister's choice.

Their meal was over.

"Oops, Affinity!" Prudence cried.

Two pair of eyes turned to her.

"What did Summit do to be sentenced to seven years in the dunville," she asked.

"Interfered with a female, a fellow director apparently, and injured her quite seriously. I don't know the details and don't want to know but I know he's deserved it, if not more, knowing him," Affinity said.

"Right."

Chapter 22
The Pick up

Prudence and Stone sat at the breakfast table opposite each other, quietly taking care of their nourishment, while quietly contemplating their day; that was until Prudence paused, dropped her utensils and glared at her food.

"Look at this food <u>Snafed's</u> served up this morning, it's not very interesting, to say the least. Actually, it's damn boring. There's been very little variety from them the last few days." Prudence complained.

Stone looked up, "There's no point complaining Pru, it's the grade you selected."

"And what was that?" she snapped.

"I think it's seven-MP (medium plenty) and I'm fed up with it as well."

"Why are we eating cheap food Stone?"

"You chose it Pru," he reiterated.

"Well can you have it upgraded, continue with the MP but let's go up to a twelve, at least."

"Right."

Prudence sighed, pushed the remaining food around the plate with her fork, then begrudgingly consigned half a mouthful. Suddenly the morning's mediocrity was disturbed when Prudence's tice ignited, which initially she ignored but noticing it was a colleague indicating she wished to talk privately, she reached for it and put it to her ear. "Good morning, Grace, what is it?" she asked and after a minute's listening replied, "Thanks luv, I'll be there as quickly as I can."

Prudence laid the tice back on the table slowly, said nothing, stared distantly, thoughtfully for a moment, then returned to her breakfast struggle, but only for a mouthful before pushing the it aside and looking up across the, "Stone, can you collect our surrogate this arvo; something urgent has cropped up at work, and I'll could be tied up most of the day."

"You mean pick up Clarity? Yeah, I suppose so, if you can't."

She stared at him, slightly annoyed by his gibe and apparent casual indifference."

"What's happening, why is it more important than collecting our baby boy's mother," he asked.

Prudence grimaced, "She's not the mother," her exasperation obvious. "She's an overpaid surrogate, I'm the mother; nothing more. Just remember that Stone!" she cracked, glaring.

"Still, what's more important."

"I'm not in the mood for your rubbish Stone. Just pick her up because there's a situation I must attend to," and she looking away, contemplating. "That was Grace on the tice. She went early into work this morning to find my chief designer Paladin dead."

"She what?" Stone exclaimed.

Prudence looked back at Stone, "Of course she doesn't know what's happened to him, but he's in his chair at his work station. That's all she knows so I've must get there promptly."

"Have the warders been informed," Stone asked.

"I assume so."

"Can I do anything?" Stone offered, out of courtesy.

"Just pick up the surrogate, and if there's anything else I'll tice you."

Stone nodded and returned to his breakfast.

Prudence was up from the table, stuck her tice to her arm, snatched her holdall from the bench and left the house.

Fifteen minutes later Prudence hurried along the corridor towards her offices, sporadically breaking into a brief trot, her gold and blue crepes flowing from her shoulders and fastened high in the front, her concession to modesty. Her loose black hair bounced on her shoulders while her piercing blue eyes studied the dramalessness at the entrance to her offices. A uniformed warder lazed against the wall beside the doorway, and looked up at the sound of her rhythmic approach. He was a slob, his ogling undisguised, his bent being for her legs. Prudence slowed to a commanding stride and approached him indifferently.

He was unconcerned at unblinking gaze, eased himself off the wall, and held out his scanner ready to read her identity implant. He glanced at the dial, looked at her and smiled, "Mornin', Prudence. Please go in," he said pleasantly, mollifying his eyes' malevolence.

The door slid open but Prudence halted at the threshold, suddenly apprehensive, and peered into the sprawling complex. The tragedy, apparently, was in Paladin's office, deep inside, but from the doorway the only contextual discrepancy were two recovery operatives lounging behind the reception bureau, talking idly, probably about something irrelevant, she assumed. They glanced up nonchalantly, one of them raising a hand pointing her down the hallway, as if she was a stranger. Convincing confidence to conquer caution, Prudence stepped inside and made her way towards the rear workrooms.

Suddenly Grace popped out of the doorway, and at the sight of Prudence dashed to her, wrapping her arms around her shoulder, and began sobbing.

"It's Paladin. He's dead. He's killed himself," she stammered, her face streaked with tears, some fresh, some old. She drew back from Prudence. "What are we going to do?"

"I don't know Grace, but let's not worry about it just now," she said easing her friend and deputy aside.

"When I came in this morning, I knew he was gone as soon as I saw him. There was nothing I could do. I couldn't touch him."

"You did fine Grace."

"I've sent everybody away until lunch time, and told them to stay together and say nothing to anyone else," Grace explained.

"Excellent, Grace," she said and Grace smiled, reassured and pleased her boss was pleased.

At the doorway to the designer's department, Prudence again hesitated studying the four expansive multi-screen designer stations standing ghostly, while the scattered ancillary paraphernalia lay forlorn on the desks. Speechless investigators hovered around the body at Paladin's station, while the air felt stale, hanging in the humidity of death.

Half a dozen operatives presumably had a reason for attendance, and they were colour coded, two in white, two in green and two nondescripts, warders she thought, but only one was attending the obscured figure slumped over the desk and appeared to be taking a saliva sample.

Prudence moved into the room, angling sideways to view the lifeless frame of her old compatriot and friend; a male who had been a significant contributor in the success of her fashion design operation. Her heart fluttered in a pit of hollowness, and she clutched her open mouth, while a moment of disbelief and senselessness reigned. She'd never seen a dead person before and she swallowed heavily as she looked at the body's flopped head against the head rest, the arms dangling between his legs, his feet splayed each side. On the floor below one of the dangling hands lay a glass file, which was being retrieved by an operative in green. He'd poisoned himself, she concluded, baselessly.

An attendant who idled turned to Prudence, expecting her to identify herself but she didn't notice, and was interested less. Her eyes were locked on Paladin's remains, while her mind filled with what had been. The incongruity was profound. The jovial face of her colleague; who was always impatient to show her an idea; his thoughtful expression as he'd slide into the chair at her desk with a suggestion; the pleasure of his presence about the office, and the male who always had a word of encouragement; time to advise, and to lend a helping hand. None of it bore any relationship to the wretchedness before her now. She moved further into room, but came no closer to his body, then her private melee was interrupted when an operative approached her, "Prudence, I'm Warder DI244, can we have a talk?" she said indicating they should move into the hallway.

Prudence didn't know if she wanted to talk or not but was happy to be distracted and understood a search for an explanation would be part of the aftermath. She turned away and led the way from the office. She was scanned again to re-verify her identity.

"For the moment it appears to be a suicide but there's further investigating to be conducted before we register a finding. In the meantime, we need to examine the background to the incident, and since, I understand he's worked here for many years, I'd like to start with you hoping you can throw some light on the incident."

Prudence turned to her "Yes, all right," but for the moment she was averse to outsiders prying into Paladin's life. Just how cooperative she was going to be was hazy, because while she knew a lot, she was in no mood for sharing his intimacies or privacies. Suddenly she realised, she should have recognised the forces which had inexorably navigated her friend to this ending but she not, even fleetingly.

Stone had his first view of the new season's Nog-Nog and Now-Now as he entered the foyer of the Pregnancy and Surrogacy Board, Surrogacy Unit, and when from the corner of his eye he spied the new Now-Now she compelled his attention. She is definitely an improvement on last seasons, or had the old one just become boring? Most likely.

They looked at him and Now-Now spoke. "Welcome Stone, we note Prudence is not with you. Since she was listed for attendance, your arrangements officer will need an explanation, and be assured no difficulties have arisen. Otherwise, you'll be please to know surrogate Clarity passed her final check-out examination this morning. She is fit and healthy, in body and soul, and your implant is secure. Please proceed to station seventeen where you're awaited."

Almost at station seventeen he stopped, staring ahead unseeing, wondering, contemplating, uncertain, seeking perspective. While Prudence was dealing with death, he was contemplating birth. So far, their parenthood planning and preparation had included some personal interactions, but mostly they had been academic. Now though, suddenly confronting the reality of the germination of flesh and blood, his flesh and blood, there was an unexpected wall to step through. He was to have a son, the die was cast, the chromosomes were aligning, the molecules were configuring, and the genome was directing the outcome according to a foreordained map. Unexpectedly visions of his own childhood with his father filled his thoughts, and he remembered his love and their bond. He'd not realised the high bar of responsibility he'd been bequeathed, and while he had never doubted his manhood, he wondered if he could measure up to fatherhood?

After a moment confidence saw-off his apprehension, and as the wave of doubt drained away, believing he'd be at least an average father, probably better, having learnt at the knees of a heavy weight. With reality, veracity and the future just the other side of the blue light door, the nuances of the hypothetical were losing their subtleties, and the theories were beginning to crystalise.

Stop thinking and get on! Stone took a deep breath and with its slow release the last of his hesitation dissipated. Besides, it was far too late for reflections or rethinking, and he took the last steps through the blue light, where two welcoming faces waited. Stone's gaze went straight to Clarity;

his mind quipping a profanity, and surprised by her allure, he was grappling with his preconception that pregnant females should look pregnant. Having had little experience with this female condition, and until this moment even less interest, he was amazed at her display of sexuality, nothing gravidness about her.

My goodness! Why would any male complain about living in a dunville. Promiscuity, not pregnancy seemed her priority this morning. She had not applied anybody toning or patterning, though her facial features were outlined lightly in scarlet, her lips in dark red, as were her nails with stripes. Her short cropped and forward layered hair was blonde with some cross striping in dark red.

Her presentation suggested she was expecting leisure, not confinement, her attire hugging, in fine milky brick with fine red cross stripes, the neck line dropping to midriff, her three-quarter tiffanys shaded, as were her legs, visible to well above her knees. Stone looked at her smile, glimpsed her tiffanys, and wondered again why she'd never bothered with the alphaspection. Of course, she wouldn't look any different being only days pregnant, and Stone was shocked his illogical impressions of pregnant females had been restricted to one spectacle.

"I hope I haven't kept you waiting," he said looking deliberately at Nemasos, afraid of being noticed, excessively noticing Clarity.

Nemasos stood and walked from behind her desk, her hand outstretched in welcome, while Clarity remained seated. With the formality complete, Nemasos and Stone sat.

"No, we've not been waiting long Stone, we've just been running through the details again and Clarity is pretty clear and happy with everything."

Stone turned to Clarity, "Well Clarity, we're underway. I'm told everything has gone according to plan and you're fine, so all that's left now is to take you home, look after you and wait for nine months. Prudence and I am excited, and pleasured with everything and hope you have a comfortable time with us." He turned back to Nemasos, "Is there anything else I need to do."

"Yes, I need an explanation for Prudence's absence since she's listed as joint acceptee. While it's probably just a formality, we need to be assured that all the approval factors are still in place. That is; you haven't separated or she hasn't lost her jay status, that sort of thing. Lastly, I need a final scan to verify that your DNA correlates with the embryo implanted. We should verify Prudence's too. Maybe later."

"Prudence had an early morning emergency call to her office. Evidently there was a serious mishap at work which required her attention. It seems, someone died in her offices overnight but that's all I know at this stage."

"Can you make sure you register the incident with Petrace (Personal Tracking Centre), and tag it with your surrogacy contract number. It's important!" Nemasos instructed.

Stone looked at Clarity, his smile ambiguous, "The merchandise looks satisfactory, thanks. But she's not displaying coding patches," he said with a quick look at Nemasos, then he turned back to Clarity.

"They're not compulsory, and she doesn't want them, but we've advised her that since she's approved for the jot, she must apply them before being in public. Not doing so, could cause her embarrassment," Nemasos said.

"Well, we'll deal with that when the time comes, I suppose," Stone said, his mind ahead of the subject and now contemplating his next awkward move. He turned to Clarity, "Are you ready?" he glanced at her two hover trunks, "Got everything you need?"

She nodded yes and stood up ready to depart, while Nemasos scanned Stone's implant.

Leaving station seventeen Stone again felt uneasy even uncertain. He'd never considered the protocols of their convoluted relationship, and he was beginning to think Prudence's dogma over the living agreement had pitfalls, not only because the threesome could become annoying and uncomfortable, but temptation was likely to be a factor.

As Stone strode along the corridor causally but upright, he sensed Clarity drawing closer, and when he turned to her, found her gazing at him, seemingly pleased with herself. When her intuition noted his approval, she slipped her hand under his elbow and gripped his forearm. Stone thought her slightly audacious, so soon in their association, but she was too becoming to rebuff, so he smiled instead. He enjoyed them walking together, stepping in unison.

Passing Nog-Nog and Now-Now, 'new edition' came: "Goodbye,

Clarity, Stone. Hope you have a comfortable nine months Clarity; and Stone, we and the Governing Council wishes you and Prudence a satisfactory outcome from this endeavour. All the best to you both." Stone looked at Clarity and raised eyebrow.

His tice sounded and Clarity unhanded him. It was Prudence on voice call.

She asked where he was, wanted to know how the pickup had gone, did the surrogate appear happy, when would they reach home, was everything under control, to which Stone answered with a series of yeses. Prudence was keen to get home and see their surrogate settled but matters at work were a long way from winding up.

The forensic investigators had finished their work, the warders had interviewed the staff, except Prudence, who they wished to further interview at headquarters. It was unlikely she'd be home for two or three hours.

"Why do they want you to go to headquarters," Stone enquired.

"I assume they want to interview me with sensual monitoring, because they must think I have relevant information I'd otherwise be reluctant to divulge."

"Do you?"

"Probably."

"All right, Pru, Well, everything's good here. We'll see you at home."

Stone put the tice back on his arm, and promptly Clarity reclaimed it.

Prudence sat in the rear of the warder's transporter, her mind wandering about the day's dramas, and the loss of her friend and chief designer. She'd known that beneath Paladin's gentle manner, avoidance of antagonym and instinct for harmony, he'd been troubled, but this solution was an answer she'd never envisioned. Maybe she should have considered the possibility. Maybe if she did but blind-sided it, convinced conveniently he'd find a way through.

Attempting to emancipate her conscience was failing knowing it was convenient, when she was acquainted with the intimate details of his troubles. Neither could she escape some encrusted responsibility for having moored his confidences, and thereby failing to help him. Had she just overestimated his strengths, and underestimated his vulnerability? As she watched the outside world whizzing past, the scenery morphed into an image of Paladin, slumped over his desk, and without warning, a wave of wounded worth washed over her. She was angry, realising that not only had he deprived himself of a future but he'd robbed the world of his talents and his charity, and the world was poorer for his unnecessary absence

For two years Paladin had been at war on a field he found foreign, perplexing and deceitful, and which became a wrestle for which he was found unqualified, unfit and unarmed. Both his flanks were exposed, firstly because he refused to believe his lover was lost; and secondly, he lacked the resilience to accept the inevitable. Twin pillars of beauty had maintained his life; his partner, and his artistic creations; his lover was his life's foundation, and with no yearning for any extra, his work provided all the self-worth he required.

It was twenty odds years ago Paladin was drawn to the tall, modestly presented female, in woven blues and yellows, with silver/grey hair who was examining one of his art pieces at a small exhibition. She seemed absorbed by his handiwork and as he approached her from behind, a sense of opportunity inspired his confidence. Almost upon her, she turned, the aura of his approach tapping her shoulder, and she smiled welcomingly, her naturally blue eyes piercing. Paladin halted, agog, speechless, heart rushing, and filling with a delight rare in his life.

"This is very good, you're very talented," she said her finger pointing over her shoulder.

She obviously knew who he was, which was a mystifying delight, and an encouragement for his sudden dream, "I'm glad you like it. I think it's one of my better works," he said moving closer to her, his move prompting her to reduce their gap even further. From that first moment they were never strangers, not for many years anyway, as their relationship immediately found its own momentum. It was inconsequential to Paladin she was a jayone, neither was it relevant he was a jok, two classes lower.

"I'm Vamp," she announced and lifted her hand for him to kiss, and with his eyes locked on hers he took it gently and lowered his lips, leaving them to linger longer than etiquettely appropriate. She made no attempt to discourage him.

Another factor he failed to assign credence was their ages, Paladin in his late thirties, while Vamp was a mid-twenty. She noticed the differences, the age more so than his rating, but as male maturity, for her, was a goal, the sophisticated eccentricity of the artist kissing her hand roused tinglings, and agitated her chemistry. Their passion evolved quickly, and when Paladin found himself, every morning, breakfasting with the female he'd spent the night with, his appreciation of life's good fortune was complete. Their companionship grew organically but time exposed an attitudinal differential, and when he asked her about becoming rebas, Vamp initially palmed his wish aside, and subsequently refused point blank.

Paladin consigned his disappointment to the dormant niches of his mind, while his sensitivities continued to relish in the gratification of having her. However, the inevitable was inbound and in his late forties another attitude disparity arose, one he could not pretend was frivolous. She began criticising his appearance, and the potential for his loss of jot status, nagging him to undertake remedial actions. Despite undertaking these programs, his love for her, and faith in their relationship, Vamp's amorous appetite was no longer being nourished imaginatively enough. Never constrained by inhibitions or fidelity, she tolerated insufficiency and frustration only briefly before finding a solution. For a period if any hint of her escapades escaped, she discounted it as gossip, and the sum of inventive minds. When the predictable eventuated and Paladin was relegated to a rap, her pretence ended and all residual passion evaporated.

Having lost his jay rating, he descended into an emotional spiral, and with his life's impetus scoffing at him suggesting to a detached relationship, he resolved to find a desperate solution. He sourced, for a price, an avenue which allowed him to remain in the jot, albeit unlawfully. Initially his ID chip was re-programmed with bogus information but this manipulation could only be temporary, as the authorities would eventually detect his false identification, and track it down.

His next step was more insidious, but as long those involved kept to the rules, he was convinced it could be successful, long term. It was known as 'twinning', whereby the avoider was tied inexorably with duplicate identity to a person with a legitimate rating, but it was expensive since the penalties for all parties, if detected, were hefty. It meant finding a genuine jay desperate for the financial reward, and judged dependable. With the genuine identity duplicated, and programmed into the avoider's chip, it became imperative the co-conspirators never circulated at the same time, in any location where there was potential for random scanning. To have both identities scanned at about the same time in different places would be fatal.

For a year this threat hovered over his clandestine life, while he strived fruitlessly to revitalise his now fanciful relationship with Vamp. His health suffered and his nerves frayed, more seriously than Prudence appreciated, and now reflecting, she marvelled how he had continued to produce innovative designs, and had endured outwardly polite and positive. It was only a few days ago he attempted to confided in her, and even then, with his turmoil evident, she failed to notice or react.

Vamp had finally disgorged her disgust for his r-rating, and her aversion to his criminal presence, and while she declined to demean his deteriorating carnal capacity, she made it clear he was no longer of any use to her. When she brought matters to a head, she gave him alternatives, move voluntarily to the dunville, or she'd betray him. Suddenly and in a haze of detachment the battle field hushed, emptied, eeried, and it lay strewn with the agonising remnants of his struggle, while she'd drawn double lines under his epilogue.

On hearing the perturbing news, Vamp arrived, running into the office, and on seeing Paladin she froze, stunned and bewildered. Prudence, impulsively wanted to go to her, but with Paladin's body in the corner of her eye, she filled with anger, and she too froze, watching. After an absent moment Vamp glanced around, tears drippling, then tottered to the body, bent over, kissed the back of his head, and ran from the precinct.

The journey home was good fun for Clarity, having only ever had a few glimpses of the jot, and her scrutiny meandered from one side window to the other. She didn't ask questions but as her eyes explored, they kept flashing glances at Stone, finally coming to rest on him. Stone had watched her fascination furtively, and when she turned to him, he too turned to looked into her eyes. His gazed glinted, his brain vorticed, and his thoughts became aspirational.

"You're very attractive Clarity, I find it hard to imagine you being pregnant," he said confidently.

"That's okay but how do you imagine me, then?" her response came quickly, and convinced Stone to capitalise on the encouragement he sensed.

"Well Clarity, you certainly don't belong in a dunville. You're far too attractive for that place, because you're a pretty and alluring female," he said, opening several gates, wondering which one would appeal to her.

She waited, smiling, teasingly Stone thought, she looked away, then back, her smile broadening, her sparkle brutal, convincing Stone the tease was indeed on, irritatingly. When her amusement was rewarded sufficiently, she slid across the bench of the transporter, stretched an arm around his neck and pulled herself into him. "Stone; how would you like to father your son properly?" she asked, her face beside his, pouting, while sombrely gazing, devilment rampant in her eyes.

"What do you mean?" he asked, after a moment, and well aware of what she intended.

"You want to fuck me; I can see that! I saw the first day we meet. And since I'm mothering your son, it'd be appropriate, don't you think?"

Stone was surprised by her frankness, so soon in their association, and despite his hallucinatory desires, she'd flummoxed him with the possibility, and had certainly snatched the initiative. Confronted with this astute insight through his transparency, he felt self-conscious.

"Well!" She tilted her head a touch, leant into his shoulder, took his forearm with both hands, then stretched up and kissed his cheek. He turned to her, their gazes squarely in each other's but still he didn't answer, her manifest effrontery, emerging charisma, and oozing sexual presence, was unexpected and disorientating, even intimidating, and she was threatening to take control of their association

She was impatient. "Wouldn't you like to feel like you've done the fathering properly Stone; after all, squirting it into a test tube couldn't have been anything like the real thing."

He was glad for the diversion even if her speculation was spurious, "The apparatus used is rather enjoyable, and it didn't take long for the requisite to arrive," he said smiling.

For an instant he considered her juxtaposition, and wondered if their consorting would complicate their contract or compromise their affiliation, but he promptly abandoned the concern, his libido having taken control. Hers was already well aflame, seemingly.

"Well!" she prompted forcefully.

He looked at her. "Yes Clarity, you know it. I'd like to fuck you."

She smiled, reached for his hand, opened his fingers, pulled them to her stomach pressing them into herself. Enthused, Clarity launched her surprising and brazen sortie knowing Stone was enlisted, and while he intended delivering on her expectations, he'd been startled by her exuberance, and now needed to sprint a catchup.

When his hand rested on her knee, almost imperceptibly, her knees began to dissociate, and Stone's hand gently slithered upwards easily finding the way under her garment. As his fingertips tracked over her silky skin, they ignited an electrifying path of delight across her body. It was exactly the way she wanted him to start, and she slipped down in the seat, opening her legs as wide as the transporter would allow.

"Resting seats, one-way vision" Stone commanded and slowly the seatbacks lowered, while the glass took on a silver tinge, allowing insiders to see out but denying outsiders a view inside.

Clarity pushed his hand aside, gathered her legs together, then drew her knees up under her chin, and smiled at Stone, in anticipation. He wasn't sure what she wanted, but neither did he care, as he knew what he was going to do. He reached across her lap with one hand, took hold her he knickers and when she lifted alice off the seat, he slipped them off.

"That feels a lot better Stone," she said, as she settled back on the seat, and stretched a leg across his thighs,

"Looks a lot better too!" was the instinctive come back from Stone. Vesuvius, lay naked and close by, the focal point for his thinking, not only because of its potential, but there was something different. Clarity was finding amusement in his apparent, sudden and puzzling hesitation. She guessed what he was looking at, and suspected why he'd paused from stroking her, and could see what he was looking at. She smiled and jiggled her leg against caesar, which was well alert, having snaked its way to attention beneath her leg. It was ample, strong; and her imagination felt the gratification of its rampaging descent into her wonderland. Stone leant back against the vehicle's door rest, and his fingers began slithered until to vesuvius's edge. He paused gazing at her. Abruptly she whacked his hand aside, gripped the neckline of her outfit, wiped the full-length seam open, flung her arms aside, to expose her entirety.

Stone perused her offering, and it was magnificent, caesar felt that too, but he was unsure about her discrepancy. She was different to any other female he'd been this close to, and although he knew what it was, it was new, unexpected and perplexing. Initially his reaction was negative but being amidst otherwise fair and tender beauty, it seemed an integral element to her appeal and charisma. Clarity had a moment of concern but when his hand returned to caressed vesuvius softly, she knew the occasion was still at her auspices.

"I know it's a bit bristly Stone, that's because I was defoliated a month ago, ready for my implantation," she explained. "A fortnight ago it was spikey and, and in another month, it'll be hairy, so we've probably linked up at a good time, for you."

"I know jay females all have hairless pussies but I'm a dunvillian girl, and many of us never bother having it purged. Some males like it anyway," she concluded.

"How do you know that?" Stone snapped thoughtlessly, and having been persuaded by caesar to accepted the societal differential, his fingers began seeking the silky path into vivian.

"As you know mum and my sisters sometimes do some whoring if they like the guy, and most of the johns come because they want hairy, which is not weird but there are other weirdos who want pregnant."

"You're joking?" The image was horrific.

"No! If one of my sisters is home and pregnant, and there usually is, she'll probably do him because they'll pay plenty for it. I'm happy just doing surrogacy though but as this is only my second contract, I might change my mind later."

Stone's shoulders shuddered at her pragmatic perspective, and the notion that his son's surrogate being randomly screwed, sapped some of his enthusiasm, for the moment anyway. Suddenly he realised Prudence's wariness was well foundered, and of her insistence, he now had no argument. Their pregnant surrogate already wanted fucking, the only consolation being that it appeared she wanted it for enjoyment, not reward. But did that make any difference? Making the apparent blatant, it was clear Clarity was palpably and uninhibited lustrous, and while committed to screwing him at the moment, would she seduce any available male, if mooded? Probably. No, definitely.

However, her mercenary and unencumbered style, not forgetting irresistibility was gusting an invigorating eagerness into far more zones than just caesar's. In his lap lay freshness, renewal, even innocence, even be it feign, and he was seeing her in new light, which neither offended or deterred him. She was compelling, her wily and alluringly smile billboarding the erotic uncultured and undisciplined panache, which exuded from her every pore.

"Where does your father fit into this?" Stone asked curiously, and as a diversion for his impatience.

"After Mum had us three girls, she threw out the lazy klutz. Then she did three surrogacies which was enough pregnancy for her but since she was still felt fit and healthy, and still in her early thirties, she decided to do sex instead. As we girls became old enough, we followed her ways, until now pata-pata and surrogacy are our way of life. We live very well from it, and don't need the alphaspection or the jot. And sure, I might be pregnant just now, but only just, and it's some honest and willing dedication I need at the moment, while I'm comfortable and able to have my way," she looked at him and smiled innocently. "I expect to be fit, able and needy for a few months, Stone, and I'm sure you will find a solution for me."

It was becoming an insightful day for Stone, and while he had always considered himself confidently savvy, this paradigm was flooding fresh plasma into his libido. The embryonic arousal of a while ago now felt pedestrian, while the prospect of plunging caesar into this professional's pussy had him yearning for the escapade. He ran his hand up and down the inside of her leg on his lap, then leaning over to her other leg, which lay stretched to far corner of the transporter. Then it was a stroking up her body, through her cleavage, a tickle to her neck, a caressing of her under chin, a fingertip across her lips, and back down a slow circuit of her tiffanys, hello dewdrops and gently back down to the centre of the encounter's universe.

"I like that Stone," she looked at him smiling.

"Good," he replied, thinking she would like it even more shortly.

Two of his fingers found their way along her moisture track and past her foyer, to pry not slowly into vivian, while the heel of his hand began an agitation for cleopatra. He was unsure how to most exploit this unexpected and invigorating opportunity, though he now made no effort at polite seduction or gentle coercion, and persisted despite her flinch of discomfort.

"Be nice Stone," she said reaching down and pulling his hand back. When he acquiesced and smiled, she paused, then pressed his hand back down, his spreading fingers clutching her ladies, as one finger slipped more gently from whence, she'd extracted it a few moments ago.

"Would you like pussy naked, Stone?" she asked. "If you'd like you can cream it later, make it soft and smooth, I don't mind."

She'd backfooted him again, and left him somewhat nonplussed, like a baffled youth blundering on in testicle aching uncertainty, while tingling to the coercion of female torment.

"Cream it Stone, make me a jay girl, I'd like to know what it feels like anyway."

"I've never done it," he excused himself.

"That's because you're always fucked jaybirds. But it's not hard."

He had no intention of jotising vesuvius; the furry concept was appealing, and he aimed to feel the prickles, as well, and he was visualising the fun of fucking a feral female. Her significance to his family was, for now, inconsequential as his fascination for the foreign and inappropriate dominated.

His hand stroked a delicate trail from vesuvius up her body, where upon his finger again drew circles around one of her tiffanys, and then the other. They were firm, beautifully contoured halves, and he leant over kissing her dewdrop, then the other one, as his hand slipped deftly back to her precinct of his thoughts. He looked into her eyes.

"No Clarity, I want you as you are. You're not a jay, and I've no interest in pretending," he said benevolently.

Definitely! He was yielding, bowing to her breeze, and while she had his libidinous fuelled compassion, she'd seize the opportunity to broach another desire she harboured.

"I know I'm not a jay but since I'm mothering your son, I have a full jot permit for the next three months, then, an after dark permit for a further two months, and there's one thing I want, while I can," she said, as her hand groped for caesar.

"What's that Clarity?" he asked warily.

"I want to go to the arena, a night with cloud. Will you take me Stone?" She gave caesar an encouragement, as she spoke.

One hand continued cupping vesuvius, while two fingers explored the succulence of her lustrous fissure, while his other hand took be back of her head and lifted it for him to kiss her. She closed her eyes and let the tip of his tongue reach in for a moment. He lowered her head back down, and looked into her eyes for a moment.

"You're incorrigible Clarity; you're becoming a spring of surprises, and I suspect you intend to profit from us, as much as you can. I suppose I should be impressed."

"Yes, I could be taking advantage, but does it matter. Look what I'm offering you at the moment. Pretty good deal, wouldn't you agree? But anyway Stone, you'll take me to the arena, won't you? I watch the holograms all the time, but they're restricted to 45 percent, so they look like dolls. I want to see real bouts, jump some, shout a lot, suck some cloud, and I want see a big mamma bash the shitta out of a little bloke," she explained excitedly, her body bouncing slightly to her imagination.

He throbbed in her hand.

"Ooh, nice one Stone. I like it," she grinned.

Her request raised two issues. Firstly, being their surrogate, she had a status, but was she expecting too much advantage too soon; and secondly, she hoped to imbibe cloud despite her pregnancy, suggesting her underlying fille de joie was close to the surface. He surveyed her beauty, and felt cleopatra hardening beneath his finger, as another finger ventured into vivian. Whore was okay for now, as was his pandering. He lifted her leg away, stretched back in the seat, arched his backside up to wrench his lower attire clear. Caesar reared immediately but Stone was not ready for his commissioning, his urge being to indulge the aesthetics and fondle her youthful tenderness. He pulled her back over his knees.

"You continue to surprise me, Clarity. I met you for an hour, about a month ago, then we met again a little while ago, and we've been together for about an hour today, and already you've suggested I fuck you, and asked to be taken to the arena. It makes me worry where this might end. I know you're important as our surrogate but you remain a contractor, and a well-paid one."

"Yes, but while we've just met, you've wanted to screw me since you first set eyes on me; so, our relationship has done its apprenticeship and although I might only be your surrogate, I can be a bundle of fun too. I'm your bonus Stone." she giggled.

"You're a bundle of something Clarity, but is it a bundle of bother?" he wondered, his fingers pushing deeper, as his palm wriggled spreading her ladies, further presenting cleopatra and her hinterland.

Stone knew she was growing impatient when she pushed his hand aside for a second time and flipped onto her side towards him, seized caesar and pumped furiously for a few moments. The transporter halted, Clarity sat up, leant over and mouthed caesar.

Although Stone had sidestepped the vesuvius clearance suggestion, Clarity's intuition suggested he could be frustrated sexually, even exasperated, and primed for stepping outside orthodoxy, vulnerable even to the bizarre. Could he cross the threshold into a jurisdiction which would fire his imagination for the untilled? "Do you think, Stone, you'd like being sexual submissive?" she asked, earnestly, releasing caesar and lifting her head to gaze into his face.

He looked at her, "What do you mean?' he said, his mind racing, his senses enthusiastic for her elaboration.

"You know! Become my slave, with a bit of bondage, a bit of biting, some spanking, being obedient, some pain, some stamina stimulation, and then when you're desperate, explode with the best finish you've ever had. You know, things like that." she explained, siting up one elbow, while pushing him onto his back.

Surprisingly her suggestion was not repulsive, not even distasteful, and when he glanced down at her short cropped vesuvius, her web seized him. "We'll be home soon," he said, desperate for a moment's interlude, while he absorbed the tingling in his spine.

"Then stop and park Stone, don't be awkward," reaching under to grip his brothers.

Stone sat up, "Park, one-hour, twenty-six degrees," he instructed and lay back down, to have Clarity rest her head on his chest.

The transporter slowed, pulled aside and stopped, and quietness infiltrated.

He turned to her, "so what's in it for you."

"A lot. Masochism gets me going big time, and I like finishing myself. I can fuck lots of things. Your leg, your face, the vehicle seat, a melon, anything pretty much, but I prefer penetration, especially devices."

Defying instinct's argument, Stone had abandoned caution, but a curious nagging persisted about his fascination for her. She was mysterious and having precipitated from a cultural back water, was it her untamed impulses, or her seeming unbridled enthusiasm, her expansive imagination, her apparent experience, which made her so enticing? There must be more to her than her prickly pussy! Whatever? He wanted to journey in her abandonment, dismiss reservations, and feel the bounds of restraint burst.

"I can't guarantee I'll comply," he said, caution in his voice, but already submissive, waited for her insistence.

"Yes, you will!" A wave of excitement whoofed from vivian through her body, sure her dominance had rooted, while for Stone, delight was in the apprehension whoofing around his hollowing stomach.

She was going to make him wait for the adventurous, and start with the usual. Stroking his erection, she looked up, "I like it," she glanced down, then back up, "Is it natural or enhanced, not that it matters?"

Stone looked down checking, "Yeah, there was some work done on it when I was about 14, I think, maybe dad or more likely mum, decided a bit extra would be useful for my future. I remember having to stopped masturbating for a couple of weeks, which was frustrating. There were a few wet dreams though."

"Yes, I can understand why it would have been your mother," she said satirically, smiling self-amused, then lowering her mouth over caesar again.

He watched her head bobbing, then glanced over her curled figure, her beauty and sensual features switching on all his sensual cathodes. He looked at her back and watched her shoulders working, and then he slapped her back, ungently.

Her revenge was immediate. "For shit's sake," he yelped and tried to pull away. She'd bitten caesar, then held on to prevented his escape. When she relented, she began soothing his pain with smarmy lips and her mooching tongue.

Despite the momentary agony, his masculinity was undaunted, rather, surprisingly his erection had gallantly held up, surging periodically. However, after a while it began to ease, so unconsciously he reached over and slapped her posterior again. Clarity smiled to herself, and knowing he wanted to be punished again, was pleased her intuition about his susceptibility for masochism. It had been a quick conquest, but how much more pain would the sentinel of his ego tolerate? More, she thought, and as she validated her authority by sinking her teeth slowly into his erection again, the sensation sent a shudder squirting about her salacious zones. Stone's head came up, his face winced, but caesar surged again. This time when the pain drained, so did the enthusiasm, and he flopped back.

"Damn, Clarity, that's enough," he said forcing a grin.

She withdrew, sat half up, looked at him, maintained her grip around the base of caesar, and asked, "Do you promise to take me to the arena?"

He took her head in his hands, and was going to say no but her charm continued beguiling, "We'll see."

It was not the answer she wanted, and her head went down again. The touch of her lips sliding over caesar again was soothing, and it responded positively until she reached his injury. He felt her teeth teetering, and feared this time it would be pain without the excitement. Then he felt her teeth closing, deliberately, slowly on the same spot; he needed to end the encounter.

"All right Clarity, not again, not in the same place anyway. I'll take you to the arena."

Her grinning face popped up, she was happy in more ways than one, "That's nice Stone, thank you." She looked down at his erection and then back at Stone. "He's still strong Stone but seems sore and sorry, poor boy, I'll kiss him better," and his pain faded quickly as her expertise became palpable.

At the warders' headquarters Prudence was confronted on the other side of the table by two officers, one female and one male, who had introduced themselves using their identification numbers only.

Prudence was irked at being brought in for interrogation, and refused to be interviewed by way of tactile monitoring, and was offended at being subject to any kind of scanning. Any knowledge she possessed about the incident was inconsequentially, so the scrutiny was pointless. She leant forward in her chair, "Listen you two, I don't know how I can help you but I'd like you to do me the courtesy, and tell me what happened to my friend and valued designer."

The female lifted her gaze from her screen, "Prudence, our monitoring shows you're quite hostile towards us. There is no need for that, and we'd appreciate your cooperation, as we're just attempting to ascertain what motivated Paladin to take his own life. We assess all suicides in an effort to determine at what stress levels people, firstly, consider suicide, and then at what level do they act upon that impulse, that's all. We are hoping you can assist us in this case. With regard to the cause of death, it was a self-administered dose of fast acting poison, taken at approximately ten o'clock last night. He would have died without pain or suffering, very quickly."

Prudence eased back into the chair, and her hackles relaxed somewhat, "It's been a stressful day so far, and you people aren't helping, that's all."

"We have examined the deceased's tice and found a considerable amount of information giving us a picture of his personal problems, but also, there's a message to you, which we believe conceals a secondary private message," the male explained.

"How do you know that? What's the message for me, you've no right to withhold it?" Prudence demanded.

"The voice analyser detected an inflection in a certain phrase, which suggests the presence of a double meaning. It's not a difficult anomaly to identify, and in the phrase which concerns us, he says to you 'remember our triple cee.'" he said, and paused for Prudence to reflect on the moment.

"What does it mean to you?" Puss asked firmly.

Prudence's mind scurried to find an answer which would satisfy or confuse the scanner without says what she knew.

"Your stress level has jumped," she announced, but Prudence was unperturbed.

"I'm not sure," she said finally, disinterested in the scanner's conclusion.

"What could it mean?" she demanded.

Prudence had had enough, "I don't know," she rebounded defiantly

"We think you do, certainly the sensor indicates you're being evasive, probably deceptive."

"I can't help that, and I've nothing more to say."

Threats to pursue the matter failed to impress Prudence, believing some spurious phase, doubtfully thought to be a code, mentioned by a suicide victim, was of little consequence, and would not convince any authority to direct any further action. She stood up, and without a word left the office unhindered.

When Prudence walked into her home, and into the entertainment centre, the scene did nothing to help her recover from the day's stresses. Stone was relaxed in his sacs, obviously cleansed and nourished, so was she. The ambience was suspicious.

Stone stood up and went to her, "You've had a big day by the look of you Pru, how did it all turned out?" he took her shoulders and kissed her quickly on the lips.

Prudence was in no mood to detail her day or respond to affection. She was glaring at Clarity, "I'm going to the shower, and when I get back, I want you in your own quarters," her hand flicked a dismissal, in the direction. As Prudence left the room, she glanced back, staring at them both, "You've fucked her Stone, that's bloody obvious."

Chapter 23
Affinity's Tragedy

At Affinity's home the security came to life, 'Affinity, the ambulance has arrived, and two technicians are seeking entry. They have been scanned and are legitimate, and are listed for your pick up this morning. Are they to be admitted?"

The months of frustration, annoyance, anger, heartache, disappointment, sadness and misery were about to come to end in catastrophe; with her tiffanys being dissolved away. A depressive anticipation began fermenting the moment her options were eliminated, and her diagnosis became irrefutable. The toll on her anguish had been accentuated lately, by Summit's stupefying situation, while for most of the week sleep had been elusive, only gracing her for brief periods, and for the last couple of days she had trembled so intensely, it was unconcealable. Her mind had devolved into a haze of self-pity, fear, and the despairing dream that a salvation might still be discovered.

The announced ambulance arrival was more akin to the mortician's arrival, and for the moment Affinity was overwhelmed, and unable to respond.

"Affinity, repeating! The ambulance has arrived and two technicians are seeking entry. They have been scanned and are legitimate. Are they to be admitted?"

"For fucks sake! Yes!" she yelled.

Intuitively she stood, staring at the door, like the condemn breathing her last, awaiting the executioner's pleasure. The slid door opened to the smiling face of a spunky young male, and immediately Affinity's slumped a little, and some tension drained. He was a jaytwo, maybe a one, his strength well expressed beneath his white, all-overs, while his face radiated trustfulness and compassion. From behind him a female peered over his shoulder, assuredly also attractive, she thought.

"Good morning, Affinity, how are you? I'm Ainsley," he said

stepping in and approaching, while Affinity's examined his assistant which confirmed her suspicions, she be a jayone or two, too. Worse, she carried high, a perfectly shaped pair of half tiffanys, beneath the all-overs.

"There is my assistant Harmony, we're here to deliver you to the clinic for your procedure, this afternoon," Ainsley informed her.

The strong, gently edged voice was assurance for Affinity, and her smile surprised herself, "Thanks for coming, I think I'm ready, I hope I am, I haven't been thinking very straight this morning."

"Never mind, you won't need anything much since we'll provide whatever you need. As long as you're happy to go, that's all we need to know."

"Yes, I suppose I am!" she splurted, her resolve solidifying, and provoking Ainsley to flick a sceptical glance at Harmony.

"Good. There're a few things to do before leaving. I'll scan your Bahs to make sure the health information we have is current, and we'll double check some other information."

"Okay," Affinity approved quietly, and eased back into her chair.

Harmony moved beside Affinity, and scanned her upper arm.

With her examination over quickly, Ainsley announced everything was correct.

"I understand Affinity that the procedure has been explained to you, so now we'll give you a sedative," he said.

"Yes, but I'm not sure I understood it all, what's this for?" she asked staring at the injector.

"It's the first step in preparing you for the procedure. By the time you're at the clinic, you'll be relaxed and lethargic but that's normal and you'll be happy." Affinity looked at him sceptically but as his words registered, she hoped it would be an escape from the melancholy.

Scarcely through the gold doors of the clinic than a proverbial refrain spoke. "Welcome Affinity, we're ready for you." Affinity had never been into a procedure facility, and what she was being wheeled into was big, pleasing and took her by surprise, thanks in some measure to the effects of her medication. The facility was cream, off white, cream and off-white variations, dark cream, light cream, amber, milky cream, shading cream, mottled dark cream, with all definitions and shapes outlined in fine gold.

Huge bunches of red and yellow flowers proliferated, in tall floor vases, in wide bench vases and in wall vases. As well the air woofed with a delicate scent, though Affinity could not identify it.

"You will remain conscious for the duration, and if our monitors detect any increase in your stress levels corrective medication will be administered automatically, so there's nothing to be concerned about. You should not suffer any discomfort. We expect your treatment will be straight forward, and will take an hour and a half, and then Ainsley and Harmony will return you home."

It was an unfortunate comment, she felt through her medicated euphoria. She'd been made enough promises before, only to end up with the appropriation of her tiffanys. And they weren't just excising from her anatomy, they were about to suck essence from her soul, her predicament the consequence of culpable promises. And now they were trying to convince her there would be no discomfort, and nothing of concern, or to suffer.

The aroma of the clinic's sterility reached well into her lungs, and she inhaled deeply for its refreshment but her euphoria was in danger. Affinity dropped her head to her chest, as her mind filled with the vision of her ten-year-old self, lying in bed one night and discovering little swellings under her dewdrops And, they were tender and she worried something was wrong. Then she smiled, discovering the answer was simple, her breasts were spawning, what would Mum say. Some news for school, let me see.

She threw the bedclothes off and clambered from bed, called for the light, and stood against the mirror. There was more to feel than see but her dewdrops were protruding a bit, she was sure. The next morning's mirror hadn't changed, Mum confirmed her delight, her school friends were jealous, and she found herself touching them every few minutes. Then the itchiness came, then the buds, and with fatty tissue under her areolas came their shading. Eventually they were real tiffanys, and of the three other girls in her group, hers were the stand outs.

By the alphaspection her tiffany had pretty much matured, and ever since she'd patiently protected them, but now she ached for those two buds she'd discovered so many years ago.

The calmative was taking full effect, and her senses found the aroma pleasing, and the trauma of the pending, was fading. She turned her head and looked at Harmony, smiling assuredly about her encroaching timeless indifference. Before she was aware, she lay on the air cushion staring at the ceiling, and a tall female in white moved in beside her, took hold of her arm in one hand, and with her other hand massaged a medication through her skin. A few minutes earlier she would have noticed her figure, and been jealous but now she was of no consequence. On her other side another female in white was suddenly there, and she was looking into Affinity's eyes and talking, explaining seemingly, but for Affinity it was slurred garble she could not be bothered trying to understand. Her body was fading, she could see everything, but her sense of touch was numbing and quietness was enveloping, all leaving her remote, impregnable and suspended in a world of disinterested contentment.

The two white figures were disrobing her upper body, she couldn't work out why but she didn't care either. They talked to her occasionally, indiscernibly, but their voices were comforting and their smiles pleasing. An apparatus was being fitted across her chest, but she felt nothing. The details of the bloodless removal of tiffany tissue by particle dissolution had been explained to her, but she feigned attention and understanding, preferring not to know.

The attendants completed the set-up work, double checked the settings, looked at each other for corroboration, stroked a dial, watched the instrumentation intently, glanced at Affinity then back at the panel, then at each other, smiled in consensus, and withdrew to sit suitably stationed to supervise the session. Affinity, from another world, watched their conversation but heard nothing. The younger one, probably a jap, was the focus of the intercourse, and as her face toiled earnestly on the conversation, Affinity watched her dark blue lips and eyes delivering a tall tale, while her companion seemed to listen keenly.

There was a persistent niggling irritation in her chest but for her it was inconsequential, and when one of the attendants left their chair and looked closely into her eyes, Affinity returned a focused gaze dispassionately.

Time had no substance, so when a red light on the apparatus began flashing signalling the completion of the procedure Affinity didn't know or care if she'd been there for ten minutes or two hours, when in fact it was over two hours. The apparatus was carefully dismantled from off Affinity's chest. One of them looked at her. "It's all over Affinity, we'll just get retract this equipment and do a few checks."

The other attendant was using an appliance to massage a substance through her skin, "Affinity, this will return you to normal, but we want you to remain here for a short while, to monitor your recovery."

Affinity heard the words and was aware of her way back to the world of pleasure and pain, affection and disaffection, dispute and determination, fidelity and fiction and 'bloody' tedium. The paraphernalia was gone, and the females in white were doing something which made her chest feel cool, but she was not going to look. It was over, they were gone presumably but Affinity's vestige of denial lingered, and she'd not look down, yet. With a hand under each shoulder, she was lifted to sit, and while one attendant steadied her the other re-robed her.

Another skin impregnation was administered; the effects this time quickly manifested itself with a revival of wellbeing and a refreshing energy. She was helped from the air bed and when her feet touched the floor she paused, looked about and took some deep breaths. She was helped to a sacs then lowered onto it. However, after only a few minutes "Affinity, you appear okay, we think you're about ready to go home. The recovery team is ready to deliver you but your reba, daughter and sister are waiting outside for you."

"Which sister?"

"Enamour, I believe."

Affinity wanted to walk and did so but with Ainsley and Harmony in close company, on each side of her. Outside the procedure room she halted, elbowed her chaperons for space then slowly raised her hands to her chest. She paused almost there but still did not look down, instead she threw her head back and looked blindly at the ceiling. Then without warning the wellbeing infusion failed, her knees folded and four hands forward to save her. She hunched over, hanging from her shoulders, her head drooped, and with closed eyes still refusing to look, she was gently lowered into a hover chair, which had been rushed to her aid. Her tears streamed.

The door across the foyer opened and a horrified Enamour appeared. She froze for an instant but the mayday call was clear and Enamour dashed to fall on the floor at her sister's side, Harmony pushed aside. Essence was close behind, at her other side, while Summit, being less prone to panic, strode to her back and embraced her head. Affinity looked at her sister, then her daughter, then with her face in her hands began sobbing uncontrollably.

"They're fucking gone, En, fucking gone, and I feel fucking shit."